MANTIS

RICHARD LA PLANTE

MANTIS

A TOM DOHERTY ASSOCIATES BOOK ■ NEW YORK

A Tor Book
Published by Tom Doherty Associates, Inc.
175 Fifth Avenue
New York, N.Y. 10010

Tor ® is a registered trademark of Tom Doherty Associates, Inc.

Library of Congress Cataloging-in-Publication Data

La Plante, Richard.
    Mantis / Richard La Plante.
        p.   cm.
    ISBN 0-312-85531—1
    I. Title.
PR6062.A66M36   1993
823'.914—dc20   93-554
                                                  CIP

First Tor edition: May 1993

Printed in the United States of America

0 9 8 7 6 5 4 3 2 1

Special thanks to Officer Michael Cullin of the Lower Merion Township Crime Prevention Unit for his advice and encouragement.

To Terry O'Neill's *Fighting Arts International*, and to Terry, himself, a good friend of many years.

To Graham Noble for his kind permission to use his name.

To Dennis Martin, of CQB Services, for relevant information concerning firearms and other weapons.

When the speed of rushing water reaches the point where it can move boulders, this is the force of momentum.

When the speed of a hawk is such that it can strike and kill, this is precision.

So it is with the trained warrior—his force swift, his precision exact.

Sun Tzu, *The Art of War*

MANTIS

All Japan Karate Championships
Nippon Budokon Hall
Tokyo, Japan
August 1976

"**W**hat is your name?" The man asking the question was Dr. Kenwa Itosu. He was a tiny man, not more than five feet in height and only 110 lbs. in weight. His face, however, was fierce, his eyes piercing and his thin lips locked in a perpetual frown.

"Your name?" the doctor repeated, squatting directly in front of the fallen competitor.

Josef Tanaka smelled the broiled *hamachi* on the small man's breath, noted the sweat on his forehead, and wondered for a moment how the diminutive doctor was managing to look him directly in the eye.

"Tanaka . . . Josef Tanaka," he answered.

"Are you able to stand up?" Itosu persisted, his stockinged feet leaving moist circular marks on the hard canvas floor.

"Yes," Tanaka replied. *Anything to escape the stink of fish coming from your mouth.* He pushed with his hands, then willed his quadriceps to complete the task of raising his six-foot-two-inch body to a vertical position. Now the doctor's head came level with Tanaka's sternum.

"Do you know where you are?"

Tanaka breathed in, attempting to focus on a row of doll-sized faces which stared from the lowest of the circular tiers of stadium seats. *Is that my father? Yes, that's him, sitting next to Toshiro Mifune, the film actor.*

"Budokan Hall," he answered.

"Can you continue?" the doctor pressed, feeling the unnatural silence of ten thousand spectators.

There was still a humming in Josef's head, like the metallic whine of a dentist's drill. Sweat mixed with blood trickled from his nose and ran in rivulets on to the white cotton of the loose jacket of his *gi*. He should have said no.

"Yes, I can continue."

Kenwa Itosu smiled with relief. Then he nodded to the referee who, in turn, nodded to the four corner judges.

A shrill whistle cut the air. Upon its signal one white and three red flags rose in unison.

"*Ippon. Hiki-waki.*" The referee's pronouncement of a full point and a tied match met with the applause of eight thousand spectators.

Josef Tanaka turned side-on to the eight-meter fighting square; he brought his right hand upwards, gripping the bridge of his nose between his thumb and index finger. He twisted his hand slightly as he squeezed, listening to the broken cartilage grind into a semblance of alignment. *He has the hardest punch in all Japan.* That's what they said about Hiro, his brother. Now Josef was convinced.

He walked briskly to his white line. One full point and twelve seconds would decide this final match. The applause died, replaced by an electric concentration.

Hiro Tanaka stood two body-lengths away, opposing him. A fresh rush of adrenalin masked Josef's physical pain. He centered himself on Hiro's dark, hooded eyes. An irrational fear threatened to rob his limbs of motion. It was a childhood fear, the fear of an older brother. As if, by virtue of age, Josef was not allowed to win. A moral dilemma began to well in his heart.

What if I beat him? In the presence of our father. . . .

"*Hajime!*" The referee's call to begin halted his thoughts.

Josef waited, holding his ground, watching Hiro's small, sturdy body flow forward. *Three times All-Japan Champion. He has won three times running.* New thoughts trickled, spreading doubt.

Hiro's gaze locked on to his brother's; he could not help but see the blue-grey discoloration spreading from Josef's nose, half-closing his right eye. He was sorry he had damaged the soft, almost pretty face. He would apologize later. But now there was no time for sentiment or compassion. It was imperative that he score, decisively. More than sport, this was a matter of family honor. He was Josef's *sempai*, senior both in age and rank. There was one other difference between the brothers: Hironori was pure Samurai, the son of Mikio Tanaka and Kamisaka Enoeda. Josef was the product of Mikio's second marriage, to an American socialite. He was not Samurai, not even pure Japanese.

Ten . . . nine . . . Josef could almost count the passing seconds by the beat of his own heart. He watched the shorter, stockier man inch forward. Indecision made Josef nervous, and there was no room for indecision in the space between them.

Hiro observed his brother's erratic breathing, sensed the disquiet in his attitude.

Eight . . . seven . . . He would take him now, just as time ran out.

Six . . . five . . . four. . . .

"Hei!" Hiro kiai'd once, short and sharp, throwing a throat-level jab with his left. Josef reacted, raising both hands, taking a half-step backward.

He's open, wide open. The realization flashed simultaneously with Hiro Tanaka's lunge. Dropping on to his forward knee Hiro fired a reverse punch toward his brother's heart.

In that split second Josef saw his target. His body reacted before—almost in spite of—his mind, his left leg lifting to aim a round kick at Hiro's unguarded head. Josef was close, too close, and it was his shin that connected. There was a loud crack, like the breaking of a tree limb. He felt something give, a burst of pain. Thought, for a moment, that he had broken his leg.

"*Yame!*" The referee's shout coincided with the loud buzzer ending the match.

Hironori Tanaka remained on the mat, kneeling as if in prayer. His body twitched. Then, slowly, he pitched sideways, his legs curled in a foetal position.

"Don't move him!" Kenwa Itosu shouted. A second later the small doctor was kneeling beside the injured man, his fingers examining the vertebrae at the top of Hiro's spine.

A hush fell like a shroud over the arena.

Josef stared, finding his brother's almond eyes, noticing as if for the first time how different they were from his own. *Samurai eyes, pure and fine.*

Behind them, Mikio Tanaka rose from the crowd, pushing forward, powerful arms flailing, clearing his path. Josef sensed his father's approach, yet he could not turn away; he was held by Hironori's eyes. They were clear, without guile; they seemed to speak, to reassure. "I am fine, really. No problem, brother, no problem . . ."

Mikio Tanaka mounted the steps of the raised platform. "Hiro, my son, Hiro."

Josef could hear the resonant voice, repeating his brother's name, over and over again. Hironori's lips turned upward in a faint smile. For a moment there was hope. Then the smile faded and his body grew still, acquiring a deadness, a solidity. Kenwa Itosu shook his head, defeat furrowing his brow.

From the corner of the arena two men carried a stretcher. Mikio Tanaka knelt beside his eldest child, whispering, pleading. And all the while Hironori's eyes remained open, alert, like the eyes of a wounded animal, searching deeper and deeper into Josef's heart. Silently, Josef began his Christian prayer beseeching his God to make his brother stand.

It was then that Mikio Tanaka turned, and looked up. He was crying, staring straight at Josef, his lips tightening, hardening his face into a mask of hatred. The Lord's Prayer died in Josef's mind.

Later he would blank out the memory of those moments, yet he could never forget his father's words as they walked, shoulder to shoulder, through the silent crowd.

"You are a *budoka*; you live by the code of the warrior. There is no such thing as an accident."

I.

LOU-PREGO-DIEU
THE ANIMAL THAT PRAYS TO GOD

The man walked slowly down the paved passageway, glass tanks and metal walls to either side. It was dark and deserted. The smells of raw, fresh-blooded meat and dried urine mixed to create a familiar perfume. He listened, his ears tuned to the faintest change of sound. Finally he heard her, calling to him, gauze wings quivering. He stopped a moment, inhaling, picking up her scent, dry and sweet. Then he continued. Walking to a grey metal door at the end of the passage. He unlocked the door and entered a small octagonal room, illuminated by a warm, violet light. Glass jars lined its shelves. Some of the jars were for storage, others were "killing jars."

The man's heavy boots came off first, followed by his outer garments and underclothes. He folded the clothing and piled it neatly by the closed and locked door. Then, naked, he walked to the shelves, silently removing the perforated lid of a storage jar. Reaching in, he grasped a large cockroach between his thumb and index finger. The creature struggled, twisting upwards to fight his intrusion, its strong, piercing mandibles closing on his flesh.

The slight, stinging grip was incidental to his purpose. He walked quickly to the work table in the center of the room.

The Mantis awaited him there. He forced his captive through the specially constructed feeding lip of her cage, shaking his index finger, dislodging the cockroach. It fell to the floor of the cage.

At first it remained still. Then, gradually gaining confidence, the dark brown insect inched forward, testing its new surrounds.

The man sat on his wooden observation bench, concentrating upon his mentor; her elegant bust, her pale green coloring, her gauze wings. Large diamond eyes found him, entering his depths, acknowledging his gift. Understanding his desire.

A fine vibration connected them, a transfer of consciousness which had evolved beyond reason, beyond guilt.

She trembled, beginning a convulsive shiver. The cockroach sensed her movement, interpreting it as vulnerability. Its body appeared far larger and altogether sturdier than the Mantis. It began a lumbering approach, mind conditioned by perpetual hunger, muscles gross and misshapen.

The man watched, excited in a way which exceeded the confines of sexuality, although there was a feeling in his genitals. He stroked himself once, disciplining his urge to use the syringe, to inject his flaccid penis, to bring himself to full power. But this was not his time to practice, this was his time to learn.

Concentrate! The Mantis' voice shattered his desire. Her next move caused him to gasp, to feel as much her victim as her student. Rising on four legs, she spread her wings like towering sails; the tip of her abdomen curled upwards, rising and falling in fast, puffing breaths, revealing a beautiful star, pure and white in its center. The man was drawn to the star, his mind pulled taut to the point of pain.

The cockroach reacted identically, sucked into a vacuum which preceded death. The Mantis was magnified in their perception, two rows of razored spikes positioned to each side of her exposed thighs. Her lower legs folded into a groove between them, yet even her delicate shins were covered by small, jagged teeth. Two open hooks, double-headed like pruning knives, grew in place of hands. Both man and cockroach stared, transfixed by the horror beneath her beauty.

Then the grapnels fell, claws digging inward as the double saws closed and clutched the hard, beetle-like body to her own. Her embrace was both intimate and final.

For a few moments her victim's mandibles opened and closed, finding only empty space, the horned cockroach legs kicking in protest. Finally the long wings closed, enveloping and entombing, Inside the soft green, her meal had begun.

The man waited respectfully, aware of his inadequacy in technique and style, comparing his mentor's display with his own crude efforts. Yet he was determined to improve, to strive for perfection. For only through perfection would he find relief.

An hour passed before the Mantis was sated. A brown, crusted outer skin remained on the cage floor.

Then her diamond eyes looked up, seeking the man.

She is like a cat in the dark
and then she is the darkness . . .

The song was as stale as the air, Stevie Nicks' voice was croaking through burnt-out loudspeakers. *Like Orson Welles on helium.* Gina couldn't remember which reviewer had said it, but it was definitely true. She leaned forward, looking at her face in the flat mirror, staring right up her nostrils, viewing the tiny white crystals which clung to the fine hairs. She lifted the straw and vacuumed the last powdered line up her clear side. The freeze felt good; she could happily have had her front teeth extracted without fear of pain.

The chorus of *Rhiannon, taken by, taken by the sky* . . . wafted up from directly below her dressing room, actually a curtained-off cubicle that the six "artistes" shared. Eighty-eight seconds 'till show-time. She tossed the used flexi-straw into a bin full of mascara'd Kleenex.

The University of the Arts; tomorrow she'd be at her easel, torn jeans and tied-back hair. Life drawing, Stan Kramer's class. He'd be behind her, his legs insinuating against her thigh. "Maybe a little shade around the eyes." She'd probably sleep with him before the end of fall term; he reminded her of her father, something in the smile behind the beard, like a weasel, a cute predator. *Where's Dad now? Fucking his latest head case? On a flight to Vegas? In the audience downstairs?* The last thought made Gina laugh.

An artificial energy flooded her. She stood up, moving her pelvis in a self-mocking grind. The last strains of the fifteen-year-old *opus* crescendoed below.

Crackle, crackle. The twenty-second pause before Z Z Top propelled her into the spotlight. She passed Jeanette on the stairs.

"Watch it, there's a Raincoat at the front table," the black girl cautioned, leaving a trail of Georgio as she pushed by.

A Raincoat, that's what the club girls called the occasional masturbator who found his way into the lounge. *A Raincoat . . .* Gina repeated the words as she mounted the first of the three steps leading into the cage.

She snapped the chrome gate shut in time to the opening guitar riff. Her audience jolted to attention. She spun dramatically, causing a stockinged thigh to flash from the exaggerated slit in her skirt. *How corny can I get?* she thought from behind a façade of studied indifference. Finally her body locked into the rhythm of the bass and drums.

That was what was good about being a little high; by the time her eyes focused, her ass was already in gear.

She spread her legs, crouching slightly, creating a hint of tension in the muscles above her knees. *Exotic dancer. Fifty dollars an hour. Must be over eighteen.* At first she hadn't been sure. She didn't need the money, Dad saw to that. Psychiatry paid well, particularly in Beverly Hills. Add in the guilt trip he ran for living with a girl two years older than his daughter, and Gina was assured of a constant cash flow. As if he could buy her approval.

What she did need, she thought, was the street credibility. It gave her that touch of reality that the other second-year "artsy-fartsys" lacked. "I work as a dancer." Just being able to say it.

Every girl's crazy for a sharp-dressed man. . . . The lyric coincided with his smile.

The Raincoat. Better looking than most, his boyish face marred only by a small, slightly crooked nose. *Like a boxer's nose,* Gina thought, unconsciously searching for the eyes behind the dark shadows of the high cheekbones. He wore a shining leather jacket and his head bobbed in time to the music. One hand was extended, curled around a tall glass. A large, ugly hand. The other was concealed beneath the table. There was a peculiar movement in his shoulder which corresponded to the hidden hand. A Raincoat. He was grinning from ear to ear.

Don't look at him, he'll think you're coming on. Don't meet his eyes.

Gina turned, refocusing on a table full of oriental coats and ties. She began to slip the silk jacket from her shoulders, holding tight to the rhythm. She let it fall, leaving only a black lace bra. Red overhead lights accentuated her outsize breasts. The Japanese gentlemen reared back in their chairs, tapping each other on the shoulders, motioning towards the cage, moving in various directions to see beyond the vertical bars.

"Sharp-Dressed Man" segued into the slower, moodier "Rough Boy." Gina concentrated on the Japs, slipping her thumbs into the sides of the waistband of her skirt, moving easily, her confidence building in steady pulses. She watched the nearest moon face nod vigorously as the skirt hit the floor. She rubbed her palms suggestively across the smooth, tanned skin above her stocking tops. She felt safe now, in control, changing direction, glancing once to her left.

A single long-necked bottle and a half-full glass of dark liquid, probably Coca-Cola, remained at the table. The Raincoat was gone. Gina relaxed as she removed her bra.

Five feet six or seven, probably a hundred and twenty pounds, big, full tits, a lot of protection above the heart. Strong legs, impeccable rhythm, a natural athlete. She's been in the sun. Maybe Atlantic City, a lot of showgirls go to Atlantic City. This one can't be much more than twenty, her face has a touch of puppy fat. Long neck, yes, that's it, long neck. Jugular vein, pulsates during respiration, collapses during inhalation; gets hard on the out breath. Gets hard. . . .

He touched a square, calloused fingertip to the fly of his trousers, pressing against the full, unyielding knob of his erection. *Four hours, I'm good for another four hours . . .* He leaned back.

"Get ya somethin'? A beer?" She stood in front of him, wrecking his view. "Are you at a table?"

No answer.

"You can't stand here, you're blocking the fire door."

The man straightened, fixing the black girl with target eyes. He remembered her act. Now she carried a tray. She stank of perfume, sweet and spicy. He held her stare; forgetting, for a moment, his purpose. Wanting to accept her challenge.

"Look, if you don't move . . ."

He didn't wait for the threat. Pivoting, he caught the curved handle in his right hand and moved through, the heavy door closing behind him. He heard her struggle with the crossbar lock, imagined her placing the drinks tray on the floor, levering with her body, straining to get the bolt back into place. She'd know, there and then, his strength, his mastery.

He walked towards the light, his rubber soles silent against the stone alleyway. Two people passed at the intersection of alley and pavement. *Enemies.* The warning voice was soft yet intense, clearer than the other voices in his head. It was the voice of his teacher, his mentor. He stopped and turned, searching the shadows for the stick-like silhouette.

The twenty-four-hour coffee shop was a hundred yards away, with a clear view of the club's entrance and exit.

The waiter winced when he saw the spatulate hand, fingers pointing to "Mineral water, $1.25."

He kept his head down, nursing the drink, ordering another before the first was finished. He practiced the cleansing breath, swallowing the iced liquid only at the end of every fifth exhalation. He was a machine, a breathing machine, senses heightened, body tuned.

"Anything else, mister?"

No words were necessary; he didn't look up, handed the waiter a five dollar bill, avoiding contact with the man's grimy fingers, noticing the dirt beneath his nails. *The hands of humanity, unwashed, untrained.* Again the voice.

"I'll be back with your change."

He waved the waiter away.

"Thanks."

Thirty seconds later, Gina walked from the club. He watched her stand a moment, talking to the black girl. Then she turned and headed east, towards the river.

He maintained his position, excited but controlled. He

downed the last of the water, holding his breath, finding his heart, measuring its beat against the second hand of his watch.

Fifty-two to the minute, excellent. No nerves. . . . This time the voice of the Mantis synchronized perfectly with his thoughts.

He stood up, catching his passing reflection in the glass door; his body appeared thinner, his facial features blurred. The change was coming.

Gina held the folded fifty-dollar bill in her left hand, pushing it deeper into her pocket as she passed Fourth. In her right she carried a Gucci hold-all. The soft leather contained her working clothes and cosmetics.

She wore white Reeboks, loose khakis—the high-waisted military drills from the Army-Navy—and a beige pullover. It was hardly the look of a stripper, except for the red silk G-string. She'd left that on; it made her feel sexy, reminded her that she was more than a student.

Her mind locked on Stan Kramer. She fantasized a private party, just the two of them. She'd do a few lines, then show Mr. K. how she worked her way through college. *How old is he? Forty, forty-five? Old enough to be my father.*

Her thoughts exhumed a buried anger. *How could he have dumped us? Just walked out, leaving me and Mom? The great shrink, Mr. Compassion, the famous head doctor.* Suddenly she felt small, cheap and totally alone. The coke was wearing off and the Gucci bag felt heavy in her hand. *A stripper . . .* She peered painfully through her tough charade.

I'll write to Mom before I go to sleep. And after tonight, no more coke. That's it. She'd made the same resolution before; this time she'd keep it.

It was 1:42 a.m. when Gina turned right on to Second Street, quickening her pace as she rounded the final corner into Queen Village. Her apartment was one of the newest in the mixed yuppie community.

She could see it now. The second floor of a recently converted factory space. She'd left the kitchen lights on. She hated dark places.

It was then that the shadow moved beside her, fast and silent, overtaking her, stopping, turning.

The Raincoat . . . Her heart froze. *Keep moving. Don't run. Don't panic.*

He was five steps away. This time he wasn't grinning, his face set like stone. Eyes bored into hers, concentrated, pupils like black holes.

Keep it together, she willed, turning to glance sideways. Nothing. No one to help.

Distends on the out breath. He focused on Gina's throat, studying the soft area of his left, above the round neck of her pullover. *Full and hard.* He imagined her jugular vein, returning blood from her brain to her heart, protected by the long sternocleido-mastoid muscle. He had practiced the strike ten thousand times, into sand, into gravel. He felt the eyes of the Mantis, watching, examining, judging. He raised his arms, as if to unfurl hidden wings.

"What do you want?" Gina managed the question, her voice breaking.

He seemed to glide towards her, as if the pavement had become a smooth sheet of ice. She stepped laterally, attempting to pass him; the lights of her apartment drawing her forward to safety.

He blocked her way, his body shifting in countertime to her own, yet she hadn't seen him move.

He was very tall and, because of his strange posture, arms spread, he seemed on the verge of enveloping her. She dredged anger from fear.

"Get out of my way!"

Perfect range. She can't run forward. Maybe swing the purse. Next time she speaks. On the out breath. Full and hard.

He raised his hooking hands, cocking his arms slightly, no tension in his triceps, tightening his fingers, forcing them to merge. A muffled, puffing sound seemed to rise from his abdomen, as if he was breathing through cloth.

She stared at the ugly callused fingers. "This isn't funny!" Her tone was desperate.

Missed your chance. Concentrate, the thin voice chastised.

The black Gucci swung up and round in slow motion. He stepped inside the arc of attack, striking downward. The bag glanced off his shoulder as his nerve-deadened fingers dug into the soft fasciae of her throat.

Gina gurgled, hunching forward, hands reaching out, grasping. She caught the heavy fabric of his trousers, just below his knees, above the hard leather of his steel-tipped boots. He stepped back and she fell flat on her face.

She is alive. The jugular did not burst. No contact with the cervical vertebrae. The Mantis was angry, threatening separation with her host.

Frustration overrode common sense; the man kicked upwards, the crotch of his trousers giving enough to facilitate the low snap. The boot-heel of his support leg shifted and he stumbled as his instep connected with her forehead.

The Mantis stood beside him, frowning.

"Please, please," Gina whispered. "Please, Daddy, help me. . . ."

The man squatted down, gripping her hair with his left hand, pulling back. Glazed brown eyes begged for mercy. A trickle of blood ran from her open mouth. A purple bruise an inch square marred the flesh of her swollen neck.

Daddy, help me, is that what she said? Daddy, help me . . . A rage filled him, threatening his control. He fought against a desire to use his teeth, to bite, to devour, to smash her body against his own.

He was trembling as he drew his hooking hand up, level with his right eye. His range became his power, harnessed and pure.

She closed her eyes as the killing hand struck. Once. Twice.

Sloppy, very sloppy, the Mantis whispered.

The loading dock was deserted; empty crates and a vacant hoist. The Delaware coursed below, sending up a faint smell of gas and oil.

He stripped her, folding her clothes in a neat pile, stopping when he got to the red G-string. He considered, then carefully removed the delicate garment.

Once he heard voices above, male voices, one rough and aggressive, the other light and lisping. They faded, hollow echoes through empty alleys.

He moved quickly, concealed beneath the lip of a walkway which led from the pavement to the mooring. He had worked with bodies before, freshly dead, but none this young and supple. Still, he knew time was against him. She would lose heat rapidly, particularly in the chill of autumn.

He began by folding her right leg at the knee, pulling her foot upwards so that the heel touched her pelvis, manipulating her left leg, bending it identically, drawing the foot over her other ankle to form what is known in the discipline of yoga as the full lotus. Then he stepped behind her, lifting her torso, pressing her head forward to her feet, listening to the vertebrae crack as her spine reached perfect alignment.

Time dissolved into pure consciousness, concentration super-seding thought until finally she was ready, fully prepared.

The man smiled, a smile of worship, kneeling before his offering, closing his eyes, turning his mind inwards. The Mantis was there, awaiting him, no longer angry or impatient.

His hooking hand found his belt buckle, opened and released it. He thumbed the buttons on his trousers, causing them to fall, freeing his drug-induced erection.

Gripping himself with both hands, squeezing, guiding, he began his work.

II.

LIEUTENANT WILLIAM T. FOGARTY

THE NIGHTMARE BEGINS

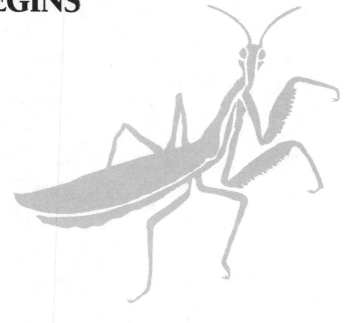

It is a medium-sized bedroom, blinds closed, curtains drawn. Six floors below, City Line Avenue intersects with the Schuylkill Expressway. The Schuylkill is the main artery connecting central Philadelphia with its rich suburbs. At 4:57 a.m., traffic is sparse. Its noise barely reaches up six floors, hardly touches the solitary figure sleeping in the four-poster bed.

The man's face is turned towards the dim light of an adjoining bathroom. His exposed skin looks waxen in the artificial glow. As if the flesh has somehow congealed, growing thick and porous. He breathes deeply, his body locked unconsciously to a second pillow. He holds the pillow in his arms, as if it is a wife or lover.

He turns slightly. The features of the other side of his face are markedly different, almost handsome. His eyes flicker, pupils dilating behind closed lids; the nightmare begins.

One, two, three o'clock, four o'clock rock. . . .

Bill Haley's spit curl remains motionless, glued to the sweating skin of his forehead.

"How does he keep it in place? What does he use?" the man puzzles, watching the singer's black-and-white image mime to the jangling chords of the record.

Five, six, seven o'clock, eight o'clock rock . . .

A short blonde with a beehive hairdo dances on to the TV screen, eclipsing Haley's white suit and black tie. Her eyes glitter behind long lashes. She smiles at him.

Nine, ten, eleven o'clock, twelve o'clock rock . . .

He knows the dancing girl.

We're gonna rock around the clock tonight . . .

Sarah. Fear accompanies his recognition. Her face changes, becomes rounder, her hair longer, darker. "Turn it up, Pop, it's a golden oldie."

Ann's voice. He is no longer watching TV: he is driving a car, the top down. His wife, Sarah, is beside him, his daughter, Ann, in the back seat.

When the clock strikes one we're gonna have some fun . . .

The music is tinny, far away; the roar of the Pontiac's V8 fills his consciousness.

"Turn it up, Pop! Turn it up!"

There is a traffic circle ahead, one of those outdated, four-exit convergences that links Route 70 with the other roads leading to and from the Jersey shore. A long Esso tanker winds its way through the junction, gleaming in the afternoon sun, its cylindrical body appearing to bend and flow with the unbanked highway.

When the clock strikes four we're gonna rock some more . . .

His fear heightens.

"Turn it up, Pop!"

The tanker pulls out of the last curve, turning left to face him; its black predatory grille rushing forward . . .

"*The wrong side of the road, the sonofabitch is on the wrong side of the road* . . ." He can hear his own voice, screaming. Fear turns to panic, jangling guitar chords mix with the screech of rubber against asphalt. A roar like an explosion, followed by the sound of hub-cap rolling across pavement. Then silence.

He tries to crawl forward. He can't move; searing pain runs the length of his legs, up into his lower back.

"Where's the ambulance? God Almighty, where's the ambulance?"

Somewhere in the distance a high-pitched sound; it is coming closer. A siren? Giving him hope.

He can see his wife and daughter through the windshield, looking straight at him, an arm's length away. He reaches towards them. In time with the first burst of flame. The blast lifts him, blowing him backwards into the gravel and dirt of the tree-lined highway.

The flesh of his face is immersed in liquid fire. He remains conscious, listening, thinking. *The ambulance, it's gotta get here soon. The ambulance.* . . .

The sound is incessant, ringing in his ears, over and over, wedging inside his memory, prying open his eyes. It is not the sound of a siren; it is the ringing of a telephone. He stares up at a white ceiling, focusing on the criss-cross of tiny cracks in the fresh stipple.

Ocean County Hospital, is that where I am?

Another ring of the phone and Lieutenant William T. Fogarty rolled on to his right side, somehow surprised that he was no longer in traction. Sarah and Ann stared at him from inside a silver picture frame. Suddenly four years and five hundred hours of therapy separated him from his nightmare. Beside the picture a digital clock read 5:03 a.m. The phone rang again.

This is going to be bad. The thought flashed a moment before he lifted the receiver.

"Bill?" It was Dan McMullon's voice, worried.

Fogarty waited a beat. "Go ahead, Dan, I'm listening."

"We got another one, Bill."

"Oh, Jesus," Fogarty replied, a rush of adrenalin sickening his stomach.

"Where?"

"On the docks, back end of Washington Avenue, the old Amoco pier."

The sun rose above the murky water, bathing the girl's body in a sallow light. From a distance there was a profane beauty in its posture, like a piece of sculpture, meticulously positioned.

The crackle of police radios and the flash of a camera seemed far away as Fogarty walked forward. For an unsteady moment, only the corpse appeared real, anchoring him inside a moving wash of sound and shadow. He was on the fourth wooden step leading down to the pier, twenty feet from the cordoned square.

As if she is praying. His illusion was shattered by the sight of torn flesh and caked brown blood.

A thin man with short carrot-red hair and a neatly trimmed goatee bent beside the body, tightening the drawstring on a clear plastic bag which encased the corpse's right hand. He straightened, noticed Fogarty and nodded, then deftly removed a thermometer from the victim's rectum.

Fogarty waited as the forensic pathologist studied the instrument. Finally Bob Moyer's stark voice cut the morning air, leaving a wispy white vapor in front of his face. "Time of death approximately two a.m."

A tall man in corduroy trousers and a black leather jacket recorded the data on a yellow medical pad. The man stood next to Fogarty, his profile obscured by his upturned collar. Fogarty concentrated a moment, trying to place him. *Must be new*, he concluded, somehow annoyed by the intrusion of a fresh face.

He continued to watch as Moyer motioned for his leather-clad assistant to join him, the pathologist now kneeling, his eyes riveted to the victim's neck. The tall man walked to Moyer's side and dropped into a full squat. There was a surprising agility to his movement and, again, Fogarty wondered who he was.

"Same as the Nickles girl. Bruising to the sternocleido-mastoid directly above the internal jugular." Fogarty listened to Moyer's voice.

"It's cleaner, Bob, much cleaner," the tall man answered, moving his hand in a circular pattern just above the damaged flesh. Fogarty watched Moyer nod in agreement.

Their voices faded as the lieutenant stepped back from the body. He'd worked with Bob Moyer for over a decade, long enough to know when to keep his distance. This was the time to let the pathologist get on with his examination. He'd get the results later. For now, Bill Fogarty would employ his intuition, trying to get the feel of the crime.

He moved to the outer edge of the dock, to a vantage point which allowed him an overall view of the wooden pier, its access points and possible overlooks. Sometimes he did a rough sketch with pencil on paper. Today he worked in his head.

Gina Genero, that was the victim's name given by the proprietor of the Birdcage Lounge. A formal identification would come later, when the deceased's mother arrived.

An extreme discomfort threatened Fogarty's concentration. *I won't meet the plane, I'll send a couple of detectives.* The resolution relieved him; Bill Fogarty hated to be the welcoming party for the bereaved. "Gina Genero," he whispered, trying not to be distracted by the plastic body-bag which was being unfurled at the far end of the pier.

"Gina Genero." Finally his mind cleared and he began his work.

The largest precinct building in the city of Philadelphia is the Roundhouse, a three-story gray-stone structure occupying the corner of Seventh Street and Vine.

Architecturally, the Roundhouse is unique, two circular buildings connected by an enclosed walkway. An aerial view would reveal its shape to be distinctly similar to a set of police-issue handcuffs. Whether that similarity was coincidental or by design had never been of consequence to Lieutenant William T. Fogarty. His office was on the second floor of the building, overlooking Seventh.

On Saturday morning, October 30th, he sat behind a desk that had been new in 1945. He sucked two Rolaids while easing his back against the orthopedic cushion of a wooden chair. Three things were prominent on his ink-stained blotter: two newspapers, *The Inquirer* and the *Daily News*, and a ten-by-twelve manila envelope. He picked up the *Daily News* and scanned the print just below the headline: "Third Dancer Found Dead. Narcotics Connection. Traces of cocaine were allegedly found in a sample of Ms. Genero's blood. Two grams of the narcotic were discovered in her apartment."

"Cunt." Fogarty uttered the expletive as he eyed the reporter's name. Then he thought of Diane Genero, Gina's mother, due to arrive on a seven o'clock flight. By then the evening edition of the *Daily News* would also be on the stands. Tough to miss. They may even hand her one on the plane. Somehow the idea of Diane Genero reading that her late daughter was not

only a stripper but also a drug user offended Fogarty's Irish
Catholic morality.

"Ms. Genero attended the University of the Arts." The line
was inserted between descriptions of the sordid nature of her
employment and the fact that her father was a Beverly Hills
psychiatrist.

It's always a matter of emphasis, Fogarty mused, dropping the
paper into a metal waste-bin. Next he lifted the manila envelope,
knowing he wouldn't like what was inside.

Crunching the undissolved Rolaids between his rear molars,
he tore the envelope along the perforated upper edge, removing six scene-of-the-crime photographs of Gina Marie Genero.
His lips tightened in an unconscious grimace.

He picked up a yellowed phone, pressing a button for an
outside line, and spoke as soon as he heard the receiver come off
the hook.

"You got anything?"

"Same as before." Moyer's voice was apologetic.

"Prints?"

"*Nada,*" Moyer answered.

"Saliva? Sperm?"

"Nothing. There was no skin or hair under her nails. She
couldn't have put up much of a fight."

Fogarty's next question was, for him, the most uncomfortable.

"Was she dead when he performed?"

The forensic man hesitated, clearing his throat. "That's hard
to say." Then, as if in concession. "We do know what killed
her."

"Go ahead."

"Multiple strikes to the anterior neck region. Drowned in her
own blood," Moyer stated.

Another silence followed. Moyer interpreted it as a signal to
continue. "Internally, he pretty well ripped her apart."

"That's enough, Bob," Fogarty said.

"Bill?" Moyer's voice took on a gentler quality. Fogarty remained quiet, listening.

"Are you guys anywhere near to finding this animal?"

"We've got a dozen confessions. After today's headlines we'll have a dozen more," Fogarty replied, knowing how unsatisfactory his answer was.

"I see," said Moyer.

"We're no closer, Bob," Fogarty owned up, staring at the loose collage of black and white photographs.

"I'd like to send somebody round to see you. He's just out of Penn Medical School. In our trainee program. He's gonna be good. Real good."

"That's fine, Bob, but what's he got for me?"

"A theory."

"Uh, uh." Fogarty was anything but interested. He suspected another fresh-faced would-be forensic genius.

"What's his name?"

"Joey Tanaka."

Fogarty conjured images of an updated Charlie Chan. He was about to put Moyer off, saying he didn't have time, but he waited too long.

"Tomorrow morning, eight-thirty," Moyer said, concluding their conversation.

The Hotel Atop the Bellevue is located on Broad Street, two blocks from City Hall, beneath the statue of Philadelphia's founding father, William Penn.

Entered from Chancellor Court, via a "European style" private drive, the entrance hall features marble floors and high corniced ceilings.

Fogarty's shoes tapped against the marble as he walked to the elevator. It was raining outside, and he was leaving wet tracks on the white stone.

He pressed the glowing button with the upward pointing arrow. The elevator arrived a moment later, its doors opening to reveal his reflection in a smoked-glass mirror. He looked at the good side of a rugged face topped by thinning, corn-colored hair. The skin was pale; he hadn't had much sun since that two-week holiday in Point Pleasant Beach, New Jersey, in 1986. The tan Brooks Brothers suit looked as tired as he did. He was still staring at the familiar stranger when the doors closed.

"Shit," he muttered, looking up to see the pale light flash three and rising. Fogarty turned and walked past two more sets of silver doors, opting for a twelve-floor climb up the winding staircase. Ten minutes later he arrived in a pillared portico. He felt, suddenly, as if he had been transported to a swank Miami Beach hotel. The enclosed room featured wicker furniture and a long, blue-watered swimming pool. It also featured two of the longest-legged black women he had ever seen. One of them lounged in a cocoon-like sedan chair while the other sat facing him. Their swimming costumes were still wet and the lieutenant detected the outline of nipples beneath the white Lycra. Both sipped umbrella-topped drinks from "bird bath" glasses.

The seated woman smiled. Fogarty turned away. *Hookers, probably hookers,* he surmised, noting that his response to attractive women hadn't changed. His therapist had termed it "evasion-avoidance," a negative reinforcement to his deep-seated guilt. "It will effectively keep you from entering into any meaningful male-female relationship," she had assured him.

"They're still hookers," Fogarty answered out loud.

"Pardon me, sir?"

Fogarty looked over his shoulder to see a small, acne-faced, grey-suited porter. He sported a gold lapel badge which read "Henry Kline" and he seemed to be giving Fogarty the once-over.

"Room twelve-fifteen," the lieutenant said.

"Is that your room, sir?" The youth made a point of giving an incredulous edge to his question. As if, perhaps, the worn-out man in the worn-out suit had stumbled in off the street and was now attempting to impersonate a paying guest.

Fogarty moved closer to Henry Kline, turning to face him. Henry Kline took a step backward. Fogarty tried to remember the line he'd heard James Caan use in an old film. He couldn't remember the film. Was it even James Caan? He wasn't sure.

Henry Kline's shock was wearing off.

"Henry." Fogarty used his friendliest voice. "What size mouth does your shoe take?"

He knew he'd fucked it up the moment he saw the puzzlement cross the acned face. *What size shoe does your mouth take? That's it, that's it, asshole.* Fogarty cursed himself. Henry Kline still looked puzzled as the lieutenant turned and walked down a plushly carpeted corridor marked Suites 1201–1219.

Diane Genero's last words began to repeat with every step. *Why? Why my Gina?* There was never an answer; always the question and never an answer.

He arrived at Suite 1215, hesitating a moment to pull his jacket down at the sleeves. Next he straightened his maroon-striped tie and wished he'd worn something more sombre. Finally he pressed the bell, positioning himself good side forward.

The woman who opened the door reminded him of the actress from the old TV series, *Hill Street Blues,* the defense lawyer married to the police captain, sexy but refined. He'd watched the show two or three times and the face had caught in his mind. The kind of woman who'd always be a television image away from his reality.

"Mrs. Genero?" He didn't have to ask. He could have told the moment he looked into the pale blue eyes. It was there, always; the desperation, tainted by anger and mixed with hope, the last emotion rushing forward while the others restrained it in their exhausting grip.

"I'm Bill Fogarty."

"Come in, please." Her voice was low, husky from crying.

Fogarty crossed the threshold, immediately noticing a copy of the *Daily News,* open to the "Third Dancer" story, lying on a low coffee table. Diane Genero followed his eyes.

"They didn't know Gina. They just didn't know her," her husky voice trembled. "She wanted to grow up so badly, to prove she was independent. Behind it all she was a child. One boyfriend before she came here. One boyfriend. . . ."

"It's best not to read them," Fogarty replied, looking up from the paper.

Diane Genero met his gaze. Her eyes registered something; sympathy, pain? Fogarty remained silent, fighting a habitual urge to explain his disfigurement. A feeling passed between them. Loneliness, something they both understood.

"I'm sorry, Mr. . . . ?"

"Fogarty." He filled in his name.

"Will you sit down? I'll ring for coffee."

His awkwardness began to pass. "I'm OK, thanks. I've been living on coffee for a week."

He took the hard leather seat of a repro colonial armchair. She sat opposite him, pulling her skirt down over long stockinged legs.

"Comfortable flight?" His question hung in the air. "From LA," he added.

She shook her head. "I came in from Santa Fe. Gina's father lives in Los Angeles. I live in New Mexico."

Fogarty almost asked, "Alone?" He changed the word as it came out. "Oh . . . I didn't know you were separated."

"Divorced." There was finality in her tone, but no bitterness. "Levenson was my married name. Gina's been with me since she was fourteen. She preferred Genero."

Fogarty nodded.

"These last couple of years have been hard," she continued. "I knew she was into drugs. I prayed she'd grow out of it. I mean, I smoked pot in college, I slept around."

Fogarty tried not to react. At the same time he was impressed with Diane Genero's matter-of-factness.

"We talked about the dancing job. That bothered me, but not as much as the kind of people she mixed with."

"At the club?" He began now, slowly.

"At the club, at school. She seemed drawn to. . . ." She hesitated, searching, ". . . a lower element. As if these people could somehow validate her ambitions."

"Ambitions?"

"Of becoming a painter. My daughter wanted to be a painter. She was very talented. And now. . . ."

Fogarty watched the tears well in the huge eyes. He hung on; this was the part of his job that he hated, the intimacy, the manipulation.

"Did she have a steady boyfriend?"

Diane Genero shook her head, holding back a sob. Fogarty firmed up, trying to dominate the mood, extract as much as he could before the inevitable.

"Where did she get the cocaine?"

There was a flash of indignation, then the tears came.

"Listen to me, Diane," Fogarty began, about to play his trump card, already feeling cheap for saying what he was about to say. As if he hadn't said it twelve times before, used it like a credential. "Four years ago I lost my wife and daughter. My daughter's name was Ann and she'd be eighteen now."

Diane Genero looked up; this time her eyes stayed with him. She saw his hurt, and looked unselfconsciously at the interweave of thin, jagged scars which ran down his left cheek all the way to his upper lip, cutting through the thickened pink flesh.

"How?" Her voice was sensitive, soft.

"Car accident." His reply was clipped.

"I'm sorry." She was sincere but somehow dismissive.

"I was driving."

Their eyes met again and the loneliness returned, swallowing them both. He could have cried then, wailed like a baby; it was in him, somewhere. Tramped down below piles of case reports and black and white photos of a hundred Gina Generos, like a rusted nail beneath a ton of earth. He could permit the guilt, the self-hate; he would not tolerate the indulgence of self-pity.

"She had a few friends at school. I think they were all into drugs."

"I'd like to talk to them."

"I have their names."

"How long will you be staying?"

"Long enough to make the arrangements. And long enough to help you in any way I can." Her voice was stronger, sincere.

He chose his moment, standing up from the chair. "We should go along to the hospital now."

Her back straightened; she braced herself. He closed the distance between them in a single step, touching her arm gently, guiding her to her feet.

"Have you got a coat?"

"In the closet, I'll get it." Her voice had lost none of its strength, but there was a hollow inside it, a vulnerability. Fogarty watched her walk to the adjoining bedroom, admiring her elegance. He remembered the body of Gina Genero, naked in the cold morning sun, bent forward, her legs twisted beneath her. The skin on her forehead had split, exposing the bone, the flesh ground away by the weight of her killer, mounting her from behind. Moyer had concluded that it would have taken at least twenty minutes to cause that depth of abrasion.

Twenty minutes. Fogarty imagined the scene. A fury crept up from the base of his spine, traveling inch by inch through his limbs. He clenched his right fist, squeezing his fingers tight into his palm.

"I'm ready." Diane Genero's voice cracked the shell of his anger. She walked from the bedroom, wearing a blue woolen coat, soft at the shoulders and belted at the waist. Fogarty forced a smile, holding the door open, catching the scent of perfume as she stepped into the hallway.

Class. The single word hung like a price tag in his mind. The last place in the world he wanted to escort Diane Genero was to the city morgue.

It was 8:20 the following morning when Fogarty returned to his office. The memory of Diane Genero's expression, frozen at the moment the sheet was removed from her daughter's face, wouldn't let him go.

No tears; not on the outside, anyway. She'd remained stone-silent, sitting in the car beside him, all the way back to the Bellevue.

"Thank you, you've been very kind." Her parting words. "Very kind."

The low thunder of a motorcycle engine jarred him into the present tense. Fogarty turned in his chair, looking from his window to see a black Harley glide gracefully into the space between his Buick LeMans and a rusty Firebird.

"Who the fuck . . . ?" he muttered, watching the leather-clad figure dismount and lock the bike. The rider wore dark glasses beneath a half-face helmet. He kept the helmet on as he walked away from the motorcycle.

Fogarty caught the phone on its third ring.

"Yes?"

"Lieutenant Fogarty?"

He recognized her voice, eased his tone. "Hello, Mrs. Genero."

"Would it be possible to see you later today?"

"Of course. Is it urgent?"

"A few things I think you should know."

"What time did you have in mind?"

"Six, seven." Her voice was little more than a monotone.

"Make it eight and I'll take you to dinner."

Silence.

"Unless you have other plans," Fogarty added.

"I have no plans. Eight is fine."

The phone went dead and Fogarty noticed the red light blinking on the receiver. He pressed the intercom button.

"Yes, Millie?"

"A Mr. Tanaka to see you, Lieutenant."

Charlie Chan. I forgot all about him. His mind raced, looking for a put-off.

"Shall I send him in, sir?"

"Yeah, OK," he said finally.

Fogarty recognized Joey Tanaka the moment he stepped through the door. Moyer's assistant wore a white shirt and grey-and-blue-striped tie under the black leather jacket. He carried his motorcycle helmet in his left hand. For a moment he seemed ill at ease, his posture too precise, spine straight and shoulders back. Fogarty thought he might be the recipient of a formal bow; he had a moment of uncertainty. *Should I bow back?* Then Joey Tanaka extended his hand.

Fogarty accepted it with light relief, surprised that it was as big as his own. In fact, Tanaka was a good bit taller than Fogarty's six feet. He was also no kid. Early to mid-thirties, Fogarty guessed. He noticed that the shirt beneath the leathers was starched, white and neatly pressed. Tanaka had a definite quality, almost a military bearing.

"Thank you for seeing me, Lieutenant." His voice bore only a trace of an accent.

"No problem. Sit down."

Fogarty watched his visitor settle into a green office chair.

"You wanna coffee?"

"No thank you, Lieutenant," Tanaka answered.

Fogarty was drawn to the large brown eyes. *Something about his eyes. . . . Yeah, that's it—no slant. He's got Western eyes.*

Tanaka stayed with him, seemingly unconcerned by the lieutenant's disfigurement. Again, Fogarty felt self-conscious.

"Bob Moyer said you had something for me."

Tanaka straightened, spreading his wide shoulders.

"A theory," Fogarty added.

"It involves the method of attack," Tanaka replied.

"Go ahead, I'm listening." Fogarty sounded gruff. He didn't mean to; it was just that he couldn't get a bead on Joey Tanaka. The man's demeanor made him uncomfortable. And Fogarty didn't like to be uncomfortable, particularly in his own office.

"First of all," Tanaka began, "the assailant isn't punching. Not in a conventional manner. The bruising is too concentrated and deep. It's going right through the sternocleido mastoid muscle and into the jugular." He illustrated by pressing his index and middle fingers into the side of his own neck. Fogarty clocked the enlargement of the first and second knuckles on the doctor's hand.

"The wounds have been identical on all three bodies. With one exception." Tanaka hesitated.

Fogarty cocked his head, discouraging any dramatic event.

"There was evidence of nine blows to the neck and head of the Lasky girl, seven to Janine Nickles, and four wounds on Gina Genero," Tanaka stated.

"So he's using a bludgeon and he's getting cleaner. Probably more confident," Fogarty said.

Tanaka ignored the interjection and continued, "The movement is downward, at a forty-five-degree angle, then in." He illustrated his words, this time with a sharp, linear movement of his right hand. He held his fingers rigid, his thumb tucked downwards. "*Nukite*—spear hand," he explained.

Fogarty waited.

"A death strike, meant to kill her instantly," Tanaka added.

"What are you getting at?" Fogarty asked.

"I've seen this method of execution before."

Execution? The doctor is suddenly talking about execution, Fogarty thought, remaining silent.

"Tokyo. Enforcers employed by the Yakuza, highly skilled in martial arts."

Fogarty stared into the handsome, almost pretty face, trying to piece Joey Tanaka together a little at a time. Most of the pieces didn't fit. "Have you come in here to tell me that the Japanese mafia are knocking off young girls and then sexually assaulting them?" His voice held a distinct edge of sarcasm.

Tanaka shook his head. "I'm saying that the striking method distinguishes our killer as much as the nature of the assault following death."

"So our executioner," Fogarty slipped the word in, "is practicing karate somewhere?"

"Is or has; the injuries correspond to that type of discipline."

Fogarty thought for a moment. Three months, three homicides, no real headway. *What the fuck . . .* "How many people in this city are involved in a martial art?" he asked.

"I don't know, but I can find out," Tanaka answered.

"I take it you're one of them?" Fogarty ventured, nodding towards Tanaka's hands.

"A couple of times a week, a little teaching," Tanaka replied.

Fogarty thought the reply was just a bit dismissive. He was about to pursue it when Tanaka added, seeming to sense Fogarty's question, "Not like in Japan."

"Find out for me, I'd appreciate it," the lieutenant said, getting up from his chair.

Tanaka stood simultaneously, assuming correctly that the meeting was over. He liked Fogarty, saw through his rough manners and valued the honesty beneath. He knew he had been scrutinized continually during the last twenty minutes. Fogarty had never let down his guard; Tanaka respected that. It was a good example of *zanshin*; perfect posture, mental alertness.

"And you'll do the leg-work for me on this karate thing?" Fogarty asked, extending his hand.

"My pleasure, Lieutenant," Tanaka replied.

This time Fogarty was attentive to the sure strength in the even grip. He wanted to say something friendly, aware that he'd been less than forthcoming.

"That's some bike you came in on," he offered.

Tanaka's face lit up. "Thanks. It's a '53 Panhead."

Fogarty looked puzzled, somewhat let down. "Hell, I thought it was a Harley."

Joey Tanaka laughed, revealing white teeth with no fillings. "It is a Harley, Lieutenant. It's called a Panhead because of the pan-shaped tops on the rocker covers." *Rocker covers?* Fogarty thought of asking what a rocker cover was. He didn't, and Joey Tanaka was gone, leaving the question on Fogarty's face.

Bob Moyer picked up his phone just as the echo of the Harley's straight pipes died in the street below.

"Who the fuck is Joey Tanaka?"

Moyer laughed. The forensics man had anticipated the call.

"You figure he's on to something?" Moyer countered.

"Maybe. But what's his background?" Fogarty remained deadpan.

"His mother was from Boston, his father is Mikio Tanaka, Japanese industrialist. Mikio Tanaka's a heavyweight; computers, automobile engines, you name it."

"So what's his son doing as a forensics trainee in Philadelphia?"

"He didn't get here that easily. I think having an American mother helped."

That explains the eyes, Fogarty thought, working the pieces into place.

"Joey served his time as a Yojimbo. . . ."

"*What?*"

"A bodyguard to his old man. Standing beside stretch limos and negotiating non-union contracts with the Yakuza."

Another piece slid into position.

"Becoming a doctor was Joey's idea, paying the toll as a Yojimbo was his father's."

"Why? Why a bodyguard?" Fogarty inquired.

"That's a long one."

"Give me an outline. I like to know who I'm working with."

"Mikio Tanaka was the first All-Japan Karate Champion, nineteen fifty-six or seven. Joey would've been about three then. By the time he was ten his father had him in training and by the age of twenty-three he was upholding the family . . . tradition. . . ."

"Which means?"

"He was in the finals of the All-Japan Championship. Then something happened, an accident."

"Like what?"

"I'm sorry, Bill, he's real sensitive about it. Maybe he'll tell you himself." Moyer hesitated. "Anyway, he's a damn good doctor. And he's as intuitive as a rattlesnake," he added.

"A rattlesnake?" Fogarty gave the word a curious twist.

Moyer laughed. "Joey's all right, believe me."

"Thanks, Bob, I believe you."

*   *   *

West River Drive is a congested exit from town on any weekday
evening at six o'clock. On this particular evening it was backed
up to the Art Museum. Fogarty did his best to relax, tuning his
radio to Kiss 100, Philadelphia's easy-listening station, while
scanning the smooth, gray-brown water of the Schuylkill.

Two eight-man rowing shells entered his field of vision, their
oarsmen pulling with long, synchronized strokes. He watched
them glide soundlessly by, then disappear round a bend in the
river. Behind him a motorcycle eased out from bumper-to-
bumper traffic, accelerating in the outside lane, free from the
snarl-up and frustration.

A '53 Panhead? Not that one, sounds more like a lawn mower,
Fogarty thought, recalling Joey Tanaka, his western eyes and
starched white shirt.

The Presidential Apartments, built in the late Fifties, are a
complex of cream-colored brick buildings. They stand ten floors
above City Line Avenue and, on a clear day, provide a south-
easterly view of the Schuylkill River, all the way to City Hall.

It was 7:10 when Fogarty walked into his two-bedroomed,
sixth-floor apartment. He'd live there since selling the Adison
Street townhouse, nine months after he buried his family. Now
everything was in 611A—remnants of his past, all accounted for
but not quite in order.

A fine mahogany coffee table, surrounded by six high-backed
carved chairs, sat just off-center at the far end of the rectangular
room; an ornate alabaster chess set lay on the table, its pieces
forming no particular pattern and appearing dusty in the sliver
of moonlight which pierced the curtained window. Lacklustre
beige carpet ran beneath the table and chairs, brightened only
by the presence of two kalims and a blue and gold Chinese
throw-rug. Nice things, some of them expensive, yet lacking the
proper care and placement.

His wife had been the decorator, the one with taste. Now the mild disarray seemed to suggest that she would return, straighten things up.

Fogarty didn't really *live* in the apartment. He used it more to store things; his clothes, his memories. He still slept in the old four-poster, drank a cup of coffee at the pine breakfast table and, very occasionally, sat in the upholstered armchair to watch television. Basically, though, Bill Fogarty's life existed outside these creature comforts, in cold city streets and public bars, in the company of policemen, officials and strangers. That was his penance.

Fogarty was in and out of the Presidential in the space of thirty minutes; a shave, a shower, a change of clothes. He met Diane Genero in the lobby of the Hotel Atop the Bellevue at eight sharp.

III.

KATANA
THE JAPANESE LONG SWORD

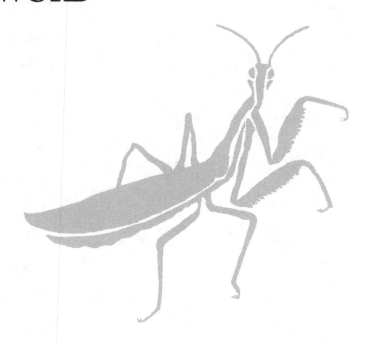

Rachel Saunders stood in the shadow of the half-open door. She was not quite a raging beauty, not in the classical sense. Her face was a shade too round and her nose a shade too wide, set between huge, ice-blue eyes. "Potato nose" was her self-appointed nickname. She'd used it more in college than she did now.

She wore her hair loose today and it hung like a shining, honey-blonde curtain down the back of a dark-blue Miyake cashmere suit. Well-shaped, rounded calves appeared from below the hemline, flowing into long ankles and beautifully proportioned stockinged feet.

Saunders loved sex, unashamedly and not always discreetly. Not quite a hobby, more a serious pastime. In the last five or six years she'd simmered down a bit, three steady boyfriends. In the past year only one. She studied Joey Tanaka as he walked, naked, from the bedroom.

"I thought Orientals were supposed to be small," she teased, estimating that she could be equally naked within the space of ninety seconds.

He looked up, not the slightest bit startled by her presence. "I'm only half Oriental," he said.

She still didn't know when he was joking and when he was serious. "That's no excuse," she continued, walking towards him.

The feeling of her eyes on his body excited him. He was semi-hard by the time she touched his penis.

"I've got Samurai blood," he added.

"So what?" she countered, encircling his growing organ with a soft, warm hand.

"The Samurai sword is three feet long."

She pulled and squeezed simultaneously.

"Worn with its cutting edge up," he added.

She let go and dropped to her knees in front of him. Her fingers touched lightly beneath his scrotum as she pretended to examine his erection. "Three feet? I would say, in that case, that this couldn't possibly be a *katana.*"

Her use of the proper Japanese never failed to add to his arousal.

"Maybe a *tanto,*" she whispered, referring to the traditional eight-inch dagger.

He rested his hands on the top of her head, feeling the softness of her honey-blonde hair. It had been the first thing he had noticed about her. She had been turned away from him, talking to one of the nurses at the Jefferson Hospital. Her hair was pulled back, hanging in a braid outside her hospital coat. It was the longest hair he had ever seen, reaching below her hips.

Turning, she had locked eyes with him. Ten months later they were sharing a single-bedroomed apartment in Rittenhouse Square.

And now she was delicately circumnavigating the head of his penis and he was having serious thoughts about giving the dojo a miss. The muffled sound of a bleeper put an end to his indecision.

"Oh, no," whispered Rachel, withdrawing her tongue and using Tanaka's *tanto* as a convenient support while she rose to a standing position.

The disconcerting signal was originating from a suede briefcase beneath the wood-framed bed. Tanaka pulled on his underwear, then a pair of thick cotton socks, watching as she switched off the bleeper and used the bedside phone to dial her office.

"This is Doctor Saunders." Her voice was professionally warm.

"Uh, uh . . ." she continued, a slight frown weighting her full lips.

"I see."

She twisted several strands of her crowning glory between her fingers, then glanced at her small Cartier wristwatch. "Tell Mrs. Stoll I'll be with her in twenty minutes."

Stoll, Stoll . . . Patricia Stoll. Tanaka linked the name with the middle-aged face he'd seen so often in the society pages of *The Inquirer.*

Rachel hung up the phone, clearly exasperated. "Christ, I just did her eyes this morning and already she's saying the right one is lower than the left."

Tanaka laughed, tucking a heavy cotton pullover into the waistband of his jeans. "I thought you told me the best part of plastics was regular hours and no emergencies."

"The best part of plastics is six hundred grand a year," she countered.

They walked together to the narrow, marble-floored hallway leading to the front door. Saunders' black patent-leather Charles Jourdans sat dwarfed beside a pair of equally black Engineer boots.

"I'll be back by nine, I'll have some dinner ready," she offered.

"I may be a bit late. I've got something to take care of," Tanaka said, tugging his boots on.

She wanted to ask what he needed to take care of. She restrained her impulse, knowing that he'd blank her. *Something to do with his work, probably that murder investigation,* she surmised. A tension grew between them.

He is half Japanese, she reminded herself, rationalizing his sometimes dark, brooding nature and his occasionally chauvinistic attitude. Every now and then she felt frightened of him. It was a passing feeling, one she couldn't explain.

He slid open the closet door to reveal an extensive array of designer label coats and one shining leather jacket. He smiled as he grabbed the jacket. *Leather so tough you can come off at a hundred and thirty and it won't even tear,* he had announced on the day he acquired it along with matching black pants. *Unfortunately, the bike won't go over ninety without rattling to pieces,* he'd joked. He wore the pants when it was cold, December onwards. Tanaka rarely went out without the jacket.

The tension had lifted by the time he picked up the saddlebags containing his black belt, towel and gi. He followed Rachel

Saunders to the elevator. They exchanged a warm, dry kiss before separating in the underground parking lot, the surgeon heading for a Mercedes 450SL while the forensics trainee walked to his Panhead.

Faces turned as he entered the changing room. He walked to a grey metal locker with "Tanaka" printed above the combination lock.

"*Oss. Oss.*" A chorus of the standard dojo greeting following his eye contact with most of the dozen men who stood in various stages of undress. Tanaka smiled and did his best to allay their anxieties. To them he would always be the Japanese giant. The man they had read about in *Fighting Arts International*, the one who had been disqualified for crippling his own brother in the National Championship. The guy everyone respected, even feared, but no one really *knew*.

"How are ya?" Ben Chagan asked.

Joey turned to see the bearded man using his right hand to tighten both ends of the drawstring of his gi. The white sleeve of Chagan's uniform came to just below his elbow, half covering the inscription "USMC/Saigon '71" which formed an arc above a red and blue crucifix tattooed on to his muscular forearm. The other sleeve of his training suit was sewn at the end, concealing the stump of his left arm.

"Fine, Ben. You?" Tanaka answered.

"All right," Chagan said, the continual hint of a challenge in his eyes. "See you on the floor," he promised as he walked towards the main dojo.

"Hello, Joey!" *Sensei* Tetsuhiko Azato called from beyond the open door of a small room marked "office".

"Welcome back, *sensei*." Tanaka answered, bowing as the solidly built, fifty-eight-year-old chief instructor appeared. "You look well, *sensei*, very tanned," he continued, extending his hand.

"Barbados is beautiful in October," Mr. Azato replied. "And your father, you hear from your father lately?"

Tanaka bristled, trying to conceal the impact of that single word, "father". *Sensei* Azato smiled, aware of his student's sensitivity.

"I spoke to him three weeks ago, *sensei*. He asked after you, said they'd missed you this year at the Budokan," Tanaka managed.

"Good, good," Azato said, his voice becoming softer. "Don't lose touch with your father, Joey. Don't lose touch."

I lost touch thirteen years ago, Tanaka thought, nodding slowly. Beyond the wood-framed door he could hear the class coming to order. He bowed to his teacher, turned and double-timed to the pine floor.

An hour and ten minutes into training and the group was separated according to grade. White and yellow belts faced each other on the near side of the floor, green, purple and brown in the center, and black belts at the far side.

Sensei Azato gave brief instruction to each group. He got to the black belts last.

"*Jiyu-ippon kumite.* One attack, semi-freestyle sparring," the *sensei* ordered.

Tanaka handled his first three opponents easily, more as a teacher than an antagonist, creating openings and counter-attacking with a practiced control.

From the corner of his eye he could see Chagan. The ex-marine was being particularly heavy-handed, blocking as if to break the attacking limb, then "digging in" with his counters. A trickle of blood was running from his opponent's nose.

"*Yame.*" The *sensei*'s command to stop and change partners.

"Remember, one attack, one killing blow," Mr. Azato shouted.

And it took four attacks to kill Gina Genero, Tanaka thought, studying Ben Chagan's callused feet as the ex-marine walked towards him. Then Joey turned, straightening his gi, glancing a moment at the dozen folding metal chairs lined up on the other side of the spectator rail. There were always onlookers, occasional winos in from the cold or friends of the participants, but mostly would-be members wanting to watch before joining. There were eight or nine in tonight, *eight or nine too many*, he thought, scanning their faces, sensing his own nerves. Joey Tanaka hated audiences; he also feared them. *Relax, breathe. It's all right. It's over, he's not there.* He coaxed himself from anxiety, chasing back the shadowy premonition that had haunted him for thirteen years. He turned again to face his opponent.

Chagan's emotionless gray eyes waited, his thin mouth set firm behind a reddish beard. They were eyes that had seen battle. Tanaka felt his own spirit harden, his nerves held in suspension. It was as if the two men had never met, exchanged pleasantries or greeted each other in the locker room. Now they were mortal enemies, about to engage in a simulated combat, using each other to perfect a killing strike, a decisive counter.

"*Hajime.*" The *sensei* ordered them to begin.

By the time they got to coffee there were tear tracks running through the light powder base beneath Diane Genero's eyes.

"Mark Pearl." Fogarty repeated the name. "You think that was where the stuff was coming from?"

Diane Genero nodded.

"And you're sure they weren't sexually involved?" Fogarty pressed, instantly annoyed with himself for not having chosen a more delicate term.

She bristled, a trace of anger crossing her face, softened only by the black hair which fell on to the shoulders of her cream silk blouse. The outline of a low-cupped lace bra rose and fell beneath the fabric.

"I'm sure," she said, holding his gaze.

A screech of brakes gave Fogarty the excuse to glance towards the window. He looked through the inverted neon A of a sign which read "Angelo's". Beyond the glass an angry driver waved his fist at a yellow cab which had stopped to discharge its passenger. Fogarty stared a moment, not so much at the cars or the passers-by, but at the white glow of the neon sign.

Angelo's . . . Twelve candle-lit tables and an overpriced wine list. Was I hoping for romance?

He was vaguely embarrassed when he returned his attention to his dinner companion. "I'm sorry," he said.

"So am I." Diane Genero's tone was full of ambiguity.

"*Jodan.*" Chagan's voice was low, announcing the upper-level attack. He shifted laterally, raising his right fist to indicate that he would be using a reverse *gyaku-zuki* punch instead of the customary left thrust.

There was little more than a body-length between them, Tanaka moving in careful countertime to his opponent's flat, hedging shuffle. He could see the *sensei* in the periphery of his vision. He felt the stern eyes, evaluating, criticizing, preparing a progress report for Tanaka senior.

He was aware of the taste of blood, mixed with the salt of his sweat. Chagan's last *jodan* punch had caught his upper lip, grinding it against his teeth. The one-armed man had turned his handicap into an advantage, developing a deceptive feint with the empty left sleeve of his gi while striking with a broken rhythm. Tanaka was aware of the way Chagan's eyes locked into him, as if to freeze and destroy the spontaneity of his movement. Still, he willed himself to relax, deepening his level of alertness, clearing himself of any preconceived defense.

Chagan shifted back, his rear leg bent at the knee, using the muscles of his support foot and calf for spring. A split second later he attacked, his right fist flying forward, powered by the counter-clockwise twist of his hips.

"Yaaah!" Chagan's kiai cut the air.

Tanaka moved forward, into the attack, drawn by the energy of the charge. A fist's distance separated his throat from Chagan's punch. His right foot swept hard, catching Chagan's ankle a split second before it rooted to the floor.

The one-armed man flew parallel to the hard wood, propelled by the combined force of his own movement and Tanaka's perfectly timed sweep. He landed on his side, his missing arm unable to break his fall. He shifted to his back, bunching his legs.

Too late; Tanaka was already behind him, bending down in a half-squat, gripping Chagan's hair with his left hand while drawing his knife-hand back.

Sensei Azato was close now. Tanaka could make out his silhouette. Behind him a spectator leaned forward against the guard rail. A flash of light caught his eye. *The glint of the steel frame of a wheelchair. His brother's distorted face sitting on top of a wasted body, mouth drawn back to form a soundless cheer, eyes bulging.* Tanaka froze in mid-motion.

"Yaaah!" Chagan's war-cry shattered the image as his foot broke inwards against Tanaka's groin guard. The fiberglass box barely absorbed the forbidden kick. Tanaka was furious by the time the one-armed man had recovered from his backward roll. He waited for Chagan to stand, then kicked him squarely in the solar plexus. Chagan collapsed, rolling on to his side. Tanaka moved above his heaving body, lifting his foot to stamp down.

"*Yame! Yame!*" Azato's command halted him, just.

"Control!" Tanaka heard the word hiss as the *sensei* brushed purposely close to his shoulder.

Later, after he had showered and changed, he found Mr. Azato waiting for him by the front door.

"Tanaka-*san*," the *sensei* began, laying a fatherly hand on his shoulder, "what happened in Tokyo is finished. Now you are here, you have a new life. You must not be held prisoner by old wound. . . . You understand, Tanaka-*san*?"

Joey tried to imagine Mikio Tanaka, reaching out to him from behind the *sensei*'s eyes. It was impossible. Since that day his father's relationship with him had been one of *giri*, a loyalty born of obligation. Josef was provided for and his activities monitored, but there was precious little *ninjo*, or human feeling.

He held Azato's eyes, controlling a deep sadness. "I'm sorry, *sensei*."

"No time for 'sorry'. You must conquer your mind, forge your spirit, become equal to life's tests." The *sensei's* voice hardened.

"Oss," Tanaka said, bowing to his teacher.

Ben Chagan appeared from the changing room, keeping a distance. "Fuckin' crazy man," Tanaka heard the muttered words as Chagan eased by. Then Tanaka turned, pulled open the glazed door, and followed the ex-marine into the night.

IV.

A SUSPECT

"**Y**ou guys let me handle this," Fogarty said, passing by the window of the gray Ford. "Just stay cool," he added before walking up the broken stone path leading to the ten-room boarding house.

Fogarty judged the man who opened the door to be in his late forties. One of those pre-psychedelic characters who maintained an air of bohemia. Dark, receding hair, streaked with silver-grey, pulled back and tied in a pony-tail, his swarthy face was hidden beneath an unkempt beard. Distaste, mixed with an air of annoyance, clouded Mark Pearl's muddy eyes.

"What can I do for you?" His voice was fat and arrogant, a touch of the Bronx. It was obvious that "Scarface" hadn't come about a room; even if he had, Pearl wouldn't have wanted to know. He was selective with his rentals, strictly college students, preferably female.

Fogarty flashed his ID.

"You gotta warrant?" Pearl was quick off the mark, the door halfway shut before Fogarty's foot slammed into the wood below the letterbox.

"Look what ya fuckin' did, man. Ya got no right to run this trip on me." Pearl's voice took on a martyred tone, his hand motioning to the dirty print of the lieutenant's size elevens.

"I'm going to give you a choice," Fogarty began, stepping into the dingy entrance hall. The smell of greasy eggs wafted from a windowless corridor to his left. "You talk to me now, be real cooperative, and I won't bust your ass for what I know you do to make your money."

A barefoot girl in a billowing, knee-length T-shirt appeared from the egg-infested hallway. She stopped, staring at Fogarty as though he were an apparition.

"S'all right, Tina, no problem." Pearl oozed fatherly affection.

Fogarty scanned Tina's thin arms, surprised there were no needle marks.

"Maybe we should talk in the other room," Pearl suggested.

* * *

The "other room" was out of context with the parts of the house that Fogarty had seen. It was clean, and the residue of burnt incense hung gently in the air.

Pearl offered Fogarty one of the two wooden chairs, square-backed and austere, the type Fogarty remembered from the priest's private chambers in his parochial school. He sat down while his host settled his corpulent body into position on top of a large, carpet-covered cushion in the center of the floor, folding one leg beneath the other into an attitude very close to Gina Genero's death posture. He looked at Fogarty, smiling without showing his teeth; a Jewish Buddha ready to dispense wisdom.

"Gina Genero." Fogarty studied Pearl's eyes as he spoke the name. Nothing moved, not even the smirk. Fogarty felt anger building.

Then, slowly, Pearl took the foot of his lower leg and lifted it up and over his right knee, drawing the heel back to his pelvis. He held Fogarty's eyes as he relaxed in the full lotus.

The policeman was halfway out of the chair before he caught himself, holding back, his insides seething. *This sonofabitch knows something. He's fuckin' taunting me.*

"Gina was one of my children," Pearl whispered, his eyes suddenly sorrowful.

"One of *my* children?" Fogarty repeated. "What does that mean?"

"She lived here. Her first year at school. All these kids are like children to me." He opened his arms expansively.

"Why don't you cut the shit, Pearl?" Fogarty said with low menace. The overweight holy man began to weep.

"Gina was a special lady; she had talent, real talent. A gift from the gods," he blubbered.

Fogarty wasn't sure how much more he could take. He waited a measured interval, then interrupted Pearl's mourning.

"She was getting drugs from you."

Pearl looked up, offended.

"Cocaine," Fogarty stated.

"No coke, man, I don't do coke. Nothin' to do with coke." He was adamant.

"When was the last time you saw Gina Genero?" Fogarty asked, changing tack.

"Coke's bad karma, man. Bad karma," Pearl continued as if Fogarty hadn't spoken.

"D'ya wanna talk here, or you want me to arrest you?" Fogarty's threat had an immediate effect. Pearl straightened and met the policeman's eyes.

"Maybe two weeks ago. She dropped by. I didn't expect her."

"What happened?"

"We talked."

"You gotta do better than that," Fogarty pressed. He stood up from the chair, his right knee on a level with Pearl's head.

"Maybe I oughta get my lawyer," Pearl suggested.

Fogarty pressed his knee forward, brushing against the bushy beard, a dangerous caress. Peal seemed to rise from the pillow in a single movement, his body deceptively agile. He stood even with Fogarty, and close enough to touch. It was the first time the policeman had felt even the hint of a threat. He stepped back, out of striking range.

Pearl smiled. "I don't like being interfered with, Lieutenant." There was a hiss in his tone.

Fogarty thought of Joey Tanaka, of his theory. He glanced at Pearl's heavy hands, noticed the shortened index finger on the right, the fingernail and top joint missing. It was an awkward moment, a psychological arena in which the table could be easily turned. *Could this be Gina Genero's killer?* Fogarty had to find out.

His next move was more instinct than premeditation. A straight shot to Pearl's gut, a fist's distance down from his solar plexus. He felt his hand enter a pocket of soft flesh beneath the denim work shirt. He half expected retaliation, a kick, a thrust.

Pearl doubled over, sucking air, heaving as if to vomit. Fogarty watched, keeping his distance, anticipating the counter-attack.

"You ugly mothafucka!" Pearl spewed. He stared at Fogarty. There was no fight in the brown eyes, indignation but no fight.

Fogarty backed towards the door, two thoughts crystal clear in his mind. *Pearl is not Gina Genero's killer. The girl's murder had nothing to do with two grams of cocaine.*

"My lawyas will fuckin' crucify you!" Fogarty heard the proclamation as he walked out of the house, leaving the door open.

The two narcotics detectives waited in the gray Ford. Fogarty nodded and the men slid out of the car and walked briskly towards the open door.

The lieutenant's next call was to a converted loft on Bank Street. The business card, tucked above a grimy entrance buzzer, read "Jeanette Key, Private Dancer."

Fogarty pressed the buzzer. A female voice crackled through the perforated speaker of a two-way intercom.

"Who is it?"

"Lieutenant Fogarty, Philadelphia Police Department."

"I can't hear ya."

"Lieutenant William Fogarty," he repeated.

"Who?"

"Police Department." He was now shouting at the broken speaker. It crackled back and Fogarty eyed the reinforced steel door, considering the merits of a forced entry.

"I still can't hear ya! Did Arthur send you?"

Fogarty didn't answer.

"Are you my eleven o'clock?"

"Yes!" the lieutenant boomed. An ear-splitting buzz and the door was ajar.

Fogarty entered. The hallway was lit by fluorescent tubes and was void of decoration. An industrial cage-like elevator awaited at the opposite wall.

"Press No. 1 for Jeanette Key." The words were scribbled on a sheet of lined paper and taped to the cage door.

Fogarty rose with the rumble of pulleys in need of grease. His ascent halted with a back-wrenching jolt. He stepped out into a vast living space.

An old-fashioned formica table and four red vinyl-covered chairs were positioned by a gas stove and a white metal sink. A feeding bowl with "Rudy" stencilled on its side sat at the base of the sink. To the left a pink velvet sofa curved ceremoniously around a glass-topped coffee table. There were two thin joints laid out on the table; beside them a humidor full of greeny-brown marijuana.

"Do a joint if you want. I'll be right out." The voice came from behind a sheetrock partition which didn't quite join the girdered ceiling. Fogarty sat down in one of the vinyl chairs.

Seconds passed, then came the sound of a tape being loaded into a cassette player. A click as the machine was turned on. Strains of Pachelbel's "Canon in D major" floated between the top of the partition and the high ceiling.

"Arthur said you were into classical stuff," the voice intoned.

Fogarty conjured pictures of Arthur, then began to become angry with the voice behind the partition. Not because of the drugs, or the obvious realm of employment, but because of the lax security; the fact that he had penetrated this far into this person's domain without being challenged or vetted. He stood up, half facing, as the door in the center of the partition swung open. A large black cat appeared first, spotted Fogarty and darted behind the sofa. An equally black woman followed.

Jeanette Key was short, sinewy to the point of muscularity. *A female body-builder*, Fogarty guessed. She wore spike-heeled red shoes, white stockings, a black bra with holes cut for the nipples, and matching panties, minus the crotch. She seemed to travel on the crest of Pachelbel.

"I'm sorry. Rudy can be so rude," she said, nodding in the direction of the cat. Then, "Here, I hope it's your size." She pushed a Tarzan-style striped body suit toward the lieutenant. Fogarty was lost for words.

"Don't worry, honey, Arthur told me you like to dress up."

Fogarty turned towards her, silent. He could see her wince,

then the confusion began in her big brown eyes. She glanced once at the coffee table, then back at the policeman.

"You are from Arthur, aren't you?" She began to drape herself with the Tarzan suit.

"I don't exactly know how to tell you this, Miss Key, but I'm Lieutenant William Fogarty from the Philadelphia Police Department." The policeman held his badge forward.

"Oh, God." She seemed transfixed by the bronze shield, her body appearing to liquefy with the fading D major strains. "It's not what you think," she pleaded, flowing forward to wedge the striped Spandex between her legs, then pulling up the straps to cover her breasts. "I do wrestling, light body contact," she continued.

Fogarty nodded his head slowly.

"No sexual intercourse, absolutely none," Miss Key confirmed, a glimmer of hope in her voice. "I'm serious, no sex," she repeated.

"Look," Fogarty began, " I didn't come here to investigate your livelihood. I don't give a damn about Arthur or the grass." He motioned towards the table. "I came here because you were working at the Birdcage Lounge on the night Gina Marie Genero was murdered."

A wash of sobriety straightened the face beneath the curling white wig. In spite of her sinew, Jeanette Key looked small and, somehow, innocent.

"May I change my clothes, sir?" she asked.

"Go ahead."

Three minutes later the Pachelbel concert had ended and a barefoot, beautifully featured black woman with short cropped hair and a blue terry-cloth bathrobe stood in front of Fogarty.

"Let's sit down," he suggested.

An hour later Rudy was positioned snugly in Fogarty's lap. They had covered the evening of the twenty-sixth in fine detail. Fogarty had a list of dancers and regulars; he also had a hazy description of the "Raincoat."

"One more time, Jeanette," he began, aware of the twitching fingers, pumping foot and repetitive speech patterns that suggested his subject was reaching the end of her concentration.

"I couldn't get a good look at him. It was dark, and there's always so much smoke," she said for the tenth time.

"He was big. . . ." Fogarty primed the pump.

"And he had dark hair, a black leather jacket, a strange face. Maybe Hispanic, or even Indian. Like an American Indian, kinda swarthy, and he had to be strong, really strong."

"Why?"

"Because he jus' lifted that crowbar lock and slung open that fire door like it was made'a plywood. You think it was him that killed Gina?"

"Where does that fire door lead?" Fogarty continued.

"Into the alley, joins the main street at Tenth."

"And why the fuck did you let me in here without knowing who I was?" Fogarty's voice was suddenly hard, ten decibels above his normal speaking voice. Rudy hissed, jumped to the floor and scurried beneath the sofa. Jeanette Key sat bold upright. She seemed on the verge of tears.

"I could see the top of your head from the window," she whimpered, pointing towards the barred glass at the street-facing end of her loft.

"So what?" the lieutenant said.

"You didn't look kinky or nothin'. I just thought you was early."

Fogarty stood up, fixing her with a stare that was midway between a policeman and a father.

"Don't be stupid, Jeanette, don't be stupid." Then he was gone, into the cage and down to the street.

He passed a small, bespectacled man wearing a silver-streaked toupee and a pin-striped suit. The man turned, glanced quickly at Fogarty, then scurried by the door with the "Private Dancer" placard above the buzzer. Fogarty kept walking, turning back once to see the nervous executive make his second pass at the loft.

* * *

The waiter at Ringwolds, "Open 24 hours", couldn't add much to Jeanette Key's description, other than that the man had unusual hands.

"As if they were deformed, you know, like the knuckles were swollen and the first couple o' fingers broken at the joint. To tell you the truth, lieutenant, the guy made me so uncomfortable, I didn't like to stare."

"Uncomfortable? Why?"

"Hard to get a handle on it. Jus' somethin' dangerous about him. He was so calm . . . No, different than calm . . ." The waiter hesitated, stretching his powers of description to find an encompassing phrase. "He was. . . ." The blue, beady eyes squinted, adding lines to the high forehead below the clumps of mangy brown hair. Finally the narrow lips pursed. "Like ice about to melt. Yeah, like ice about to melt."

"What?"

The waiter looked up, hurt that Fogarty had not appreciated his metaphor. "Like he was completely uptight, but keepin' it together. I mean seriously uptight. You know, like too far gone to even talk. He never said a word. . . ."

"Yeah. But could you identify him?" Fogarty pressed, clearly irritated.

The man shook his head. "I never saw his face."

V.

THE AUTOPSY

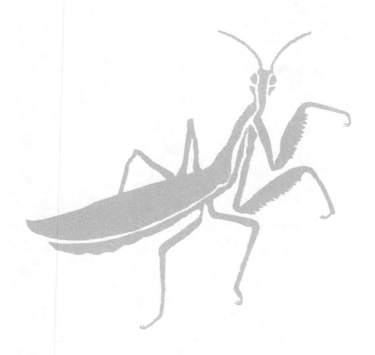

The smell of the mortuary never failed to sicken Fogarty. It was a combination of Gorgonzola, burning rubber, stale urine and rotten eggs, all swirling through the ducts which pumped the recycled air into the windowless rooms.

His long relationship with Bob Moyer allowed him the privilege, on occasion, of watching the pathologist's work. In this case Moyer had postponed the autopsy for a day, giving the lieutenant time to make some inquiries. The pathologist understood that the policeman's instinct was sometimes primed by viewing the body during dissection. A disfigurement, a seemingly random bruise, anything to align him with the psyche of the killer.

"They're just beginning, sir," the attendant stated while helping Fogarty with his boots, hospital gown and green plastic apron.

"Won't need those," Fogarty said, leaving the rubber gloves in the attendant's hands. "Thanks," he added, walking from the garment lockers towards the double doors of the operating room.

Gina Marie Genero's body was naked, her head hanging backwards over the edge of a green metal table. Moyer and Joey Tanaka stood close by the body while a third man, probably a student, hovered in the background, pencil and notepad at the ready.

Moyer acknowledged Fogarty with a sharp nod of his head, then motioned for Tanaka to proceed. The young doctor stepped forward, gripping the body beneath the lower lumbar area, pushing with his right hand and rolling Gina Genero on to her right side.

"Some rigor mortis evident in the extremities," he began. "No superficial evidence of decomposition. Palpation of the breasts and abdomen reveals no abnormal swellings. Evidence of bruising and discoloration to the flanks and outer tissues of the rectum. External vaginal area normal. . . ."

Tanaka's voice droned on, finally losing any semblance of human warmth, like a computerized signal transmitting data. The student with the notepad recorded furiously.

Moyer sidled up to Fogarty and said under his breath, "We've had the X-rays and done the preliminaries on the rectum. Nothing up there; a lot of torn tissue, but no objects. We know what killed her, so this is going to be a partial. I'm going to let Doctor Tanaka do it."

As Moyer spoke, the student assistant went to the worktop and lifted an enamel jug of steaming water. Tanaka arranged the body in a supine posture as the assistant poured the water into a basin to the right of the corpse's head.

Next, Tanaka picked up a long-bladed knife and made three cuts that opened the body. The first two were at the sides of the neck, joining above the breastbone; the third was a longer cut which severed the tissue of the abdomen. He was careful to avoid the umbilical tendon below the navel.

Tanaka then placed the knife on the worktop and quickly cleaned his gloved hands in the hot water. Fogarty watched, quietly impressed by the young doctor's dexterity and confidence, hardly able to associate the distinguished robed figure with the leather jacket and roaring motorcycle.

Tanaka pulled back the skin flaps, exposing both ribs and breastbone, taking a pair of long-handled shears to cut through the cartilaginous tendon. He removed the front ribs and breastbone in one piece. The internal organs of Gina Genero's chest glistened beneath the overhead lights.

Fogarty noted that her right pectoralis was marginally larger than her left. *Right-handed* he thought, and suddenly recalled Diane Genero's voice. *A painter, my daughter wanted to be a painter.* He inhaled, shutting down the part of him that governed his emotions.

He looked again to see Tanaka raise the neck flap, folding it up over the chin. Gina Genero's face maintained a vague, close-lipped smile. Then the young doctor took a curved scalpel and circumvented the inner edge of her jawbone. Her tongue appeared in the aperture. Tanaka grasped the tongue and manipulated it into the opening of the neck. Continuing his pressure, he liberated the pharynx, epiglottis, larynx and trachea, cutting them free from their attachments.

Fogarty backed up a full step, breathing deeply to maintain perspective. He had always reserved a certain awe for Bob Moyer, and now that reverence was extending towards the tall half-Oriental in the green robes. As if within this small putrid theatre, unseen by any audience, these men were capable of feats that bordered on magic.

Moyer moved forward, viewing the damaged organs. Then Tanaka spoke, his voice cold and matter-of-fact.

"Superficial laceration of the internal jugular, caused by contact with the cervical vertebrae. Severe contusion of the carotid artery. Contusion of the vertebral vein. Contusion of the hypoglossal nerve. Contusion of the vagus nerve. . . ."

The student assistant wrote with a speed to match the staccato voice.

"Contusion of the phrenic nerve, laryngeal nerve. Haematoma in the carotid sheath. Hyaline cartilages shattered, driven clean through the larynx, shredding the trachea."

Drowned in her own blood. Fogarty repeated the cause of death in his mind, closing his eyes a moment, drawing pictures on the dark screen behind his lids. *A man, a big man. Striking like an animal, swiping, clawing over and over in a frenzy. No. There was no frenzy. There was control. He was attacking with a deadly, studied control. Like an animal with a human mind, disciplined. His victim too frightened to resist.*

Fogarty opened his eyes.

Tanaka stood away from the body with the mutilated organs in his outstretched hand. "This took a hell of a lot of force," he said, his voice, at last, sounding human. It also sounded strangely respectful.

VI.

A PRESSURE DAY

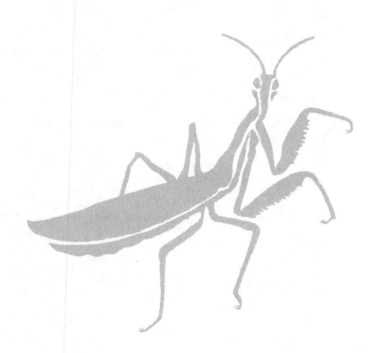

The lieutenant rolled down the window of the silver Le Mans. A blast of cold air blew in from across the river. The dark water almost looked clean in the bright sunlight, as clean as the Schuylkill could ever look. Fogarty glanced at his watch; seven o'clock. An hour from now and the expressway would be jammed. But now, right now, it was a straight gray ribbon, all the way to Vine. He kept the car at sixty, eyeing the road for the potholes that made it notorious. *The Sure-Kill Expressway*; they seemed to appear overnight.

Today would be a "pressure day." Mark Pearl had proved a dead end, not much more than a dime-bag dealer, seducing little girls and playing guru to half a dozen college students. The bust had uncovered an ounce of cocaine and a cache of FX, the latest in designer sex stimulants. Enough to close down his rooming-house and, theoretically, enough to put the ageing beatnik away for a few years. Fogarty doubted it would happen, though; Pearl's lawyer was already claiming that his client had no knowledge of the drugs being on his premises. This, on top of "police brutality" and Pearl's impeccable record within the community—working at the day center with reformed junkies—pointed to the case never seeing a courtroom. A slap on the wrist, some heavy lawyer's fees, maybe a term of probation, but no incarceration for the corpulent Mr. P.

At any other time this would have infuriated Fogarty to the point of obsession. He would have been all over Pearl like a cheap shirt. Now he couldn't afford to give the fat man even a little harassment. *Well, maybe a little. . . . A couple of plainclothes and a gray Ford outside for a few days. Just so the asshole knows I haven't forgotten him,* Fogarty concluded as he followed the road left towards the Vine Street off-ramp.

A pressure day. He'd call Moyer first thing to see if the autopsy had turned up anything else, anything at all. He knew it hadn't, Moyer would have been on to him, but he'd call anyway. Sometimes listening to the same details gave him fresh ideas.

* * *

Chief Inspector Dan McMullon was waiting as Fogarty entered the pine-scented, air-freshened office building. "Bill, how are you?"

Fogarty smiled and nodded.

"I think we got a major problem," McMullon continued.

Fogarty could hear the embarrassment behind the Chief Inspector's tone. It had been there for three years, ever since McMullon, the younger man, had received the promotion which had been slated for Fogarty. Snapped it up. There was a rumor that McMullon had testified to the lieutenant's "head problems" following the automobile accident. Only Internal Affairs knew for certain, but Fogarty suspected it was true.

He dropped his smile. But the time the elevator arrived, Bill Fogarty was aware of just how major a problem it was.

Diane Genero was gone, her daughter's body with her. Before she left she had been corralled by Bev Richards, WPVI's Voice of Philadelphia. The result was an expertly edited two-minute interview with a grieving mother, as much in the dark as to her daughter's killer as when she had arrived in the City of Brotherly Love. She'd even given Bill Fogarty a nice mention, probably an attempt at gratitude but, with the help of some judicious cutting, a testimonial to his incompetence.

"There's nothin' we can do to block it. I've already twisted a few arms. No result, they know they've got something big. It'll get networked."

As McMullon spoke, Fogarty recalled Diane Genero's blue eyes and elegant manner. Then he thought of Bev Richards, a five-foot-two-inch fire-haired stick of ambition.

"Where'd they get hold of the Genero woman?" he asked.

"In the driveway of the Bellevue, on her way to the airport. Oh, it's a fuckin' beaut."

Fogarty and McMullon exited the elevator and walked side by side down the gray-green corridor. "The gutter press'll grab it by tonight an' tomorrow Philadelphia will have the hottest serial killer since Gary Heidnick."

Fogarty looked at McMullon, remembering the six naked women, strung up and tortured in Hydenik's basement. They'd hardly looked human by the time they were found. More like animal carcasses.

"This is gonna get crazy, Dan," Fogarty said soberly.

"An' we're gonna look like the Keystone Cops," McMullon added.

Fogarty sat down on his orthopedic cushion, glancing at the name scrawled on his blotter.

"We gotta do something, quick," the tall, hulking Chief Inspector said, settling into the chair facing Fogarty's desk.

"Look, Dan, this is an outside shot, but I may have something." Again Fogarty looked down at the name on the pad: Joey Tanaka.

VII.

THE FACE

Walter Dromgoole had a fleck of saliva hanging from the hairs of his waxed moustache. He licked upwards as he worked, the tip of his tongue touching the hairs, adding on to the glistening saliva.

Five years ago, when he fronted *Drawing Can Be Easy*, a half-hour show on local television, the waxed Salvador Dali 'tache had been his trademark.

Until the infamous "Donkey" sketch. Performed while still intoxicated from a party held the previous night, in celebration of his forty-fifth birthday.

"Now ladies, here's one you all can do. . . ." His patented lead-line preceded the drawing of a slender lady performing oral sex on a well-endowed donkey.

After that it was a small art supplies shop in Havertown and, occasionally, a brief assignment with the Philadelphia Police Department.

Today he was working for Lieutenant W. T. Fogarty. Hunched over a desktop easel, following the instructions of a young black woman by the name of Jeanette Key.

The colored likeness of a man's head was taking shape in chalk on the thick white paper attached to his easel.

An elongated head topped by longish dark hair combed straight back. Large brown eyes positioned wide apart above high, well-defined cheekbones. The lips were full, yet there was a cruelty in their set, as if they were being held taut against the release of some undesired emotion.

"Make his nose smaller," Jeanette Key instructed.

Walter Dromgoole complied and within seconds a smaller version of the same, slightly aquiline nose replaced the existing image on the paper.

"Now you can bend it slightly at the bridge. Like it's been broken and maybe badly reset," she continued.

Dromgoole's pointed tongue licked twice as a third version appeared on the face.

"Yeah. That's sorta like him. Can you darken his skin? Just a shade."

Another lick, a new chalk, and the face took on a slight suntan.

Fogarty didn't want to believe what he was seeing. The man he had just requisitioned to work full-time with him on the investigation was now clearly depicted in Dromgoole's drawing.

"I thought you said you couldn't see his eyes," the lieutenant interjected, already beginning a mental defense against his deep discomfort.

"If his hair was dark, they'd probably be brown," Jeanette Key answered, apparently satisfied with "her" work. "This is amazing," she added, staring first at the smiling Dromgoole then at the chalk drawing.

"Print it," Fogarty ordered.

He sat in his office, staring at the drawing so hard that finally all he saw were the tiny lines forming the whole.

"Could be anybody," Fogarty mumbled, placing the sheet of paper on his desk, standing up and looking down at it again. Then he thought for the thousandth time of the description of the black leather jacket and the deformed hands. "It's fuckin' crazy!" he said out loud, knowing that it was just crazy enough to be true. Hadn't Tanaka come to him with a theory? Didn't these types of freaks love to confess? "Oh come on, asshole, you're getting desperate." Again he spoke out loud. "Joey Tanaka. Joey Tanaka." He listened to his own voice repeat the doctor's name.

He stood up, hands resting on his desk, and looked straight down at Dromgoole's artwork. This time the resemblance was not so clear. He felt greatly relieved.

"Joey Tanaka." He spoke the name again, and the image seemed to refocus. Fogarty stepped back, turned and stared through the window, up into the metal-gray sky. A terrible anxiety threatened his equilibrium. He closed his eyes. A vision of Dr. Tanaka, resplendent in his hospital gown, filled his mind.

The doctor's hand was extended. Gina Genero's windpipe lay like a torn piece of rubber tubing in his open palm. "It took a hell of a lot of force to do this." Fogarty recalled Tanaka's words. Even then he had detected the essence of pride. Pride? Pride or respect. He wasn't sure which. Something had caught his attention. Something that was just that bit out of context with the flat atmosphere of the mortuary. Yet it was also in that room, watching the young doctor work, that Fogarty had begun to trust Tanaka. To sense the skill of his large hands, the precision, the control.

He opened his eyes, looked down at the parking lot, remembering the Harley, the man in the helmet, sunglasses and jacket. That was also Joey Tanaka. He recalled how awkward he'd felt in the doctor's presence. But it was his own awkwardness, his own reaction to the younger man's sureness.

I must be losing it, Fogarty thought, inhaling deeply. But his mind wouldn't quit, hurling details and fragments of suspicion inwards upon itself. *What was the accident that Tanaka was so sensitive about?*

He picked up the print of the drawing, folded it, and tucked it inside the pocket closest to his .38 police special.

Moyer's office was located at 321 University Avenue. A ten-minute shuffle through the lunchtime traffic around City Hall, then west into University City.

Fogarty left his car in a No Parking zone and walked briskly through the smoked-glass doors.

He found the pathologist at his desk, bent over a stack of medical reports.

"Bill," Moyer said, looking up. He stood, removing his glasses at the same time.

"Keep 'em on, Bob. I want you to see something."

By the time Moyer had repositioned his half-lens reading specs, the drawing was unfolded and lying on top of the medical files.

Moyer gazed down, nodding his head as if deeply in thought.

"What do you think?" Fogarty pressured.

"Is this our guy?" Moyer asked.

No, it's your fucking assistant, Fogarty wanted to say.

"Who ID'd him?" the doctor continued.

"One of the girls at the Birdcage," the lieutenant answered. Why wasn't Moyer reacting? Couldn't he see it?

"Pretty distinctive. What d'ya figure, Asian, Hispanic?"

Fogarty was at breaking point. What the hell was the matter with Moyer's eyes? Did he have to say Tanaka's name? He couldn't.

"Where's your assistant?" he asked, trying to add inference to his tone.

"Josef's in the lab. I understand I'm going to lose him for a few days," Moyer answered, continuing to study the compu-fit.

Fogarty nodded.

"If it weren't for the eyes, this guy could be Oriental," Moyer concluded.

Come on. Say it. Say it, Fogarty willed.

"You mind if I keep this?" Moyer requested, lifting the eight-by-twelve print from his desk.

"I'll send you one over," Fogarty replied, taking the picture from Moyer's hand.

The lab was in the basement of the building.

Joey Tanaka sat, shoulders hunched, studying a single human hair through the bi-optic lens of a microscope.

"Hello, Lieutenant," he said softly, never looking up, yet completely aware of Fogarty's approach.

"Hello, Doctor," Fogarty answered.

"Please, there's no need for 'Doctor'. Call me Josef, or Joey, even Tanaka."

Usually Fogarty's response would have been, "Okay, Joey. And since we're going to be working together, call me Bill." But he purposely held back, walking to the lab table and unfolding the drawing.

The picture lay like an indictment beside the man Fogarty thought it so closely resembled.

Tanaka backed away from the microscope, rubbed his eyes and stared down at the compu-fit.

"Who's he?" he asked.

Fogarty thought a moment before answering. "Suspect *numero uno.*"

Tanaka nodded, slowly. "Pretty distinctive face. Looks part Chinese."

Here we fuckin' go, Fogarty thought, moving a step closer to the seated man. "Why do you say that?"

"Aside from the coloring, it's the cheekbones, the way they rise up high, just beneath the eyes. There's a certain. . . ." Tanaka hesitated, finding the word. ". . . delicacy to the bone structure in general. Who put this together?" he asked, meeting Fogarty's eyes for the first time.

"Probably the next to last person to see Gina Genero alive," the lieutenant answered.

"One of the girls from the club." Not a question, more a statement.

Fogarty nodded.

"It gives us a starting point," Tanaka said.

"What d'ya mean?" the lieutenant asked. There was a certain nonchalance to Tanaka's manner and it was throwing Fogarty off center.

"The first places we should visit are the kwoons."

"Kwoons?" Now the lieutenant was asking questions. Yet the single question he had come to ask, the "What was your 'accident' in Japan?" question, slid uneasily to the back of his mind. *Not a good time,* he told himself.

"Kwoon in Chinese. Dojo in Japanese. Means 'training hall,' the place where the martial arts are practiced."

"Oh yeah?" Fogarty mumbled.

"There's five of them in Philadelphia, maybe more that aren't listed."

"How do you know that?"

Tanaka got up from the chair. He smiled broadly, then winked at the lieutenant. "Yellow Pages, Lieutenant, Yellow Pages."

Fogarty half laughed as he returned the smile.

Then, as if on cue, Tanaka glanced again at the picture.

"Did it ever occur to you that the drawing looks a bit like me?" The nonchalance had returned to his voice.

Fogarty laughed again, an uneasy mixture of nerves and amusement.

VIII.

LIKE A LADY DANCING

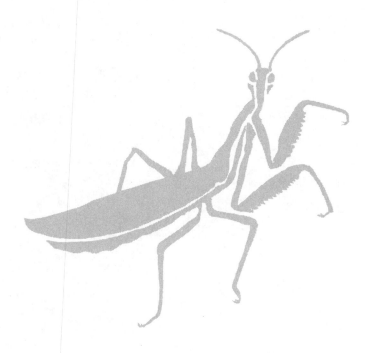

Philadelphia's Chinatown begins at Eleventh and Race, three blocks from the Roundhouse. It is a small area, alive with flashing neon dragons, shops selling herbal remedies and, seemingly, more restaurants than residents. It is the hub of Philadelphia's Chinese culture. Four of Philadelphia's five listed kwoons are in Chinatown.

"Like a Lady Dancing, Like a Tiger Fighting." The white shingle with the gold lettering was positioned prominently above a door with "Pakua" printed in black, center frame.

Inside, a narrow stairway led down into a damp stone basement. Fogarty and Tanaka entered the matted training area through red bamboo curtains. The main room was illuminated by twin-tubed fluorescent ceiling lights. Fogarty counted seven men in the room. One, a diminutive Chinese man with a wispy silver beard and a domed, hairless head, was apparently the instructor. The other six were non-Orientals and could have easily passed for college professors from the nearby university. Glasses and goatees seemed as much a part of their training attire as the buttoned white tunics, baggy black canvas trousers, and rubber-soled cloth slippers. "Moyer would fit right in here," Fogarty whispered.

The instructor glanced over at his guests, gave a quick nod, and continued his explanation of a practice he termed "walking the circle." As he spoke he demonstrated, arms extended, hands open, his palms turning inward then outward as his arms twined in various patterns to correspond with the distinct foot patterns and turning motions of his body. In fact, he did seem to be following the imaginary circumference of a circle.

"Like a Lady Dancing." Fogarty remembered the gilded words above the entrance. He surveyed the goatees. "I'd put a grand on not one of 'em being able to fight like a tiger," he concluded, growing noticeably impatient.

"Now, please, work in twos." The instructor's voice was barely above a whisper.

The lieutenant watched the college professors pair up, one man standing still while the other walked the circle around him. Then the stationary partners began to attack, striking outward with the heels of their palms. The defenders evaded, turning, backing up, using their hands to protect head and body, all the while adhering to the line of the circle.

"Interesting," Fogarty granted, but neither this kwoon nor the six they had previously visited looked like the breeding ground for a sociopath.

In fact, Fogarty hadn't seen anyone yet who he thought could handle a good clean right cross. He had, he reminded himself, been the Police Athletic League Heavyweight Champion from '64 to '66. Not that "Blubberguts" McMullon had provided much competition, but Fogarty did know a good punch when he saw one.

"*Sifu*, thank you for allowing us to visit your kwoon." Tanaka's voice lifted the lieutenant from past glories.

Sifu? Fogarty repeated the word in his head. What had Tanaka told him—in Japanese the instructor is *sensei*, in Chinese, *sifu*.

"May I introduce Lieutenant William Fogarty."

Fogarty extended his hand.

"I am Paul Ke-shan," the *sifu* said, accepting the big hand, and bowing simultaneously.

Paul Ke-shan, Joey Tanaka, Charlie Chan; it was all getting too much, Fogarty thought, smiling and nodding as he parted his jacket enough to extricate the photofit from his pocket, while revealing just a hint of his "Rapid-draw" cowhide shoulder holster containing the blue-barrelled .38.

Fogarty unfurled the police drawing while Tanaka, as agreed, handled the chat.

"If you would be kind enough, *sifu*, to look at this police likeness of the suspect, and try to recall anyone—perhaps a student or teacher from another kwoon, even a former student of your own—who resembles it in any way."

Fogarty held up the drawing. In the background the students had shifted position. Now it was the dancing ladies' turn to remain stationary and fight like tigers. Fogarty was becoming impatient.

The *sifu* shook his head thoughtfully. "What did this man do?" he asked.

"Possibly nothing, *sifu*," Tanaka replied tactfully.

"We're investigating a homicide," Fogarty cut in.

"Homicide?" Ke-shan repeated.

"Murder." Fogarty added bite to the word.

Tanaka turned toward Fogarty with a clear look of warning on his face.

The *sifu* bristled. "You think maybe I have such a man in my kwoon? That I teach such a man?"

"Absolutely not, *sifu*," Tanaka answered, willing the lieutenant to hold his tongue. Couldn't the *gaijin* understand the implications of his rudeness? It was the first time Tanaka had thought of Fogarty as an outsider or foreigner.

"We have come to ask for your assistance," he continued, doing his best to rescind the insult. "A man in your position would be instantly aware of a weakness in character, in either a student or a teacher."

He was relieved to see the Chinese man's tight, thin lips relax. He was also acutely aware of Fogarty clearing his throat.

"Never seen this man before," Ke-shan answered.

Fogarty remained mercifully silent.

"Most teachers in Chinese community take only students from families they know. I am close to campus," the *sifu* explained, glancing over his shoulder, "so I instruct certain men from University."

I knew it, Fogarty thought. *Fucking academics. Sandals and socks.* Again he contemplated his own right cross.

Tanaka nodded thoughtfully. Then, tentative at first, "Is there anyone you have come in contact with, even heard of, who would be teaching or practicing in any way to bring shame upon your community?"

Fogarty refocused, studying the *sifu*'s dark eyes. They seemed to harden with thought.

"One man. Not Chinese. Teaches system based on Wah Lam."

"Praying Mantis?" Tanaka asked.

The Chinese man nodded. "Calls it Wah Lam, but is not. Uses hooking hand, and claw hand, but his technique is without art."

"What's the guy's name?" Fogarty asked.

"He is American man," Ke-shan answered, wrinkling his nose, centering his conversation on Tanaka. "Teaches students in old shop-front, Bainbridge Street, South Philadelphia."

"How 'bout his name?" Fogarty pressed.

"That is all I know," Paul Ke-shan concluded, holding his gaze on Tanaka.

Tanaka bowed and Fogarty managed a grudging "Thanks" before they exited through the bamboo curtain.

"Why wouldn't he say the guy's name?" the lieutenant asked as they headed south in the Le Mans.

"It would have been beneath him," Tanaka answered. There was a sharpness in his tone.

"Give me a fuckin' break!" Fogarty retorted, swinging hard to the left of a gaping pothole.

"Lieutenant, you should try a bit of respect with these people," Tanaka said, his voice growing taut.

Fogarty had had about enough. "Listen, Doctor. So far we've spent five hours and forty minutes watching a bunch of guys in pajamas and slippers balancing on one leg imitating cranes, or 'dancing like ladies.' With due respect to these people and your theory, so far I haven't seen one of 'em who could punch his way out of a paper bag."

Tanaka remained silent.

A slushy rain began, and the Buick's wipers grated against the windshield before smacking loudly into the rubber base of the screen. Tanaka gazed out of the side window, watching two black men complete some hard-fought transaction with the exchange of a folded bill and the slapping of hands.

"Maybe I'm missing something," Fogarty ventured.

Tanaka turned towards the good side of the lieutenant's face. A half-smile flickered in the headlights of the oncoming traffic.

"You know, I was once precinct boxing champ," Fogarty continued, his smile widening.

"Oh yeah?" Tanaka replied. He sounded surprisingly American, just the appropriate edge of sarcasm.

"Yeah," Fogarty said, willingly rising to the bait.

"Heavyweight division?" Tanaka continued, eyeing Fogarty's mid-section.

"Beat the son of a bitch in thirty seconds of the first round," the lieutenant confirmed.

"Is he still on the force?" Tanaka asked.

Fogarty chuckled. "Oh yeah, he's still on the force. . . ."

Now Tanaka was grinning, his curiosity aroused.

"Who was it?"

Fogarty glanced over at him. Even in the semi-darkness Tanaka saw the twinkle in the lieutenant's eyes.

"Didn't even hit 'im in the head. Stuck one straight in his gut. Sent him right down on his ass. And, I swear to God, he dropped the loudest fart I ever heard when he hit the canvas."

Tanaka began to laugh.

"The boys in Second Precinct heard it four rows back."

"Who was it?" Tanaka asked again. He was relaxed now. It was the first belly laugh he'd had in as long as he could remember.

Fogarty turned towards him again.

"Dan McMullon."

The Chief Inspector's name sent guffaws ricocheting off the windshield, fogging the glass.

"Then do ya know what the sonofabitch did?" Fogarty managed, between intakes of breath.

Tanaka shook his head.

"Refused to get back up. Said the whole thing was childish. He quit . . . so the guys booed him and the ref counted him out! I don't think he ever got over it," the lieutenant added, swiping his right hand through the condensation of water which limited his vision to a thin strip of glass at the bottom of the windshield.

Sure as fuck he never got over it, Fogarty thought. *Probably why he badmouthed me to Internal Affairs. Dickhead's got my job.*

The Buick hit a particularly uneven set of trolley tracks. It shook and shimmied as Fogarty fought the wheel.

"Damned thing's all out of alignment!" he cursed.

Tanaka laughed again.

The Keystone Cops; McMullon's description played aptly in the back of Fogarty's mind.

Twenty minutes later, after a slow cruise of the dingy premises which lined either side of Bainbridge Street, the silver Le Mans pulled to a halt in front of a derelict laundromat. To the left of the deserted building stood a single-storey shop with a paint-blackened plate-glass window. "Temple of the Mantis" was etched in blood-red script into the thick paint. "SURVIVAL AT ANY COST" was printed in smaller white capitals below it.

"'Like a Lady Dancing,' is a lot more poetic," Fogarty commented as he and Tanaka arrived at the entrance. There was no handle on the closed door. Fogarty pushed the grimy white button. A loud, grating buzz resounded from behind the steel-reinforced wood.

"Maybe no one's home," the lieutenant said, depressing the buzzer again. This time he held it.

Within seconds, the door opened.

"This is a closed session." The voice was low and gruff. The words distinguishable before either the lieutenant or the doctor could focus on the backlit features of the big man's face. Then the door slammed shut.

"That's a little more like what I expected," the lieutenant said, leaning again on the buzzer.

The door opened wide, its frame almost entirely filled by a man in a black training suit, his huge feet bare.

"I said it's fuckin' closed." The words hissed from a mouth which lacked front incisors. Shoulder-length, oily black hair framed a wide, flat-featured face. Pig eyes stared from beneath a forehead tattooed, dead center, with the crudely conceived likeness of a standing spread-winged insect. The insect was, Fogarty assumed, a mantis, but it could as easily have been a snake's head, or a crucifix with eyes.

Tanaka maintained a prudent distance while the lieutenant met the human barricade head on.

"We've come for private lessons," Fogarty said, deadpan.

Tanaka came a step closer, getting a bead on the pig eyes, watching them decide whether to issue a last warning, or commence with the "private lesson" right there and then, in the street. The man's long, thickened fingers twitched beneath the black canvas sleeves of a training gi that stank of mildew and sweat. Tanaka's abdomen tightened. He became conscious of his breathing, lowering and centering it. The old tournament nerves twitched and fluttered. This wouldn't be a points competition.

"Would it help if I told you that I'm a police officer?" Fogarty relaxed as he spoke, smiling.

"Let them in, Elmo, it's all right." A quiet, clipped voice came from behind the big man.

Elmo emitted a low, guttural growl as Fogarty brushed past. Tanaka paused, a strange thin smile playing on his lips, then vanishing as he locked eyes with the man in the black gi. A familiar mixture of fear and rage began a coiling ascent upwards from the pit of his gut. He felt his self-control slacken. He hated intimidation, had hated it when he'd worked for his father, hated it now. It was a personal thing.

"You ought to wash that gi, it really stinks," he said, low enough so that only Elmo could hear him. Then Tanaka turned and followed Fogarty into the training hall.

The black partitioned walls which formed the entrance hall displayed a cache of medieval weaponry. Spears, long-bladed curved swords, fighting axes and a spiked ball and chain were mounted within easy reach of the tall man with the clipped, elegant voice.

"And what brings you gentlemen to the Temple of the Mantis?" he asked politely.

Even in the dismal light it was apparent that their host was wearing make-up. A pale powder base made his face appear death-like, accentuating slate-grey eyes which seemed somehow liquid behind black tinted lashes. His hair was dyed and close-cropped, cut purposefully into a widow's peak. His moustache was razor thin, divided in the middle and arched above a cruel, painted mouth. A further line of hair dropped from beneath his lower lip, spreading above his chin to give emphasis to his hard, square jawline.

He wore a black cashmere cape above a dark turtleneck jersey, tight stovepipe trousers and black, Cuban-heeled boots. He held a lacquered walking stick with a silver handle in his right hand.

"I am Count Dante, Grandmaster of the Black Mantis Fighting Society."

Under other circumstances this preposterous man with his preposterous title would have elicited a good laugh and a long list of expletives from the lieutenant. But here, in a rectangular space maybe twenty feet long and six wide, with an arsenal of weapons hinged to the wall and a human gorilla blocking the only exit to the street, Fogarty decided to take the count seriously.

He was happy to see Tanaka flanking him, half turned, keeping an eye on both Pig-eyes and their host, and remembered fleetingly that his partner had been a Yojimbo in a former life.

"Would you care to see my credentials?" Fogarty asked, reaching for his wallet. His voice was pitched low, giving it a seasoned resonance.

"That's not necessary," the count replied. "Just state your business and be on your way." Aside from the minimal movement of his lips, Dante's face remained fixed, mask-like, as he spoke.

"We don't look for any trouble with the law, but this is a

private club," he added in time with a resounding thud from behind the thin, plywood door which separated the entrance hall from the training area.

Another thud was followed by a muffled cry of pain.

"You have come at a most inopportune time," Dante noted, as whatever was taking place behind the door seemed to move away until the sounds were less perceptible.

"Then why don't we take care of what we came for, and," Fogarty paused, nodding towards the thin door, "leave you in peace."

"Could you take a look at this picture for me."

Dante stared at the drawing. Fogarty wasn't sure if it was his imagination, maybe even wishful thinking, but he thought he detected just a glimmer of something in those lifeless gray eyes.

"Don't know'm," the count stated curtly, his impeccable English slipping slightly.

"Maybe if we take it into a better light?" Fogarty suggested, moving forward, towards the count and the door behind.

Tanaka watched Pig-eyes shift, nervous, watching the Grand-master, waiting for a sign, a cue.

"I really do insist," Fogarty pressed.

"I cannot allow that," the count answered, lifting his head to make eye contact with his gorilla.

"I can be back here with a warrant in six hours, confiscate your weapons, and probably close you down."

"You will be interrupting an initiation of blood and honor!" the count said grandly.

"Open the door." Fogarty's voice was flat.

Dante nodded curtly towards Pig-eyes, and Tanaka expected a move.

Instead, Elmo appeared to relax. Then the count turned and opened the door.

Tanaka reckoned they'd been inside the Temple for less than ten minutes. His adrenal glands had turned on and off so many times it felt like ten hours, and his mouth tasted like battery acid. He remained purposely sensitive to his accelerated heartbeat.

He was aware of the mental fatigue that could dull a man's awareness when repeatedly taken to the threshold of violent action only to have the threat removed. He wondered if the count and Pig-eyes were playing a game with them. He admired the lieutenant's control under pressure. Very professional.

Still, Tanaka was infinitely better prepared for the scene that greeted them behind the closed door.

He had spent three years in the special instructors class of the Japanese Karate Association; he had seen men tested to their physical and mental limits. "Beyond mind and body lies spirit"—that was what Keino had promised him on the afternoon of his own initiation. Forty-five minutes later it was only his spirit which forced Tanaka to his feet, to stand again before the two-hundred-and-forty-pound monster with the hooded eyes and anvil head. He had certainly discovered his spirit on that day. Yet, even then, Keino's beating had been practiced and methodical. An exercise in attrition, in which, by virtue of physical strength and experience, the new student was the guaranteed loser. But the loss was more of ego and self-importance than eyes and teeth.

The initiate currently being gripped by his throat and held securely against the far wall, his head pressed flat on to the gray cinderblock, had already parted with several teeth. They were lying in a small pool of saliva and blood in the center of the cold concrete floor. A small, wiry man in a gi identical to Pig-eyes' administered this phase of the "blood and honor", while three more stood by.

Tanaka watched the pinioned man try to swing his left fist in a circular punch. The fist got halfway before the wiry oppressor rammed the heel of his hand into the shoulder of the attacking arm. There was a dull popping sound, followed by a garbled scream. Then the five-fingered vice closed tighter around the victim's windpipe and the scream died.

"What the fuck is this?" Fogarty spat the words into Dante's face.

The count bristled. "It is an initiation of blood and honor," he repeated.

"It is also a felony, so call it off!" Fogarty reaching in for the .38.

The count tapped twice against the concrete with his lacquered cane. Pig-eyes reacted with a forward lunge, catching Fogarty by the right shoulder and spinning him crudely towards the closest wall. The lieutenant's head had smacked once against the concrete by the time Tanaka had a grasp on Elmo's oily black hair. He pulled sharply, and long, slippery strands came loose in his hand. Pig-eyes spun round. Spittle flew from his mouth. He sounded like a rabid animal as he clawed in the direction of Tanaka's eyes. Tanaka felt sharpened fingernails tear a patch of skin from his forehead.

It was the last thing he felt before his rage erupted. He wrapped his attacker's arm as it swiped forward again, looping his own arm up and over, securing it as he levered against the elbow joint. A second hand pulled against his cheek, a thick thumb inside his mouth. Tanaka bit down, tasting blood. The hand tried to withdraw and he opened his mouth, allowing it to escape. Then, with the hand clear, Tanaka punched straight forward. A short punch, his fist connecting like a hammer, half turning as it entered the softness at the side of Elmo's throat. He sensed an immediate slackness in the trapped arm, released it, brought his left hand back and struck again. This time with a reverse strike, impacting with the knife edge of his open hand.

Elmo grunted, his eyes glazed and he buckled at the knees. It was only the wall which held him upright.

Fogarty had recovered sufficiently to draw his weapon, yet even with gun in hand he felt strangely impotent. He was only a body-length removed from Tanaka, close enough to see the darkness in the brown eyes, close enough to feel the vibration of the deep war cries, close enough to know that he was about to witness a murder. *I'll get him off for self-defense,* the thought flashed in the lieutenant's mind as Tanaka drew his close-fingered 'spear' hand back for a final strike.

"Stop!" Now it was Fogarty's voice that resounded in the low-ceilinged room. And it was Fogarty's gun that pointed directly into Joey Tanaka's face.

"Fucking stop!" the lieutenant bellowed.

There was a moment, a dangerous, black moment, when Fogarty thought Tanaka was going to turn on him. He wondered if he would shoot, then knew that he would. It was in that moment that Tanaka's eyes relaxed, their terrible concentration seeping downwards as if to release the deadly instinct of his body.

As if he's waking from a dream. Fogarty filed his observations, warding off a sickening dread.

"Now, back off!" Fogarty demanded, glancing towards Dante and the group of men that had gathered.

Pig-eyes remained slumped against the wall, the anterior region of his neck already blue and swollen.

A sobriety had descended upon the Temple. Its members, including the bloodied initiate, appeared somehow chastened by the intensity of Tanaka's violence.

Pig-eyes began to mumble something, rubbing the side of his neck as he straightened.

"A-nother t-time, Shithead. . . ." His words were garbled. Then he fell sideways on to the concrete.

The count smiled, his eyes surveying Tanaka as if he'd just discovered the *Mona Lisa* amidst a warehouse of fakes.

"That," he turned towards his students, "is killer instinct. Only that will overcome your basic weakness for self-preservation!"

"Shut up!" Fogarty ordered.

"This man is not afraid of dying," Dante continued, nodding towards Tanaka.

"How bad is he?" Fogarty asked. The lieutenant's question and the matter-of-fact tone of his voice seemed to lift Tanaka to another layer of consciousness. It was as if he was switching characters in a stage play.

The doctor squatted down beside the body, gently examining

the damage to Elmo's neck. His face was placid when he looked up.

"It's a haematoma in the jugular sheath. A tear. It has sealed itself."

"How do you know?" the lieutenant asked.

"If it hadn't—he'd be dead."

And you'd be up for Murder One, Fogarty thought, searching the doctor's eyes. He saw deep shame, at least, he hoped that was what he saw.

"He should probably spend the night in the hospital . . . for observation," Tanaka added.

"Fucking great. That's just fucking great," Fogarty replied. In his head he was already working on how to bias the incident report.

"And you're coming downtown," Fogarty stated, waving his .38 in the direction of Dante.

The count remained poker-faced. "I don't believe you have just cause."

"I've got about twenty 'just causes', so pack your overnight bag."

Then Fogarty turned towards the initiate. From what he could see, aside from the missing teeth, the man had a broken nose and a dislocated shoulder. "Anything you can do?" he asked Tanaka.

The injured man cowered in the doctor's presence, wincing as Tanaka's fingers explored the ball-and-socket joint, thumb positioned beneath the armpit.

"Relax," Tanaka whispered. Then, too smooth and too quick for resistance, he jerked downwards on the man's extended arm. The joint popped as it found realignment.

Tanaka nodded, then looked into the blood-drained face.

"It's a multiple fracture. His nose should be reset and held by a splint."

"Fine. He can ride with Quasimodo in the ambulance," Fogarty agreed, glancing at Elmo before looking again at Tanaka.

Like an animal with a human mind. Yesterday's intuition drifted back into consciousness. He imagined the photofit, mentally comparing it with the face in front of him. For the thousandth time.

An acute anxiety threatened his composure. He tightened his grip on the .38. It felt heavy in his hand, but good heavy, like an anchor in a storm.

It isn't possible, he told himself. *You're projecting your own guilt, free-floating anxiety.* He'd heard the psychiatric jargon enough times to perform the quick self-analysis. Anything to get him moving, away from what he knew could become a fixation. Tomorrow he'd introduce Josef Tanaka to Jeannette Key.

Rachel Saunders was still awake when Tanaka got in. As accustomed as she should have been to his irregular hours, she could never sleep deeply until he was there, beside her. Then the apartment felt secure, complete. She heard him removing his clothing, knew he was trying to be quiet.

"It's all right. You can turn on the light," she said, rising so that the sheet fell away from her breasts.

Tanaka pressed the button and lowered the dimmer. He smiled when he saw her. It was a sad half-smile, tinged with defeat.

"What happened?"

He didn't answer. Instead, he dropped his white shirt on the floor and walked towards the bed.

She saw the blood stain on the wrinkled cotton, searched his body and face for wounds.

"Come on, tell me," she urged as he sat beside her. Her voice was moving towards a professional mixture of hardness and compassion. Her doctor's voice.

He smiled again. The defeat showed in his eyes.

She wanted to touch him, but knew better, wary that he would withdraw. She remained quiet, waiting for some more subtle psychological link to form between them.

"Not a lot of tit, but what nipples," he whispered, reaching across to stroke her.

She permitted his hand a mild caress, felt her body respond, knew it was the wrong time. Gently she placed her palm on top of his fingers, preventing their movement.

She knew he'd been requisitioned to work on the homicide. She knew the police lieutenant's name, Fogarty. Other than that she hadn't pried. Now something was wrong.

"What the hell is it?" She attempted a stronger tack.

He removed his hand. His eyes hardened and, instinctively, she pulled the sheet up, covering her chest.

"Nothing."

"Nothing?" She repeated his word.

"When I went to talk about it, I will," Tanaka snapped, standing up.

She could have softened then, let it drop, but, somewhere deep down, it was against her nature.

"Oh, thanks," she said sarcastically.

The barrier began its descent, making them uncomfortable strangers.

"I'll sleep on the sofa," Tanaka said, turning.

"You can sleep in the street for all I care!" she countered, regretting her words instantly, but not taking them back.

He turned angrily, glaring. Then Rachel Saunders really let go.

"You come home in the middle of the night, so fucking uptight you can hardly speak, blood all over your clothes. . . ." She was beginning to remind herself of her mother, the original voice of inquisition.

"I'll talk when I'm ready to talk," Tanaka hissed.

"And in the meantime I'm supposed to put up with your comings and goings. I'm supposed to respect your silence."

"Yeah, that's right," Tanaka said sharply, backing towards the door.

Rachel wanted to stop, to let it end, but she couldn't. She was furious now, the past few months of frustration finally finding release.

"And what are you going to do for me?" she continued, turning to glance at the Big Ben bedside alarm. "Perform the rhinoplasty on Jane Rosenthal at eight o'clock?"

The bedroom door slammed in reply.

"If you want some subservient slave, then earn enough money and I'll retire!" she yelled at the closed door. It was a cheap shot and she knew it.

Half an hour later Rachel Saunders was still wide awake, feeling like the type of bitch she dreaded becoming. She'd waited a long time to find someone with the strength and energy to match her own, and here she was doing her best to screw it up. She slid naked from the bed, pausing at her dresser for a quick spray of Paloma before opening the door and walking quietly to the sofa.

Even in the clouded moonlight she could see that the sofa was vacant, the apartment empty.

IX.

QUIET DESPERATION

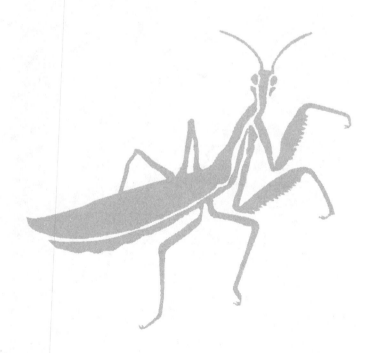

He sat hunched against the door, his buttocks aching, his hair wet and disheveled, and the ragged oilskin doing little to keep the rain off his jacket. He lifted the half-empty whisky bottle to his lips, swilling long and hard, holding the water that the bottle contained in his mouth as, slowly, he turned his head, first right, then left. The street was, for the moment, deserted. The neon Ringwolds sign looked like a lonely beacon amidst the single-story row of closed shops. He could make out the vacant seats at the long formica counter. To his left, adjacent to where he was positioned, the Birdcage Lounge and Nitespot began to empty.

A car door slammed, an engine started, and tires squealed against slick asphalt. Two men in blue-and-white naval uniforms supported each other as they strolled towards him. He swallowed the water, hung his head down, watching their feet as they passed.

He measured the time in heartbeats before he looked up again.

Only a few remained. A cigarette lighter sparked in the moonless gloom, a choked laugh cut the air, then a fine rain began. The stragglers dispersed quickly.

To . . . where? he pondered. What dismal little pits did they inhabit? What purposeless monotony substituted for human life? Quiet desperation. He knew all about quiet desperation. He'd lived with it, immersed and struggling. Until he learned the secret that separated him from its shoddiness. The discipline, the hardening.

His thoughts subsided with the return of stillness to the street. Any minute now she would appear. He silenced his mind and waited.

Jeanette Key walked from a fire exit, euphemistically termed "the stage door". Stopped beneath a flickering arch of birdcage-shaped neon. She had been nervous since the police lieutenant had visited her. Nervous and vigilant.

She looked up, then down the street, noticing the drunk who sat hunched and asleep inside the doorway of Simms Drycleaners. Nobody else, nothing out of the ordinary. Just a drunk. She pulled the black bomber jacket tight to her body. It was going to be a cold night. She glanced again at the sleeping man. Wondered how he survived. Wondered how any of them survived, those men and women who lived on the streets. There seemed to be more of them now than when she'd arrived six years ago. . . . Six years ago, on her way to New York to be an actress, all the way from Atlanta, Georgia. Well, New York was still a hundred miles north and she was still going to be an actress. It was just that she'd been temporarily detained by a lopsided love affair with a married man. At least, she thought it was a love affair; Winston Bright, city-slick and on the rise, had considered it no more than a diversion. A black politician, the first black politician she'd ever met, her own Jesse Jackson. Picked her up when she was waiting tables at the Palace. Dropped her down when he needed to "maintain a clean profile." It must have been clean enough, because he was way up there now, and she was "acting," saving money for the big trip to the Big Apple by prancing around in high heels and crotchless undies for a select clientele of balding bankers, aging attorneys and Japanese businessmen.

"C'mon, it's rainin', I'll give you a ride." Arthur's voice intruded upon her thoughts. She hadn't even noticed that the club lights had been turned out.

"What? All the way to the next block?" she replied, knowing what kind of ride her "business" manager had in mind.

"We'll have a drink, do a line," the tall, razor-thin black man coaxed, sliding a deceptively strong arm around her shoulders.

It was tough saying no to Arthur. He'd helped her over a few rough patches and he was always discerning as to her client list. He was also generous with his split, fifty-fifty and no rough stuff. Never. Arthur was no pimp. He had contacts all over town.

Managing the club, hiring the girls was a useful front. Out of the six, four did tricks on the side. Arthur never pushed; after they got hip to what exotic dancing had to offer they usually approached him. Gina Genero was an exception. Either she figured it out or she didn't want to know. Gina Genero—Jeanette stiffened, glancing again at the vacant street. Not much had changed. The drunk had rolled a little forward, his straggly head buried between his knees, the bottle lying empty on its side in front of him.

"Would you be pissed off if I said I was tired?"

Arthur smiled, great white teeth in a coffee-colored face. "Some a' my Peruvian'd have ya dancin."

Jeanette laughed. "It ain't the dancin' that worries me." She slid a quick hand along his crotch. "It's wrestlin' the alligator afterwards."

Arthur broke up. "There ain't another one like you!" Then, more seriously, "Sure I can't give you a ride?"

She stepped back, out from under his arm. She would have liked the ride, but she knew it wouldn't end there. And she just didn't feel like waking up with a runny nose and Arthur's over-the-calf banlons languishing at the foot of her bed.

"I figured I'm good for the hundred yards to my front door," she said.

"All right." Arthur stayed smooth—no sense pushing. Jeanette was a good earner. "Might have somethin' for ya' tomorrow anyway. There's a Mitsubishi convention at the Four Seasons."

"I'd better get some rest then," she joked, walking away.

Arthur trailed her with his eyes, then turned and quickstepped across the road, ducking into the narrow sidestreet that concealed the midnight-blue Mercedes 300E. Dropped suspension, alloy wheels, front, rear and side spoilers—you name it, the Merc had it. A hundred thousand bucks worth of German steel, leased and loaded. He climbed into the leather bucket, locked himself inside and relaxed. A quick toot of the Peruvian and he turned the ignition key. Stevie Wonder's "Superstition" blasted from the six wrap-round Blaupunkt New Yorkers. A wiper slapped in four-four time across the tinted windscreen.

The Merc slid through the night like a shark through water, turning west towards Market. Arthur noticed the drunk as he passed. Standing up, there was something about the guy that caught his attention.

He watched him in the rearview mirror; the man appeared to glide along the sidewalk, the oilskin like a cape across his shoulders. His movements, graceful, purposeful, seemed strikingly out of context with the discarded whisky bottle and the desolate street.

A thought began to form in Arthur's mind, a premonition. Erased by the mirrored glare of headlights.

"Asshole." He cursed the unknown driver. The offending car pulled closer, its lights blinding.

"Right, motha fucka!"

Arthur stayed in first, slowed down a fraction, then gunned it. The Merc's exhaust spat a volley of smoke, the extra wide cat-grip tires squealed . . . and the headlights were history.

He knew the black girl would be stronger, more cunning than her white friend. He'd sensed it when their eyes had met in the darkness of the club. She had an edge, a challenge. He had almost taken her then, abandoned the softer kill. Instead, he'd obeyed the thin, reedy voice in his head.

But now he was stronger, closer to permanence. The practice and repetition had honed and sharpened him. He had experienced very little separation in the past week. Very little conflict within the internal dialogue of his mind. The reedy voice had become his voice. The pulse of gauze wings was the beat of his heart. And, like his mentor, he yearned for harder prey. Soft, undisciplined flesh was no longer satisfying. The need for confrontation, for the precise moment of kill, for the sustenance that the merging provided; these needs were constant. Soon he would select a male, a worthy opponent, but, for the moment, the black girl would suffice. She would provide a final trestle in the bridge between the world of reason, bound by intellect and its inherent pain, and the world of the senses, the freedom into which his mentor was leading him. For only in that world was perfection a permanent state.

He had known this for years, understood it with his human mind. Yet the truth had only manifested itself since the killing exercise had begun, taking him beyond the cheapness of thought and into the light.

Killing cracked the shell of his intellect, and merging provided the nectar of enlightenment.

He was no more than twenty paces from his prey. She hadn't turned; the refinement of his being, his vibration, was beyond her perception. He continued the "stalking breath," inhaling slowly through his nostrils, retaining the breath for five paces, then exhaling with a mild contraction of his abdominal wall.

Three people passed. One woman and two men, talking loudly, laughing, never so much as glancing in his direction.

Jeanette Key turned left, walked the ten yards to her door and stopped. She searched her handbag for the palm-sized leather key-case.

He halted in the shadows at the corner, drawing the outside edges of the oilskin across his body.

There was a familiar tingling in the center of his forehead, like the flutter of wings, a death song. He experienced a sublime tension, an acid hunger.

He concentrated on the broken white pattern of her breath in the night air. Knew that she would soon be aware of his power, longed for that moment.

Jeanette slid the brass key from its case, standing on tiptoes to reach the masterlock. The electric mechanism shot the double belt into its retainer with a sharp, percussive snap.

She pulled on the handle, intent on getting inside, closing out the night.

A splinter of light cracked the pavement as the heavy door opened. The Mantis stepped from cover. He stood stone-still, every fiber of his being aimed at the black woman in the red coat.

She turned, her instincts suddenly tuned to his presence.

A tall, broad silhouette against the backlight of the street-lamp. Out of focus . . . yet still she knew him, recognized him innately. As if she had known he would come for her. He appeared to magnify, looming larger as he rushed forward. Blocking out all hope of escape. She could see his eyes now, dark and glowing, locked on to hers.

"Please, no. God, no." She froze for the moment it took him to wrap her in his arms. To crush her face against his leather chest as he forced her through the doorway.

Then she fought. Gasping for air, twisting, screaming in muffled rage, all her energy concentrated on survival.

She dropped down, found a pocket of space inside his grip, reached inside her handbag and touched the cold metal cylinder. Releasing her handbag, she brought the aerosol upward.

The propellant discharged with a sinister hiss, finding only the leather and a patch of skin above his collar. He swallowed, gagged, and backed away in time for a second burst.

"Get away. I'll blind you—swear ta God. Blind you!" she screamed. He raised his arm, protecting his eyes. The ammonia-based liquid rained against the oilskin. He sprang towards her.

"Away!" Her voice broke as he seized her attacking arm, wedging his thumb into the belly of her bicep, tearing inward.

The can flew from her grasp, smacked against a wall and rolled uselessly along the concrete floor.

Her adrenalin masked the pain of separation between bone and muscle. Her arm was numb, hanging uselessly when he released it.

He slid a half-step back in time with her kick to his groin. Smothered by his left palm against her knee. Countered simultaneously with a single knuckle strike to her forehead.

"Control. Perfect." He knew the instant she dropped to her hands and knees, dazed but not unconscious. There was a spreading discoloration around her eyes when she stared up at him.

He never blinked. As if his lids had been removed or sewn upward into their sockets. His eyes were round, enormous, and seemed to burn with a dark spiralling power.

He was smiling, at least she thought he was smiling. His thin wide mouth stretched taut across his long face. Ugly pearl-white hands hung loose and shining from the cuffs of his jacket.

Say anything. Buy some time. It was a strangely lucid thought, followed by a desolate fear.

He remained still, his breathing imperceptible. Waiting.

"I'm sorry about the tear-gas," she began, fumbling. "You see, I didn't recognize you." Her voice quivered.

Silence.

"I mean from the club. You know, from the other night." As she spoke she adjusted her posture, glancing furtively at the closed door.

"Please can I get up?" Completely submissive.

He cocked his head, looking down at her from the line of his small, beaked nose.

"Is it all right?" she continued, rising to her knees.

He jerked his head to the side. Short and quick, reminding her not of a man, but an animal. Then he viewed his quarry from a slightly different angle, attuned to the subtle nuances in the varying shades of her voice.

He heard fear, pure and simple—he also heard cunning. All in the vibration of the vowels and syllables. It was the oscillation of sound waves that gave the true meaning of words, identical to the language of wings or the twitching of mandibles.

He moved a measured step backwards, inviting her to stand.

"Thank you." She began to rise, but the trembling in the muscles above her knees prevented balance.

"I'm sorry—too nervous," she apologized, then settled again into her kneeling posture.

His eyes left hers, scanned the hallway, found the elevator. He motioned with a precise nod of his head. She began to crawl towards the steel cage.

Jeanette Key had a fair understanding of fear. In the past four years she had been threatened with everything from a leather strap to a carving knife. Clients who got carried away, took the play-acting too far. Not often, but enough to know that when it got down to the real nitty-gritty, she had only herself to rely on. Panic was the true killer. And now she was finding it difficult not to panic. She could feel his warm, even breath on the back of her neck as they entered the dimly lit loft.

Rudy looked up from his bowl, arched his back, hissed and appeared to rise vertically before vanishing beneath the pink sofa.

He touched her shoulder. She stopped, facing forwards, away from him.

"What do you want me to do?" she whispered.

Again he touched her shoulder, very gently, drawing her round to face him. It was the first time she had noticed the reason for the color of his hands. He was wearing gloves, sheer latex gloves. The type of gloves a surgeon would wear to perform an operation. The fear began to sicken her stomach.

I'm not gonna die. Not gonna die. The vow strengthened her, repeating like a chant inside her head.

He concentrated on the body beneath the jacket; Lycra pants and high-heeled boots. Concentrated hard, eyeing her slowly up and down.

She lowered her head. An image formed: a short, blue-barrelled .22, lying beneath the pillow of her bed. *Far away . . . too far away. I'd never make it.* Another image. The kitchen drawer, directly behind her, and the long serrated-edged carving knife. *Maybe.*

He hit her then. Fast and unexpected, as if he had read her thoughts. More a sweep of his leg than a hit, so hard and clean that it lifted her completely from the ground, dropping her in a seated position, legs front. Her left ankle burned above the heel, where his foot had made contact.

His eyes bored into her. He began to make a noise, a terrible puffing noise, his abdomen rising and falling as he stretched his arms outwards like a crucifix.

Her threshold of terror dropped in steady pulses. She was too stricken to move.

He watched the pupils of her eyes contract, studied the involuntary twitch of muscle beneath her cheeks, saw her full lips tighten. Her tears came last, falling in time with her shallow, broken breaths.

He was controlling her, her mind and body. As he had never controlled the others. They had all been so quick, so rushed. He had been plagued by the separation, had focused anxiously on the critical voice of his mentor. Now the voice was internalized. His discipline was near fulfilment; his orthopterous spirit finding freedom within the confines of his human shell.

He had never revealed the change to any of the others, all had been dead before the final transition. This black offering would be the exception. She was different, stronger. Her survival instinct was seasoned. She refused to surrender.

A knife. Long and saw-toothed. He had lifted that image from her mind, exposed and neutralized it. A demonstration of his power.

He dropped the oilskin, unzipped his jacket and tossed it to the floor. Willing her to watch, to look closely, to validate his work.

Veins and sinews, long and serpentine, coiled and interconnected beneath the smooth, hairless skin of his torso, winding down from his shoulders to form tubular pathways. Thick and heavy with blood at the inside elbow, then spidering out along his forearms to seep beneath the join of latex and flesh. A detailed circuitry of veins and capillaries streaked the squared pectoralis muscles of his chest, while a gnarled, rocky wall of muscle descended into the belted waist of his black trousers. There was a precise symmetry to his development, as if all the striated tissue and tendon had been constructed to rivet the observer's eyes to the star-shaped patch of waxen scar tissue which covered his sternum, centered beneath the place where his nipples had been amputated.

Jeanette Key wanted to run, to scream, to hide away. To deny his reality. Yet she could not move; she could not divert her eyes. She was hardly aware of the warm urine as it began to seep between her legs.

The 300E had just reached the turn-off for City Line when the hard-on struck. Pushing relentlessly against the inside leg of his Armani tweeds, it pulsed in time with the insistent bass-line of Robert Cray's 'Another Woman'.

Arthur Stubbs thought once again of Jeanette Key. He rarely, if ever, imposed upon any of his ladies. Tonight, however, was going to be an exception.

He glanced at the dashboard. The clock read 2:40 a.m. *A little over half an hour since I last saw her. Enough time to get home, get out of her clothes. . . .* He slowed down, took the exit ramp to City Line, turned right; then left at the lights, placing him alongside the Presidential Apartments. Heading straight back along Kelly Drive, towards the city.

Suppose she's got someone with her. . . . It was an outside chance, but one requiring consideration. Arthur pressed the third recall-dial button on the console-mounted cellular phone.

Seconds later, Jeanette Key's number rang.

The Mantis was naked when the phone began to ring. He had just begun the deep, lower-level power breaths, and the electronic bleep cut into his concentration.

He lowered his arms and stared hard at the equally naked black girl who sat in full lotus at his feet. There was both fear and apology in her eyes.

A third bleep. Neither prey nor predator moved.

It'll catch on the fifth, Jeanette Key knew, awaiting the caller's voice as if it were a rescue party.

Four bleeps. She stared into the Mantis' eyes. They appeared to loom with a glowing incandescence. As if they had doubled in size since he had removed the tangled black wig.

There was not a visible hair on his body. Armpits, legs and genitalia were clean and smooth. He had no eyebrows; that was the detail she had missed when recalling his features for the photofit.

Also, there was something wrong with his sexual organs, something unnatural in the angle of his penis and the way his scrotum pulled tight and lopsided at its base. As if he was wearing a rubber prosthesis—the organ seemed attached to, but not part of, his body.

Five bleeps and her music began, the edited intro of Tina Turner's "Private Dancer", Where the lyric should have come in, Jeanette Key's voice started. "Hi! I'm not exactly sure where I am right now, but if you know where you are, I'll get back to you. Leave your name, the time, and your number. Bye bye!"

Her own recorded voice sounded amazingly confident and somehow reassuring.

"Hi babe. On further consideration I'm gonna have to insist you try some a' this blow. If ya got somethin' else happening I'm on the car phone. If I haven't heard from you in ten minutes, it's too late."

She tried not to react, not even to hint at the joy of reprieve she felt swelling inside her. *Ten minutes.* Ten minutes and this would be over. One way or another.

The Mantis' face revealed nothing, but the human mind which lay deep beneath his orthopterous consciousness knew the exact meaning of this change in circumstance. His mentor was sending him an opponent.

He discontinued the power breath and waited.

Arthur saw the dim overhead light in the loft as he whipped the Merc's driver-side wheels on to the kerb outside number three, Bank. The car's door shut with the authority of a bank vault, locked and alarmed with the press of a button. Arthur had his own key to the loft. He kept a key to all the girls' apartments, just in case of emergency. Like now. He was happy to see that Jeanette had not deadbolted the door from the inside. He hesitated in the entrance hall, just long enough for two good spoons of powder, lifted straight from his art deco snuff box. He

got a kick out of thinking that sixty years ago, someone, somewhere was tootin' from the same lid.

He felt good, a nervous kind of good, as he rode the elevator
car to the first floor.

The cage clanked to a halt. Arthur stared through the girdered bars, realizing instantly that he'd made a big mistake. He
could see a man in profile. A large man, unusually muscular.
Naked. With a hard-on.

"Jesus Christ!" Arthur muttered. He was about to press the
button marked with a downward arrow when he noticed Jeanette Key sitting at the man's feet. The whole scene suddenly
focused. Arthur's embarrassment gave way to anger. *Bitch has
been turning tricks on the side. Put me off so she could do some business.*
An unpleasant revelation, coupled with the indignation of a
business manager who had dealt fairly, even generously, with his
client.

Arthur opened the door. The Mantis half turned, his legs bent
slightly at the knee, his hooking hands formed but resting at his
sides.

Jeanette prayed silently.

Instinct told Arthur that something was wrong, very wrong.
Instinct, and the fact that the closer he got to the stationary man,
the more he could make out the details of the freak body and
the face. He was about thirty feet from them when he heard the
strange puffing sound.

He saw the oilskin on the floor, the disheveled wig, the boots.
His mind made the link-up with the bum from the sidewalk. He
could probably have turned, sprinted to the cage, got away, but
the coke was giving him a brittle courage. And getting away had
never been his style.

"You all right, babe?" His words sounded hollow in the vast
space.

Jeanette Key nodded quickly, her legs numb from lack of
circulation and the urine now stinging the inside of her thighs.

"OK, man, whatever you're doin', you're not doin' any more.

So pick up your shit an' get the fuck outa here," Arthur said, levelling his eyes on the Mantis.

Arthur took two steps forward and paused, bending slightly to withdraw the six-inch knife from the side of his boot.

The Mantis watched the stainless steel blade appear, like an extension of the long brown hand.

"Are you gonna split, or are we gonna party?" Arthur asked, inching forward.

Jeanette Key felt it coming, knew Arthur would go all the way. She also knew the freak wanted him to.

She wondered if she could move, run for the knife, or the gun.

Arthur held the blade low, drawn back, his left hand guarding to the front. Just like he'd learned it in infantry school, eighteen years ago, in North Carolina. It worked then and it had worked a couple of times since, once in 'Nam, and once in prison. *Thrust straight in—nothin' fancy. Aim for the third button of your target's shirt.*

In this case the third button was an ugly mass of scar tissue in the centre of a hairless chest. Added to that, the freak had begun to move. Not like a boxer, or a wrestler, but like—Arthur wasn't sure. Karate, kung-fu came to mind, but it wasn't so much the extended arms or open, claw-like hands, nor the bandy, shifting legs that unnerved him. It was the dead concentration in the freak's eyes, and the steady rhythmic breaths produced by the accentuated rise and fall of his abdomen.

The crazy, sick thing was that the guy was still hard. He was actually facing Arthur's blade with a fucking rod-on.

"Does the idea of gettin' cut up turn you on?" Arthur sneered. His words bore a cocky false confidence.

The Mantis stopped his breathing, listened. Picked up the uncertainty in the vibration of his antagonist's voice. With his peripheral vision he monitored the black girl. It was difficult tuning to two minds at one time. Their shared fear, however, gave minimal variation to the thought-waves. He had them both now; he was the center of their triangle of consciousness, the controller.

He tilted his head, giving himself a better view of the room. Remained poised, breathing subdued, capable of striking in any direction.

Like a fuckin' animal, a fuckin' insect, Arthur thought, still hoping against hope that he could intimidate the guy enough to make him split. Knowing, deep down, that the longer the stand-off went on, the slimmer his chances.

"I'm gonna cut that thing off an' stuff it down your throat." He flicked the blade outward in the direction of the freak's cock. His voice sounded less convincing than last time; he decided to shut up. But if he shut up, he'd have to do something. Attack? He shifted forward.

The puffing breath began again in that instant—loud and demanding, accompanied by the long, spreading arms and expanding chest.

A star. A perfect star! Arthur's eyes locked and held on the precise six-pointed formation of scar tissue. Intellect blocked spontaneity, freezing him in a perilous vacuum. In that instant, the Mantis struck—once, fast and sharp with a blurred down-ward motion of his hooking hand.

Arthur's next awareness was of the deep burning centered in the hollow above his cheekbone, where his eyeball dangled on its thread-like optic nerve below the socket. It took him another second to realize what had happened. By then Jeanette Key was shrieking and he, Arthur Stubbs, was instigating a wild, forward lunge with his shining blade.

The Mantis caught him before the attacking arm left its cocked position. Wrapped him in a steel embrace, squeezing the breath from his body. His hands numb, Arthur felt the knife fall from his grip. Heard the steel blade ring as it hit the wooden floor. Then the pain struck, bigger than the pain in his face. Terrible, suffocating, as his ribcage began to cave inwards, compressing his lungs.

"Oh, Jesus Christ, Jesus Christ. . . ." He heard his own voice, lost in the hollow of space between consciousness and oblivion.

He became aware of an odor, a pungent, animal odor.

Breath? Sweat? The Mantis was close to him now. Close like a lover, hot breath pulsing against his flesh.

Then the wide, muscled jaw opened and Arthur stared into a cavern of teeth. A heartbeat later, pointed incisors tore into the cartilage of his nose.

"Jesus Christ—help me—"

The Mantis growled, whipped his head sideways and tore through the flesh and gristle. Over and over again.

There was a noise inside Arthur's skull. Like a howling machine, loud and grating. The pain was everywhere.

"Please God. Please—"

Then darkness.

The Mantis released his grip, allowed Arthur's body to fall to the floor. Then he swallowed, tasted the salty flesh—and something more. A foreign taste, acidic, chemical. Impure. He registered the thought as Arthur Stubbs' nose entered his stomach, its residue of cocaine leaving the Mantis' tongue and gums mildly numb.

The Mantis turned in time to see Jeanette Key crawling towards the door of the partition. She looked like a cockroach, a whimpering black cockroach. He caught her in three strides, lifted her effortlessly and threw her beside the half-conscious man on the floor.

He handled her roughly this time, reshaping her body into the submissive offering posture.

Then he adjusted the man. Listening to him groan and whine, stripping him naked, folding his legs, bending him forward. Ready.

He would permit the girl to watch. Wanted her to see him transmit the fading essence of his human spirit into the hollow shell of Arthur Stubbs. Wished her to witness his Mantis soul harden and crystallize as his orgasm discharged his humanity in empty convulsions.

Then he would work on her.

X.

HE ATE THE CAT

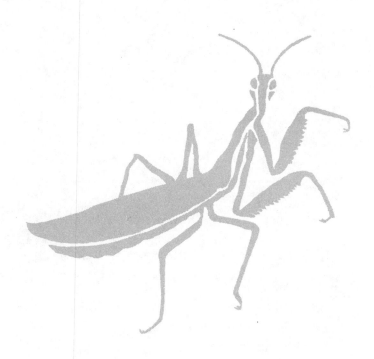

"**H**e ate the cat. . . ."

"What!?"

"He ate the fuckin' cat." The young detective's voice was a mixture of revulsion and amazement.

Fogarty pushed by the stricken man and walked into Jeanette Key's loft.

The two body-bags were laid out in the far corner of the room, near the familiar pink velvet sofa. The clock above the gas stove read 9:05 p.m.

Bob Moyer had concluded his preliminaries, and two forensic men were powdering a large circumference surrounding the naked bodies. Lying to the immediate left of Jeanette Key was the hollow carcass of a black and white cat.

Rudy. Fogarty remembered the big tom's name. He also remembered holding him on his knee less than a week ago. Now most of Rudy's internal organs were missing and a pool of viscous brown blood surrounded his body.

Fogarty walked forward, circumnavigating the silver print-powder, eyes riveted to the cat. As if by concentrating on the least of the three horrors he could function within his own swirling pool of shock, guilt and frustration.

"This time we've got footprints, bite marks and pressure indents from his fingers," Moyer said. His tone was one of consolation.

Fogarty stared at Jeanette Key. She looked small, pitiable, the soles of her feet pink in comparison to her brown posterior.

Arthur Stubbs was positioned beside her, perhaps a yard away. His feet seemed absurdly large compared with his skinny ankles and lean, sinewy thighs. A single-piece stainless-steel knife lay beside him. There was a boot clip on the handle and the trade name "Body Guard" in clear black print on the blade.

Moyer followed the direction of the lieutenant's eyes.

"Nothing on the knife, no flesh, no blood. Just prints from the first victim."

"First victim?"

"His name is Stubbs. Arthur Stubbs."

Fogarty clocked the name. Arthur. Jeanette Key's pimp.

"Time of death precedes the female victim by approximately two hours," Moyer added.

"Two hours. Are you telling me that. . . ." Fogarty hesitated, almost saying "Jeanette." Somehow he couldn't, just couldn't allow himself the proximity, ". . . that the second victim was alive for two hours while—" He balked again.

Moyer shook his head. "I'm sorry, Bill. This one is a lot uglier than the others. The nature of wounding, the bruising. I'd almost say it was a copy, except that I know this was the girl who gave the description. That gives motive—"

Fogarty's glare cut Moyer dead.

"Where's Josef Tanaka?"

"He's still in the hospital." There was a note of surprise in Moyer's reply.

"Doing what?" Fogarty pressed.

"Recovering from the accident," Moyer answered.

"What the hell are you talking about?" Fogarty was taken aback.

"Josef was involved in an accident early this morning. Hit an' run. Pretty bad, totalled his motorcycle, damn near totalled him."

"Where? What hospital?"

"I'm sorry, Bill, I thought you knew. He's in the University of Penn."

"No, I didn't know."

Fogarty felt suddenly blank, as if his emotions had been sucked from his belly. Responsible for everything, yet helpless to intervene, to control. It was a debilitating psychological impotence.

"You all right?" Moyer's question seemed incongruous amidst the flashing bulbs and milling policemen.

"I knew this one, Bob," Fogarty replied, looking down at

Jeanette Key. *Christ, I'm going to cry. Fucking cry.* He managed to stop the tremor before it reached his voice box.

"I told her not to be stupid." His words sounded hollow.

Moyer wanted to put an arm around his friend's shoulders. He resisted.

"Give me a few hours and I'll have something for you," the pathologist promised.

"Right," Fogarty said, then he turned and walked towards the elevator.

Across town, in the high-rise Society Hill Towers, overlooking the Delaware, Mayor Winston Bright was settling down to a late dinner.

His two children, Andrew, aged five and Stella, aged seven, were tucked in for the night, two doors down, in one of the five bedrooms in the mayor's stately apartment.

Winston Bright's political career had been tempestuous, highlighted by the infamous "stampeding horse" débâcle in the mid Eighties.

Despatched to maintain order, a dozen of Philadelphia's mounted policemen had ridden headlong into a three-thousand-strong "Gay Activist" demonstration.

Two marchers were killed and five hospitalized. A single "stampeding horse" was given as the official reason for the tragedy.

Winston Bright bore the brunt of the blame; he had proposed the use of mounted police in the first place.

In spite of the incident, he survived to be re-elected twice, and remained a charming, witty, black figurehead of a rapidly changing city. "Accessible to both business people and ordinary citizens." Or so Mayor Bright said.

He was just cracking the seal on a bottle of Saint-Emilion Château Ausone when the telephone rang. His wife lifted the receiver from the kitchen wall.

"Hello. This is Shandy Bright."

Dan McMullon could all but see the woman on the other end

of the phone. Her face was as articulate as her speaking voice. Small, perfect features, "like a white woman with a black skin." McMullon always said when describing the mayor's wife. And smart as a whip; she had graduated *cum laude* from Bryn Mawr in '76.

"Hello, Shandy, it's Dan McMullon. Sorry to break in on your evening."

"S'all right, Dan. I guess it's important?"

"It is important," McMullon answered.

"I'll get him," she replied, eyeing the pork roast through the glass oven door. Twenty minutes later and they'd have been eating. She pressed the intercom button marked "Dining Room."

"Yeah, honey." Bright's tone was as smooth as the wine, *premier grand cru.*

"It's the Deputy Dog," Shandy Bright announced.

All the way to the Roundhouse, Winston Bright sweated over what McMullon would do if he found out about his affair with Jeanette Key. *No reason to think he's going to find out,* Bright told himself as he slid into a reserved slot at the back of the building. "It'll be the fuckin' press that'll do the digging," he grumbled, sliding from the Chrysler and heading towards the back entrance. McMullon was waiting inside his ground-floor office.

"This is it, Dan. This is it. The last one. Do you understand me, the last one!" Bright's expensively trained voice assaulted McMullon from twenty feet.

The overweight chief inspector raised both hands. When he lowered them his face was flushed red.

"We're on it, Winston. Believe me, we're on it. This time we're gonna have some good forensics. Bite marks, footprints."

The mayor calmed down, eyeing McMullon suspiciously.

"It turns out that one victim was a prostitute and the other was her pimp. The guy had a record a' misdemeanors a mile long. He even did time. Three years for drug trafficking," McMullon stated, then shut up.

Bright used the silence, holding the chief inspector's gaze, nodding his head slowly. McMullon felt pressured to offer more by way of appeasement.

"Stubbs. The male victim's name was Arthur Stubbs. He was still dealing. Coke. Pretty heavy."

"So what?" Bright asked. He knew the answer, but he wanted to sweat McMullon anyway, just in case. Keep him under his thumb.

"So it isn't like the victims were. . . ." McMullon searched for the word, "innocent."

Winston Bright reached up slowly, pursed his lips and ran his thumb and index finger over a coarse stubble of newly grown moustache. Somewhere, hidden beneath several layers of self-preservation, he still had a touch of feeling for Jeanette Key. When this was over, and he felt safe, completely safe, he would allow himself a little remorse. She'd been, in her own way, a good friend. Discreet when he was at his most vulnerable. He owed her something for that.

"Anything else? Diaries, phone numbers?" he asked.

McMullon thought it was a strange question. He'd expected something about the press and television.

"Nothing yet," the chief answered.

Bright considered. She'd never had his home number anyway, not even his private number at City Hall. "Now 'bout next of kin?"

"None for the dealer. The girl had a grandmother in Atlanta. In a home—senile."

Bright was feeling more righteous now. The tragedy was almost reaching him.

"What about the press?"

"Bev Richards is pushing for an interview," McMullon answered, prepared for the mayor's tirade.

Bright lowered his head, licking his lower lip with the tip of his tongue, thinking. Finally he looked up. "And you're telling me you've got something this time? Prints?"

"Footprints," McMullon confirmed. Winston Bright nodded.

His paranoia had all but evaporated. How many times had he actually seen Jeanette Key? A dozen, two dozen times in the course of a year? Basically, she'd lived on hope. It must have been a sad life. A sad little life.

"Let me handle Bev Richards."

Fogarty arrived at the reception desk at the University of Penn Hospital and was promptly informed that visiting hours were over. The curly-haired redhead with a name tag that read 'Smart, Hazel RGN' viewed him down the bridge of her bifocals.

"It *is* eleven o'clock at night."

"I'm aware of the time. I'm also a police officer in the process of an investigation."

Hazel Smart was considering signalling for a couple of orderlies when Fogarty produced his ID.

"I'm sorry, Officer. I wish you had shown me that to begin with."

Fogarty waited.

"I'll just ring the ward and make sure Mr. Tanaka is awake."

"Doesn't matter. I'm going to see him anyway."

"Very well," Hazel Smart answered, shuffling the papers on her clipboard, fingering the patients' list.

"Floor number seven, room 7A. . . . It's a private. . . ." She trailed off as Fogarty turned towards the elevator.

No mirrors in this one, the lieutenant noted, relieved not to have to look at his own reflection. He was sure it was written all over him. He was certain that Tanaka would see it the moment he walked through the door.

Tanaka had known that Jeanette Key helped put together the artist's drawing. He'd known she could identify the man in the club on the night of the Genero murder. Fogarty had seen Tanaka nearly kill a man, had studied his morbid fascination with the mutilated organs at the autopsy. He'd suspected, when no one else even dared note it, the striking similarity between

Josef Tanaka and the artist's likeness. Yes, Josef Tanaka would see the accusation the moment Fogarty laid eyes on him.

The lieutenant marched down the blue-green corridor. He stood a moment in front of the closed door of Room 7A. He could hear the faint whispers of a conversation. He knocked, twisted the handle and entered.

Saunders smiled as the lieutenant approached. Then she got up from the side of the bed, extending her hand.

"You've got to be Lieutenant Fogarty."

The lieutenant accepted her hand, but withheld an apology for barging in. He nodded curtly.

"I'm Rachel Saunders."

"How do you do," Fogarty managed, looking from the pretty blonde to the dark-haired man on the bed.

Tanaka held Fogarty's eyes and shook his head.

"Doctor Moyer called me an hour ago . . . I know about Jeanette Key."

An awkward silence followed, broken by a soft, feminine voice.

"I'm going to go home now." Rachel kissed Tanaka once on the lips, then turned towards the lieutenant.

"Some evening, when you have time, Josef and I would love you to come to dinner."

She brushed close to Fogarty's arm as she walked to the door and out of the room.

"Your girlfriend?" It was the best he could do for pleasantries.

"About a year now," Tanaka confirmed. "She's one of the top plastic surgeons on the east coast," he added.

"Christ. Doesn't look old enough to be a doctor," Fogarty replied, loosening up, but not enough to be friendly. Another pause. Tanaka changed the subject.

"This time Bob's got something. Maybe even saliva."

"Saliva?"

"From the bite on the nose. It's going to be tricky, there was a lot of discharge, even a residue of cocaine," the doctor continued.

Fogarty took a step closer to the bed, his eyes fixed on Tanaka's blackened right eye and the seven stitches just below his hairline.

"Any other damage?" he asked.

"Yeah. It was a mess. Took his eye out, pulverized his testicles." Tanaka hesitated." C'mon Bill, you were just there."

"I'm talking about you, Joey."

"Oh, sorry." Tanaka seemed to settle down. "Nothing much. Mild concussion. That's why I'm here overnight. Nothing broken."

Fogarty nodded.

"Except the bike. . . ." Tanaka added forlornly.

"How the hell did it happen?" Fogarty began his inquiry.

"Some asshole ran a light on Market, caught my back tire an' I lost it."

"Lost it?"

"Control of the bike. I think I hit the curb, then a parking meter. The bastard never stopped. I don't even think he saw me. I couldn't get the bike up. Just too heavy."

"What time did it happen?"

Tanaka studied Fogarty's face. He saw concern in the blue-gray eyes, and something more.

"About—two . . . I'm not certain. What time did we get through?"

"Twelve twenty-three."

Fogarty's answer was clipped, precise. Tanaka took the cue.

"It took me fifteen minutes to get home. Another fifteen in the apartment, and maybe half an hour riding around."

"Joey, there's something I don't quite understand."

"What's that, lieutenant?" Tanaka replied, deliberately dropping the "Bill."

"Why, after five hours of going from one little kwang—"

"Kwoon, lieutenant. I think you mean kwoon."

"—kwoon to another, then after all the shit that went down at the last place, why were you riding around on a motorcycle at two o'clock in the morning?"

Now Fogarty really reminded Tanaka of his father. He resented the prying.

"May I ask you a question, Lieutenant?"

Fogarty nodded.

"Why, when you've just discovered two more victims in a murder hunt that's so far turned up nothing in the line of leads, why are you so interested in my private life?"

There was a barely controlled edge beneath the quiet of Tanaka's voice.

Fogarty smiled, sat down in the chair beside the bed. Readjusted his position, allowing the .38 to sit clear of the armrest.

"They bring you in here by ambulance?" His voice relaxed a shade.

"What's this all about, Bill?" Tanaka decided not to let it go.

"What it's all about is this," Fogarty started. "We've got a murder case that's been going on for five months. We've got twenty-six officers on it, a dozen full-time, and, until I met you, no leads. No theories. Then you come in with this 'death blow' shit, convince Boy Moyer that you're the new Charlie Chan and—" Fogarty hesitated.

"And what."

"And then convince me by nearly killing a man."

Tanaka sat up. He was exhausted, his head throbbed and he couldn't quite figure out where the lieutenant was headed.

"Then there's Jeanette Key. The only person who could have given us an ID on the guy from the club. And she's dead . . . twisted in the shape of a pretzel, lying next to her pimp—"

Fogarty hesitated, studying Tanaka's face.

"But we do have the drawing. The Oriental face, or half-Oriental. . . ."

Now Tanaka understood. Found it hard to believe, but understood. He stared silently as the policeman stood up from the chair. Watched him step backwards from the bed. Began to grow angry at the man's exaggerated wariness.

"I was going to introduce you to Jeanette Key."

"Why?" Tanaka asked, knowing the answer but wanting to force Fogarty into the open.

It was, at that point, as if Josef Tanaka was divided cleanly into two people. His western, rational, self demanded explanation and reason, while his eastern, Samurai self begged for vengeance. A tenuous thread held both halves together, denying action.

"Why?" he asked again, his steely tone shooting warning signals through the policeman's body. Fogarty wondered if he could draw his gun before Tanaka reached him. He backed nearly to the door.

In Japan there was honor. Beyond all else, in spite of all else. Mikio Tanaka had raised his son, both his sons, to understand that without honor a man was nothing. The *gaijin* who faced Tanaka now was about to deny him his honor, an unpardonable insult. Yet, as surely and as poignantly as this truth entered him, there was another truth equally clear in Tanaka's mind. The truth that, as a policeman, Lieutenant William Fogarty had reason for suspicion. Even their mutual friend, Bob Moyer, had mentioned the similarity between the artist's drawing and Tanaka's face. Jokingly, but not without substance. And there was the karate, added to by the incident at Dante's. That reasoning, and only that reasoning, inhibited Josef Tanaka's fury.

He shook his head slowly as he got up from the bed, dressed in a hospital gown, tied at the back of the neck and open behind. Tanaka focused his eyes on the detective, his two selves wrestling with a bitter indecision.

Fogarty stayed loose, as loose as he could, trying not to get caught up in the paranoia of what Tanaka's hands could do to him. He thought of his gun; didn't want to draw it, not unless he had to.

"Jeanette Key was the only one who could identify the killer." Fogarty's words dropped like bricks.

Tanaka glowered, his indignation and fury tipping the balance. He let go. Hunching forward, contracting his diaphragm as the mouthful of saliva slid the length of his tongue and fired from his lips.

Catching Fogarty's face dead center, the spittle spread across his nose and attached itself evenly to both his good and bad side.

Then the lieutenant and his suspect stared dumbly at each other, both at an immediate loss.

Tanaka spoke first. "Take that to Bob Moyer. Tell him to match it with the forensics sample. . . . Or do you need a footprint to convince you?" he added menacingly.

Fogarty scowled, eyeing the opposition as he withdrew a wrinkled handkerchief from his pocket to mop his face.

"*Baka-yaro.*" Tanaka spat out the word.

"What was that?" the detective challenged.

"Idiot," Tanaka translated.

Another silence.

Then the door opened; its handle caught Fogarty in the small of the back and he lurched forward, halting an arm's length from Tanaka.

"What on earth is going on in here?" the ward nurse demanded, studying the two men as if they were misbehaving children.

"Police business," the lieutenant answered.

"Police business, indeed!" she snapped, her dark, deep-set eyes drawing a bead on the detective. Suddenly Fogarty did feel like an idiot.

The nurse spun around, addressing Tanaka.

"And you, sir, are supposed to be recovering from a road accident. Get into bed."

Tanaka obeyed, revealing tight, black-haired buttocks as he climbed beneath the sheets.

"Five more minutes, then I must insist you leave," she added, looking again at Fogarty before closing the door as she left the room.

The lieutenant glanced at Tanaka, then down at his handkerchief.

Finally, Fogarty looked up, apologetic. "Well, what the fuck did you expect me to think?"

Tanaka shook his head. He appeared neither angry nor particularly dangerous.

"You missed some," he said, eyeing Fogarty's face. "Right in the center of your forehead."

Fogarty mopped the wet area.

"And Charlie Chan was a Chinese man . . . I'm Japanese," Tanaka added. Then he smiled.

At 12:17 a.m. Fogarty's Le Mans pulled into a lighted space at the rear of the medical examiner's building. Fogarty felt light, almost unsteady on his feet; a strange giddiness brought on by a combination of deep exhaustion and the relief of knowing that Joey Tanaka was not his man. He had wanted to feel that Tanaka could be a friend, someone he could trust, rely on, and now the gateway to that feeling was clear. He also felt that he was on the edge of a breakthrough—maybe it was Moyer's confidence, maybe his own intuition. A *couple more days and we'll have 'm,* he promised himself as he trudged across the asphalt, towards the rear door of the building.

Moyer's tone was dismal on the other end of the entry-phone. The forensics man looked up as Fogarty passed the six white refrigeration units lining the entrance to the lab. Fogarty noted the two semicircular impressions beneath Moyer's fatigue-rimmed eyes. They were a perfect match with the double optical lens of his microscope.

"Fingernail. Jeanette Key's," Moyer explained, twisting his red goatee into a nervous point as he glanced at the seemingly clear slide at the base of his microscope.

"And?" Fogarty asked.

Apology furrowed the doctor's brow.

"It's not as good as I thought, Bill. Nowhere near. No skin under the nails, no body hair from the killer."

"You mentioned bite marks, saliva. . . ." Fogarty interjected.

Moyer shook his head. "Maybe something in the saliva, but the bite marks are indistinct. The guy must have been wrenching his head from side to side to tear the victim's nose off. Massive laceration but no clear pattern on the teeth."

Fogarty nodded, tightening his lips.

"How 'bout the footprints, indents. . . . ?" he continued.

"Footprints are funny, Bill, not like fingerprints. I've got a couple that are relatively clear, but the guy had to be moving a lot, some kind of circular pattern, like a dance. . . . He sweats, but not enough to give me definite lines." Moyer pressed a button on the side of his metal desk and the microscope dimmed. He stood up.

"Sometimes we can get a decent fingerprint right through a glove. You'd think in this case that would be true. I mean, the guy is pressing inwards at over five hundred pounds per square inch. . . ."

Fogarty nodded, but there was uncertainty in his eyes.

"That's enough to compress your skull. And he's doing it with just his hands, his grip. There's something odd about his fingers. It seems his hands end in hardened bulbs."

"Which keeps taking us back to Joey Tanaka's theory," Fogarty interjected.

Moyer glanced up. A thin film seemed to clear from his gray eyes and a look of guilt drew his tired features further downward.

"Christ. How is he? I never even asked. . . ."

"Joey's all right, Bob. He'll be out in the morning." Fogarty touched Moyer's wiry shoulder, then added, "Our boy's fine."

Moyer relaxed, as if something unspoken had been resolved.

"I can do the autopsies first thing tomorrow. Do you need to be there?"

"Not this time. I'm holding a couple of gorillas overnight, and if I don't get in for questioning, they're gonna walk out on me. . . ."

"One of them is the guy that Joey hit, isn't he, Bill?"

"How did you know about that?" Fogarty asked.

"Joey came over here last night. He'd had a run-in with his girlfriend, or vice versa, and he was pretty upset. Plus," Moyer hesitated, "he didn't feel you trusted him."

"Well—I do now, Bob. I do now," Fogarty stated.

"Good," Moyer said, adding, "There's still some shoe prints in the hallway, and in the elevator. Size twelves. I'm going to take a look at them before I go home."

"I'll call you tomorrow, before noon," Fogarty said, walking from the room.

"I'm sorry I came up short," the forensics man said softly.

Fogarty stopped and turned. Moyer appeared small and suddenly older than his forty-eight years. His entire presence seemed faint, as if he was being absorbed into the somber yellow glow of the overhead lights.

"Don't take it all on yourself, Bob," the lieutenant said. "How the fuck do you think I feel?" Then Fogarty eked out a weary smile, and departed.

Fogarty woke up on the sofa. He had taken valium, and had slept so heavily that last night seemed like last year. He didn't like to take the valium; it was an old prescription, given to him to relax his back spasms following the accident. Now he kept a bottle handy for occasions like this—his body so tired that the drive from Moyer's to the Presidential became an exercise in following the center line, while his mind ticked over on its own energy source. He never unplugged his phone, but sometimes, when he knew it was important to be sharp for the next day, he locked the damn thing in the bathroom, shut his bedroom door, and camped out on the sofa. Seven o'clock—five hours' sleep. Heavy. Like jet-lag sleep. What was that they'd told him at Fort Bragg? A combat soldier can function efficiently on three hours' sleep a night for four to six weeks. Well, he'd had five hours. A cup of black coffee and a cold shower would move the residue of muscle relaxant through his system, then he'd be ready to face things again.

He was going to get this freak. Soon. He could feel it—the

same way he'd felt it when he'd brought Hydenik in and, before that, Rita McCall, the baby strangler. The trouble was—and it was always the same—freaks never had a rational motive. Their patterns were scattered or nonexistent, and no matter how many psychiatric profiles the police shrinks came up with, no matter how many meetings they held to discuss the sociopathic profile of the killer, nine times out of ten it was a random detail or off-the-wall clue that gave them away. With Hydenik it had been a passing comment to one of the tellers in the bank he managed, with McCall a particular perfume on a cheap scarf found near the scene of the crime. This time it would be the same, Fogarty could feel it.

The phone was ringing as he slammed the door of 611A. Probably McMullon. He'd see him soon enough anyway.

Joey Tanaka walked from the tall glass doors of the University Hospital complex and into the cold gray morning. He'd been awake since four, waiting for his doctor to OK his discharge. Waiting and thinking. His life had seemed to him to be a network of incompletions. Japan, his father, his brother Hiro, Rachel Saunders, Bill Fogarty; all open-ended relationships, plagued either by his retreat or his inability to commit himself. Fogarty, perhaps, was the exception—at least that was now out in the open. But only because the lieutenant had chosen to resolve it. In the hours before dawn, Josef Tanaka had inspected his life and decreed himself a failure. A failure and a coward, propped up behind the guise of Eastern ethics and Western rationality, slipping easily from one to the other, according to which suited his need or purpose. He had consciously run away from Japan, eager to embrace a society which, he had imagined, offered greater expression and personal flexibility. Only to find that the rigidity was within him, cultivated by him, used by him. And now he employed this Orientalism as an excuse for his own isolation. He never let anyone too close, not even Rachel. He knew she'd leave him—a month, a year? Eventually their communication would cease. And he would be the loser. Yet somehow, as much as he despaired over this prospect, he welcomed it, invited it. He had set it up. And why? Because he deserved nothing from life. Hiro had nothing. Well, not quite. Hiro did have a fully automated wheelchair, and a visiting team of nurses who bathed him, massaged his atrophied limbs, and changed his underclothes as though they were a baby's diapers. And Hiro did have his father's love. Somewhere, deep within Josef Tanaka's heart, he hated his older brother for that. And then hated himself for his own weakness. It had all seemed very bleak at four o'clock in the morning. Yet now, as Tanaka entered the peaceful apartment on Rittenhouse Square and saw that the hall closet was still full of Rachel Saunders' designer-label coats, and as he watched a bright slice of late autumn sun pierce the sky, entering the south-facing window to turn the grey clouds to silver, cutting a white path across the onyx dining table, he felt a sense of reprieve. *After all, isn't consciousness the gateway to awareness. And awareness is the seed of change.*

He sat down on the sofa and thought of Bill Fogarty. The lieutenant had seemed almost brittle during his visit to the hospital, riddled with his own private guilt and burdened by self-doubt. The investigation was killing Bill Fogarty, not as fast as a bullet, but just as surely. Yet the lieutenant was still fighting, somewhat misdirected, but nonetheless fighting. Tanaka smiled, remembering Fogarty's expression following the saliva sample. Then, as abruptly, Tanaka's smile faded, his face set. A shadow crossed the floor in front of him as the sun withdrew behind a cloud. The room felt cold. And in that moment Tanaka knew, by instinct, by intuition, that he was close to the killer, that their minds were in some way connected, linked. For a time he sat motionless, almost paralyzed. His thoughts struggled with the irrationality of his intuition, yet he knew—simply *knew*. It was going to come down to the two of them, man against man. Then Josef Tanaka contemplated death, his own death. And with this contemplation the pettiness and indulgences of his life fell away. He looked at his watch, it was 9 a.m. exactly, that meant 10 p.m.

Tokyo time. He picked up the telephone and dialed his family's number.

"I see you got a room to yourself," Fogarty commented, walking into the six-by-ten cubicle with its cracked, faded green walls and single cot.

Dante looked up, smirking.

"Probably the title that impressed them, Count," Fogarty continued sarcastically. Dante stood, and the lieutenant was surprised at the man's height—or lack of it.

"You must be packing six-inch risers in those Cuban heels."

"Fuck you, Lieutenant," Dante answered coolly. "When do I get out of here?"

"Depends on whether or not I file charges," Fogarty answered, matching the count cool for cool.

"I'll beat 'em. I got lawyers," Dante snapped, no longer disguising his South Philly twang.

"If you talk to me, you won't need to beat 'em," Fogarty promised. "Elmo's already back in training."

"Oh yeah. Wha'd he tell ya?"

"Nothing to worry about . . . he's very loyal." Fogarty mocked reassurance as he pulled the solitary wooden chair from the corner of the cell. Then, straddling it back to front, he faced the standing man. Dante took the cue and sat down on the edge of the cot. Fogarty noted the delicacy, almost effeminacy, of the count's manicured hands and bare white feet.

"What d'ya wanna know?" the count offered.

"First of all, *Walter*, I'd like you to take another look at this picture," Fogarty began, bringing both the photofit and a well-thumbed copy of *Fighting Arts International* from his inside pocket.

"Walter?" the count repeated, a barely disguised protest in his tone.

"Yes. Walter Purdkok. That is your name, isn't it?" Fogarty said, staying smooth as he handed the count a fresh print of the artist's drawing.

Walter Purdkok, a.k.a. Count Dante, studied the picture, shaking his head. Finally he looked up.

"My name, Lieutenant, is Count Dante. I believe you will find that officially registered in the County Court."

Next Fogarty handed Purdkok the magazine, opened to page twelve. There, written by Graham Noble—Fogarty wondered if everyone in martial arts invented high-sounding pseudonyms—was an article entitled "The World's Deadliest Fighter."

"According to this, Count Dante died in 1975, in his sleep, from a perforated ulcer. . . ."

"The picture sure as hell looks like you, though," Fogarty added, smiling. "Although it says that Dante was six feet tall. . . ."

"All right, all right, Lieutenant. You made your point . . . I was a student of John Keehan—that was Dante's real name. I—" Purdkok hesitated, searching for the appropriate word, "studied with him in Chicago from '68 to '73."

"Then you moved back home and borrowed his title."

"I didn't change my name officially until '81. What the fuck, man, John wasn't using it no more."

"Yeah, Walter, that's true. And besides, your old one was a little dirty. Seven assault charges, three with grievous bodily harm. Even two attempted rapes. . . ."

"What d'ya want outa me?" Purdkok snapped, targeting Fogarty with his dead gray eyes.

"Look again at the picture," Fogarty instructed. "The way this animal operates fits right in with your instruction. 'Maiming, mutilating, disfiguring, paralyzing and crippling' "—isn't that what you advertise?"

Count Purdkok studied the drawing.

"Had a guy come in once. Looked like this," he stated. "Wrong kinda guy for the Black Mantis."

"What do you mean?" Fogarty primed.

"I mean the guy was a fuckin' freak, man."

"The guy I'm looking for *is* a fucking freak," the lieutenant said. Then, for the first time, he let some of his fury through:

"He killed two people less than twenty-four hours ago. Killed 'em an' sodomized them. One woman and one man. The woman had a pet cat . . . an' this fuckin' freak ate the cat.'' Fogarty was standing now, looming menacingly above the count.

Purdkok studied the angry, disfigured face, searching deep into Fogarty's green eyes. He seemed unruffled by the lieutenant's anger.

"The only reason I remember'm, is because of the nose.'' Purdkok looked again at the likeness. "Too small for his face, ain't it?''

Fogarty stayed silent.

"Been busted once. Before he came to us. Kinda gave him a weird look, like a bird or some kinda animal. Made his eyes big an' his mouth seem too wide. I mean, Lieutenant, I'm not sayin' it was the same guy. But the nose looks the same.''

"His name. Give me his name,'' Fogarty insisted, bending forward.

"Never got the mothafucker's name, he only showed once.''

"Oh come on. Do better . . .'' Fogarty pushed, resisting an urge to collar the count.

"If I do better, am I outa here?'' Purdkok propositioned.

"Yeah,'' Fogarty replied.

"All right . . . The guy I'm thinkin' about came in one time, maybe a year, even eighteen months ago. He said he was interested in joining, but he wanted to see if we was for real,'' the count began. "Somethin' 'bout his attitude got to me. Like he was above what we were doin'. Anyway, one thing led to another an' one of my boys invited him out on the floor. . . .'' Purdkok hesitated, looking down again at the drawing. He shook his head, and when he looked up at Fogarty there was an intense, somehow demonic, glint in his eyes.

"He was good. I gotta hand'm that. Not good like your buddy the other night. Different than that. More dangerous.''

"More dangerous?'' Fogarty repeated, wondering just how much more dangerous a human being could be.

"Exactly,'' said Purdkok. "Not so much in his movements or strength, but in what happened to him when he performed.''

Fogarty noted the word "performed."

The count stopped, studying the drawing for what seemed to Fogarty to be the hundredth time.

"Get to it!" the lieutenant ordered.

"He practiced the purest 'Mantis' I've ever seen." The count formed his own hands like open claws, illustrating his description with several quick jabbing movements.

"Don't know where he learned it, but it was clean. An' that son of a bitch actually looked like an insect when he fought."

Purdkok was on a roll now, his eyes wide and his head nodding. "Took four of my best boys to get a handle on 'im—the guy was that outa touch with his own pain."

"Whatdya mean by that?" Fogarty interjected.

"This sucker was really way out there. He hissed, he spread his arms like wings. A fucking freak-show. . . . Until Elmo managed to get a shot at his nuts. I mean a hard shot. Shoulda put'm down. Must have crushed a testicle. He never flinched. Face never changed expression. He coulda killed my boys if he'd wanted."

"So how did it end?" Fogarty pressed.

"After the shot in the balls, the Mantis—that's what we ended up callin' him—backed right out the door an' disappeared."

"Disappeared?"

"Yeah. Gone. Musta hit the street and sprinted. By then one of my guys had a fightin' sword down from the wall an' I think he'd a cut the bastard in half . . . if we coulda found him. The foot in the groin musta done some damage; he mighta been bleedin' inside." The count smiled. "Check your police files for a one-balled psychopath."

"I will," Fogarty said.

"Now when do I get out of here?" the count asked.

"As soon as you give me an exact date on when the 'Mantis' visited your place."

The count bristled. "How the fuck am I s'pposed to do that?"

"Don't you keep records?"

"No."

"Maybe one of your members could help?"

"Let me call Elmo. He might remember somethin'," the count said flatly.

"All right," Fogarty agreed.

Forty-five minutes and six phone calls later, Elmo had recalled some Christmas decorations on the adjacent shopfront. Christmas, 1989.

Fogarty then put a trace on every in-patient facility in every hospital in the Philadelphia area.

"The Mantis, a one-balled psychopath"—the lieutenant was about to strike lucky.

It was 8:21 a.m. when Fogarty escorted Walter Purdkok from the police lock-up. The lieutenant half smiled as he watched the elegant leader of the secret fighting society leave in the back seat of a converted hearse, Elmo at the wheel.

Then Fogarty walked back into the Roundhouse and rode the elevator to the third floor. He could imagine McMullon doing a flatulent quickstep around his desk, and prepared himself for the inevitable grilling. He had not anticipated the added threat of the infamous Winston Bright.

The black man's tightly pressed blue three-piecer and red silk tie with white polka-dots gave the game away.

"Going on the TV, sir?" Fogarty asked pleasantly as he entered McMullon's office.

Bright glanced quickly at his eighteen-carat Patek Philippe and stared sharply at the lieutenant.

"In one hour and thirty-two minutes. Live."

McMullon nodded, a yes man's nod.

"An' I plan on doing a whole lot better than you did, Lieutenant," the mayor added, undisguised rancor in his voice.

Fogarty stood silent a moment, looking first at Dan McMullon then at Winston Bright.

"I'm sorry, Winston, I missed that interview, but—" He was about to add the punchline when McMullon intervened.

"Which reminds me, Bill. . . ." The chief inspector's voice was artificially friendly, and Fogarty remembered one of the reasons why McMullon had jumped the line for Chief Inspector— "loves to lick assholes." Fogarty wondered if the credential was buried somewhere in Fatso's CV.

McMullon cleared his throat and Fogarty cleared the hostility from his face. McMullon continued, "That woman's been trying to get in touch with you. Called the department two or three times. Said she lost—"

"What woman?"

"Mrs. Genero."

"Miss Genero. . . ." The correction in title left Fogarty's mouth before he could check his tongue.

"The case, gentlemen! Let's get down to the case!" Winston Bright fumed.

"Diane Genero *is* part of the case," Fogarty countered.

"I am aware of who Diane Genero is. I *did* see the interview," Bright replied. His black skin appeared to have a flush beneath the epidermis.

"Now, what am I going to say to the people of our city?"

The media, or the ordinary citizens? Fogarty wondered. He fixed his gaze on the mayor's clear brown eyes.

"We're close," the lieutenant stated.

Suddenly the atmosphere in the room changed, as if two words could turn a tornado into a vacuum.

"Very close," Fogarty added, then wondered why he'd said "close" in the first place.

Bright nodded and McMullon narrowed his eyes.

"When?" the chief asked.

"When are we going to have a suspect?" the mayor elaborated.

"I don't know," the lieutenant replied.

Bright threw up his hands. "Come on, Bill! You can't say 'we're close' and in the next breath tell us there isn't a suspect. . . ."

"There isn't," Fogarty confirmed. "What there *is* is a developing profile of a suspect."

"That's great. Fucking great!" Bright ranted. "I'm goin' on with that little red-haired cunt to announce that Philadephia's finest are developing a profile of the killer. . . .Well, that would have been fine if Jeanette was victim number one and this was twenty-four hours afterwards, but she's victim number six and this has been going on for five months!"

Both Fogarty and McMullon caught the mayor's use of "Jeanette" when referring to Jeanette Key. Almost as if he was speaking of a friend or family member.

"Winston," Fogarty said, "our profile is getting pretty focused."

"How focused?" McMullon insisted, making an obvious attempt to tally points with his superior. So far he'd been scoring about zero.

"I'd prefer not to talk about it," the lieutenant answered.

"Well you'd better fucking well talk about it, Lieutenant. After your last television performance we got over two hundred telephone calls from the public—"

"Business people, or ordinary citizens?" Fogarty inquired. McMullon winced.

"Demanding that you be replaced on this investigation," Bright continued, "plus the front page of the *National Examiner.*"

"Christ, Winston! I didn't know you read those kind of papers," Fogarty retorted.

"Bill," Bright tried again, toning down his voice, "before this conversation ends up in hard feelings, let's both remember—"

McMullon's face fell. He looked injured, neglected.

"—let's all three of us remember," Bright corrected himself, ever the politician, "that we're on the same side."

"All right," Fogarty said, settling down. "But what I'm going to tell you, Winston, must not be repeated on A.M. Philadelphia."

"Sometimes, Lieutenant, I get the distinct impression that *you* are the mayor of this city and I am the—'' Bright wanted to say ''cop,'' but chose ''investigating officer.''

''He doesn't mean it that way, Winston,'' McMullon spouted.

Silence followed. Broken by Winston Bright's promise:

''Agreed.''

''What we've got is this,'' Fogarty began, editing out a piece or two before he began. ''A psychopath who wears a size twelve boot, is over six feet tall and weighs in the vicinity of two hundred to two hundred and fifty pounds. He is also highly proficient in some form of martial art, and is very probably practicing a type of 'death blow' on his victims.''

''Jesus Christ!'' McMullon gasped.

''No prints, no blood?'' Bright asked.

''No.'' Fogarty answered.

''Right,'' Bright mumbled as he nodded his head. ''Black or Caucasian?'' the mayor asked , as an afterthought.

''At this point it's tough to tell. We've got no skin samples, and no body hair. His victims don't get much of a chance to retaliate,'' Fogarty answered.

''Fuck me. Not a lot to work with. . . .'' Bright said, as much to himself as to the two officers.''

''For you or for us, Winston?'' Fogarty asked.

Bright looked up, his face harder, more businesslike.

''In case you gentlemen don't realize it, what I am doing is as much an exercise in police public relations as it is a fulfillment of my duty to keep the people informed and alerted.''

''I think we all realize that, Winston,'' McMullon said.

Bright nodded, offering his hand first to McMullon, then to Fogarty.

''Wasn't George Bush wearing an identical tie in his last television interview?'' Fogarty asked, eyeing the white polka dots.

McMullon cringed and Winston Bright chuckled. ''Find the mothafucker, will you, Lieutenant . . . Find him.'' Then Bright turned and departed, leaving only the musky fragrance of Armani.

* * *

McMullon trailed Fogarty through the corridor and towards the stairs.

"I must say, you're pretty frisky considering the amount of shit we're stepping through," McMullon said, catching up with the lieutenant.

"It won't be long now. It won't be long. . . ." Fogarty promised, eyeing McMullon's maroon tie with the beige polka-dots, and wondering what the fuck everyone was doing wearing the same tie.

"What are you keeping back, Bill?" the chief inspector probed.

"Nothing," Fogarty replied.

"Then how can you tell me it won't be long?"

Fogarty thought of a dismissive answer, then reconsidered. He had nothing against McMullon, except that he was an asshole.

"Because the killer is getting sloppy. And when they get sloppy, it means they want to get caught."

Fogarty did not wait for a reply; instead, he turned and took the flight of stairs up, two at a time.

Heads turned as he marched by the desks *en route* to the glass door with his name on it.

"Bob Moyer's been in three times in the last half-hour. . . ." Millie said as Fogarty passed.

He looked at the silver-haired woman, beyond the half-lensed reading glasses and into her hazel eyes.

"Did he say anything?"

"Just that he needed to talk to you," the secretary confirmed, then added: "He sounded tense."

"Get him on for me, will you, Millie," Fogarty said, and walked into his office, closing the door.

"We got something." The forensics man's first two words vindicated Fogarty's instinct.

"Go ahead, Bob."

"The killer left footprints in the hallway. It was raining so, initially, I assumed the stuff was mud, off the heel of his boots."

"Yeah?"

"It's not mud, it's animal feces. . . ."

"Dog shit?" Fogarty asked, beginning to feel let down.

"No way, Bill. This doesn't analyze like domestic animal feces. First of all, it's specially formulated—the feces appear to have been encased in a fibrous skin. Indicative of small pellets, like deer droppings. Secondly, it's protein-enriched, and has a particularly high oil content. On top of that, it comes off both boot heels, which makes it less likely that he just happened to step in it haphazardly."

"You sure it isn't some special breeder's brand of animal food? You know, for house cats or something?" Fogarty tried to keep the pessimism out of his voice.

"Bill, I don't think this stuff is consistent with anything that a domestic animal would eat. It would require too much digestion."

Fogarty was silent, thinking. *Deer shit.* Maybe their man was a hunter. Deer season? Wasn't it deer season now?

"And it's definitely a laboratory-based preparation."

Moyer's statement put a halt to the lieutenant's speculation.

"How long before you've something more?" Fogarty asked.

"Josef's working as we speak. First, I want to eliminate any chance of domestic animal food, then there's the exotics—"

"Exotics?" Fogarty repeated.

"Jungle cats, monkeys—anything sold special order."

"Probably time to put a team on the pet stores. Check the SPCA for anything registered above a canary," Fogarty said, thinking out loud.

"Give us another hour on this, Bill. Another hour should do it."

"Good enough. I'll see you in an hour."

"You coming to the lab?"

"Yeah. I want to see Joey," Fogarty answered then rang off.

XI.

WILLARD NG

Less than five miles from the Roundhouse, east across the Delaware River, in Camden, New Jersey, Willard Ng sits in the full lotus posture on the floor of his small, shingle-fronted house. He is naked and his porcelain-smooth head is tilted forward at a slight angle. He is breathing, drawing air in through his nose, then forcing it from his mouth in sharp, staccato bursts.

For thirty-six hours he has eaten no solid food. Not since the entrails of the cat.

Willard Ng has been very sick. Vomiting, diarrhea. Now he is trying to cleanse himself. His body, his mind.

The illness had done more than debilitate him, it had exposed him. Taken him from the realm of perfection in which he had finally achieved a unification with his mentor, to the frail, pitiable depths of humankind. His naked body flat against the cold, moist tiles on the floor of his bathroom, his arms outstretched, fingers touching the smooth, round base of the toilet, covered in vomit and excrement. How quickly his illusions had been shattered, how tragically he had descended into the lonely, abandoned child that Willard Ng had once been. How the years and distance between his beginnings and his fulfillment had dissolved. The sickness had gone on all day and into the night and before it had ended, he had wanted to die. Wanted it like he had wanted it once fifteen years before, in the orphanage in San Francisco, when his ears had become so agonizingly inflamed that a cotton wick had been inserted into each of them, enabling his medication to be dripped inwards. When his lungs and nasal passage had burned with each rasping intake of air, as if the oxygen was fueling some scorching, pulsing fire. And all he could do was lie alone in his darkened room, curled naked in the fetal position beneath the starched sheet and single woollen blanket, and silently beg for death to take him.

''Primary meningitis''—that was what the doctors whispered

to the sisters who attended him, those habited nuns who walked the corridors, monitored the dormitories and gave up their lives to instruct on Mission Street. Primary meningitis brought on by a fracture to the base of Willard Ng's skull.

"Look at 'im—he ain't white, he ain't black, he ain't even a Jap. He's a geek, a fuckin' half-breed geek!" That was what the older boy had decreed to his circle of accomplices before planting the regulation steel-tipped army boot into the back of Willard Ng's head. Once, twice, three times he kicked the fallen thirteen-year-old.

"C'mon, cry—we wanna hear what kinda sound a half-breed makes when he cries!" the instigator had commanded as he positioned himself for another try at a field goal. But Willard Ng wouldn't cry. In fact, he could not cry. He did not know how; he never had. Not in the thirteen years and three orphanages that had comprised his life. So he lay on the pavement, knees pulled up tight to his abdomen, while his hands covered his face. And listened as his tormentor's voice grew more intense, anxious, finally pleading.

"C'mon, say somethin'. Anything an' w'll stop. C'mon, geek." Then came the sharp, penetrating impact that opened the gates of darkness and allowed Willard Ng to float through.

"Whatever did you say to Patrick to make him do such a thing? Whatever did you say?" Willard listened to the voice through his shattered consciousness.

"Now Patrick will be punished. Paddled. And I'm certain you started it, Willard, certain," Sister Marie concluded.

Why? Why are you certain? he had wanted to say, to challenge. But he already knew the answer. He'd started it because he was Willard Ng, the outsider, the newest kid in St. Thomas', the kid with no friends, the kid nobody wanted.

Three days later the earache started, first in his left ear. Then the throbbing pain, which seemed at times to be in perfect tune with his beating heart, traveled the circuit of his skull to balance in either side of his head. He told no one, accepting it as punishment for his transgression, for being Willard Ng. The pain deepened, making it impossible to sleep. So he lay awake, his narrow cot in line with the row of cots on which boys slept to his left and right, separated by a walkway from a dozen identical cots in front of him. All around was the sound of humanity; the murmurs and cries, the grunting and farting, the creaking of bedsprings in the night. And inside was the sound of his heart, pumping, his blood coursing through his veins.

Willard began then to separate the inside noises from the outside noises, feeling more secure inside, concentrating on the beat of his heart. It was easy; it coincided with the throbbing pain in his temples. Until the pain became familiar—exquisite and private. And the pain brought him closer to his specialness.

Bangkok, 1966. That is when I was born. In Bangkok. And in his mind, somewhere between memory and fantasy, coinciding with the rush of blood to his temples, red images exploded. Neon images of rain slick streets and milling people, of a single woman, a girl really. Not much older than himself. Her skin was taut and brown, her teeth flashing white, and her body moved towards him with a sinewy, snake-like motion, along the glistening sidewalk. And there was a marine, an American on R&R. On leave from Vietnam. Tall and white and hard. His penis like an iron bar inside his trousers. The marine stared at the snake woman, at her long, skinny legs at her tight waist and flat chest, at her shinning hair and jet-black eyes. Skin stretched tight against the bones of her face. So tight that, if he blinked, she resembled the face of death, a grinning skull with ivory teeth and marble eyes. And he hated the thought of death. He had been close to it several times. Yet he was drawn to it, obsessed by it. So he took the snake woman from the rain-washed streets, led her to the threadbare linen of his hotel and fucked her with his iron dick. Fucked her with all the hate and fear inside him. Fucked her in defiance of death, until she bled. Red neon blood. And upon that river of blood a baby came. A child of death; the son of Sergeant Raymond Willard and Taew Ng. A child who was permitted no sense of life, no joy, no sorrow. Punished if he laughed, punished if he cried. Beaten with a leather belt and heavy brass buckle until he had welts upon his skin, until he would never laugh or cry again. Beaten in the name of discipline, peace and tranquility.

And the pain of unexpressed emotion gradually grew, finding no release. Expanding and filling him, it became his silent possession. Something that could not be prised from his fingers or jerked from his arms.

He carried his pain with him from Bangkok to the naval base in San Diego. And then the squalid apartment in Oakland where his mother went, a year before she died, to escape Raymond Willard's sadistic tyranny. *Something just exploded inside your mother's head.* That was the way the social workers described Taew Ng's brain hemorrhage to her five-year-old son. He was sure it was his fault; it must have been. Otherwise why would he had been taken away, moved from orphanage to orphanage, placed behind locked doors? Beaten by the other boys, kicked in the base of the skull? *Pain.* He had come to cherish it, the earaches, the isolation. Until the day that the cough began.

The cough was a different kind of pain to the earache. Different because it deprived him of his thoughts, his images, his distorted memories. Blotted them from his mind, made them superfluous to his survival. It was as if each time he coughed his lungs would collapse, wrapping like burning, clinging tissue around his heart. Strangling him inside. And when he heaved inwards, his breath fanned the fire in his lungs. His temperature soared, 102°, 103° and the pain in his head spread downwards through his neck, radiating outwards through his lower spine until it filled his legs. The coughing induced vomiting, and the vomiting continued until Willard Ng was aware of nothing but his burning, retching body. And a thin, high pitched cry, like the cry of a dying animal.

Weak and afraid, he listened . . . unaware of the origins of the whining sound. Until he realized that for the first time in his life he was listening to his own cry. Frail and pitiable, a thin, lonesome plea. And from somewhere, unlocked from the recesses of a mind conditioned by beatings and deprivation, came the shadow of death.

For two days and two nights Willard Ng cried. Cried until the shadow of death hovered like a cool specter above his bed. Listening and deciding, watching, and waiting, until the child's fever waned, and his yelps became faint, distant less demanding. Until death departed, closing the gulf between pain and release. And, finally, Willard Ng began to recover.

It was during his convalescence that Willard first encountered his mentor. Pale and drawn, unable to walk, the sisters had parked his wheelchair beneath an orange tree in the far corner of St. Thomas' east garden.

The air smelled sweet and fresh, and a light breeze carried the fragrance of early summer. Willard was staring into the sky, his mind adrift, lulled by his lack of physical vitality and, somehow, enjoying the fact that little, if anything, was expected of him; no classes, no chores. He had even been allowed to stay in his private room, although the curtains had been opened, allowing the daylight to wash the remnants of his sickness from the cracked plaster walls and bare wooden floor. The days passed in a singular haze, punctuated only by meals which were brought to his room, and at night he slept his heavy dreamless sleep.

But this particular day was to be different; it was to change him. The meeting began with a shrill voice, coming from a branch above Willard Ng's head. Like the chirping of a cricket, but more desperate and intense. He looked up, and at first saw nothing. It was only as his eyes focused that he saw the Mantis, its green gauze wings blending perfectly with the leaves of the tree. The Mantis was standing straight up, like a tiny horse rearing on its hind legs. In front of it was a slightly smaller insect, with long transparent wings and a hard, twig-like body. A cicada, that was the name the sisters had given the twig-like insect on one of the St. Thomas' nature walks. It was the cicada that was screeching, the volume of its shrill cry in extreme disproportion to its matchstick body. The two insects were engaged in a fierce battle, the cicada screeching and biting ferociously, while the Mantis circled, maintaining a hair's-breadth length distance from the other's razored jaws. The longer the fight continued, the more Willard Ng was drawn towards the Mantis, as if the young man was being sucked into a vacuum in which the essence of life and death was symbolized by the struggle before him. He observed the definite pattern of combat which the Mantis employed. Lightning strikes with its two front limbs were followed by a quick withdrawal. Then the creature circled it, while leaving its coinciding limb extended, crouching down and springing forward, grabbing and tearing with the hooking hand of its extended limb. Unlike the cicada, there was no confusion in the movement of the Mantis, only simple intent, clear and certain. Another exchange, and the cicada retreated, the Mantis opening its wings as it pursued. Then, wrapping them around its beaten prey, the Mantis bit long and hard into the cicada's neck.

Willard Ng watched all of this, feeling a surge of excitement so strong that he did not realize that he was out of his wheelchair and standing, his face not more than twelve inches from the Mantis. He was positively entranced by the small creature. The Mantis was equally aware of the young man, stopping its meal to view its audience with sharp, piercing eyes, concentrated and aware. For a moment, Willard felt in mortal danger. He had no doubt that the Mantis could leap from its perch and tear the flesh from his face. The creature was omnipotent. Willard's fear caused him to stop breathing, as if even his breath could disturb and enrage the Mantis. Again, a vacuum seemed to form, and the Mantis appeared to magnify to human proportions. Then the humming began. Like the sound of electricity vibrating through a high-tension wire; originating in the center of Willard Ng's forehead, a finger's width above the bridge of his nose, and extending outwards towards the Mantis, connecting them. A joy descended, healing the boy's spirit, completing in him some secret fulfilment . . . until, finally, the Mantis turned away, lowered his head, and recommenced its meal.

Willard Ng dreamt of the Mantis that night. And in the

morning he was refreshed, rejuvenated. He dreamt of the creature many times after that. . . .

It was four years later, after Willard Ng had departed from St. Thomas', and while he was employed as a night janitor in the Oakland Public Library, that he stumbled across a slim black book entitled *Praying Mantis Kung Fu*. The author's name was given as H.B. Un, and beside the Chinese characters on the cover was an artist's rendition of a praying mantis.

Ng devoured the eighty-four-page text, studying the pictures and reveling in the fact that three hundred years before his own experience in the gardens of St. Thomas', the Chinese fighting master, Wong Long, had witnessed a similar encounter, between a mantis and a grasshopper. So impressed was Wong Long with the style and ferocity of the mantis that he incorporated the insect's movements into his own system of combat.

This knowledge came as nothing short of a revelation to Willard Ng, awakening in him a dormant sense of hope and purpose. And something else—something which he could not quite identify, something else—something which he could only feel, in the same way he had felt it on that June day in the gardens of St. Thomas'. As if a part of him—his soul, his spirit— had been summoned for some higher purpose. His destiny.

He scoured the telephone book and the classified ads in the newspapers. Forty-eight hours later Willard Ng was a member of the Fan Yook Tung kwoon in Berkeley, California. He lasted three years, long enough to learn the rudiments of Mantis-style kung fu, and long enough to give his instructor a premonition of disaster. Willard Ng was going to injure someone—badly. He appeared impervious to his own pain, and intent on causing pain to others. He needed to make the techniques work. And although Willard was a dedicated student and, potentially, a gifted practitioner, he was very bad for business. No one wanted to train with the tall half-caste.

Four years and as many kwoons later, Willard Ng justified his first teacher's fears. It began during sparring practice in the advanced class of a garage-based training hall in Oakland.

"Control. You have no control." The criticism was accompanied by a spray of sweat and saliva from the thin, pale lips. Ng stepped back, seething, at no time breaking contact with Miranda Morgan's dark, condemning eyes. The sturdy thirty-three-year-old social worker rubbed her right elbow vigorously, shaking her head as if to reinforce her criticism.

"Five times, on your own," the *sifu* instructed from the opposite end of the garage. The five pairs of students responded by continuing their prearranged sparring practice. When Miss Morgan attacked, using a thrusting right fist, Willard Ng was supposed to deflect the blow with his corresponding wrist and counter with a left-handed chopping movement to her waist. In fact, Ng had become increasingly weary of the monotonously predictable two-man sets. When he was certain that the *sifu*'s attention was directed elsewhere, he would improvise. In this case he was using the "claw"—a fist formation in which the index and middle fingers were thrust forward, supported by the thumb, while the other two fingers bent back toward the wrist, imitating the jagged teeth of the praying mantis' claw—to catch, grip and twist Miss Morgan's extended elbow. He was making sure that the tip of his middle finger dug good and deep into her joint, above the extensor tendon, twanging it like a guitar string, and giving the suffering social worker the repeated sensation of striking her funny bone. She was close to tears by the time the small Chinese *sifu* appeared.

"What is problem, Miss Morgan?" the *sifu* asked, casting a suspicious eye upon the towering twenty-four-year-old Ng.

Ng returned the *sifu*'s gaze, looking deep into his teacher's eyes. He felt a defiant hostility coil like a serpent at the base of his spine. Then Ng directed his gaze at Miranda Morgan, daring her to answer, to humiliate him in front of the others.

"He is not doing the exercise properly, *sifu*," she stated. There was a self-serving arrogance to her tone. As if, under the protection of the teacher, she could reprimand Ng without fear of reprisal.

"I see," the *sifu* replied, examining the red fingermarks and fresh bruising above her elbow.

"Perhaps, Mr. Ng, you would like to demonstrate your technique on me."

By now the other eight students had converged in a somber circle. Ng felt awkward, embarrassed; his childhood had conditioned him to fear the attention of others.

"Mr. Ng." the *sifu*'s voice contained both challenge and authority. "You do not belong." The Chinese man's voice grew more powerful, his words a repetition of persecutors before him. Willard Ng listened. Until, finally, he recognized the truth. He did not belong. Not in this filthy, dark garage. He was not one of them. He was not a pretender. He had seen the way many years ago; he had tasted the essence of something that this small, self-important man would never know or understand.

Ng smiled. A dangerous, tight-lipped smile. He straightened, squaring his shoulders, towering above the Chinese man. He could see fear in the *sifu*'s slanted brown eyes. He glanced quickly at the others. The same fear was present in all their eyes, contagious and malignant. Yet he, Willard Ng, was not afraid. Because he understood.

He stared again at the Chinese man, imagining the lithe, sinewy body beneath the black training suit. Long yellow fingers hung from the *sifu*'s cuffed sleeves; his hair, dark and cropped, accentuated high cheekbones and a narrow, skeletal face. The *sifu* barely appeared to be breathing.

"Go from here . . . now!" the Chinese man demanded, his voice high, screeching. Ng paid no attention to the command, concentrating instead on the familiar shrill tone. He breathed inwards, slow and wary. As the oxygen filled him, a memory rose to the surface of his mind. The cicada, hard and lithe, stood before him. Without thought, without self-consciousness, Willard Ng raised his arms, like wings. His hands tingled, his fingers merged. He was invincible.

"Now this is going too far. . . ." Miranda Morgan's voice trailed off, dissipating in mid-air. Then stillness, electric stillness. Broken only by the *sifu*'s shifting movement, flowing forward, his rear leg supporting the weight of his body while his front shoe pulled like a black-gloved hand against the canvas. His eyes were hard now, fear controlled by determination. His honor and the sanctity of his kwoon were at stake.

Ng watched the small man's attack as if it was being performed in slow motion, the *sifu*'s left fist flying forward towards the center of his face. He responded by snapping his left wing inwards, deflecting the blow with his open hand while swinging his right palm towards his opponent. His palm cracked loud and hard against the sternocleidomastoid muscle of the Chinese man's neck. The *sifu* appeared stunned, reeling backwards. Ng could have ended it then, certainly the Mantis would have done so. But for some reason, which Ng would later explore and re-explore a thousand times, his concentration slipped and he began a wild flailing charge.

The *sifu* stepped inside Willard's windmilling arms, and launched a short, circular kick to his thigh, cramping Ng's leg. He followed through with a palm-heel strike, which broke Willard Ng's nose and knocked him to the floor.

Willard's next memory was one of grappling from a kneeling position. People shouting. Hands pulling at him, attempting to drag him off. Miranda Morgan screaming.

The image of the Mantis, which he had held like a crystal in his mind, shattered in the mêlée. And by the time Ng felt the short, steel-hard fingers wrapping round his windpipe, he was equally aware of a wet jelly-like substance in his own right hand. Until the fingers on his throat relaxed, and he was on his feet, looking down at the *sifu*'s face. Blood ran in a torrent from the hollowed socket of the Chinese man's left eye. A horrified silence fell over the onlookers, as Ng backed towards the exit door. He was still barefoot, and his carry-all, containing his shoes and clothes, was in the small shed adjoining the kwoon. He considered stopping, then wondered if someone had, by now, called the police. Finally, Ng turned and ran barefoot down the hard pavements, never altering his stride in the five miles to his rooming house.

His feet were blistered and bleeding when he entered his room. He stopped only long enough to bolt his door. Then, still heaving deep, heavy breaths he stripped naked. There was a long rectangular mirror on the wall adjacent to his single closet. He walked to the mirror and turned, facing it full-on. Moonlight cascaded through the open window, backlighting his face and shoulders. He stared, restraining his impulse to blink, until the moonlight formed an incandescent silhouette around the darkness of his body and head. He concentrated on the darkness.

Slowly, so as not to disturb the vibrating molecules of air, he raised his arms, like wings. Invincible grapnels formed where his hands had been; a beautiful star glowed from the center of his chest. Sharp, piercing eyes stared from a wide, diamond-shaped head. As if his own mirrored image had been the larva of transition, and this vision was the archetype of his completion. Finally, the humming began, an oscillation in the center of his forehead, filling him with the same warmth and fulfilment that he had known as a boy in the gardens of St. Thomas'. This time, however, the humming was clearer, more defined. And Willard Ng heard a voice within the sound. Thin, like air forced through the reed of a musical instrument. His concentration heightened as he turned his being to the voice. *Perfection.* The voice was saying *perfection.* The word was the catalyst, dividing Willard Ng's mind cleanly in two. One half retained the Mantis consciousness while the other reviewed his human life in quick, successive flashes: the loneliness, isolation and repressed pain.

The moon rose until he could see himself clearly in the mirror; his nose bloodied and crooked, his body coarse and misshapen. Without symmetry. Like his life. Yet, superimposed upon his flesh shell was the body of the Mantis. As if its invulnerable grace was a blueprint for Willard Ng's own perfection.

He recalled the evening's encounter at the kwoon. He had been all-powerful as the Mantis, his wings spread and breath centered. He had functioned in perfect harmony with a force which had been dormant inside him. Then he had faltered, broken the thread of contact, fought without clarity. Flailed his arms, succumbed to human frailty. He had wounded his opponent, but his victory had been hollow, meaningless.

Willard Ng was on the precipice of enlightenment. He studied the features of the Mantis body, imprinting them forever upon his divided mind. Until, finally, it came. The resolve, his awakening. Willard Ng would become the Mantis.

When the student is ready, a master will appear. It had not been easy; his fulfilment required study, training and sheer dedication. Until, after three years, six cities and countless visits to a succession of dojos and kwoons, Willard Ng returned to the source of his inspiration. Recognized the source as his master. Pure and simple.

And the master inspired the killing exercise.

He took another sip from the china mug. The water was cooler now, no longer burning his throat as it passed into his stomach. He breathed in; the sickness retreated. He glanced to his left, eyeing the door which led to his power room. Considered a work-out with the strength stones. It was not physical work he needed. He forced his mind to recall the last killing exercise, visualized his movements. Each step. From the stalking to the kill, and finally his unhurried exit with the rising sun. He had been both confident and careless. And *she* would not abide his carelessness.

There was a city dump on Delaware Avenue, a place with huge incinerators and smoldering piles of garbage. He would burn the clothes that he had worn, even his boots—they had become too tight anyway, his feet now hardening and splaying from his daily repetition of "stamping on stone," Yes. He would do that today. Then, when the night came and he was assured of privacy, he would visit *her*. Tonight would be a special night, an intimate night.

XII.

A TRIP TO THE ZOO

The Philadelphia zoo is the oldest zoo in the United States. With twelve sections and one hundred and seven animal houses, it is also one of the largest. Positioned four miles west of the center of the city, at the intersection of Girard Avenue and Thirty-fourth Street, the zoo is as accessible to the suburbs as to Philadelphia proper.

Even on a Thursday morning in November, the old iron turnstiles at the entrance revolve steadily with an influx of tourists and local visitors.

"The excrement, Bill, comes from some type of large mammal. Not domestic. Nearest I can come is a camel."

"A camel?" Fogarty had repeated.

"Yes. That's what the fibrous skin and high oil content is all about. It's a food preparation," Moyer continued.

Tanaka had been there, standing next to the wiry pathologist, nodding his agreement. He appeared fully recovered, with the exception of seven stitches and an eye that had faded from black to blue-gray.

"Your killer, aside from wading in camel shit, wears a size twelve D boot. Rubber-treaded soles with the left worn clear to the nail on the outside of the heel."

Ten minutes later Fogarty had pointed the Le Mans west in the direction of Girard Avenue, and headed for the Philadelphia zoo. On the way, the lieutenant filled his partner in on Count Dante's story.

"What did you say he called him, Bill?" Tanaka asked.

"Mantis," Fogarty replied.

Mantis. Tanaka repeated the word in his head as the Le Mans shimmied and shook over the last of the potholes before the Thirty-fourth Street exit.

"I'm not flashing any tin. Let 'em think we're tourists," Fogarty said as he and the doctor walked past a stone statue of a

lioness and her cubs, towards the turnstiles. The lieutenant paid
for the tickets and asked for directions to the camels.

Once inside, Fogarty stopped for two quart-sized containers
of dry popcorn.

"No salt," he said, offering one to Tanaka. "No matter what
happens, Joey, let me handle this."

"You think I fucked up last time, don't you?"

Fogarty noticed a new vulnerability in Tanaka's voice. He
shook his head as he pressed the container into the doctor's
hand.

"As a matter of fact, you probably saved my ass. It's just that,
well, I'm the cop and it makes me look bad."

They both laughed. Then they were walking, keeping a moderate pace, munching their popcorn, like tourists. Twenty feet
above their heads an open double car, like an old-fashioned
trolley, sat perched on a single steel rail. A sign which read
"Monorail Closed For Repair" hung on its side.

"Three accidents on that thing last year," Fogarty said, looking up. Tanaka noted the practiced calm in the lieutenant's
voice. *Very professional.* He remembered thinking that before. He
also recognized the slight flutter of nerves in the hollow of his
own stomach.

"We're close, Bill. We're damn close," Tanaka said, listening
to his proclamation as if it had been delivered by a third party.
His voice sounded dry and hollow amidst the laughter of children and the light patter of people passing.

Fogarty turned towards him and, just for a moment, their eyes
met.

"I know it."

That was all the lieutenant said. Then both men walked
quietly along the signposted pavement.

An iron guard-rail, a girdered fence and a six-foot moat separated the visitors from the residents of the African plains. Beyond the brown water and black iron, a half-dozen camels
roamed the concrete sand dunes of their enclosure.

"The four on the left are Bactrian, the other two are Arabs," Fogarty remarked. Tanaka looked puzzled.

"Humps. Arabs have a single hump, Bactrians two," Fogarty explained. "I've been coming here since I was a kid," he added. Tanaka tried to imagine the lieutenant as a kid. He couldn't.

Fogarty walked to the guard-rail, leaned his chest against it so that his arms rested on top, and continued to survey the camels as he ate his popcorn. Tanaka joined him.

"What we're gonna do is this," the lieutenant said. "We're gonna spend the next hour or so walking around, making mental notes, looking at faces." Fogarty hesitated, glancing at a double-humped Bactrian. The animal began to defecate.

"One thing's for sure—"

Tanaka waited.

"We're not gonna step in camel shit on this side of the water," Fogarty stated.

Tanaka nodded, wondering if police work was always so sophisticated.

As they watched, two attendants appeared from a door concealed by slabs of stone; assembled, Tanaka presumed, to replicate the drifting desert sands . . .

"Check their boots," Fogarty whispered.

Tanaka locked on to the knee-high rubber boots. Both attendants wore them, along with khaki overalls and waxed cotton jackets. The taller of the two men carried a hose, while the other wielded a flat-backed shovel. Tanaka watched the men walk, their heads bobbing in time with their footsteps. Relaxed—but untrained. The killer would walk from his center, his head level, his steps sure and certain. The way a man walked after many years of treading barefoot on the pine wood or canvas mats of a dojo floor. The man they were after would be a real mover. Tanaka knew this. And he knew something more, something he did not want to face, not yet, not ever. His thoughts hung suspended.

"Another thing for sure," Fogarty chuckled. "Those guys definitely have shit on their shoes." Fogarty's tone brought

Tanaka back, drawing him like a thread through the eye of a needle.

"You all right?" Fogarty asked.

"Wrong kind of boots, Bill," Tanaka covered. "No nails in the heels of those boots. They're all rubber, no joins."

Fogarty looked again, nodding slowly. Then, as if to contradict his acquiescence, a third man entered the compound. He wore a quilted plaid jacket, blue jeans and leather boots. The type of boots with rigid-edged rubber soles. The man was talking, waving his arms as if to demonstrate something. He walked straight into the camel shit.

"You see, Josef, that's how it's done," Fogarty said.

The zoo's executive office building had, at one time, been a private stately home. Christened "Solitude", and erected in 1785, the white stone building now occupied a one-acre plot adjacent to the flamingo exhibit.

Fogarty and Tanaka followed a stone path, beneath a spreading maple tree, to Solitude's brass-handled door. The door opened onto a beige-colored room, leathered chairs and a gas-log fireplace. A receptionist looked up from her desk.

Fogarty did the talking.

"We've come to see Mr. Anthony Galenti. I believe he is the chief administrator?"

"And have you an appointment?" the dapper suited lady asked.

"No. We're here on police business. Also, I must insist that you keep our visit confidential."

"May I see some identification?"

Fogarty presented his wallet; shield in place.

The prim, middle-aged woman did a double take.

"Lieutenant Fogarty! God, I've just been hearing about you on the news. Is this about that dreadful killing?"

Fogarty grimaced, and Tanaka noticed a flush travel upwards across his face. The lieutenant didn't answer. The secretary, as if to compensate for the policeman's silence, continued. "Mayor

Bright said you were close to bringing in a suspect . . . any day now, any day,'' she added hopefully.

Fogarty nodded reassuringly, secretly infuriated by the mayor's promise. He studied the eyes behind the blue contacts. The practiced calm modulated his voice.

"May I ask your name?"

"Doris Herman," the secretary answered.

"Well, Doris, I missed the mayor's interview and I don't exactly know where he got the ''any day'' from, but I can tell you that we need all the cooperation we can get with this investigation."

"Certainly, lieutenant." Then, picking up the phone: "I'll see if Mr. Galenti is free."

Anthony Galenti was a fiftyish, sandy-haired man, with a craggy face and strong, callused hands. His skin was currently pale, but had the weatherbeaten texture of too many suntans. He wore a light tweed suit: he would have looked more at home in khakis and a pith helmet. He listened with deep concern to Fogarty's description of Jeanette Key's murder. Finally, when the lieutenant had finished, Galenti picked up his desk phone and punched the amber glowing button marked "Personnel".

"Alice, how long would it take to access the employee records?" Galenti waited, listened, then shook his head slowly.

"Thanks, I'll get back to you." He put the phone down, turning to Fogarty.

"It's going to be a matter of days, not hours," Galenti explained.

Fogarty nodded.

"Unless you can give me a specific name," the administrator added.

Fogarty slipped the print of the artist's drawing from his pocket. He unfolded it and handed it to Galenti.

"You recognize him?"

Galenti studied the picture, sneaking a discreet glance at Tanaka, before looking again at the lieutenant.

"Not immediately, but that isn't saying much. We've got a hundred and fifty full-time people here, plus, until the busy season ends at Christmas, there's at least a hundred extras. Fogarty nodded, looking over at Tanaka, noting that the doctor was unusually quiet. Tanaka couldn't shake the feeling. It had come and gone a hundred times since he had walked through the old turnstile. As if he was on the verge of some vital connection. As if he *knew*, but just couldn't define *what* he knew. Then there was the other feeling, the one that needed no definition.

"I'll tell you what I can do, lieutenant," Galenti said, standing as he handed the likeness back. Behind him was a wall full of pictures. Galenti standing safari-suited beside a Landrover, surrounded by several similarly attired men, Galenti with a twenty-foot python draped across his shoulders, Galenti standing beside a cage containing a great white tiger, Galenti and another man flanking an enormous gorilla. The bottom picture caught the lieutenant's eye.

"I can introduce you to Gordon Forrest. He's my head keeper. Does all the hiring and firing."

"That's him there, isn't it?" Fogarty said, pointing to the photograph. It was a black-and-white facial study of a man and a lion, side by side. So close together that the long white streaked hair of the bearded man mixed into the white of the lion's mane. The man's eyes were deep set, one intense and penetrating, the other strangely vacant. The skin of his forehead was etched with lines. Beside him, the lion appeared placid, relaxed.

"Yes. Do you know Gordon?" Galenti asked, surprised.

Fogarty nodded, smiling without showing teeth. "I haven't seen him since he was importing alligators from the Everglades and selling 'em mail order."

Galenti relaxed. "That would have been before his employment here."

"Seven, eight years ago," Fogarty answered.

"He doesn't have a criminal record, does he?" Galenti queried.

Fogarty hesitated. He remembered the first time he saw

Gordon Forrest. A drunken wild-man, stark naked and tattooed, waving a flare pistol from the window of a fourth-floor apartment. The flare had landed on the domed ceiling of a mosque below, causing panic. Followed by the impassioned cry: "The Israelis are coming!"

Forrest was laughing and cracking jokes, oblivious to the commotion below. Fogarty had warmed to him instantly. Managed to get him off on a plea of combat stress. Forrest had, after all, received a Purple Heart in Vietnam. They became occasional drinking buddies after that, sharing more than one tequila and lime. That was before Fogarty's accident. He hadn't shared much with anybody since.

"Does he have a record, Lieutenant?" Galenti repeated. Fogarty smiled now, completely.

"No. Gordon's a fine man . . . Just tell us where we can find him."

"What the hell's the matter with you?"

Tanaka ignored the lieutenant's question and kept his head turned towards the line of cages.

"You haven't said a word in an hour," Fogarty continued. The jaguar was jet black, curled in the corner of the cage. The big glowing eyes seemed to follow Tanaka. Fogarty changed tack, stopping.

"You know, those cats actually get darker when they're kept in captivity."

Tanaka focused his attention on the jaguar.

"Their coats take on the color of the bars. Camouflage. Sick, isn't it?"

Tanaka exhaled audibly, turning towards Fogarty.

"I know something about this guy, Bill." His voice was dead and dry. It was more the tone than the words that caught Fogarty. He moved closer, whispered:

"What is it, Joey?"

"I'm the one who's going to take him down," Tanaka answered.

Fogarty put a hand on Tanaka's shoulder, looking directly into his eyes. A steady line of people passed, making a wide arc around the two men.

Fogarty kept his voice hushed.

"I pulled you into this because I had nothing, and Bob Moyer said you might. I've kept you on because I respect you, and the truth is you did save my ass. But when it gets down to the collar, it's going to be a police officer who does the honors. Not a forensics doctor. You understand me?"

Tanaka was motionless, his eyes locked to Fogarty's, but without light. His unreflected thoughts picked up momentum.

Fogarty interpreted the silence as anger. He remembered the scene in the hospital.

"This isn't a case for honor or pride," he began, treading carefully. "It isn't about ego. It's about you not being a trained police officer." He toughened his voice. "You are my responsibility. Do you understand what I'm saying?"

Tanaka nodded. It was a curt, formal movement, almost a bow. The kind of acknowledgment that might precede a contest or duel.

Fogarty felt a pulse in the pit of his stomach, a warning. He tightened his grip on Tanaka's shoulder. The tension felt like electricity through his fingers.

"Loosen up, Joey, you're making me nervous. . . ."

Tanaka's eyes stayed with him; they seemed strained, his face set hard, mouth poised to speak. As if he was on the verge of some proclamation. Then, suddenly, he relaxed, smiled.

"Good!" Fogarty said. "Now let's go to see Gordon."

He steered the doctor down a paved walkway, back past the Arabian Plains, to the side of a large, gray building, where they pushed through a door designated "Staff Only". Fogarty and Tanaka were two steps down the passageway when the low groans began, deep and resonant.

"Christ. I hope there's nothin' wandering around loose back here," Fogarty whispered. To either side were high concreted

walls and closed doors. The groans were coming from somewhere on the other side of the wall.

"Hey! What are you guys doin'?"

Tanaka turned in time to see a man in a khaki shirt and
trousers follow them through the door.

"You're on the wrong side of the exhibition," the burly
attendant accused, ambling forward.

Fogarty stepped in front of Tanaka.

"Department of Health and Sanitation," he said, flashing his
shield, too quick for the man to focus. "Mr. Galenti said we'd
find your head keeper back here."

The attendant relaxed, then chuckled as if at some private
joke. Another groan erupted from behind the wall.

"Yeah, you'll find'm, but I'm not sure you'll want to disturb'm. Not just now. . . ."

"Now is the only time we've got," Fogarty assured the attendant.

The man shrugged his shoulders. "OK." A crooked smile
crossed his round, fleshly face. "Follow me."

The attendant's ankle-high work boots left dusty footprints on
the grey stone. Ten yards later, the three men stopped in front
of a door, slightly ajar. The groans were coming from behind the
door, along with a suffocating stench.

"You're looking for Gordon, Gordon's in there," the man
said, standing aside. Fogarty walked forward, knocked on the
door. Another groan, resonant but somehow submissive.
Fogarty rapped his knuckles against the old iron.

"Not now!" the voice was harsh. Tanaka detected a trace of an
accent. Not American.

"Gordon. It's Bill Fogarty. I gotta talk to ya'!"

No answer. Another groan, more a bellow, and the quick
exchange of words between two male voices.

Fogarty pushed against the heavy metal.

"I wouldn't go in there," the attendant warned.

On first glance it appeared that the man standing on the ladder
beside the enormous giraffe had only one arm. On closer

inspection, it became apparent that his right arm was buried shoulder-deep in the anus of the standing animal. An arm-length latex glove did little to prevent the discharge and feces from splattering against the plumed serpent tattooed into the swarthy flesh of the man's broad chest and shoulders. He glanced quickly at the policemen as they entered the room. Tanaka spotted the glass eye and noticed the gold front tooth. The beard was gone.

"Bill. How the hell are ya?" Gordon Forrest's voice was friendly, his accent just hinting at his origins in the outback of Australia.

"Jus' stay put a minute—any sudden move an' they'll call me Sheila," he continued, winking his good eye at Fogarty. Then he turned back to the giraffe and pushed his arm another inch into the opening. Another man stood to his side, supervising, keeping well out of range of the animal's steel-hard hoofs.

"OK Doc, I'm there."

The vet inched closer. "OK, OK—now gently move your fingers along the curve of the ovaries."

Forrest followed his instructions, and was rewarded with a loud, clapping fart.

"Smooth. Very smooth," he reported, ignoring the fart.

"Keep going. All the way round."

Forrest rotated his arm. "Oh yeah. Got something now. On the underside."

"Go to the other one."

"There's a couple there too. Jesus, mate, these feel like golf balls," Forrest said.

"Yes. They can be extremely large," the vet agreed. "You can come out now."

Slowly, with the gentleness that belied his sturdy body and rough, grizzled features, Gordon Forrest withdrew his arm. He stepped down from the ladder, away from the giraffe, then turned towards Fogarty. There was a glimmer in Forrest's good eye.

"It's been a few years, Bill." He extended his dripping gloved hand in the lieutenant's direction.

"You won't be offended, will you, Gordon—" Fogarty said, declining the hand.

Forrest laughed, then pulled the glove from his arm. He glanced towards the giraffe.

"Poor ol' Nellie here can't seem to get pregnant."

"Follicles. Cysts on the ovaries," the vet confirmed.

"Sorry to hear that," Fogarty said.

"An' aside from Sturgis, her husband, I'm the only man the ol' girl'll let near her."

"You always had a way with women," Fogarty answered. "Last time, if I remember, it was a four-hundred-pound ape."

Forrest laughed. "Bamboo wasn't a woman."

"Sorry, Gordon. No insult intended."

Forrest laughed louder. "By the way, this here's Ed Reeves. He's a proper animal doctor."

"Just can't get near the animal!" Reeves quipped.

"An' this is Doctor Tanaka—of the human variety," Fogarty said, completing the introductions.

"Christ, Bill, we're in distinguished company," Forrest commented, using a towel on his chest and upper arm. "Now, after five years I know you're not here 'bout my traffic tickets. . . ."

"Na. Nothin' like that," Fogarty replied, turning slightly more serious. "Got an investigation we could use a hand with. Just a flyer, Gordon, but maybe you could help." Then the lieutenant glanced at the vet, clearing his throat. Ed Reeves took his cue.

"If you fellas will excuse me, I've got a tiger with a stomach ache." Reeves looked at Nellie. "She can stay here for the time being. Get a little rest."

"Lie down, Nellie," Forrest demanded. "Lie down," he repeated.

The giraffe folded its legs and settled into a mattress-size clump of straw.

"Don't know how he does it," Reeves said. Shaking his head, he left the room.

Fogarty waited for the door to close before he took the drawing from his pocket. He handed it to Forrest.

"Can you tell me who he is?"

Forrest studied the picture a moment, looked up and said, "Sure."

Tanaka kept his eyes glued to the lieutenant. Even now there was only a hint of change in his expression.

"Give'm long hair and a pair o' glasses an' ya got Willard Ng," Forrest answered, pronouncing the last name as "Nigg." "He works here."

"Where?" Fogarty asked.

"The bughouse."

"Can you take us to him?"

Forrest shook his head. "Ain't been in for a few days. Called in sick . . . this is serious, heh, Bill?"

"Do you read the papers?" the lieutenant asked.

Forrest raised his hand to the front of his scalp, shaking his head. "Don't have a TV either."

Tanaka noticed the faded pink scar which ran in a thin line back into the long, receding hair. Forrest caught the doctor's glance.

"Bullet missed my brain by a millimeter. Broke my skull. Now I got a steel plate in there. Suffered from migraines ever since. They get bad enough to make me wanna top myself. Can't read nothin'. Can't really focus my eyes."

Tanaka nodded.

"We want this guy on suspicion of murder, Gordon," Fogarty said.

"Fuckin' hell. . . ." Forrest wheezed.

"Five women, one man," the lieutenant continued.

"Jesus, Bill. I hired the mothafucker. He's a bit peculiar, guess you'd call him introverted, but nothin' ta make ya think he was violent. . . ."

"He's worse than violent," Fogarty answered.

* * *

The lieutenant's bleeper sounded just as they were examining Willard Ng's working boots. A pair of Timberlands, leather uppers, ridged rubber soles. Hardly worn. Size twelve D.

"I'm gonna need a phone," Fogarty said.

Forrest pointed him in the direction of a small storeroom adjacent to the employees' lockers. Tanaka stayed behind.

"What exactly does Mr. Willard do here?" Tanaka asked.

"Nothing specific. General maintenance, a little animal feeding, cleaning. . . ."

"Has he always worked in the same section of the zoo?"

"Yeah. That was the strange thing about'm. Said he didn't care what he did, as long as he worked with the insects."

Tanaka reached in and lifted a khaki workshirt from a hook at the back of the locker. It was neatly pressed and smelled of chlorine bleach.

"Standard issue?" he asked, unfurling the garment.

"Yes. Washed and ironed here, in the laundry."

Tanaka held the shirt up against his own body. The sleeves were too long and the shoulders overstretched his own by two inches either side.

"Mr. Ng is a large man," he commented.

"The guy's a giant," Forrest confirmed.

"Can you recall his hands?"

Forrest squinted. "Only when I shook with him. Once. When I hired him. Big hands, like a catcher's mitt."

"Anything unusual about his fingers?" Tanaka continued.

Forrest shook his head. "I gotta be honest with you. I never paid a lot of attention to Willard. I don't see him that often, and he's not given to much chat. A lotta the time he works late shift."

"When's that?"

"Six 'til midnight. After the place closes. Clean-up, late feeds."

"When the lieutenant gets back, would it be possible to take a look at the exact areas in which Mr. Ng works?"

"Pretty general, really, mate." Forrest shrugged.

"Even so, it might help."

Fogarty bustled back into the locker room. There was no containment to his energy. His jaw was set and his step brisk.

"Ng's our man. Ninety-nine per cent sure."

Tanaka raised his head.

"Got hospital reports from Norristown. December 1989. A Willard Ng checked in for two nights. Had a right orchidectomy."

"What's that?" Forrest asked.

"The removal of a testicle," Tanaka answered.

"That checks out with Dante's story," Fogarty said. Then he turned to Gordon Forrest. "I'm gonna need to put some men in here. Starting this afternoon."

"You gottit, Bill," Forrest answered.

"A full surveillance team on the entrance and exits and a couple of men on the inside. Is he gonna suspect something's up if he sees some new faces?"

"No. Not this season. We have'm come an' go."

"Gordon. This is gonna be down to you and Anthony Galenti. Nobody else is going to know a thing about it. That's real important. This guy's been workin' here for the entire time he's been killing people, so if you don't ruffle him, then it's not likely he's gonna get crazy. But if he even sniffs it—"

"Nobody'll know," Forrest assured him.

"Can you handle it. I mean, are you going to be able to see him, interact with him?"

Forrest smiled. His gold tooth gleamed. "Remember, I'm the fella who scratched Bamboo's belly. Damn near cost me my job."

"This could cost ya a lot more," Fogarty said, his gaze meeting Forrest's good eye.

The zookeeper straightened. He was half a head shorter than the lieutenant, but there was a built-in quickness to his muscular body.

"I don't rattle easy, Bill."

"Good. My men'll be here within the hour. Till then, I'll wait with you." Then, turning to Tanaka, "Would you go to the administration building and try and get access to Willard Ng's records. We need a street address on'm."

Tanaka hesitated, about to speak.

Fogarty intercepted: "He paid in cash at the hospital. Didn't give an address, said he was travelling."

"Bill. I'd like to have a look at the areas in which Ng worked."

Don't start trying to take over my investigation, Fogarty thought. He said nothing. Instead he looked at Forrest and nodded his consent.

The Backyard Bug exhibit was in the children's zoo at the rear end of the main compound. It was one of the zoo's minor attractions. It was also a seasonal exhibit, spring until early fall. Now it was closed, its exhibition tanks locked inside an octagonal metal shelter.

"Shit," Tanaka whispered, staring at the locked doors of the small building.

"What are you lookin' for, Joey?" Fogarty asked, his patience wearing thin.

Tanaka answered with a question to Forrest.

"Did you keep praying mantis here?"

Praying mantis . . . Fogarty repeated it in his mind. Dante had described Ng as "the Mantis". Suddenly the lieutenant and the doctor were on the same wavelength.

"Sometimes during the season. We let'm go in the fall," Forrest answered. "They're difficult to exhibit," he added.

"Why's that?" Fogarty asked.

"Nasty little buggers. If they don't get a good scrap every so often they start fightin' amongst themselves. Pull each others eyes out, turn cannibal."

Fogarty nodded.

"An entire system of combat evolved from studying the way they fight," Tanaka interjected.

"Better that than the way they fuck," Forrest said.

Tanaka half smiled, and Fogarty looked quizzical. Forrest caught the lieutenant's eye.

"After a good seeing to, the female rewards her mate by biting through his neck. Last August we had a bus load of day campers in here. Fascinated by these two insects fucking away. Until the bitch turns around with lover boy's head between her teeth. Counselor shoulda known better. She wrote a letter of complaint to Galenti. 'Corrupting the morals of minors.' He closed the exhibit."

"May we take a look in here?" Tanaka asked. He had stopped in front of a thin steel door sealed with a padlock.

Forrest lifted a keyring from his belt. It took him three keys before the padlock opened.

The space inside was lined with empty glass tanks. A dark walkway, twenty feet long, ran the length of the bughouse. The place smelled of wet mops and antiseptic cleaning fluid.

"Any storage rooms? Out-of-the-way places?" Tanaka asked.

"This is it for the bughouse, Doctor."

"I'm referring to the entire zoo," Tanaka said.

Forrest considered. "Maybe two hundred storage rooms, closets. A dozen feed rooms. More or less."

Fogarty looked at Tanaka.

"What have you got in mind?" he asked.

"Four hundred years ago, when the Mantis style was developed, the temple monks spent days in seclusion, studying their insects. Caging them, starving them, feeding them larger and stronger prey. . . . Imitating their attacks and counters. . . . Somewhere, Willard Ng is going to have a place, a private place—"

Fogarty swallowed another little bit of ego. This really was getting to be the doctor's case.

"How long will it take to see'm all, Gordon?"

William Ng's address was listed as 1605 Rising Sun Avenue, in the northeast section of the city. He had no prior arrests. His file also included a letter of recommendation from City Bank and

Trust, where he had worked as a nightwatchman/custodian. The letter included such accolades as, "Mr. Ng is both fastidious and punctual."

Fogarty called Boy Moyer from his car, asking, pleading for anything that would link Ng with the murders. A fiber of clothing, a hair, anything. Moyer came up negative. He was apologetic but firm. Still Fogarty drove on, down Allegheny to the intersection at Broad Street, then up Rising Sun. Towards a rooming house that Ng had not inhabited in two years.

XIII.

MY WAY

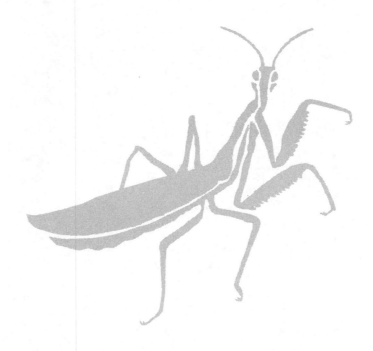

Leather boots are tough to burn. They simmer at first, until the heat builds up enough to cause flame. A few squirts from a squeezy bottle of barbecue lighter helps. It may take several trys but, finally, the hide will catch. Willard Ng squeezes for the seventh time. The boot closest to him ignites, the hard rubber sole is melting. Satisfied, he turns away. He is surrounded by similar smoking mounds of rubbish. Like rolling hills. He walks the narrow path to a VW van, old but immaculate, the model that was once known as a Microbus. He climbs in and drives away. Slows down at the guard house just before the open chain-linked gate. Hands the black security man two brand new quarters. They look like tiny silver discs dropping from his hardened brown fingers.

"Cheap fuck," the black man grumbles. Not loud enough for the dome-headed man to hear. The guard stares after the metal-gray van. Makes a mental note not to let the big man into the yard again. His job isn't worth much, but it is worth more than fifty cents.

Willard Ng drives north along Delaware Avenue, towards Penn's Landing, continuing until the intersection with Route 95. Then he turns right, joining the traffic for the Ben Franklin bridge.

He pays his toll. Follows the signs for Camden, Broadway, relaxing as he heads home. Fiddling with the tuner knob on his radio. Finding the clearest reception on WMMR, a Philadelphia FM rock channel.

The song began with a single chord, played on a synthesizer, sliding down the musical scale, ending in a melancholic puddle of blue notes. Then a guitar, soft, almost etheric, and finally the voice of Sid Vicious.

> *And now the end is near*
> *and so I face the final curtain*

Willard Ng listened. It was his song, Willard's song; he understood the words. And the singer's voice, the vibration, the tone. *Death.* That was it. There was death inside the voice. The singer was courting death, yearning for it. Singing to Willard.

> *I've lived a life that's full*
> *travelled each and every highway*
> *and more, much more than this*
> *I did it my way*

He turned up the volume.

The music changed, shifted gear. Guitars and drums, power chords and rhythm, the singer's voice jumping two octaves.

Ng's left foot was tapping now, the energy running up his leg. He drove faster, hit a hole in the road; the radio crackled and died. He wrenched the tuner knob, desperate to hear more. Swerved away from the rough patch of highway and headed in the wrong direction down a one-way street.

Jack Tucker was enjoying a little down-time, finishing the last of two double-layered peanut butter and jelly sandwiches, when he saw the van approach.

"Gotcha!" he whispered, aiming his spotlight directly into the windshield of the oncoming van.

"Son of a bitch," he growled as the VW drove by.

Tucker threw the Ford into drive, wheeled around, and took off in pursuit.

He was ten yards behind the VW when he hit his siren; this time directing the beam of his spotlight into the offending vehicle's rearview mirror.

Willard Ng raised his right hand to block the glare.

Blinding me. Trying to blind me. He was very angry when he pulled to the curb.

The police car continued behind him, finally stopping with its grille alongside the VW's sliding side door. The spotlight remained trained on Willard Ng.

"May I see your licence and registration?" The nasal voice came from inside the blast of light. A moment later, Jack Tucker stepped forward, his body blocking the beam.

Ng's eyes refocused quickly.

He looked down at the small police officer. There was a purple globule of jam on the man's shirt, three buttons down, above his heart.

"Licence and registration, please," Tucker insisted.

The VW's door began to open.

Tucker took a step back, his hand poised above the holster of his weapon. "Please. Do not leave your vehicle."

Ng considered a moment, then reached into the rear pocket of his overalls and produced a worn alligator wallet. Handed his licence to the cop.

Tucker studied the attached picture. It depicted a man with glasses and thick curly hair. The face was the same.

Alopecia, he presumed. "Mr. Nigg, do you know why you have been stopped?"

"The name is pronounced 'No one,'" Willard answered. There was no expression in his tone.

"You were driving illegally up a one-way street," Tucker continued.

Ng nodded. He was becoming impatient.

"In the state of New Jersey, it is an offense to drive the wrong way up a one-way street. . . ." Tucker laid it on.

Ng stared at the policeman's belly; it hung over his wide leather belt and holstered gun.

"May I see the registration for your vehicle?"

Ng felt the puffing breath wanting to rise up the center of his abdomen. He held it in check, barely.

"Please." Tucker's tone turned the request into a command.

"Don't have it with me," Ng replied.

Tucker nodded. "Wait here, please." Then he walked to his patrol car.

There were no traffic offenses or prior arrests on Willard Ng, and the VW van was registered in his name. Tucker was glad of this, he really didn't like the idea of taking Ng in. Ng looked like trouble. Still, he would give him a ticket.

The policeman could hear the strange, puffing breaths from twenty feet. *The son of a bitch is crazy, he told himself, walking cautiously towards the VW.*

The breaths had stopped by the time he arrived, leaving a frightening deadness in Ng's half-slanted eyes.

Tucker handed him the driving licence and a yellow form.

"If you pay the fine within thirty days, you won't have to go to court."

Ng held the licence and ticket in his hand. He appeared to be looking through the policeman.

"You should keep your vehicle registration with you," Tucker cautioned.

Ng detected a slight vibration of fear in the man's voice. He paid no attention to the words, keeping his eyes steady on the policeman's, locking the man with his mind. Heightening his fear at will.

"Now turn your car around and proceed in the appropriate direction."

Ng started the VW's engine, then drove straight ahead, ignoring the policeman's order.

"Goddamn it!" Tucker swore, wondering if he could ignore the infraction. Then, squaring his shoulders, he double-timed to his car, got in, and followed the gray van.

Once on Ferry Avenue, Ng headed straight for Benson, parked on the curb and went inside. He felt clean now. Burning his boots and clothing had reinstated his self-esteem. As if the guilt of his carelessness had disintegrated with the leather and the fabric. He entered his bedroom and stripped naked.

Then, gripping the wooden floor with the long toes of his muscular feet, he walked to the power room. It was the largest room in his single-storey house, nearly twenty feet square. His reflected image cascaded inwards, caressing him from every angle. Mirrors mounted from floor to ceiling covered each of the four walls, and two strips of silvered glass were riveted to the ceiling. In the far corner of the room were three sets of strength stones, each stone impaled upon a foot-long wooden pole. The stones were made of concrete in strict gradients of ten to twenty-five pounds. Facing him was the Mon Fat-Jong, a training device which resembled a human figure, with a spring-mounted head, and extensions representing arms. A single piece of curved wood came forwards from the dummy's base, simulating a knee and lower leg, giving the framed contraption balance. Ng had constructed the dummy himself, out of seasoned timber, hard and resilient. At one time all of the vital striking points had been padded. A year ago, one month before he began the killing exercise, Ng had removed the pads, preferring to condition his hands against the hard wood. To the left of the dummy three striking pads were mounted against a wood frame, one of straw, one a canvas bag filled with beans, and one a canvas bag filled with sand. To the left of these, hanging as if in some medieval scaffold, was a human skeleton, its bones dry and yellow-white. Ng never struck the skeleton. He used it, instead, for accuracy. Pulling his blows short of the vital points along its brittle surface.

He stood a moment, viewing himself in the eight-foot-high mirrors. The overhead track lighting cast his body in imposing shadow, the striations above the pectoralis muscles of his chest looking like taut wires. Perfection. He was nearly there. And what remained then? After perfection. Death, of course. Now that *was* something to look forward to.

He closed his eyes, reliving his encounter with the black man. Recalling the strange acidic taste, followed by numbness, as the man's nose broke away in his teeth.

The bite had been difficult, requiring six partial rotations of his neck. Too difficult.

He walked to his strength stones, squatting down beside a twenty-pound circle of concrete. Carefully he removed the weight from its handle. Then he picked up a specially crafted piece of hard rubber. The rubber was black and had been cut from the treaded portion of a car tire. Cut into what looked like a boxer's gumshield; there were teeth marks on both sides of the rubber and a heavy iron-linked chain attached to the V-shaped outer side. He threaded the chain through the hole in the strength stone and placed the black rubber in his mouth. At first it was dry, and Ng could taste the salt of previous sessions.

He envisaged Arthur Stubbs' nose and immediately began to salivate. Biting down hard, his top and bottom incisors found their ready-made grooves. He bit deeper, trying to bite clean through the hard rubber. At the same time he lifted his head, bringing the twenty-pound weight off the floor, "Bite, twist, tear . . . Bite, twist tear." He repeated the command, all the time rotating his head from side to side, just as he had seen her do in the final stages of combat. Closed his eyes, thought again of the black man. Bit deeper. After an indeterminable time his jaw ached and the muscles of his neck began to seize. He lowered the weight and relaxed his bite.

He could taste blood. That was good. It meant the pressure of his jaws had caused his gums to bleed. He inhaled. The air made a whooshing sound as it passed through the gaps between enamel and rubber. Then he exhaled, lifting the weight, twisting his head from side to side. Growling as his sharp canines met midway through the exercise device.

Outside 31 Benson, directly across from the Santa Isabel Social Club, less than twenty yards from the immaculate VW van, Jack Tucker wondered exactly what he should do.

Probably the guy hadn't even heard him; he'd certainly made no attempt to outrun the patrol car. In fact he had appeared oblivious to the policeman behind him. Tucker had intended to follow the VW to the bridge, watch him cross and forget it. *Outa state, not worth the aggravation.* Besides, the sonofabitch was an ugly mother and Tucker was on traffic control, not felony.

Still, why did he go into the small house? Why did he have a key?

Tucker lit a Marlboro and waited. His shift was up in twenty minutes and he was starving. There was also a good film on TV, *Predator* with Arnold Schwarzenegger.

Christ, this guy was as big as Schwarzenegger and looked a hell of a lot meaner. That was really it anyway. The guy had intimidated him and it was supposed to be the other way around. So what if the ape was living in Jersey and driving on a Pennsylvania licence, so what if he'd ignored the order of a Camden police officer?

Tucker was halfway out of his patrol car when a splinter of light, the kind cast when a door opens in a dark room and the light from an adjoining room spills inward, illuminated the window of number 31. Tucker froze.

A blackened silhouette filled the frame behind the parted curtains, like a statue, stone and still. *He's watching me. He knows I'm out here.*

A moment of indecision was followed by a prudent retreat to the blue and white Ford. Tucker rolled up the driver's-side window, shutting out the cold night air.

The silhouette had not moved. Tucker thought of Sally and the two kids. His shift had now officially ended.

He picked up his phone. "Officer J.R. Tucker calling in. . . ."

"This is Preston, go ahead Tuck."

"Gene, I'm goin' home, but will you do me a favor; run another check on a Willard Ng. See if there's anything listed with department of transport on a change of address. Check 31 Benson."

He could hear Preston groan on the other end of the phone. "It's gonna take a little time, Jack, the computer's backlogged."

"All right, forget it, Gene, I'll do it myself in the morning."

Ng watched the patrol car ease its way past his van and continue up the street. It was the same cop that had stopped him. The same cop he could have killed half an hour ago. Not a worthy opponent. He observed the tail lights flicker and die, then he returned to his power room and resumed training.

Fogarty left Hawkins and Magee on all-night surveillance, dropped Tanaka off at Rittenhouse Square and headed west towards the Presidential. His body ached with fatigue but his mind wouldn't quit. He considered valium, but only for a moment. He needed rest; he also needed to be sharp. What he really needed was a good woman. Someone he could talk to. Someone to take the pressure off his head. Diane Genero. Christ, she'd called him . . . Diane Genero had phoned him twice.

He caught himself on the verge of fantasy, then tried to erase the unformed thoughts from his subconscious. Thinking of her that way was sacrilege. She'd be calling about the case. He'd return her call in the morning. Too late to phone now. He wanted to say *We got him. No,* I *got him. Yeah, I got him. Me, Bill Fogarty, I took him down. And I did it for you, Diane. You and Gina, Sarah and Ann* . . . and suddenly Bill Fogarty was crying. Big wet tears running down his cheeks. *Let go. That's it, Bill. It's all right. The tears wash your mind.* Isn't that what his therapist had said the first time he had broken down. The first time he had ever really spoken to anyone about the accident. *I've never cried in front of a woman,* he'd lied. He had cried. When Ann was born. He'd cried in front of Sarah. And that was all right too. Then his thoughts cleared and he refocused.

He picked up his phone and got through to highway patrol. His voice held no trace of anguish; it was a mask of hard authority. "Anything new on Willard Ng?" Fogarty too pronounced the name "Nigg."

The voice on the other end of the line sounded broken, far away. "Nothing, Lieutenant. No address change, no out-of-state offenses. Nothing in the past eighteen months. We haven't had a full reply from Jersey. Computer back-up. They're promising us a full read by morning."

"All right, stay on it. I want anything. Anything at all."

"I understand."

"No matter what it is," Fogarty emphasized before hanging up.

Josef Tanaka had deserved to die since that moment in Tokyo. Since he had taken Hiro's life from him. He knew he was pushing himself towards it, knew that some time, somewhere, he would reach the brink. Then he would decide. To live or to die. It motivated his actions. He didn't see it at first; it was clear now. He had thought that it would probably happen on the bike. Sometimes he rode that way. When he was alone, on a run, maybe up along Route 309 towards Allentown or when he got off the main roads and hit the country lanes. Bends and hair-pin turns, leaning the Harley so low he could hear the underside of the frame grind against the gravel, letting the rear wheel slide out enough to lose it. Almost. Now the bike was gone; his obsession remained. It had put an end to three lovers before Rachel Saunders. Eventually they just couldn't take it, his pre-occupation with pushing everything as far as it would go. Seeking the freedom, the relief from guilt that lay on the other side of . . . of what? Sometimes it happened at the dojo, looking for that single punch, that one movement, measured in the psychological nuances of what constituted a killing blow, registered by the fear in his training partner's eyes.

At first he thought it was justified, his personal quest for perfection. And then he began to understand it as something more; it was his personal quest for atonement. A life for a life, a death for a death. For after perfection, after the freedom of enlightenment, surely came death. Josef Tanaka had a death wish.

Before Rachel Saunders there was Lynda Bellings. He'd managed to drive her to the threshold of a nervous breakdown. She had finally confessed to an addiction to tranquilizers before seeking solace in the arms of her therapist. But Rachel was different; she was also driven. In a healthier, more conventional manner than Josef Tanaka, but none the less driven. She could match him for energy and match him for endurance. When Rachel Saunders wanted something she usually got it. He wondered if she wanted him enough to see him through what he was stone-sure would happen. If she could, and if he survived, he would marry her.

He recalled the recent phone call to his father. He had

intended to tell Mikio Tanaka of his plans, to ask his approval. Instead he hung up the phone the moment he heard the low, hoarse voice. He wasn't ready to speak to his father after all. Something remained undone. Something concerning perfection and death. He wasn't sure what it was when he'd made the call; he knew now.

"Are you still awake?" Rachel's voice was soft and quiet, filling the empty space at the conclusion of his thoughts. She pushed her warm hips against him, the back of her thighs molding into the front of his own. He was half hard and it was easy to find the wet between her legs. She moaned as he pressed inwards, tilted her hips slightly so that he could enter her. Wrapping both his arms around her chest and resting his lips lightly on the back of her neck, he became silent and still.

XIV.

AN EVENING OF
INTIMACY

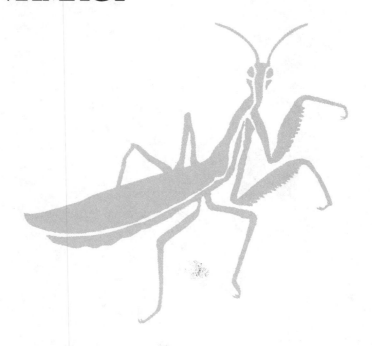

It was 2 a.m. when Willard Ng arrived at the zoo. His first visit in three days; he knew she would be hungry. He left his van in Zoological Avenue, across from the railroad tracks, and walked to H. Gate. Knelt down in front of the chain-linked barrier, turned on his back, pulling his body along the rough gravel between the bottom bar and the courtyard. The method he always used when he came late at night. The security guards were generally lax but he saw no need to take chances. It was not so much his own safety that concerned him; it was her's. He could not bear the thought of someone discovering her room, of the penetration of her sanctuary. As if the very presence of another human soul would cause an irrevocable imbalance. She guided him towards perfection and, in exchange, he provided her with inviolability.

He stopped in front of the door which led through the rear corridors of the reptile house. Listened a moment. Heard the faraway cry of the leopard and the call of the night owl. Nothing more.

He found the correct key, amongst a ring of keys that matched the ones he turned in when his shift ended each day. Keys that he had paid to have duplicated. Opened the door and slipped inside. The passageway was dimly lit by the glow from the exhibition tanks, the humidified atmosphere made more close by the antiseptic smell of cleaning fluid. The rubber soles of his training shoes padded softly along the concrete floor, through the door marked "Employees Only" and down the narrow stairs into the Feed Room. After a few steps he paused and stood still, acclimatizing himself to the darkness, listening for her voice. He was uncertain if the tremor which began in the center of his forehead, above his nose and between his eyes, that same point which had been touched so many years ago in the garden of St. Thomas', was an internal or an external emanation. It was certainly a connection. He breathed in, deep and slow, savoring the warm electricity of their contact. The sound was like a buzz, whirring inside his skull. Then her voice, forming from the fine line of vibration.

Tonight I am hungry, Willard. Hungry and lonely. Starving . . .

He began to run in the direction of her voice. Long, fluid strides, stretching into the darkness. Her room was at the end of the passage, interconnected with the Quarantine Room. Behind a wall of cages, filled with new arrivals. Diamond-back rattle-snakes, Peruvian lizards as long as a man's arm, small piercing eyes that stared warily into the darkness.

He slid the cages aside, revealing the iron door. The door had been painted gray, with the kind of paint that was once used on warships, thick and glossy. The same color as Willard Ng's VW van. It was locked with a Yale padlock, round and heavy. A lock which Willard had installed, retaining the only existing key.

Inside, the room was bathed in a warm glow, infrared replacing ultraviolet. He had turned the heat lamps on five days ago and now the temperature was a constant eighty degrees. Humid. He began to sweat as he walked toward her bamboo temple. She shivered slightly as their eyes met. *Hungry. Starving. Lonely.* Her thoughts were clear. She watched patiently as he stripped off his clothes. Finally he stood naked in front of her. He was acutely aware of his inadequacy. Her eyes penetrated the core of his being, assessing his evolution. *I am hungry, Willard. Starving and lonely.*

Is the season right for love? It was a personal question. The question he always asked before a coupling.

The season is perfect. Like a warm August night. And I am lonely.

He smiled at her. She made him feel so innocent, so inexperienced; she permitted him such freedom within her discipline. He walked to the rows of storage jars, picked up the last jar on the long shelf, looked inside. Two male mantises huddled lazily on the bottom, wings closed, camouflaged in the straw and grass. He turned. She was standing now, following his movements, drawing him inside her consciousness. He placed the jar on the table, beside her. Reached in. *No, Willard. The smaller one first. Always begin with the weaker.* She reared back slightly, acknowledging that he had chosen the correct offering. His groin tingled as he forced the slender male through the feeding flap. At first she backed away, shy. Then her shyness was replaced by indifference. She lowered her head and waited. Willard sat naked on his round wooden stool, elbows on the table, his chin resting in the palms of his hands. There was an exquisite stillness to the atmosphere, as if all time had stopped. Warm and dreamy. The smaller mantis moved forward towards her. Moved so slowly that his motion would have been lost in the blink of an eye. Willard Ng did not blink. He had learned not to. The heat from the overhead lamps pulsed against the flesh of his neck and shoulders. His entire being was centered on her. Waiting for her sign. He knew what would happen next. Should happen. But it did not, and as he became more aware of waiting, so his ability to concentrate faded. A single rivulet of sweat ran from his brow, traveled slowly down his cheek. He could taste the salt in his mouth. Was the room temperature incorrect, too humid? Was she displeased with his offering? Should he reach inside and withdraw the male? He studied the smaller of the two insects, drawn for the first time to the stick-like frailness of the creature. *She* turned her head; the movement seemed almost mechanical, her diamond skull pivoting on the stem of its neck. Her eyes aimed into his; Willard felt the familiar sensation inside his forehead, the electricity that preceded contact. He wanted to turn away, to deny this presence. His mind opened. A new, unfamiliar consciousness invaded him. A consciousness instilled with the primordial knowledge of death. Great sorrow threatened to overcome him, a sorrow which was at once sad and beautiful. Willard closed his eyes and looked inside the sorrow, saw himself. Realized in a single lucid moment that it was death that stood before him, death that hung like a shadow. Death that guided him towards fulfilment, death that was close to him now. He felt a fresh flood of energy in his loins. Experienced a hunger that was at once undeniable and final. He looked again into her eyes and detected the satisfaction of a shared knowledge. Then the eyes withdrew and the diamond skull turned from the naked man. The mating dance began, the small slender insect rushing forward, wings spread, towards the waiting female. For the first time Willard was aware of the clear abandon in the creature's movements, freedom in the face of death. The final lesson.

The male mounted from behind, clinging to her back as he steadied his hold. She quivered as he entered her.

Willard was sweating profusely as he stood up from the stool, backing to the shelf, never removing his eyes from the Mantis and her mate. The small metal box was cool in his hand; it opened easily, the amber phial and metal-based syringe falling into his palm. He popped the needle through the rubber cap, retracted the plunger of the syringe and emptied the phial. His flaccid penis felt moist and spongy as he held it level with the tip of the needle. Pinching some skin towards the base of his organ he penetrated the flesh slowly. It required a full thirty seconds to inject the papaverine. The drug lumped and swelled before he massaged the area to disperse it. Then the tingling began, an electric warmth. His penis began to fill, thick and hard.

She was bucking ever so slightly, her head bowed forward in submission as her lover increased the tempo of copulation.

Three hours passed. Willard maintained a wide straddle-legged stance in front of her temple. He clenched his buttocks, savoring the burning pain in his thighs. Masturbating slowly. Keeping a gentle rhythm, prolonging his orgasm in the same way that he delayed it when he accomplished the transition. He was in ecstacy, his entire being undulating with the sexual vibrations of the room. The buzzing was all around him, inside and out. He was completely connected. Both male and female; he had transcended gender, transcended humanity. Both hands stroked up and down along his shaft, centering his consciousness, guiding him along the fine smooth tunnel to permanence. Another hour, another lifetime; a slow dissolving of ego. He shuddered as he climaxed, in time with the convulsive twitching of the slender male. His testicle throbbed, pumping in dry spasm.

She was rising up now, tossing her expired lover aside. He

shook and trembled as he fell away. She loomed above him, her darkened eyes assessing the quality of his performance, judging him as she had often judged Willard. The male appeared pale and weak, diminished by his loss of seed. Willard stared, fearful of her dark eyes. Stillness descended. He shifted position, allowing the circulation of blood to disperse the lactic acid in his quadriceps. His penis remained engorged, swollen and chafed from the masturbation. For a tortured moment it was as if his mind had split and he was at once both mentor and offering. The moment extended and an acute fear threatened to rob him of clarity. Fear of rejection, buried deep in the recess of his human mind. He was a child again, naked and vulnerable. Unable to express emotion. Unloved, unwanted. Rejected by his parents, rejected by his peers. And, finally, rejected by death. A nausea began in the pit of his gut and rose upward. He coughed and his heart burned. He wanted to cry out, opened his mouth. His scream was silent. Then he felt the tingling take him, grip him like it had never gripped him before, anchoring him to the Mantis.

She had begun to move. Creeping forward to her lover, head raised, eyes certain. Willard felt his moment of reprieve. The exhausted male remained still. Yet there was a dignity to his stillness. She had accepted his performance; he had pleased her. Willard breathed inward, a long fluid breath. The vacuum, which had held him so perfectly, returned. He knew what was to come, as did the slender male. She was close now, and Willard could imagine her short, hot breaths against his throat. He watched mesmerized as her jaws opened, revealing perfect rows of razored teeth. Her first bite was quick and decisive. He gasped as it tore through the gristle below the male's jaw, to the side of its neck. Her initial bite did not kill the male, nor was it intended to. He remained upright, standing before her. Proud and complete, finally on the cusp of fulfilment. Her second bite was not so deep, and as she lifted her head Willard was able to see the flesh inside her mouth. Observe the satisfaction in her eyes. Revelling in the taste. The male fell on the third bite. She had gone deeper, severing his head completely. She turned towards Willard, the head still in her mouth. *Death is permanence. Simple and complete. Without death we revolve forever on the wheel of imperfection. Victims of what we have been, tortured by what we can never achieve. Look at yourself, Willard Ng.* Her jaws moved as she transmitted her thoughts, crunching inward against the diamond skull, sucking the brain.

Once the head was consumed she started on the body, eating slowly and deliberately until only the pale gauze wings remained.

It was just before five when Willard closed and secured the door to her chamber. His erection had subsided and he walked with a solemn gait of one who has just buried a close friend. He saw no one on his way down the stone footpath and out of H Gate. Not that it would have worried him to be seen; he was beyond that pettiness. He was going to die. Soon. That was certain. It was necessary.

Had Tyrone Johnson looked up from his eggs-ranchero and glanced once in the rearview mirror of his blue Ford sedan, he would have noticed an enormous man in khaki-colored overalls walking slowly in the direction of his car. The man's head and face were void of all hair and he was talking to himself, in fact he was deep in conversation. There was a peaceful, dream-like quality to his features and he moved his hands in a strangely flowing manner to emphasize whatever it was he was saying. Because of his size and proximity Johnson would have identified the giant as Willard Ng. The surveillance cop would have phoned his sighting in and Ng would have been picked up. He may even have gone quietly. Instead, with Jeb Hawkins asleep and snoring in the passenger seat behind him, Johnson kept his head down and concentrated on not letting any of the egg yolk run on his Harris tweed jacket; it was an old favorite, his lucky jacket. Behind him, not more than thirty yards from the Ford, Willard Ng rounded a bend and disappeared.

XV.

THE HOUSE CALL

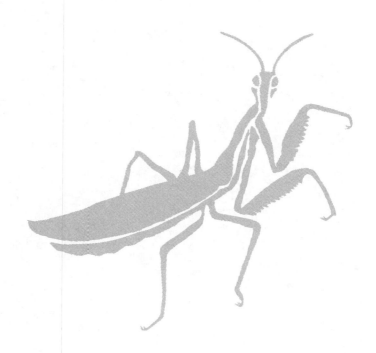

Fogarty was just about out the door when his telephone rang.

"Lieutenant Fogarty?" It was a male voice, not one that he recognized.

"Speaking," he answered.

"My name is Jack Tucker and I'm with the City of Camden Police Department. Traffic control," the voice added reluctantly.

Fogarty's stomach tightened and he experienced the unsettling feeling of *déjà vu*. He knew where the conversation would go.

"I've seen your request for anything recently issued involving a Pennsylvania license under the name of Willard Ng."

"That's right, Officer, what have you got for me?" Fogarty attempted to sound off-hand, routine.

"Yesterday at 5:15 p.m. I stopped a 1973 Volkswagen van operated by a man identifying himself as Willard Ng," Tucker replied.

"What was he doing?" The lieutenant kept it light.

"Going the wrong way down a one-way street." Tucker felt foolish saying it; he had bigger things on his mind.

"Have you got a current address for him?" Fogarty continued. "The one we've got here is out of date."

"As it happens, I had reason to follow him," Tucker said, sounding cagey.

Here it fuckin' comes. Fogarty waited for the punch.

"Would this be in connection with your investigation of the serial killings?" Tucker's tone was patronizingly solemn.

Oh yeah, the Lieutenant thought. *Another uniform looking for the big time.* He was about to snap, only holding himself in check at the last. New Jersey was close, but it was still out of state. He would need cooperation. He assumed his most confidential voice and lied. "We have reason to believe that Willard Ng may have inadvertently made contact with the killer in the past several months. It isn't much, but anything we can get right now could turn this thing around.''

The last thing in the world Fogarty needed was a New Jersey detective making the collar. Or, worse still, some traffic control cop getting killed trying.

"Shall I have Mr. Ng picked up, Lieutenant?''

Fogarty waited before answering, making sure his desperation was buried. "Officer Tucker—'' He hesitated purposefully.

"Yes, Lieutenant.'' Tucker waited. He'd seen the TV news reports, read the papers. He knew he was on to something. Sensed it. Intuition. This guy Fogarty must have thought he was an idiot.

"Because of the delicacy of this situation, it's probably best if I handle it myself. I certainly appreciate your cooperation though. Now would you give me Mr. Ng's address.''

Tucker stayed silent, thinking. He wondered if he could get away with bringing Ng in on a misdemeanor, disobeying a police officer. Then he recalled the ominous silhouette at the window and wondered if he really wanted to try.

"The address, Officer Tucker, please.'' Fogarty's voice was beginning to take on an edge.

"31 Benson St. Right over the bridge, off South Fifth,'' Tucker answered. He felt as if he'd just been robbed. "That's where I followed him,'' Tucker added.

"Thank you very much, Jack. Thank you very much.'' Fogarty put the phone down; he wondered if the traffic cop would attempt any heroics. He knew the man was suspicious.

Camden. Seven o'clock in the morning. Twenty minutes if he hustled. No time for a warrant. No time to organize a back-up. Got to make it before Officer Tucker. He just knew the guy smelled a promotion.

Fogarty wrote the address on a slip of paper, stuffed it in his pocket and turned to leave. His leg brushed against the side of a maple chest. In the sun the wood looked like polished gold. Today was overcast and the maple was the color of honey. A fine piece, picked up by Sarah on one of her jaunts to the outdoor markets near New Hope. She'd used it as a drinks cabinet. Since the accident Fogarty had used it for something else. He thought a moment then knelt beside the chest, running his hand along the underside. The key was there, beneath a strip of masking tape. He opened the chest. The faint aroma of metal and oil preceded his vision of the Colt Officers Models. The compact .45 automatic was loaded, cocked and locked. A hundred rounds of hollowpoint ammunition lay in neatly ordered boxes beside the weapon. *Christ. What am I going to do? Blow the bastard up before I arrest him?* He corrected himself. *I can't arrest him. Got nothin' on him.* Then he took off his jacket and removed his shoulder rig, exchanging it for a Milt Sparks Summer Special; hanging the holster from the double belt-loops above his right kidney.

His five-shot Smith and Wesson 'snubby' was fine for conceal-ment, reasonably accurate at close and middle range. Fogarty just didn't trust its stopping power. Not completely. Not since it had taken three reloads to drop a single male suspect one clammy July night in '86. The guy had been out of his mind on a mix of PCP and methadrine, a little acid thrown in for visuals. Strong as an ape and unaware that the Teflon bullets that were entering his body from a distance of twenty feet were meant to make him drop his three-foot Samurai sword and desist. He had already decapitated his wife and pet dog when the lieutenant arrived. He continued to thrust and slice as they netted him. The added weight of fourteen rounds of .38 "Thunder Zap" didn't appear to slow him down at all.

The .45 made an obvious dent in Fogarty's rear vent, but he'd sacrifice style for peace of mind any day. Particularly on the day he was going to interview Willard Ng. He'd have to get a couple of Jersey detectives to make the arrest, then he'd extradite the suspect. Just a hitch, a formality. Shouldn't be a problem, he was owed a couple of favors there anyway. As long as nobody got greedy. "Jack Tucker, please don't be an asshole." Fogarty said it out loud as he dropped two spare clips of ammo into his side pocket. Then he closed the door to 611A and thought of Willard

Ng. *What if it isn't him? What if after all this I'm back at square one?*
Too painful a thought to entertain. And if it was Ng, how clever
was the guy going to be? He had to know there wasn't any hard
evidence. No witnesses, no nothing. And he'd be right. Except
for the artist's drawing and size twelve shoe-print with the trace
of camel dung. Thank Christ they hadn't released the drawing
to the TV and press. Fogarty had gone to war over that one.
Better to hold it back. Gave him a hidden card in the psychological hand he was going to have to play. It would probably get
down to that. Trip the suspect up. Get him to incriminate
himself. But how?

Fogarty checked in with Johnson and Hawkins from his car
phone. Nothing, except that Johnson had terminal diarrhea
from a suspect batch of eggs-ranchero and he was threatening to
bust the local McKinneys Diner. "Drop a couple of Rolaids and
stay with it for another two hours," the lieutenant instructed.
Then he called the Roundhouse and arranged for detective Jim
Ratigan to meet him at 31 Benson; Ratigan was always a safe bet
as a back-up. Plus he'd been working the case nearly as long as
Fogarty. His final call was to the forensics lab.

Willard Ng was in that first hour of deep, dreamless sleep that
always followed a contact with his mentor. It was a sleep beyond
peace, almost a death sleep. His body's natural rhythms shifting
slowly, heart beating at less than thirty beats a minute. He lay
naked on his double-width futon, the firm padding on the
mattress holding him rigid support. His face was placid, and had
it not been for a certain hardening of his features, a cruelty that
appeared more a mask than something innate, he could have
been described as pretty, in a strong, non-human way. His closed
eyes were set wide apart, matching his thin wide mouth. His nose
was small and pushed vaguely to the left side while his ears were
in perfect proportion to the long, wide formation of his skull.
His skin was flawless, smooth and yellow, and the fact that
neither his face nor head was desecrated by a single hair or the
slightest shadow of beard added to the fineness of his being. A

single cotton quilt covered him to the shoulders, rising and falling gently with the shallow breaths of his lower abdomen. There was a quality to him not unlike one would imagine a mummy to look before age and decay caused the freshly embalmed corpse to shrink and wrinkle.

The new light of morning was blocked from his window by heavy, dark curtains and the door to his bedroom was closed and bolted from the inside.

Now Willard Ng's deep phase of slumber gives way to the next plateau of sleep, REM—rapid eye movement or the dream phase. And, following a contact, the dream is always the same. Willard Ng is a little boy, six, maybe seven years old, about the age he was when his mother died. He is naked, running alone through a patch of woods on the outskirts of the vast lawns and gardens which surround a stone building. He recognizes the building; it is St. Thomas'. He has been naughty again, crying in his sleep. Now he is going to be punished. He is running hard because he is being pursued.

His father is coming. He is gripping a bat, like a baseball bat but plastic and hollow. He has used the bat on Willard before, many times; it makes a sharp smacking sound as it whips against the bare flesh behind his thighs. Sometimes, if Willard's father is really angry, he pushes the tip of the bat into Willard's anus. Deep. Willard can't walk after his father is finished with the bat. He can only crawl.

Willard picks up his pace. His father is gaining on him. He won't make it to St. Thomas'. Then he sees *her*. She is poised on a branch, in a tree whose limbs overhang the dirt path. She spreads her wings as Willard approaches. Her wings unfurl like welcoming arms. Willard runs towards her. She is big now. Bigger than Willard. Bigger than Willard's father. Her entire body trembles as he gets close, then she wraps her wings around him. Protecting him.

This morning's dream is different. She has opened her mouth, not her wings. Willard can see her razored teeth. He is frightened, but not as frightened as he is of his father. He runs

forward. Her mouth opens wider. He can see inside now, beyond the needle teeth. First there is blackness, like a cavern,
then there is a staircase, winding upwards. He is inside now. The
teeth have closed behind him, like a white gate, blocking out his
father. He can hear Raymond Willard's voice, shouting, threatening.

The further he climbs the fainter his father's voice becomes.
He continues up the staircase. There is a light at the very top. An
overhead light, cascading like a single ray of sunshine. Focused
on a solitary figure waiting for Willard. Now Willard is truly
scared. Maybe his father will not force the bat into his rectum,
maybe he should turn and run back down the staircase. He is
somehow compelled to look at the figure.

God. He is beautiful. Half man and half mantis. The body of the
insect and the head of a man. The man-mantis is smiling. He
knows Willard. And Willard knows him. The man-mantis' face is
a reflection of Willard's. Yet it is not a child's face; it is Willard as
a man. Willard's man-eyes are huge and forgiving. They know
how hard Willard has tried to be a good boy, how hard he has
tried to conform to his father's discipline. The man-mantis has
no fear.

Willard stands at the feet of the creature. The man-mantis
towers above him, looking down. There is great compassion in
his eyes. Willard is at peace. . . .

Until the knocking begins. The terrible banging on the gates.
Over and over. It must be his father. Determined to punish him.
The incessant noise is destroying his peace, fogging his vision.
The man-mantis is becoming displeased, shaking his head from
side to side. He begins to smell the fresh cotton of bed sheets.

Willard Ng is coming round, being forced from his dream by
the vibration of a closed fist, striking palm side forward against
the wood of his front door.

"Don't break the fucking door, Bill. If he's in there he'll come
out." Ratigan's breath was like wispy smoke in the cold morning
air. His nose was still red and bulbous although he hadn't had a

drink since the family barbecue on July fourth '88, the first and last time he'd hit his wife.

Tanaka sat in the passenger side of Ratigan's car, waiting.

The knocking had a distinct authority. It wasn't going to stop till he got up and did something about it. Willard Ng slid from the covers and stood naked beside the low bed. He considered putting on the six hairpieces he kept on the mannequin heads inside his closet, then decided it was not necessary. Instead, he removed his Chinese silk dressing gown from its hook, and wrapped and belted it around himself. Then he slid the bolt from his bedroom door and walked calmly through his small sitting room to the source of his disturbance.

The two men who stood on the small patch of pavement below the sill of his front door were policemen. It was obvious by their assumed importance. One was a good head taller than the other and had something wrong with his face. He was half turned, more out of habit than self-consciousness. A third man was getting out of one of the two cars parked in front of Ng's house. It was this man that interested Willard. He was different from the policemen. More graceful, his footsteps smooth and centered. Ng stared at the new man, trying to make eye contact, drawn irrevocably to the facial features which so closely mirrored his own. And as Ng stared, concentrating his mental energy on Josef Tanaka, he began to see in a way that he had never seen before. Swirls of light appeared to encircle the new man's head: gold and green, a flash of red. Light in constant motion, emanating outwards searching for and touching Ng's mind. And as Ng concentrated on this aura of light, he began to experience the buzz. The same buzz that had accompanied his first contact with his mentor, like a connecting strand of electricity.

Finally, Josef Tanaka met the Mantis' eyes. And it was as if the cold electricity entered him, freezing his heart, drawing him towards the enormous domed head. It was the same feeling that he had had at the zoo, that feeling of inevitability. He had been able to turn it off then, to deny it. Now it was right on top of him.

"Mr. Willard Ng?" Fogarty's voice served to disconnect Tanaka from the Mantis.

Ng took a long time to answer. As if he was withdrawing from another plane of consciousness, reluctantly entering Fogarty's reality. "No one. My name is No one." His voice was almost metallic in its monotone.

"Mr. Ng," Fogarty pronounced the name properly, "my name is William Fogarty and I am a lieutenant with the Philadelphia Police Department." He held his shield forward.

Ng nodded. He had expected them to come, eventually. It had always been a matter of time. Thankfully, the time had been adequate. There was really nowhere else to go with the killing exercise.

Fogarty removed his attention from the blade-like formation of scar tissue that ran upwards on Ng's chest from the join of his dressing gown. "May we come in?"

"Why?" Ng asked, shifting his posture so that he was squarely filling the frame of the door. He had prepared for this confrontation. In fact, he did not mind confessing. It was just that he would never confess to a policeman. He was not a criminal.

Ratigan sensed Fogarty's agitation. "Mr. Ng," the bulbous-nosed detective began, "we're here to ask for your cooperation. We have no warrant and you are not under arrest."

Ng nodded again.

"May we come in?" Fogarty repeated, removing any threat from his voice.

Ng looked at Josef Tanaka. It was like looking at a brother. He ventured a half-smile.

"We'd like to ask you a few questions," Ratigan continued, looking up and down the row of houses. "It'd be better inside. You don't want your neighbors talking."

Ng stepped aside, permitting the policemen access to his sitting room.

There were no chairs in the eight-by-seven room. Instead, six meditation mats formed a square pattern around the room's perimeter. Ng nodded appreciatively as Tanaka removed his shoes before stepping upon the tatami-covered floor. Had it not been for Tanaka, Ng would have shut the door in the police-men's faces. But Tanaka was different. Tanaka had been sent.

Ng closed the door. The room was adjoined by a small, white-tiled kitchen. Fogarty noticed that the kitchen door was secured by a single Yale lock. *Probably leads out to a backyard or garden,* he thought, making mental notes. Three further doors connected the main room to the other sections of the house. They were closed.

The proximity of the four men made the atmosphere claus-trophobic. Ng was acutely aware of the body odor of his visitors. The smaller, bulbous-nosed man reeked of dried sweat and no sleep; the scar-faced lieutenant smelled of lime cologne and gun grease; while the warrior was clean. Willard Ng was not nervous.

Fogarty had to clear his throat before he could speak. He was uneasy, in spite of their odds and firepower. "Mr. Ng, we are here to investigate a series of homicides that began last Febru-ary. We have reason to believe that you may be connected with these murders." Fogarty went in direct, studying the pupils of Ng's eyes for any dilation. Sometimes when an interrogation subject was shocked by a question or was preparing to lie, his pupils would dilate. Ng's pupils showed nothing, no reaction at all.

"Do you know what I am referring to, Mr. Ng . . . do you read the papers?" The last part of Fogarty's question was tacked on to elicit a positive response. Anything to get Ng talking.

Ng shook his head, studying the curious configuration of scars that marred the square, almost handsome face of the detective.

"Would you be more comfortable if we gave you a lift down-town and talked to you at the police station, Mr. Ng? We have a lot more room there. We could all sit down," Ratigan inter-jected, just a touch of sarcasm below his sincere tone.

Ng turned towards Tanaka. "Why are you here? With these men. Why are you with them?"

Tanaka met Ng's tight-lidded eyes. They reminded him of some sort of reptile, a snake—or an insect. A mantis.

"My name is Tanaka. I am a police medical doctor. I've been assigned to this case."

The frank simplicity of Tanaka's answer pleased Ng. There had been the color green in Tanaka's aura, and green was the color of the healer; there had also been red, the color of violence, the warrior. . . .

Ng needed to talk to Tanaka, it was imperative. He knew they were destined for a great intimacy. "May we speak in private?"

"Yes," Tanaka answered, as if by compulsion. He felt the instant agitation of the two policemen.

"Can't do that, Mr. Ng," Ratigan said.

"Why?" Tanaka's voice was a quick snap.

"You're not an officer of the law."

Fogarty considered a moment. "It's all right, Jim. Doctor Tanaka will be all right," he said, putting his arm around Ratigan's shoulder, guiding him to the door. "We're right outside, Doctor, right outside," the lieutenant added. Then the door closed and Josef Tanaka and Willard Ng were alone.

At first there was silence.

Then, "We should sit down," Ng whispered. There was something so estranged yet so intimate in Ng's tone that had Tanaka not seen the thin lips move he would have sworn the voice came from somewhere else in the room.

Tanaka sat on the nearest cushion. Ng sat facing him. Then, slowly, Ng removed his dressing gown. Squaring his shoulders, he folded his legs into the position of the lotus.

"I have been waiting for you." Again the hollowed whispered voice.

Tanaka stared at the white, waxen scar in the center of Ng's chest.

"I know," he answered. Again his words seemed to precede his thoughts. It was as if he was being drawn into a powerful and alien field of consciousness.

"It is my wish that you understand me completely," Ng

continued. "I will do whatever it is that is necessary to heighten your understanding."

Tanaka looked up from the scar into the dark eyes; he saw his own face in reflection. Ng held him there, on the precipice of revelation. The stillness became unbearable for Tanaka, as if his mind was being stretched beyond its limits. He wanted to speak, to take control but he was unable. Instead he retreated into memory. Another time, his brother's eyes. Almond eyes . . . Samurai eyes, pure and fine. Hironori stared at him through the veil of consciousness. *Our Father who art in heaven. Hallowed be thy name.* . . . He remembered saying it, the Lord's Prayer. He remembered when he could no longer believe—

"Thy kingdom come. . . ." Ng's hollow voice spoke the words out loud. Took them from Tanaka's head, stole them from his mind. Tanaka jerked upright, a defensive reflex. The Mantis mirrored his movement.

"We are in perfect tune," the Mantis said softly. "I have listened to your mind. Now you listen."

Tanaka experienced a pressure in the area of his forehead above and between his eyes. Had he wanted to turn away it would have been impossible. Then the buzzing began. Like a soothing flood of soft electricity. And with it came peace.

Tanaka stared at the naked man in front of him. And in that moment of perfect peace he saw beyond the embodiment of Willard Ng; beyond the broad, hairless torso and wide domed head, beyond the scarred disfigurement and tortured eyes. Beyond the guilt and pain of human existence. He saw death. Death, like a dark trestled bridge between them.

Then, slowly, very slowly, Ng raised his arms outwards, fingers stretched. Standing, he began the power breaths.

Tanaka stared, his vision untainted by fear. Each of Ng's power breaths had the effect of heightening Tanaka's concentration, centering his vision on the evolving creature before him. Arms became wings, wide and outstretched, fingers like long-bladed claws. And the waxen scar tissue in the center of Ng's chest seemed to glow like a perfect six-pointed star, drawing Tanaka forward like a magnet. Only a small section of Tanaka's rational mind remained disconnected from the illusion. It was that part of him which, finally spoke to the Mantis.

"Why? Why the killing?" he asked.

"I am evolving," the hollow voice answered.

"Evolving?" Tanaka repeated.

"Into a state of permanence. Beyond the human condition," the Mantis replied.

"Why have you chosen to tell me?" Tanaka continued.

"You have been sent. You know this as well as I. The path of your life has guided you to this place. To me."

"For what purpose?" Tanaka's voice was soft, the way it had been when, as a child, he had whispered to his mother in church.

"Atonement. . . ." The Mantis' voice was also soft, soothing.

And somewhere, far back in the recesses of Tanaka's mind, he was frightened. It was a dark foreboding fear, a fear without hope or rationale. A child's fear. Like the fear of a devil or bogeyman.

Finally the Mantis nodded, as if in understanding, then closed his eyes and bowed his head.

Cautiously, Tanaka stood, his instinct for survival serving to separate them. "So you are admitting the murders." His voice sounded loud and unsure, awkward within the context of their connection. He felt suddenly coarse and stupid.

Willard Ng lowered his arms, picked the dressing gown up from the floor and wrapped the garment around his body.

"Another time," he whispered.

A moment later Fogarty and Ratigan reentered the room. They seemed, to Tanaka, to emerge from another reality. "Playtime's over," Ratigan quipped, looking first at Ng and then at Tanaka.

"Anything?" Ratigan enquired.

Tanaka shook his head. Fogarty thought the doctor looked somehow confused, slightly off-center. "You all right, Joey?"

Joey. Joey . . . The Mantis made a mental note of the doctor's first name.

"Fine, Bill. I'm fine," Tanaka answered. He just wanted to leave, to put as much distance between himself and Willard Ng as he could. To sit down and think.

"Mr. Ng." Ratigan's voice was becoming abrasive. "Would you mind showing us around your home?"

The Mantis took a single step in Ratigan's direction. The short detective visibly tensed and Fogarty was, for the first time during their interview, conscious of the weight of the .45 in his belt.

"I think I have been both tolerant and cooperative." Ng's tone was purposefully controlled.

"Not with me you haven't," Ratigan answered.

"Now I insist that you leave my house," Ng concluded.

Ratigan was about to object when Fogarty gripped the sleeve of his jacket.

"Mr. Ng, if we feel we need to speak to you in the future, we'll be in touch," the lieutenant said. He sensed Tanaka's discomfort. He also knew that Willard Ng would not be pushed. *I'll get a warrant and come back,* Fogarty thought as he stepped out on to the pavement. He noticed a City of Camden patrol car turn the corner on to Fifth as he opened the door of his Le Mans. He remembered Jack Tucker. Looked again as the police cruiser disappeared. Coincidence? He hoped so.

"Joey. Why don't you ride with me?" Fogarty suggested.

Ratigan caught the lieutenant's eye.

"It's all right, Jim. I'll bring him down to my office, we'll talk there. See you in half an hour."

Willard Ng's silhouette filled the front window of his house. He made no effort to conceal himself as he watched the three men drive away. *Doctor Tanaka. Joey Tanaka.* The name played gently in his thoughts. He would go to the zoo today, back to work. Resume his normal life. Now that he had met Joey Tanaka, he knew that permanence was close. He could count the time in heartbeats.

* * *

Tanaka was silent as Fogarty flashed his shield and drove through the turnstile, across the old bridge and into Philadelphia. Fogarty respected the doctor's silence; he also needed to know what had taken place between the doctor and the suspect.

They were caught in a traffic snarl at the top of Vine when Fogarty cleared his throat. Tanaka anticipated his question.

"It's him, Bill. Willard Ng murdered those women. As sure as we're sitting here."

"Are you telling me you got a confession? Is that what you're saying?" Fogarty asked.

"It wasn't like that, Bill. It wasn't like straight talk," Tanaka answered, then hesitated.

"Come on, Joey. You know I took a risk letting you do that. You know Ratigan would love to haul my ass over a bed of hot coals."

"Bill, have you ever had a premonition?"

"Please don't go mystical on me, Joey," Fogarty said. The traffic was moving now and the lieutenant wondered just how long he could drag out the five-minute ride to the Roundhouse. He needed to know something before Ratigan, McMullon and the rest of the investigation squad caught up with the doctor.

"Do you remember, Bill, at the zoo? When I said I'd be the one to take the killer down?"

"Yes, I remember," Fogarty answered. He thought he'd cleared that matter up then. Maybe he was mistaken.

"I've had this guy in my head, Bill. As if I'm connected to him. Like I almost know what he's going to do next."

"What did he tell you in the house, Joey? I really need to know."

"He told me he had been waiting for me. He told me that he wanted me to understand him completely."

Fogarty was in the parking lot now, driving slowly towards his space.

"Did Willard Ng confess to the murder of—" He almost said

"Gina Genero", checked himself and came out with,—"any of those girls?"

"It wasn't *like* that, Bill," Tanaka answered.

Fogarty turned off the ignition key. "Then how was it?" His voice was hard and cold.

"Look, I'm not playing games with you." Tanaka hesitated. "Willard Ng crawled right inside my mind. He read my thoughts. He's been drawing me to him."

"Oh fuck," Fogarty said. *Tanaka's cracking. He can't take the pressure and I can't blame him.* He tried one more time. "Did Ng confess to you?"

"He did it, Bill, I'm telling you he did it," Tanaka answered.

Fogarty sensed the doctor's agitation. Knew it was pointless to push. He reached across and placed a hand on Tanaka's shoulder. "All right, Joey. All right . . . Now, when we get inside there's gonna be a lot of frustrated people. They're gonna ask you a lot of questions. Probably the same questions. Over and over again. Please don't get involved with discussing mindreading and premonitions. You and I can discuss that, but leave it out with them. Do you understand me?"

Tanaka listened through the words and heard the sincerity of the lieutenant's tone. "Yes, I understand you, Bill."

"Good. And after this, you're back in the lab."

Tanaka jerked his head upwards; he felt as though he had been slapped in the face.

Fogarty caught his reaction. "Don't be crazy, Joey! Nobody has given me as much in this investigation as you have. Christ, you put the fucking thing together for me. I'm not forgetting it. It's just that it's going to get down to warrants and procedure. Police work."

It's not going to go that way, Bill. I wish it was, but it's not. Tanaka thought it, he couldn't say it.

Fogarty interpreted the silence as Tanaka's acceptance. He squeezed the doctor's thick shoulder. "After this, you're back on forensics and off the beat. You're out of it, Joey."

* * *

Two hours later a warrant had been requested by the Philadelphia Police Department, through the State of New Jersey, for the
arrest of Willard Ng. Tanaka's story had tipped the scales. That,
aided by the forensic evidence on the approximate height and
weight of the suspect, his shoe size, and the artist's drawing,
would give them enough to hold Ng for as long as it would take
to break him.

If they pushed, Fogarty reckoned they could have Ng locked
up within forty-eight hours. In the meantime, they weren't
letting him out of their sight.

Dan McMullon was beaming. Not only was his team about to
make an arrest, but one of his officers had turned up a diary,
hidden beneath a mattress by the late Jeanette Key. It was a piece
of evidence that he was guarding jealously. Gossip had it that the
diary bore no relevance to the Mantis investigation, but did
contain some detailed descriptions of the strange sexual behav-
iour of a prominent figure in Philadelphia politics. Speculation
was rife as to who that figure was. Only McMullon and the
detectives who had made the discovery knew for certain.

Mayor Winston Bright, on the other hand, was surprisingly
reserved in view of recent events. His expected cry for a press
conference was even held in cautious abeyance.

Fogarty took Tanaka back to the lab. While he was there he
pushed Bob Moyer for any other shreds of evidence that the
pathologist could produce before Ng's arrest.

"Once this thing hits the press it's gonna be a circus, Bob,"
Fogarty said. "Every public defender from Herbie Pressman to
that ambulance chaser Izzy Weiss is gonna want to defend Ng. I
just don't want to watch him walk on a technicality."

Moyer appeared strained as he met the lieutenant's eyes. "If
we only had the actual shoes the sonofabitch was wearing when
he attached Jeanette Key. I could link him then. So tight he'd
never walk."

"Nothing's turned up at the zoo. He's in there now, wearing
his new Timberlands. Same ones we found in his locker. Clean,"
Fogarty answered.

"How about his house?" Moyer asked.

"Didn't have a goddamn warrant," Fogarty felt guilty as he answered.

"Too bad." That was all the pathologist said. Fogarty read the rest in the faint glimmer from Moyer's eyes.

"Leave it to me, Bob," the policeman promised softly. "This guy ain't gonna walk."

By the time Bill Fogarty closed the door to the lab his plan was forming, driven by a sense of personal and moral obligation that overrode a sludge of fear, police ethics and just plain instinct.

Willard Ng would not "walk." Bill Fogarty would make sure of that.

XVI.

THE SECOND HOUSE CALL

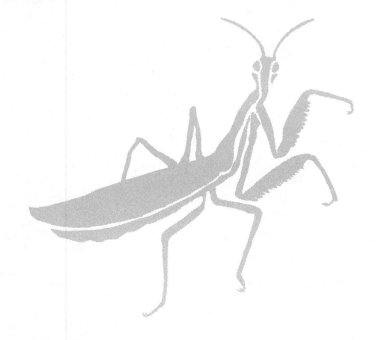

Fogarty was halfway back to the Roundhouse when he placed a call to Tyrone Johnson. Johnson relayed that Willard Ng was currently working as a replacement for a sick keeper in the Arabian Plains section of the zoo and that Gordon Forrest had agreed to Ng's request for a double shift. That would keep him at the zoo till way past the six o'clock closing time. Maybe as late as midnight, depending on what additional assignments Forrest came up with. Fogarty instructed Johnson to make sure Forrest understood that he wanted Ng to work late, as late as possible.

Then he envisioned the old Yale lock that secured Ng's kitchen door. That was it, no internal bolts, not even a chain. *A piece of cake*, he told himself. Still, he was edgy. Very edgy.

In all the years that Bill Fogarty had been on the force he'd never broken the law. Stretched it, yes, many times, but never actually broken it. This one was different; he owed on this one—Gina Genero, Jeanette Key, his wife, his daughter. This one was like a purge.

It was lunchtime when he walked into his office. Ten minutes later he was dialing Diane Genero's telephone in New Mexico. He remembered his feelings from the other night; he'd actually cried when he'd thought of making this call. "Stress reaction", he mumbled as he heard the number ring. "Misplaced anxiety." *God, I'm getting good at self-analysis. Either that or I'm becoming an expert at looking up my own asshole.*

The ringing of Diane's Genero's phone sounded particularly distant. As if he was listening to it down a long, hollow pipe. By the tenth ring Fogarty was slightly nervous, a part of him hoping that no one would answer. After all, in two days they would actually have Ng locked up. Then he'd have something to say. This was going to be bullshit, and Diane Genero was not a lady that Fogarty wanted to bullshit. Thirteen rings. He had begun to sweat, his telephone elbow hurt where it rested against the edge of his desk top. He had begun to lower the phone when he heard the crackle of a connection.

"*Ola.*" A small foreign voice speaking Spanish.

"May I have Diane Genero, please."

"*Uno momento, por favor.*" A thud as the phone was placed on a wooden tabletop.

A long pause followed by another sound, echoing, the breath that precedes speech.

Fogarty felt his stomach tighten.

"*Señora no aqui.*" The same voice.

Fogarty sat mute for several seconds, racking his brains for the residue of his ninth-grade Spanish. He hadn't even passed the fucking course.

"*Ola. Ola.*"

Christ she's gonna put down the phone. "*Donde? Donde?*" He hoped he'd somehow hit on the word for "where".

Hesitation.

"*Donde esta Sēnorita Genero?*" Now it was coming back to him. All of it. His entire repertoire.

"*Nuevo Yak.*"

"*Pardonnez-moi?*" Christ. Now he was speaking French. He'd failed that too.

The small Spanish voice cleared its throat. Fogarty could detect the frustration.

"*Sēnor,* Meesees Genero have gone to Noo Yaark." The voice now resembled a computerized director message.

Fogarty felt a rush of excitement. "*Muchos bien* . . . Have you got a num. . . ."

"*Gracias.*" And the line went dead.

New York. She's a hundred miles from here. An hour and a half. For some reason the thought gave him a rush of strength, hardened his resolve. As if he had unexpectedly acquired an ally within his battle plans. He lifted a recent copy of the *Daily News* from his desk, opened it to the second page and checked the time of sunset. 5:43. By 7, 7:30 it would be dark.

Fogarty spent the rest of the day hustling his friends in the Jersey police for the arrest warrant and extradition papers.

"Another day," they kept telling him. "One more day for the paperwork. Then the Jersey boys would make the arrest, transport Ng to the Philadelphia side of the bridge and complete the handover to Fogarty and Ratigan.

Just one thing remained. The size twelve boot with the worn left heel and the trace of camel dung on its sole. The crucial piece of evidence. *Chances are it's lying in a closet or underneath his bed,* Fogarty reasoned. *I can get in and out of Ng's place in less than five minutes,* he told himself.

He checked in with Johnson on his way to the Presidential. Nothing much. Willard Ng was working quietly, shovelling shit and wetting down the outside areas of the concrete nature reserves with a fire hose. Gordon Forrest had been briefed and nobody was letting Ng out of their sights. "Big mothafucker. Take an elephant gun to drop him." Johnson added philosophically before signing off.

Fogarty caressed the finger knurls on the handgrip of his 45 resolving to carry the heavier piece till the Mantis was caged.

Once inside the Presidential he stripped and showered, replacing his working clothes and heavy shoes with a navy blue training outfit that he had purchased when he decided to take up squash. He had only worn it once before. The air-filled soles of his Nikes made him feel slightly disconnected from the floor as he walked to the hall closet. "After you get used to them, you'll think you're flying," the salesman had promised as Fogarty handed over the hundred and twenty bucks for the silver air-soles with the white bolt of lightning down their sides. He pulled a dark brown wool-lined windbreaker from the closet. *Take an elephant gun to drop him.* He recalled Johnson's assessment as he tucked the spare boxes of hollowpoints into his right front pocket.

Each bullet carried an "Inspector" load, comprising 200 grains of hollow projectiles which, when fired from the three-and-a-half-inch barrel of his compact .45, had a one-shot stop average of 83 per cent. Nicknamed the "flying ashtray," the

"Inspector" was known to leave an exit wound that you could put your fist through without touching the sides.

He was just a touch nervous as he drove past the art museum, heading east towards New Jersey. The doorman had asked him if he was going to the gym, noted the air-soles and inquired as to their performance enhancement. Fogarty answered that he didn't know yet; he'd have to really use them first. *Try me tonight, after I've committed the felony.* He'd thought of it and smiled. The doorman had wished him a good workout.

At 6:30, another call to Johnson. 'Yeah, Ng's still here. Just stepped into the back for a piss. Bobby Spinks followed him. Better Spinks than me; I couldn't piss in a million years standin' next to that weird sonofabitch.'

Fogarty drove on, City Hall and the Roundhouse on his right. He kept telling himself that he could still turn back, not go through with it. He was strangely paranoid; something didn't feel right. *Nerves, just nerves,* he forced the thought, navigating the sparsely trafficked lane and pulling up next to the ticket booth on the Jersey side of the river. His hand went for his wallet and shield and found no inside breast pocket. "Fuck!"

"Excuse me, sir?"

Fogarty looked up into the acned face.

"Your ticket or your fare, sir."

Swear to God it's the same asshole who was working as a bellhop at the Bellevue.

"Please, you're holding up traffic." The same incredulous, whiny voice.

Fogarty looked from the small, washed-out blue eyes to the attendant's identity pin. *Arthur Kline.* "Christ, I don't fucking believe it."

"Pardon me, sir." Now there was the impatient tone of authority within the nasal voice.

"Sorry, Arthur, I think I've met your brother," Fogarty said, fishing in his pants pocket for a dollar bill. He found one and handed it over. He didn't wait for his dime change or his receipt.

* * *

Bobby Spinks sat on the plastic toilet seat behind the closed door of the small cubicle. He kept his trousers up and buckled, in the event that he had to move fast. The man next to him, invisible behind the thin metal side-panel had diarrhea. It was coming in loud, convulsive spurts and the stench was nearly unbearable.

Spinks had graduated from the police academy one year ago and this was his first surveillance assignment. One to tell the boys about, locker room talk: suspect asphyxiates patrolman. Christ, what had this turkey been eating? Monkey shit?

Willard Ng hated to defecate in public toilets. He resented the lack of hygiene which they imposed. For ten years he had practiced colonic cleansing; it was necessary for success in breath control and concentration. He did not use toilet paper. Instead he squatted in his partially filled bathtub, immersing his anus an inch below the surface. He used a strict abdomino-muscular movement to suck the water up through his rectum and into his colon. He held it there for ten heartbeats before releasing. That was clean. Perfect cleanliness.

Toilet paper was disgusting. Besides, after ten years of proper cleansing, it gave him a raw, itching rash.

Today he had been caught short; he shouldn't have come to work. Not until his stomach had settled completely. Three times he had been forced to use the employees' toilet. Three times and his rectum was blood-sore. He flushed, zipped up his overalls, opened the door to the stall and walked to the wash basin. He heard the second toilet flush behind him. He washed quickly, trying to avoid the occupant of the other stall, angered by the invasion of his privacy. He was halfway out the main door when the other man appeared. Ng was repulsed by the fact that Bobby Spinks did not stop and wash at the basin. Instead, the policeman turned and followed Ng to the door.

Ng took a right turn once outside the lavatory; he had decided not to continue work. He could call Forrest once he was home, explain that he had been taken ill. Or not call at all, it was no longer of any consequence. His job was now temporary.

Hey man, you're going in the wrong fucking direction. The wrong fucking direction, Spinks thought, studying the suspect's wide, spreading shoulders and low, gliding footsteps as Ng disappeared beyond a turn in the long narrow corridor. The policeman's hand went instinctively to his hand set, then he thought of the sound that the crackling voices would make. He hesitated. *Follow him.* But there was no one else in the back section of the mammal house. Surely Ng would get suspicious and God help the rookie detective who blew this case.

Follow him. His mind repeated the command. *What if the freak knows he's being tailed. He might have planned this. Might be waiting for me. Everybody on the case knows that Ng eats human flesh.*

Follow him. That's your job. Spinks did his best to affect a casual, somehow curious walk as he covered the thirty feet between where he stood and where Ng had taken the corner.

By the time the policeman rounded the second bend in the passage the suspect had exited through the rear door and was walking unmonitored towards the south gates.

Finally, Spinks did use his radio. "I lost him." The three words that Tyrone Johnson dreaded. "I lost him," Spinks repeated.

"Where?" Johnson asked.

"I'm standing at the rear exit of the mammal house, looking at the back gates of the zoo. I don't see him." Spinks would have explained that Ng had taken an unexplained turn after his trip to the can but Johnson was no longer on the line.

The phone at Fogarty's apartment rang twenty times before Johnson gave up. The phone in the lieutenant's Le Mans, parked four blocks away from 31 Benson Street, was still ringing as Fogarty walked past the blue Plymouth with the two Jersey detectives in it, sidestepped a streetlamp and cut into the shadows on the far side of Ng's house. It took him less than a minute to pick the old Yale lock.

The musky aroma of incense, mixed with the faint odor of

human sweat and an even fainter fetid odor, grew stronger as he walked through the kitchen and into the main room. The doors to the adjoining rooms were closed, as he had remembered them from the previous morning.

He chose the door closest to him. Opened it and entered. The room was tiny, windowless. Fogarty closed the door behind him, then aimed his flashlight at the lines of jars which occupied the wall shelves. Some appeared to contain rice, others grain, while others were stuffed with crumpled tissue paper, their lower portions filled by a shallow layer of sawdust. He lifted one of the killing jars and with his gloved hands prised the cork lid from its opening. A second later he was reeling from the impact of cyanide gas. He managed to reinsert the cork, nearly dropping the jar as he pushed it back onto the shelf.

Get what you came for and get out. The warning flashed as he switched his flashlight off and backed out of the cupboard.

The next door he tried led into Ng's bedroom. A thin blade of moonlight cut the single white quilt which covered the futon. The lieutenant closed the door, killing the moonlight. The room was pitch black. He switched on his flashlight, the light flickered once and held, revealing a low bedside table supporting a reading lamp, a telephone, a compact digital alarm clock and a thin hardbound book. A fine cone of dust spread outwards from the reflector of his flashlight as it swept the periphery of Willard Ng's bed. No boots, no shoes. He walked to the low table, his rubber soles silent against the tatami mats. *Find the fucking things and get out.* He knew what he had to do. Still, he was drawn to the few personal effects in this very personal place. Drawn towards an insight into Willard Ng's mind.

He bent and picked up the thin book. *Praying Mantis Kung Fu* by H.B. Un. Opened it and found that all of its pages had been meticulously removed, replaced by a single sheet of rice paper. There was pencilled handwriting upon the paper, random notes. "Enlightenment is intuition . . . Thinking is no longer necessary, emptiness has no style, no shape . . . Written instruction is a map to freedom . . . Freedom is a secret forbidden the common herd . . . Jealousy guarded. Once freedom is found, the map should be destroyed . . . Freedom is awareness. Total awareness is perfection. Beyond perfection is death. Death . . . Death.'' Then a line drawing of two stick-like insects. Praying mantis. The larger of the two was very clearly holding the other's severed head between its oversized mandibles. There was nothing crude about the drawing; it could have been done by an artist. Fogarty didn't have time to contemplate the philosophy.

There was nothing beneath the low frame of Ng's bed. An incense burner, in the shape of a seated Buddha, stood in the far corner of the room. A small dusty pile of recent ashes lay at the statue's feet. The other odor, the less pleasant one, came from a bathroom which adjoined the room. A closed door concealed what Fogarty hoped was a clothes closet. He walked to the door and pulled it open.

Tyrone Johnson was getting desperate. Not only had they lost the suspect but he was unable to locate Fogarty. He considered a call to Dan McMullon, then put the idea on hold. *Why bring down the walls till I'm certain the house is on fire?* he reasoned.

No one had seen Ng leave the zoo. Maybe it was only a matter of time till he reappeared. Johnson wouldn't let a beginner loose with him again, that was certain.

Willard Ng drove easily across the Ben Franklin bridge. No traffic, and a chilling wind slicing in through his opened window and beating against his face. He removed his hair piece, tossing it down on the passenger seat, as he approached the ticket booth.

Arthur Kline punched a small hole in Ng's seasonal pass and watched as the gun-metal van cut across the maze of concrete ribbons and disappeared up the off-ramp to Camden.

Ng twisted the tuning knob on his radio, hoping to find that particular song that had played in his mind since the evening at the dump. *And now the end is near, and so I face the final curtain.* He could remember some of the words but not the tune. Really, it was the singer's voice that he wanted to hear.

He stopped on a Philadelphia news station. "Police claim they are close to making an arrest in connection with the brutal serial murders that have shocked and paralyzed Philadelphia for the past—"

Ng switched off the radio. *Close. The police are close. That's good. Close. So am I.*

Fogarty stared at the six mannequin heads. Only one was bare, white and porous in the beam of light. The others were covered with wigs, full wigs. The third from the left was pompadored and swept back, like a Fifties rock 'n' roller. It was the exact hairstyle that Jeanette Key had described. *Put that piece on Ng and he is the guy in the artist's drawing. No maybe's, no stretch of the imagination,* Fogarty thought, reaching in and lifting the wig; it was surprisingly light, like a bird is light, all feathers and no bones. He stuffed it inside his jacket. Next he squatted down and began searching the various shoes, boots and trainers for a particularly worn left heel.

Willard Ng was mildly annoyed that, once again, the parking space in front of 31 Benson had been stolen by his neighbor's Chevrolet pick-up truck. He slid into a space on the opposite side of the road, across from the Santa Isabel Social Club, switched off his engine and looked across at his window.

Fogarty stopped, the crepe-soled desert boot in his right hand. He listened for a moment. Nothing. His senses seemed to heighten. *Do what you got to do and get out!* Again the warning. Stronger. He was being careless. He reached and pushed the door of the closet; it snapped shut, sealing inside the spill from the beam of his flashlight.

Willard Ng watched the subtle shift in the texture of darkness beyond his window. Someone was inside his house. Inside the bedroom of his house. Violating the inner regions of his sanctuary. He thought of Josef Tanaka. A mild electricity stirred in his groin. The freshly lubricated hinges of his car door opened quietly. He slid from the seat, bouncing lightly on the balls of his feet as he hit the pavement and ran for his front door.

One of the New Jersey detectives jotted down the suspect's time of return as Ng removed his boots before slipping his key into the lock.

Once inside Ng closed and relocked the door. Then he stood still. Completely still. Tuned to the vibrations of the air. He thought again of Josef Tanaka and, for a moment, considered taking off his clothes, preparing. Impossible. His syringe and kit were beneath the mattress of his futon. Maybe later. A rustle from the bedroom, someone crawling. Someone large but without Tanaka's grace. Someone who would provide a further exercise in his refinement. Another soul drawn by the power of his being. One more hollow vessel for the discharge of Willard Ng's last imperfection.

He controlled his breath, slowing his heartbeat, rendering his vibrations imperceptible. He knew he was close to invisibility.

Fogarty stood in the bedroom, his flashlight extinguished, Ng's desert boot still in his hand. There had been no sign of the working boots. *Probably long gone,* he surmised. *If the wear on the heel of the suede boot matches Moyer's plastercast then this was worth it.* His initial flow of adrenalin had dispersed and his mind was rambling. *One more room. One more minute. Then I'm gone.* He took three steps across the darkened floor, opened the door and stood a moment in the lighter outer room. He looked to his right and noticed that the door to the third room was slightly ajar. He hadn't remembered it being open. In fact he distinctly recalled the three doors being closed. Or was that just the way they were this morning? *This morning! Christ, it feels like a year ago.* He looked down at his watch. 8:06; he had been inside Ng's house for fourteen minutes. Over twice the length of time that a good B&E man would take. He considered calling it a night; then knew he couldn't live with himself unless he was certain that he had overlooked nothing.

He pushed open the door and looked into the third room. Noticed that the darkness was different from either the closet or the bedroom. As if the space was illuminated by a soft, indirect light. The rubber air-soles of his Nikes made a cushioned, gripping sound as he stepped on to the polished wood floor. He closed the door behind him, the room blackened. He remained still, waiting for his eyes to adjust. Was about to switch on his flashlight when he focused on the huge silhouette in front of him. His breath caught in his throat. For a moment he was incapable of action. The desert boot was still in his right hand. His preferred shooting hand. Still the figure had not moved. Fogarty stepped sideways, dropping the boot and reaching with his right in a single fluid draw. The butt of the Colt felt cold and solid. The figure remained motionless. He hesitated.

Either he was mistaken or the man in front of him had four arms and a single leg. Cautiously Fogarty stepped closer touching the Mon Fat-Jong with his left hand. The training dummy felt hard and dry beneath the sweat of his fingers. Then he turned, gasped and drew his gun. Centering his aim on the dark form which faced him. Realized a moment later that it was his own mirrored reflection, frozen in mocking self-parody. Fogarty nearly laughed. It was beginning to remind him of one of the killing rooms that had been a requirement in his VIP Close Protection course. The type of room which was set up to test the trainee's ability to perform under pressure, to think and react. The type of room Fogarty had exercised in before Senator Kennedy had visited the Liberty Bell. Thank Christ it wasn't. He would have been dead twice.

He exhaled, relaxing his grip on the .45. His breath sounded loud, somehow ominous in the confines of the mirrored space. He breathed in again and held it. Behind him, the sound of respiration continued.

Tyrone Johnson tracked Jim Ratigan to his bimonthly meeting at Alcoholics Anonymous. Ratigan was midway through recounting how he had backhanded his wife Alice at their fourth of July barbecue when the message came. It was the first time in four months that he seriously considered a whisky. He fought the urge, telephoned Dan McMullon and filled him in. Then, on a wild hunch, Jim Ratigan decided to take a trip to Camden.

Fogarty spun round, dropping to one knee, his gun following the flow of his body, rising in a two-handed straight-armed position. For a split second he thought he saw the silhouette of a crucifix standing in front of him. The crucifix was breathing, deep, puffing breaths. The lieutenant's finger began to tighten on the trigger of the Colt. He aimed to the center section of the crucifix, slightly to the right. Directly towards Willard Ng's heart.

Willard Ng hesitated, restraining his first strike, thriving in the tenuous space between life and death. The man facing him was trained, not impeccable, but trained. Excited but not dominated by fear.

"Don't fucking move." Fogarty stood as he spoke.

Ng recognized the voice. He could just make out the scarred features of Fogarty's face. He hated imperfection. Why had he been sent such an imperfect vessel?

Fogarty was bluffing. He couldn't shoot. He had no business in Ng's house, no warrant, not even his shield. As it was, Ng could have him arrested. He held his gun in position and stepped cautiously backwards.

Ng moved with him, like a dark shadow. He had no intention of allowing Fogarty through the door.

"Get down on your knees, hands on top of your head," Fogarty ordered.

Now Ng was getting a sense of his prey, his initial negativity had dispersed, clearing the space between their minds. He tuned in. Knew that his prey was confused; there would be no initial attack.

"Down!" Fogarty shouted, moving the sight of his gun level with Ng's forehead. Then he watched the large hand sweep across from the left periphery of his vision. Like a predatory hawk, the hand seemed to fly in a slow, wide arc. He could have pulled the trigger then. . . . Later, many times, he would tell himself that he could have fired, that it was only his knowledge of being outside jurisdiction that prevented him from killing the bastard then and ending it. At other times, when he was more vulnerable, alone in his private room, drifting in a semi-sleep, floating on an ocean of codeine-based painkillers, he would admit that the Mantis had taken control of him, sucked his mind from his skull, and he had been powerless, impotent. That, finally, he had wanted death. Those thoughts terrified him. As if there was a part of him that had not been returned. Would never be returned.

"Did you hear somethin'? A shout. A cry?" Detective Hugh Howard asked his partner.

"Nuthin'. I heard nuthin'," Murphy answered.

"I'm goin' up, take a look," Howard said, moving to open the door of the Plymouth.

"Don't be crazy, Hugh, the guy never even turned on his lights. He probably just fell into bed. We go fuckin' around we're gonna blow it. Christ, we can pick'm up tomorrow. Legally. He's our collar."

The bulky detective hesitated, turning in the car to meet his partner's eye. There was a sallow wisdom inside the tired gaze. "You're right, Murph, I'm gettin' anxious."

The Colt flew sideways from Fogarty's hand. Easily. Like his fingers had never been attached to its cool metal. He never heard it land. As if it just disappeared.

The second blow caught him flush on the side of his head. The striking hand was open and the Mantis palm cupped perfectly over his ear, forcing a rush of air through the auditory canal, bursting the thin-skinned membrane of his eardrum, deafening him. Fogarty felt the biting pain all the way to the back of his throat. Shock followed. An inability to respond. He just stood and stared.

The Mantis stepped back, arms raised, bent at the elbows, fingers pointed towards the eyes of his prey. It would be so easy, fingers embedded in the soft, wet tissue. Blood mixing with tears. But he wanted more. He wanted trial, refinement. He wanted exercise. The Mantis stepped laterally, edging his shoulder towards the door. Fogarty followed the movement, instinct alone telling him to distance himself from his attacker. He stopped dead center of the room. The Mantis blocked the door.

Fogarty's head was clearing, his ear numb. He knew he had to fight. Or die.

The Mantis could have transmitted his next message with his mind but he was unsure if the subtlety of contact would have the desired effect. Perhaps his prey would misread his flow of thought, the filters of social consciousness misinterpreting his intent. No, he would speak. He searched for his voice, found it buried beneath layers of discarded humanity.

"I am going to—" It was coming now, thin and reedy. An alien sound. "—fuck you. You know I fuck the people I kill." There. He'd said it. Crude, and hardly descriptive of the process, but sufficient.

Fogarty reacted with a rage born of fear and revulsion. He struck out with a low, grunting breath. A right cross, his hand bunched into a loose, beefy fist. He felt it land, and followed it with a left hook, pivoting his hips, trying to punch through his adversary. Then a straight right. And a left, elbows tight in to his body, coming off flat feet, rooted to the floor.

"Fucking bastard. Gonna kill you! Kill you!" His voice was harsh and rasping. His arms were beginning to feel like lead.

The Mantis tuned to the vibration of Fogarty's words, felt them merge with the torrent of physical blows which rained against the folded, protective wings of the Mantis body.

Then the voice quieted as the punches began to lose their sting, finally becoming soggy and slow.

Fogarty was punched out. The Mantis was still standing, arms across his body, guarding his face and chest while his left knee was positioned slightly ahead of his right, pushing inwards, protecting his groin. Then, with a grace and fluidity that belied the speed of his movement, he opened his arms and surged forward.

Fogarty was out of breath, too tired to keep his hands up, back-pedaling, shifting awkwardly on the balls of his feet when the Mantis caught him.

Jack Tucker spotted the silver Le Mans with the Pennsylvania plates the second he turned the corner of Mickie Street. He drove this route so often that he was familiar with almost all the vehicles that parked in the front of the rows of small, dilapidated houses. The Le Mans rang a bell. *Christ! It's the lieutenant's car!* He remembered it from the previous morning. He pulled up parallel to the Le Mans, got out of his patrol car and peered in through the window. Saw the police radio.

The Mantis used a short sun fist, fingers tight, palm sideways, for his first attack. It was a quick snapping movement, his hardened foreknuckles digging deep beneath the lower frontal ribs and into Fogarty's diaphragm. The effect of the strike was respiratory paralysis, forcing the lieutenant to wheeze inwards, gulping for air in spite of the contraction of his intercostal muscles pulling his ribs like iron girders against his lungs. He would have dropped like a stone if the Mantis had not secured and supported him with one arm.

Fogarty, aware of steaming hot breath against his face, straightened inside the strong grip and lifted his right knee in the direction of his assailant's groin.

The Mantis met the attack with a flat fist, knuckles down, into the kneecap. Cartilage and ligament ruptured beneath the blow, transmitting a burst of pain through the nerve endings, running the length of Fogarty's body and exploding in his brain. Then he felt the steel hand lock on to his testicles, pulling out and away from his groin and he began to scream . . . A vacant scream, rendered silent and hollow by the wide, muscled jaw which locked around his throat.

* * *

"Look, Officer. I'm tellin' you for the last time, no one but the suspect has entered that house," Detective Murphy insisted.

Tucker backed away; the detective's breath reeked of onions.

"Then can you explain why a Philadelphia police officer's car is parked three blocks from the suspect's home?"

Murphy was irritated now and Hugh Howard wasn't far behind. Murphy made a point of staring at Tucker's traffic control insignia as he spoke. "Mr. Tucker, I don't believe we have to have this conversation with you, let alone explain anything. Now do us all a favor and go home."

Tucker nodded slowly, holding Murphy's gaze as he backed away from the car, turned and walked in the direction of his own vehicle. His eyes scanned Willard Ng's house as he passed.

Fogarty lay in a fetus position on the wooden floor. He was drifting in and out of consciousness. Huge, hardened hands were stripping the clothes from his body. He did not have the strength to resist. Once, when the hands pulled his underpants down, catching on his knees before ripping them from his legs, he tried to straighten. The focused weight of two knees pinioned him until he was still. At times, when there was a lull in the process of disrobing him, he imagined he had died. Purgatory, that place of purging, between heaven and hell. That place he had learned about in his Catholic school. He was in purgatory. Then the movement started again and he knew, to his fear and sorrow, that he had not died.

He heard a gurgling sound, close. Didn't connect it with his own breathing. His trachea was clogged and swollen, his Adam's apple splintered and blocking the passage of air to his lungs. He was being lifted, manipulated. *No, not my legs, don't bend my legs that way. My knee. Please, no, don't touch my knee.* Then blackness. Awakening to find himself positioned face down against the floor. *My ass is in the air.* His mind tripped and a vivid memory surfaced. He was in the Lankenau Hospital, prepped for surgery. Hemorrhoids. In the operating room. He was groggy. He'd had the anaesthetic but he was still aware of his physical posture. Like he was praying. An instrument was going to be inserted into his rectum. Too big for the opening. Christ, it was going to hurt.

The Mantis retrieved the phial and syringe from beneath his mattress. He was just carrying his equipment to the power room when he heard Fogarty scream.

"No, I'm not asleep. Don't do it. NO, NO, NO!" Then Fogarty was kicking his legs, flopping like a fish on the dry floor.

Tucker heard the muffled shouts. Drew his gun and sprinted towards Willard Ng's front door. Voices yelling "Halt!" trailed behind him, then came the screeching of brakes as Jim Ratigan's gray Ford skidded to a stop in the middle of the street.

Ng swallowed the small phial a second after he heard the thud against his front door. By the time the door collapsed he had crushed the syringe in the callused palm of his hand and forced the needle and broken glass down the drain of his bathtub. He picked up his telephone. The lights went on just as Jack Tucker exploded into the bedroom.

Brian Murphy and Hugh Howard were a step behind.

"Against the wall!" Tucker screamed, embarrassed instantly by the hysterical pitch of his own voice.

"I was just calling the police," Ng whispered. It felt, to him, as if he was being sucked by some form of gravity into a coarser, uglier realm of consciousness.

"Oh, Christ, Jesus Christ. Bill, Bill, can you hear me?" Jim Ratigan's voice came from the next room. "Call an ambulance! Call a fuckin' ambulance!"

It was midnight when the telephone rang beside the double bed in the third-floor apartment at Rittenhouse Square. Rachel Saunders was exhausted and wide awake. She had finished some particularly delicate reconstructive surgery that afternoon at six and returned to a five-hour battle with Josef Tanaka. By the time it had ended, neither Tanaka nor Dr. Saunders could actually remember what had brought it on. Something about commitment, or lack of it. The important thing was that Josef Tanaka was leaving. Finding somewhere else to live. That was until the phone call. Afterwards, the pettiness of their argument faded into perspective.

Tanaka was ashen-faced when he put the phone down.

"Joey, what is it? What's happened?" There was nothing professional in Rachel Saunders' tone. None of the coldness that he had accused her of an hour ago. There was even a trace of fear in her eyes.

"Bill's had an accident. Very bad. Bob Moyer says they don't expect him to live."

"Accident?" The same sincerity in her voice.

Tanaka was already out of bed and dressing. He turned towards her and she could see the desperate frustration, like a disfigurement, distorting the features of his face. The look frightened her more than the call.

"Bill went around to Willard Ng's house. Broke in. Was turning the place over, looking for evidence. Ng caught him. God, they think he's going to die." Tanaka's tears started then.

Rachel Saunders stood naked from the bed. She had never seen him cry. She had wondered if he could.

"He's been like a—" Tanaka struggled with the word.

She approached tentatively, uncertain as to whether he would accept her comfort. She was crying, too. She wrapped him in her arms, his head buried in the softness of her hair. His sobs subsided and he pulled back to see her face. Stronger now.

"Like a fath—" No, that wasn't it. "He's been like a brother to me."

She searched his eyes, finding their sorrow. Then they began to harden.

"Bill didn't have a warrant. Didn't even have his badge. Ng's pressing charges." Tanaka stopped talking, stared into her eyes. "Do you understand what I'm saying?"

She stayed with him but didn't speak.

"If Bill lives, that sonofabitch is going to have him arrested."

Rachel Saunders wanted to say, *No, that's impossible. He can't do that. Don't worry.* But she was a doctor not a lawyer and she was smart enough to say nothing.

"I'm going to meet Bob Moyer at the lab and drive over to Camden with him," Tanaka continued.

She nodded her head.

"Instead of me moving out, why don't we get married." Tanaka's voice was clipped, his words blurted out.

"What?"

But he was gone. Out of the bedroom and out of the front door. And Rachel Saunders wasn't sure what she'd heard or if she really wanted to hear it.

Bob Moyer drove a BMW 320I. The car was as quiet as a tomb. His voice was thin and, at times brittle as he did his best to recount what Dan McMullon had told him.

"Bill was naked when they got there. Stark naked, face down on the floor. His right knee was shattered, his windpipe crushed and his testicles nearly torn from his body. There was also a blow to his neck, contused his carotid vein. They're afraid he's got cerebral thrombosis."

"And Willard Ng is going to walk?"

"Self-defense, Joey, self-defense. They found a non-police issue weapon with Bill's prints on it, bullets in his pocket that matched the gun. He had a three-inch jewellers pick in his jacket. No badge, no ID. . . ."

Tanaka shook his head. "Why, Bob, why?"

Moyer drove on in silence. Finally he turned towards Tanaka. "He did it 'cause I came up short on evidence. Because I told him we could make the case if I had the boots that Ng wore the night he killed Jeanette Key. He did it because," Moyer hesitated, "because it needed to be done."

"You couldn't wait for the warrants?"

"Sometimes you can't, Joey. The Jersey thing fucked everything up. Too much red tape. Too many variables. Too many people protecting their territories. All adds up to time. Evidence, even suspects, have a way of disappearing. That's the facts of this business."

"What are Bill's chances?"

"For his life or for his job?" Moyer's reply would have seemed ludicrous had it not been for the sincerity of his tone.

"What do you mean, 'for his job'?" Tanaka asked.

"Winston Bright is already pressuring Dan McMullon for Bill's badge. Come tomorrow morning, with the press and television, and he'll demand it."

"Oh . . ." Tanaka felt a terrible defeat settle over them. His next words were nearly whispered. "Is Bill going to be alive in the morning?"

Moyer drove to the right side of two motorcyclists. Tanaka looked over, noticed the men were wearing their colors. The name "Warlocks" was printed in an arc on the filthy denim of their cut-off jackets. They were riding Harley Shovelheads, the engines turning over with a low, throaty rumble. Tanaka's mind flashed to his own bike, piled up in a rain-soaked gutter. Finished. An insurance claim. It all seemed a long time ago.

"The trauma center at Cooper is one of the best," Moyer answered.

"Yes or no, Bob?"

"It doesn't look good."

"And Willard Ng is going to get away with it. How about excessive force?" There was more than a trace of anger in Tanaka's voice.

"Bill had a gun, Joey. He broke into the guy's house."

"You said Bill was naked when they got to him. That's how that fucking freak operates."

"Ng was on the phone when the police came in. Said he was in the process of calling them. Claimed he'd stripped Bill to search for weapons."

"Oh, come on, Bob. You sound like a case for the defense. The guy's a freak, a sick fucking freak."

Moyer looked across at Tanaka. His eyes were hard and his voice audibly restrained. "I'm telling you the way it is, Joey. And sometimes that's the only way that counts."

Then a lonely silence fell between the two men.

XVII.

SCARS

Cooper Hospital is a modern, white-stoned building. It is ten stories high with five hundred and fifty-two beds and has one of the finest accident-emergency units on the eastern seaboard of the United States.

Lieutenant William T. Fogarty had ceased breathing by the time he had been admitted to Cooper's street-level trauma wing. The tracheotomy performed by the paramedic in the ambulance had failed to penetrate or dislodge the pieces of shattered thyroid cartilage that had slipped from Fogarty's epiglottis and into his windpipe.

Dr. Gabriel Forner had seen almost everything in his seven years in Trauma Unit 1. Yet, as he delicately removed the splinters of gristle from the open incision, his fingers careful not to dislodge the oxygen hose which had been inserted at the base of his patient's trachea, he had to focus his concentration away from the clear set of bite marks on either side of the swollen throat. Deep and open, they suggested that a rabid animal had gripped and torn at the man's windpipe.

Four hours later, his breathing restored to a rasping gurgle, Fogarty was taken to a small private room and pumped full of anti-coagulants. If he could survive the next few hours there was a strong likelihood that the drugs would cause the clot to disperse.

Tanaka and Moyer stood with Dan McMullon, Jim Ratigan and one of the New Jersey detectives who had collared Willard Ng. Ng was currently in the main Camden lock-up being interrogated. Officially, he was not under arrest.

"He's sticking to his story." Brian Murphy's voice was hushed. The kind of respectful pitch that Tanaka had grown used to hearing in the corridors of hospitals. An "out of respect for the dying" tone. "He came home, the lights was out. Big guy comes at him outa nowhere. Wavin' a gun. So he defends himself."

"By biting a hole in the man's throat?" McMullon asked sarcastically.

Murphy shrugged his shoulders. "Hey . . . guy's fightin' for his life. I seen worse down on the docks. Believe me." Nobody did.

"Tell ya what's gonna happen now," Murphy continued with unbridled authority. "Tomorrow morning, as soon as our public defender gets this on his desk, you guys are gonna get asked to make a deal."

McMullon had known it would be coming. He tightened his mouth, as if to prevent himself from uttering some obscenity. Ratigan noticed that the overweight chief was looking tougher than usual.

"You drop your case against Willard Ng and the State of New Jersey will drop its case against the City of Philadelphia." Murphy's words landed like lead. "Maybe even talk Ng out of a civil suit against your lieutenant."

Dan McMullon's outburst was only prevented by Gabriel Forner's exit from Fogarty's room. The doctor was a swarthy man of medium height and had been occasionally mistaken for the actor Robert De Niro. He liked it when that happened; it added a touch of levity to his daily life in Trauma.

Moyer stepped in front of him, introduced himself and got right to business.

Gabriel Forner's voice was almost a monotone, his words only slightly hopeful. "If the clot is dispersed the likelihood is that the lieutenant will survive. However, he was deprived of oxygen for an indeterminable time and until he regains consciousness it is impossible to say whether there is permanent brain damage. That's the worst it—"

"What else did he do to him?" Tanaka asked.

Forner looked down once before meeting the intense brown eyes. "The lieutenant's right knee has been crushed. The patella was broken inwards against the cruciates. Both anterior and posterior ligaments were ruptured. Maybe they can be sewn back together, maybe not. Depends on when we get him into OR. His scrotal sack was partially detached from his groin but his testicles are still intact. I've sutured his scrotum and it shouldn't be a problem.'' Forner hesitated. ''You already know about the bite to his throat. Shattered the hyaline cartilage lining his esophagus.''

''When can I go in?'' Tanaka asked, looking at the closed door of Fogarty's room. It was hard to believe that his friend was behind it, lying there, helpless. It was a strange, suspended feeling. Tanaka had had the feeling before. Once. After the finals of the Japanese Karate Association Championships. Then it was his brother, Hironori, behind the door and Josef had put him there. He shut the memory off.

''Doctor Tanaka has been working with Lieutenant Fogarty on this case and they had become quite close,'' Bob Moyer explained.

''I understand, Doctor, believe me,'' Forner replied. Then he turned his attention to Tanaka. ''If we're successful in breaking up the clot, then it will be helpful to have someone there who the lieutenant trusts and is comfortable with when he regains consciousness . . . I understand there is no immediate family.''

No immediate family. The words stuck in Tanaka's mind. A hollow loneliness descended. He thought of Rachel Saunders.

''I can arrange a room for you till morning,'' Forner offered.

''Thank you, Doctor, but I'll wait here.''

Forner nodded his agreement and walked away from the two men.

McMullon, Ratigan and Murphy were still going at it in the corner of the room.

''You'll never convince anyone there was a fight,'' Ratigan argued. ''Ng doesn't have a fuckin' scratch on him.''

''There's bruising on both his arms,'' Murphy countered.

''Gimme a break.'' Ratigan sounded disgusted.

''Doesn't matter anyway,'' Murphy went on. ''It's the gun that's the fuck-up. A loaded weapon with the safety catch off.''

''Too bad you didn't lose the gun,'' Ratigan said.

Murphy's voice lowered. ''If it'd been down to me I would

have. Jus' got too complicated.'' He didn't sound that convincing.

"Yeah, I forgot. First man through the door was a traffic cop,'' Ratigan said bitterly. "Wasn't for him, our man'd be dead,'' he added.

Brian Murphy looked, for a moment, like he would take a swing at Jim Ratigan. Then he appeared to visibly deflate. "We'll get Ng, we'll get'm,'' he mumbled, then walked towards the men's room.

Bob Moyer watched the New Jersey detective open the door and disappear. He put a hand on Ratigan's shoulder. "We're all tired, Jim. This has beat the shit out of all of us.''

Tanaka drifted in and out of sleep, the occasional sound of rubber-soled footsteps sometimes making him jolt upright. The police officers and Bob Moyer were gone from the hospital by four o'clock. He'd called Rachel Saunders' answering service then. Left a message that he'd see her some time tomorrow. He'd wanted to tell her he loved her but couldn't bring himself to say it to the cold voice at the message center. When he'd returned from the telephone he'd found the nurses had set up a chair for him outside Fogarty's door. It was green and soft and the springs had gone beneath the seat. He sank into it and slept almost instantly. For one hour. The last three had been in spurts and his eyes felt raw and red-rimmed.

"Doctor Tanaka. Doctor Tanaka.'' The voice was coming from above him. At first he thought it was the overhead loudspeaker, a doctor being paged. Then he recognized his own name and realized that he had drifted off again.

"Doctor Tanaka.'' A woman's voice.

He looked up and into the eyes of the ward nurse. Gabriel Forner stood behind her. Another man stood to Forner's left. The doctor had a black stubble of beard shadowing his features. He looked exhausted, beaten.

Tanaka stood up. He waited. Expecting to hear the worst. Forner cleared his throat. "The clot has dissolved.''

Tanaka began to smile.

"However, we are still uncertain as to the damage to Lieutenant Fogarty's brain." Forner turned towards the taller, bald man. "This is Doctor James Reed; he runs our department of neurosurgery."

Tanaka extended his hand. Reed's fingers were long, delicate and cool to the touch. He nodded.

"Because of the instability of your friend's condition, I'd rather not take him down to OR for a scan. Not for a day or so anyway." Reed's voice was a perfect match for his hands. Milky smooth, vowels extended.

"If you would be prepared to sit with him, talk to him, maybe your voice would elicit a response. We just can't be certain as to the extent of his cerebral damage. Not yet, anyway."

"Of course I will," Tanaka answered.

"Don't expect much," Forner added as he led Tanaka to the door of Fogarty's room.

Two nurses stood by the monitoring system beside the bed. A white computerized ball bounced across the blue screen of the monitor. The patient's heartbeat. Tenuous on the incandescent screen. An electrode connected the patient to the monitor. "Fogarty, William T." was printed on a placard at the foot of the bed.

The figure of a man lay beneath the white sheet and single blanket on the bed. Thick bandages covered the man's neck. Where they ended, a swollen mass of purple-red tissue ascended like an angry flame up his temple and face. The other side of his face, the scarred side, was blown up like a yellow balloon. Two drips were connected to the man, one on either side of the bed. His eyes were closed and the sound of his breathing resembled the wheeze of a broken reed.

Same wounding as on the bodies of the women, Tanaka noted as his attention lingered on the wounds of Fogarty's neck. Then his emotions seemed to align with his eyes, pulling him back from the escape of professional observation. He experienced a surge of adrenalized fury, tempered by the sentiment of pity.

His voice was a whisper. "Bill . . . Bill. What happened? What happened to you?"

One mile away, sitting on a folding metal chair in one of the small interrogation rooms of the Camden police station, Willard Ng was the center of attention. A steady stream of police officers had filtered in and out of the interrogation room all through the night. Willard could feel the pent-up anger in many of them; he was equally aware of their awe. He had been reminded several times that he was not under arrest. That he was cooperating of his own volition. By eight o'clock in the morning he had retold the story of the previous night at least ten times. Of his terror in discovering an armed man in the darkness of his home. Yes, he had, perhaps, overreacted, he'd admitted that. But the man was large and strong and held a gun to his head. No, at no time did the man identify himself as a police officer. Yes, he was aware that he was under investigation in connection with the series of murders in Philadelphia. No. He had not committed the murders.

He suspected one of the men who interviewed him was a psychiatrist. The man was different from the policemen. More enjoyable to talk to. He was very polite, respectful. And he had a way of rephrasing Willard's answers, changing them into the next question. "Have you ever had a sexual experience with a man, Mr. Ng?" "Once, maybe twice at St. Thomas'," Willard answered. "Once, maybe twice?" the fresh-faced man repeated, adding his own inference. Then he waited silently. Willard understood that he was supposed to fill in the space. Elaborate. Sometimes he did. Other times he simply sat, staring into the clear lenses of his inquisitor's glasses. There was hardly any magnification to the lenses and Willard was certain that the doctor wore them to add age and authority to his otherwise bland and unlined face. Willard never turned his mind on, feeding, instead, on the energy of those who interviewed him. It was like changing a battery. The more tired and haggard they became, the more rejuvenated Willard felt.

"And have you had sex with a man in the last year?" The young doctor kept his eyes on Willard as he spoke. He was attempting to remain passive, neutral. The tick that had begun on the outer edge of his mouth, in the tiny muscles that outlined his thin pink lips, gave him away. He was mildly excited. "Have you?"

Willard had controlled his thought, curbed his tongue. He took a long time to answer, but when he did it was worth it. "I can't have sex at all."

"Can't have sex at all?" The young face appeared sincerely wounded.

"Several years ago I was injured in an athletic competition. A blow to the groin. I lost a testicle. Some of the nerves to my prostate gland were severed. I am impotent." Willard lowered his head, for effect.

It took the young face several twitches, a deep blush and one long clearing of the throat to recover. "Has no one asked you about this before?"

"I have been questioned," Willard replied. He was tuned effortlessly to the mind that was seeking to probe his own. It was a new, quick mind. Without depth. It made Willard long for Josef Tanaka. As a lover might long for another of equal experience.

The fresh face turned from Willard, caught the eye of the police officer who stood vigilant at the door. "I think I'd better see the officer in charge of this case." Then, turning back to Willard, "Is there anything I can get you. Coffee. Water?"

Willard shook his head.

"I believe I can clear this mess up for you, Mr. Ng."

Willard smiled.

"Would you be prepared to submit to a physical examination by a police medical doctor?"

Willard allowed a passivity to settle upon his features.

"To substantiate what you have just told me. It will be done in strictest confidence."

Willard nodded.

* * *

Tanaka sat silent by Fogarty's bed.

"Anything. Just say anything. Sometimes it's the sound of a familiar voice that brings a response," the ward nurse urged.

Tanaka considered. Looked up. "How about leaving me alone with him?"

"We can't do that. If there should be a respiratory failure—"

"I am a qualified doctor." He motioned towards the machinery. "I know how the monitors work. I did a year interning on the accident ward at Philadelphia."

"All right," she said, signaling the other two women to follow her from the room.

Tanaka waited until the sound of their footsteps faded in the corridor. Then he pulled his chair closer to the bed, reached out and gently touched Fogarty's arm. At first Tanaka was silent, strangely self-conscious. At last the words came.

"There's something I always wanted to talk to you about, Bill. It's the reason I'm a little fucked up in the head."

Fogarty wheezed in long, painful breaths, his eyes concealed behind pale, heavy lids. His face was ashen.

"It's about what happened in Japan. Before I wanted to be a doctor. Before I ever really thought of coming here." Tanaka hesitated, glanced once at the closed door, lowered his voice and continued.

"I was in the finals of the All-Japan karate tournament. That's a bit deal in Japan, Bill. Kind of like the World Series in American baseball. Newspapers, television, twelve thousand spectators. But it's more than that for us, because it is also about tradition, like a tiny oasis of our culture that has been guarded against Western influence. And, for those three days, in that arena in Tokyo, the highest virtues are skill, courage and honor . . . Jobs, clothes, money; they mean nothing.

"You should see the old masters demonstrate with their *katanas*, the long swords, performing the ancient fighting forms. You can feel the heart of feudal Japan. The pride of the Samurai. My father is Samurai, Bill. Pure Samurai. His ancestors were the guardians and teachers of the strongest shoguns in Japanese history.

"And my brother, Hiro, was—" Tanaka hesitated, forcing himself to rephrase his sentence. "My brother is Samurai. Different mother than me, Bill. Before my father deserted his proper wife for an outsider."

Fogarty groaned, appeared to be trying to move his damaged leg. The heavy bandages held it rigid. His eyes remained closed and, gradually, he grew still again.

"Are you listening to me, Bill?" Tanaka grasped the lieutenant's hand. "Don't try to talk. Just squeeze my hand." Fogarty's hand remained flaccid.

"Hiro was four years older than me. I idolized him. His looks; just like one of those black-and-white photographic plates from a history book on sixteenth-century Japan, a Samurai, a young warrior. He was so proud. When we were growing up we shared a bedroom. I remember sitting on my bed, watching him comb his hair, studying his face in the mirror. Wondering what was the matter with me, why I didn't look like him. I mean, you could tell we were brothers; it was just, well, my features never looked as refined, as clear-cut as Hiro's. It was like he was the aristocrat and I was the peasant. I wasn't jealous, Bill. Confused sometimes, but not jealous. He seemed too far above me for that. It was the same with our temperaments; I had the rages, the tantrums, and Hiro had the charm, the humor. I was always getting into scraps with boys I knew I couldn't beat, and Hiro would rescue me, smooth things over. When I look back, I realize that I set it up that way, to confirm my own inadequacy.

"He was a gentle guy, Bill, a great athlete but never aggressive when he wasn't competing. He probably wouldn't have got into martial arts if it wasn't for my dad. Our father had to have someone carry on the family tradition. My father was a champion. Hiro had to be a champion.

"Hiro got me interested in karate, encouraged me to try out for the team at Waseda University. He just wanted the best for me, wanted me to succeed." Tanaka lowered his head.

"I didn't want to fight him in that tournament; it was like a nightmare. Our father watching, everybody in Japan watching. The half-breed brother against the Samurai. Watered down Japan versus tradition. It was too big inside us, all out of perspective. Hiro couldn't allow me to win. No matter what. Too much loss of face. And I couldn't just lie down. Couldn't take that humiliation. It was like I finally understood that something inside me had been lying down all of my life, letting Hiro fight my fights for me. And I was afraid of him, but I was more afraid of living the rest of my life in his shadow."

Fogarty was listening now. The words were without meaning, drifting on a broken stream of consciousness. The voice was male, emotional, familiar.

"I broke his neck . . . Broke my brother's neck. Paralysed him from the neck down. Wrecked his life. Took it away from him. Paid him back for everything he'd ever done for me by making him a cripple."

Now the voice was bitter. Fogarty was being pulled upwards, towards the bitterness.

Dan McMullon was chalk white when he put the phone down. "Willard Ng is going to sue the city of Philadelphia." He repeated the New Jersey public defender's threat over and over to himself, shaking his head in disbelief.

"Let me hear that again!" Winston Bright controlled his voice; it still sounded like a strangled scream. He stood up from his wrap-round mahogany desk.

Dan McMullon held his hands tight to his sides, his thumbs twitching nervously. He could feel the mayor's rage; it seemed to seethe from every pore in the black man's body. The chief inspector took a step backwards, shaking his head.

"Willard Ng submitted voluntarily to both a physical examination and a polygraph test. The polygraph test is negative, and the police medical examiner for the state of New Jersey has sworn that Ng would have been incapable of sexual contact with any of the victims.''

"And Bill Fogarty. What about Bill Fogarty?'' Winston Bright asked, his voice compressed to a hiss.

"Still not conscious, but it looks like he's going to live—''

"I don't give a fuck if he lives,'' Bright cut in. "That's not what I'm asking you.''

McMullon began to feel his own hackles rise. He'd had plenty of disagreements with Fogarty over the years. Hated his guts from time to time. Testified against him once. To Internal Affairs. Fair testimony, Fogarty was fucked up. Drinking heavily. Unpredictable. *Christ, I didn't know I was gonna get his promotion.* McMullon still felt guilty. Always would. Worse because Fogarty had swallowed it, never called him out. And Fogarty was a cop; he was also white. Dan McMullon owed Bill Fogarty.

"Did you authorize the lieutenant's trip to New Jersey, to the suspect's house? Was that an example of your fine fucking idea of investigative work?'' Bright's voice bombarded McMullon, whose face had gone from white to puce.

"No,'' he answered sullen, The single word hinted at a challenge.

"I'll tell you what you're going to do, Dan.'' The mayor was pulling it back together now. "You're going to issue a statement to the press saying that William T. Fogarty was suffering severe mental disorders, following his breakdown four years ago, was under police psychiatric supervision and was acting completely outside all jurisdiction. You are going to take the lieutenant's badge from him and arrange a minimum disability payment—purely out of the compassion of this office.''

"And what about Willard—''

"Don't interrupt me, Dan.'' Winston Bright was on a roll. McMullon shut up.

"Then you are going to resign your command as chief inspector.''

McMullon couldn't quite believe what he was hearing. He

wanted to retaliate. His mind stalled. He'd played whipping boy so many times, he couldn't shake the role.

"When the stink blows over, I'll set you up with a good job," Bright promised.

That was it. Dan McMullon. A bad boy, rightfully chastised. He almost said "thank you."

Then, one by one, his faculties returned. His thinking process resumed. How many times had he been Winston Bright's scapegoat? Defenseless, at the mayor's mercy? Owing him his job, in his pocket? But things were different now. For once, he had a weapon. Anger and resentment began a spiral upward from the pit of his stomach.

Winston Bright forced a smile. Extended his hand. Waited.

Until McMullon's voice broke, like a wave. A tidal wave. Catching Winston Bright unsuspecting and unguarded.

"You black sonofabitch. You lying piece of shit." McMullon lurched forward. Restrained his body and concentrated on his mouth.

"I'll give a press conference all right. No problem. And I'll read excerpts from the diary of Jeanette Key. How you liked to tie her up, push her around, urinate on her. You filthy bastard." McMullon caught himself. Knew he'd gone over the line. Too far to stop. "By the time I'm done they'll have you marked as suspect number one!"

Winston Bright's eyes were bulging and his lips held so tight that they were white around the edges. His face resembled a special effect from a cheap horror film, just before the head fragments and explodes. In his heart, beneath the wide silk tie and expensive white shirt, a war was raging; the smooth black politician who had worked his way through Temple University law school on a basketball scholarship was forcibly restraining the tough kid from the concrete jungles of Lehigh Avenue; the kid who wanted to stomp the honky Irish pig into the ground. As always happened, with the exception of the gay activist incident in the mid-Eighties, Winston Bright's more polished, political self prevailed. His face deflated, molding itself into a mask of practiced passivity, while his eyes, like the pressure gauge on a steam boiler, regained a sub-danger level.

He shook his head sadly. "Dan, we've been in this game too long to start taking cheap shots. Let's sit down and run this thing through. Find a couple of alternatives."

McMullon sensed victory. For once he was smart and guarded enough not to show it. He nodded thoughtfully, accepted the mayor's large, extended hand and allowed himself to be guided to one of the three vacant chairs facing the wrap-round desk.

Josef Tanaka was certain that he felt Fogarty's hand tighten. He stopped speaking and bent over the lieutenant's bed, bringing his mouth to within inches of Fogarty's ear.

"Are you listening to me, Bill. Squeeze my hand if you're listening." He wanted to believe that he felt the rough, dry hand tug against his own. "You want me to keep talking? Tell you the rest of it?"

Another tug of the hand, or was it his imagination?

"After Hiro got out of the hospital, came home, that's when it got real bad. The doctors try and prepare you but nothing can do that. Somewhere I hung on to the idea that Hiro was going to walk through the door, that he was going to be all right." Tanaka's voice trailed off. Fogarty's hand tightened.

"Then the ambulance arrived. They lifted Hiro out, carried him into the house. I looked down at him as he went by, into his eyes. It was like I was looking for something. Hate. Anger. Anything that would—" Tanaka hesitated, groping for words, the same way he had groped at the time. "Anything that would reconnect us.

"You know what I saw, Bill?" It was all coming out now, Tanaka's voice floating on haunted memory. "I saw shame. Hiro was ashamed. Ashamed." Tanaka hesitated, cleared his throat. He was sure Fogarty was listening. Needed him to be listening.

"They put him in the room that my father had prepared for him, all his trophies lining the bookcases. I asked him not to do that but my father was ignoring me by then. The nurse stayed for the first month, making sure we knew the routine. How to feed him, how to change his clothes, how to change his diapers.'' Tanaka's voice was breaking up.

Bill Fogarty opened his eyes.

''At first I promised myself I'd never put another gi on as long as I lived, but, finally, the dojo was the only place I could go to get away from the nightmare at home. Our house was divided, my father and mother quarreling, my father refusing to acknowledge me. Yet when we went into his room, Hiro's room, we pretended that everything was fine. He wasn't stupid, he knew what was going on. Finally, as some sort of reconciliation, I took a job as bodyguard to my father. Tough stuff, Japanese unions, Yakuza. I was trying to get myself killed. Like punishment. And I think my father was helping me do it.''

Fogarty tried to speak. He wanted to tell Tanaka that he understood. That he didn't need to say any more. The words caught like white-hot razor blades inside his throat. His eyes began to water.

''I got back on the tournament circuit, fighting. I hated it. That made it good. Punishment . . . Until he started to come. Every time I fought, he was there. Sitting there, in the front row. Cheering. Shouting for me.''

Fogarty pushed with his arms, straightening himself against the pillow. He forced a single word through his dry mouth. ''Who?''

''My brother, Bill, my brother. In his wheelchair. Shouting his lungs out. And I hated him for it. For his support. For his forgiveness. I wanted to fucking kill him. For not allowing me to suffer . . . For not allowing me to be alone with what I'd done. I wanted to kill him and, finally, I wanted to kill myself. That's why I ran, came here. But I can't get away from it. I can't get away from that feeling, that feeling of death, wanting death.'' Tanaka moved closer, stared into Fogarty's eyes. ''Do you understand me, Bill?''

Now Fogarty was trying to speak. To say yes, he understood. That he had his own nightmare, that it only got better when you opened up with someone, talked it through. That it never went away. He was gripping Tanaka's hand tightly, pulling him closer. Struggling to form the words. His mind raced, ahead of his tongue. Hadn't he been guilty of the same thing? Trying to even the score. Pay his eternal debt to his wife and daughter. Balance the scales in his own guilty conscience.

"Willard Ng understands me." Tanaka said it like a confession.

"No! That's bullshit!" Fogarty's words came with a spurt of crimson blood, flying from his mouth, splattering the front of Tanaka's shirt. The lieutenant struggled to get up from the bed. Tanaka restrained him, at the same time pressing the emergency buzzer. The doctor and two nurses were there within seconds.

"The sutures around his trachea have ruptured," Tanaka stated. His voice had a professional detachment. "He's regained consciousness."

Fogarty was still grasping Tanaka's hand, trying to speak, when Gabriel Forner injected the pre-med, preparing him for surgery.

XVIII.

A STAR IS BORN

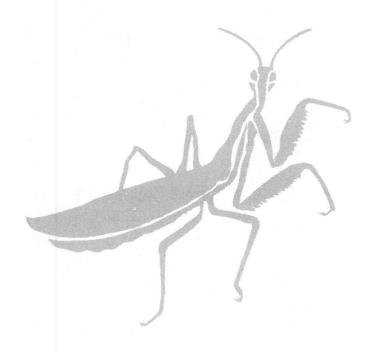

The lie-detector test had been easy, a simple exercise in breath and mind control, but the lawyers and press were an entirely different matter. It seemed impossible for them to comprehend that Willard Ng was not interested in suing the city of Philadelphia; that he was not interested in the half a million settlement that such a suit would guarantee. The newspapers were having a field day, dredging up records of police brutality and minority-group discrimination. The fact that Willard Ng was still way out front in the hunt for a murder suspect was taking second position to the media's need for a hook to their coverage. The hook was in developing Willard Ng as a national hero, a man capable of and unafraid of defending his home against intrusion. A single man standing alone against the evolving police state. Half-American, half-Vietnamese, Willard Ng was an innocent son of America's dirtiest war.

Behind the banner headlines, behind the media's chief concern that Ng was not exactly talk-show material, Bob Moyer had confirmed that Ng's sexual impairment was by no means a testimony to his innocence. Any blunt object could have been employed for penetration. It was, also, not the first time that a guilty suspect had beaten the polygraph. Ng had as much as confessed his guilt to Josef Tanaka, and the wounds to William Fogarty were almost identical to the wounds inflicted upon the female victims. Ng's physical size and strength matched the police profile of the killer and he was apparently proficient in a Chinese system of empty-hand combat. Philadelphia police psychologists agreed that impotence alone could have sparked the killing rages. Then there was the size twelve footprint with traces of camel excrement, and the artist's drawing. A massive amount of evidence, all circumstantial.

Willard Ng was their man. Every police officer on the special task force believed it, Bob Moyer believed it and Josef Tanaka was certain.

Mayor Winston Bright declined all but one network news

conference. Questions concerning Willard Ng were met with a tight mouth, a concerned grimace and a sincere "Regretfully, I am unable to comment at this particular time." And what compensation, if any, would the former suspect receive from the city of Philadelphia? The same regretful "no comment". How about the police lieutenant who unlawfully entered Mr. Ng's home and allegedly threatened Mr. Ng with a loaded pistol?

The police officer in question was under indefinite suspension pending a full investigation of the circumstances surrounding the incident. No formal action was being pursued at this time. No comment as to the circumstances.

On one point Mayor Winston Bright was remarkably clear. Chief Inspector Dan McMullon would continue to head the murder investigation.

Diane Genero switched off the television set and lifted the newspaper from beside her on the bed. "Philadelphia Detective Faces Felony Charges." She read the article for the third time, her eyes continually shifting to the accompanying picture of Bill Fogarty. His face was fresh and unscarred. Handsome in the way that the captain of the high school football team was handsome, a mixture of courage and naïvety. The kind of handsome that seemed to invite tragedy.

An untouched bowl of Caesar salad and a half-empty bottle of low-alcohol white wine sat on a walnut table at the window side of her hotel suite. Behind them, a partially drawn curtain revealed the setting sun. Beneath its cool glowing light, Central Park was nearly deserted.

Ever since her divorce, Diane Genero had stayed at the Plaza Hotel whenever she visited New York City. At first her visits were to buy fabric for her small but exclusive design company and then became, with increasing regularity, trips to see friends. One friend in particular had been Vincent Bellows.

Bellows was a partner in Madison Avenue's most powerful advertising firm; he had handled the p.r. for everything from DeLorean automobiles to the last presidential campaign.

Vincent Bellows knew bad press when he saw it. That afternoon, the body-building fifty-year-old had informed Diane Genero that her friend Bill Fogarty was in deep trouble. "Certainly his career is finished, he might even be sentenced."

Her friend. She reviewed the arrogant choice of words. What had Vincent meant by calling Fogarty her friend. She had come to Bellows for solace, mentioned that she owed the Philadelphia policeman an apology for the inadvertent results of her attempt to thank him. An attempt that had been edited and released on national television as a condemnation. She had buried her daughter less than a month ago, the last thing she needed now was some ludicrous insinuation from Vincent Bellows. *Maybe I'm being too sensitive,* she told herself. She looked at Fogarty's picture again. Even his eyes had changed, had lost their hope. "What the hell ever happened to you, Bill Fogarty," she whispered. She was still contemplating the question when the phone rang.

"Be there in an hour," Vincent Bellows said. He never identified himself. *He must assume everyone in Manhattan knows his voice,* she thought. That really annoyed her.

"All right," he continued, not so much a question as a fact.

"Yes, that's fine," Diane Genero answered.

"See you." The confident voice assured. Then the line went dead.

Diane Genero removed the phone from her ear and stared into the tiny plastic holes in the mouthpiece, unsure, for the moment, whether she wanted to see Vincent at all. Whether, in fact, she even liked Vincent Bellows. She'd slept with him three times. That wasn't quite true. Two and a half times was more accurate. His mobile phone had rung midway through their last attempt and she had point-blank refused to continue while he carried on his conversation.

After he'd left her room she'd stood, naked, looking at herself in the mirror. She was lonely, that was for sure, but never lonely enough to become an executive armchair.

She glanced a final time at Bill Fogarty's picture in the paper. There was something about his expression that was so familiar.

"What the hell happens to us?" she whispered. *Life, Mother, life is what happens.* The voice in her head answered. Gina's voice.

She picked up the phone again, leafing through her diary, finding Fogarty's office number. She was crying. Crying for Gina, crying for herself and crying for Bill Fogarty. For a moment she was going to hang up. Then the number connected and she regained control.

Diane Genero got nowhere at the Roundhouse. Fogarty's whereabouts was classified, his condition reported as stable. Dan McMullon, the chief inspector, was unavailable. By the time she put the phone down, her tears had dried, to be replaced by determination.

The telephone call from Wheels came almost as a surprise to Josef Tanaka. He'd completely forgotten the Harley Davidson Softail. He'd ordered it two days after returning from hospital, following his own accident. The bike had seemed important then, obsessively important. Now he couldn't have cared less. If he hadn't paid in advance for the cross-over exhaust system and customized paintwork he would have asked the dealer to sell the Harley to someone else.

As it was he picked the bike up joylessly, forced a few comments about the fine quality of the black laquered paint and rode to the Philadelphia Karate Club.

Sensei Azato intercepted him as he walked towards his locker. "Josef . . ."

Tanaka turned. He would rather have avoided the *sensei*; he didn't feel up to any personal conversation, let alone the inevitable "How is your father?" routine. He covered his discomfort with a formal bow. Azato's face reflected a sincere concern. "Come in, Josef." The *sensei* stepped aside as Tanaka entered the small office. Azato closed the door behind him.

"Three weeks, Josef, three weeks since you have been to dojo."

Tanaka looked thoughtfully at the sturdy little man in the white gi. The canvas of the *sensei*'s training suit had been pressed immaculately, and the black silk thread of the belt which encircled his thickening waist was worn to the coarse gray cotton beneath. There was something reassuring about Tetsuhiko Azato, a firmness, a resolution.

"Problems, *sensei*. Problems at work." Tanaka lowered his eyes after he answered.

"I have seen the newspapers. The serial killings. That is the case you were working on?"

"That is the case I *am* working on," Tanaka corrected.

"And this man, Fogarty, the police lieutenant. You admire this man?" Azato asked.

"Bill Fogarty is a friend of mine," Tanaka answered.

"Your friend is in a lot of trouble."

"I know," Tanaka answered.

"Is it true? What I read? That he broke into a suspect's house? Tried to steal things, held a loaded gun to the man's head?"

"I'm not sure if all of it is true, *sensei*, but whatever happened, my friend had good reason," Tanaka replied.

"Your friend lost his way," Azato stated.

Tanaka looked up. He felt a tinge of anger.

"I'm sorry, Josef. But I must say these things to you. It is my responsibility. You are connected to this man Fogarty and you are connected to me. He chose the path of a policeman and there is a correct way to his path."

Don't be so naïve, Tanaka thought.

"I understand that in certain situations a man is tempted to go against what he knows to be correct, but the consequences are always negative."

"*Sensei,* I respect what you are saying, but you must understand the pressure that my friend was under."

"I do understand, Josef, because I recognize that pressure in you. In your eyes, the tone of your voice."

"I am not a policeman, I'm a doctor."

"You are also a warrior, Josef. And a warrior cannot afford to be impetuous. Your friend was impetuous. It is not for me to condemn him. I don't know what was driving him, what pressure, as you call it.''

"He was being driven by the fear that unless he came up with some hard evidence a self-confessed killer had a good chance of going free,'' Tanaka answered. He was eye to eye with his teacher now. His thoughts were concentrated and he was agitated by the intrusion of Azato into his professional life.

"It appears that because of his poor judgment his fear is about to actualize,'' the *sensei* persisted. Beyond the thin office door Tanaka could hear the rustle of starched fabric as the other students changed into their gi's. He was growing increasingly uncomfortable. *A bad idea to come here tonight,* he thought.

"You have bad feeling for this man who injured your friend?'' It was as much a statement as a question.

Tanaka exhaled. Azato's inquisition was getting hard to take. "Of course I have, *sensei*. I'd like to—'' His anger rose uncontrollably. —"Fucking kill him.'' The words hung dead in the air. Azato's face tightened and Tanaka prepared for a tirade. He'd probably said enough to be expelled from the dojo. He waited.

"You lost control once, Josef, and you have suffered. Have you learned nothing from your life?'' The *sensei*'s brown eyes drilled into him.

Tanaka felt small and foolish, impotent in the face of the truth. He didn't answer.

"What you learn here, in this dojo, on that floor, is that not part of your life? Or do you keep it separate? Like a hobby. Like some child's toy, to be picked up for your amusement, then put down and forgotten. You are in a dangerous mind, Josef, without clarity. Same mind as your friend.''

Tanaka remained silent. *Sensei* Azato relaxed slightly, half smiled.

"Sometimes life sends us an opponent. Something or someone to test our beliefs, our discipline. Can be a situation, a disease, a person. Something which pits us against everything that we think that we are. If we run from such a test, we must face it again and again in other forms. If we continually let it stop us, we die." Azato hesitated. "To stop growing and to die are same thing."

Tanaka was feeling stronger, as if his thoughts and emotions were unraveling, gaining distance one from the other, finding perspective. The accident in Japan had opened something inside him, a chasm in his spirit, like a tear in the fabric of his being. He had tried to run away from it; he had succeeded only in causing the wound to fester, widening the chasm. In his soul and in his mind. That was his affinity with Bill Fogarty; somewhere the policeman had a similar wound. And it was through that wound that Willard Ng had entered both their lives.

"OK now?" Azato asked, placing his hand on Tanaka's shoulder.

"Thank you, *sensei,* much better," Tanaka answered. Outside the office, Ben Chagan was calling the class to order.

"Train hard. The enemy is close," Azato said before opening the door.

Willard Ng closed the door to his power room. He had understood that this would be a difficult time. He had not realized just how difficult.

A mob of reporters had virtually camped on the lawn outside his front door. He had nothing to say to them. He felt nothing but scorn for the obscenity of their profession. The same applied to the money-mongering lawyers who had offered their services on contingency, bombarding him with propositions that were of no interest.

He tried consciously to halt his internal dialogue as he stripped naked and examined his body in the mirror. He appeared tired, his eyes red and rimmed. His face had a rough stubble of beard and his head was dark where his hair was growing at the level of his skin. Other areas of his body, his chest, pubis and armpits, were still smooth and clean. They were the areas that had responded to his self-administered electrolysis. He breathed in, expanding his lungs, spreading his shoulders, stretching the scar tissue which covered his sternum. Nothing, no flash of realization, no feeling of contact. He closed his eyes, envisioning the face of his mentor, opened them again to find himself alone and disconnected. The scar on his chest looked thick and ugly. There was the smell of sweat and leather, a pungent, vinegar-like smell rising from his feet. He turned. His reflection was everywhere, chastising him.

He could still sense the policeman's presence within the room. His eyes searched, at last focusing on a small plastic bag which lay on the floor at the base of the wooden dummy. It was the type of bag used for gathering evidence. Left behind by the police investigators. He picked the bag up, opened it. A single reddish-gold hair was curled inside. Bill Fogarty's hair. He withdrew the hair, holding it delicately between his thumb and index finger. Perhaps it was Fogarty's presence which was separating him from his perfection. He placed the hair in his mouth. He could taste the bitter alcohol-based dressing which lingered on the filament. He swallowed, the hair tickling his throat as it passed towards his stomach. Resealed the bag and laid it beside his desert boots. Then he stood and confronted the Mon Fat-Jong, extending his hand in a long eagle's claw as he drove inward towards the wooden throat. The hardened flesh of his claw felt bruised and sore as it impacted. He cocked his arm and struck again. The sensitivity traveled up the extensor muscles of his forearm and transmitted the length of his body. His efforts reawakened him, rekindling his intent and purpose. Soon the buzzing began and Willard Ng was awash in the sea of his senses, his physical pain transforming past, present and future into *now*.

His concentration, coupled with the opiate-like endorphins flooding his bloodstream, released by the extremes of his exertion, distanced him from the barrage of questions as he left his house. The buzzing continued, acting as a homing device, calling him to her.

"Do you intend to sue the City of Philadelphia, Mr. Ng?"

"Are you still a suspect in the murder investigation?"

"Lieutenant Fogarty is expected to live. How do you feel about that?"

"Mr. Ng. Mr. Ng. Could you just turn this way."

They're all pronouncing my name incorrectly. Nigg. It is not Nigg, he thought, adjusting his pompador with both hands, repositioning the artificial hair as he walked the gauntlet of parasites. It was the same wig that he had worn on the night that he killed Gina Genero.

Snap. Flash.

And then he was gone, locked inside the safety of his gray van, motoring away from their confusion.

He knew he was being followed. The black Ford was a half-block behind, two men in the front seat. He led them to the bridge, driving easily, feeling under no particular pressure.

Another police car, also unmarked, picked him up on the Philadelphia side.

It was an unusual feeling. So many minds concentrated on his being. Like rough, sucking tentacles, probing and searching his consciousness, attempting to tip the balance, to cause him to become careless, disordered.

Then he noticed that the buzzing had stopped, as if the other minds had interfered with her connection.

He had intended to drive to the zoo, to see her. That, for the time being, was an impossibility. He would never lead strangers to her sanctuary.

He changed direction, turning left before the art museum and heading towards Walnut Street before making another turn which pointed him east, back in the direction of Camden.

"He's made us," Ratigan said matter of factly.

"So. Whaddya want to do?" Johnson asked, watching the red taillights of the VW van twinkle and disappear.

"Nothin' we can do," Ratigan rasped, purposely allowing Ng's van to outdistance them.

"You gonna let him go?"

"What do ya want?" Ratigan snapped. He didn't wait for the

black detective to answer. "You want me to pull him over so we can both empty our pieces into the side of his head?"

Johnson felt stupid.

Ratigan calmed almost instantly, then continued. "McMullon's already gone to bat for Bill Fogarty. He can't pull that kinda stroke twice. We get called in on harassment an' we're outa here. Suspended. Fucked. And that freak Nigg, or No one, or whatever his name is, is gonna walk."

Johnson waited a respectful interval." So what are we gonna do?"

Ratigan accelerated slightly, looked for Ng's taillights, couldn't see them, picked up his phone. "We're gonna stay in touch with our friends in Jersey. Keep as good an eye on Ng as we can, and for the next coupla weeks we're gonna let this bastard run. Then, when the press dies down an' Nigg thinks he's clear, we're gonna come down on him like a ton of bricks. I don't give a shit if he's guilty or not. That bastard stomped a cop," Ratigan added with resolve.

Ng checked his mirror; they were gone. He slowed down, finally pulling into a metered area at the curb. Turned off his engine and waited. Nothing. He contemplated turning around and continuing to the zoo. Sat a moment listening to the spill of music from a corner bar. A gentle, pulsing beat. He slowed his breaths, regulating his breathing.

"*She is like a cat in the dark. Then she is the darkness.*" The familiar lyric caught him. Caused him to turn towards the bar as the glass-fronted door opened and a single college-age girl walked out. Ng couldn't quite make out the features of her face. He followed her footsteps. She wore cowboy boots and blue jeans, loose in the leg and tight across her small, muscular hips, visible beneath a black motorcycle jacket. Her hair was streaked blond and cropped short. She moved confidently.

A dancer. A gymnast, Ng guessed. He viewed her with a curious detachment. She would have been easy. Yet there was no longer any necessity. Nothing stirred inside him, no longing, no hunger. No connection. The realization gave him a feeling of solidity. He checked again in his rearview mirror, then turned completely in his seat. Nothing beyond the ordinary run of traffic. No patrol car, no foot policemen. He was free. Standing securely on the final plateau. And free. He could feel it.

He experienced an amazing clarity as he pulled back into the main stream of traffic, driving towards Rittenhouse Square. He opened the driver's-side window and let the chill of late autumn caress the skin of his face. "Thirty-nine days till Xmas," a sign in a clothing shop read. A street vendor was roasting horse chestnuts by the side of the road; their aroma filled his nostrils. He heard voices, laughing, talking as groups of people passed in the street. He was happy. He could not remember ever being happy before. He didn't want to return to his home, with the milling reporters and nosy neighbors; he didn't want to visit *her*. He had had enough discipline. His whole life had been discipline. He wanted to remain in this capsule of freedom, connected to the noise and the smells and the laughter. Connected to life. He wanted to keep on driving. Into this sea of happiness.

At first the couple standing at the entrance to the driveway of the apartment block and examining the black and chrome motorcycle were no more than another super-imposure on his happiness collage. Then his thoughts focused and the buzzing began again.

Josef Tanaka. It is Josef Tanaka. Talking to a pretty woman with long hair. The woman held a briefcase in one hand; her free hand rested easily on Tanaka's shoulder.

Ng followed the road left, away form their line of vision. He threw the van into neutral, cut the engine, and free-wheeled into a shadowed space on the far side of the tree-lined square. He was little more than a hundred yards from Tanaka and Rachel Saunders. He rolled down the window of the passenger side and watched. Twice he felt the beginning of a connection with the tall, dark-haired warrior. Both times Tanaka looked up, an animal sharpness to the twist of his head, Ng changed the pattern of his breathing, slowed down, calmed himself, preventing contact.

The couple's concentration on the motorcycle didn't last long and soon Tanaka and the woman seemed engrossed in other matters. He was shaking his head and she appeared to be consoling him. Ng sensed their intimacy. It inflamed him. The woman rose upwards on her toes and kissed Tanaka on the mouth. Ng could not remember having kissed anyone. Ever. He hated the woman. Hated her with everything left in him that was human. *Why have you guided me here?* he asked. Then he began to truly understand. Of course she had called to him tonight. Called him away from the smallness of his life, the incident with the policeman, the lawyers and reporters. Guided him through the elusive maze of human happiness and out the other side. It was no coincidence that he was here, now. There was never such a thing as coincidence, not on the path to enlightenment.

Tanaka was mounted on the motorcyle. The machine came to life with a low, throaty rumble. The long-haired woman watched as he disappeared down a ramp and into an underground garage. Then the woman turned and walked towards a high glass door. A porter opened the door, nodding as he greeted the woman. *He knows her. She lives here, or comes enough to be recognized. Maybe Tanaka lives here. It's possible they live together.* And then Willard Ng knew what he had to do. It was as clear as the buzzing inside his mind.

He dreamt of the Mantis that night. Entered her mouth, climbed the staircase, found the light. Recognized his fulfilment inside the light. Experienced perfect peace. His father was gone from his dream.

XIX.

THE VISITOR

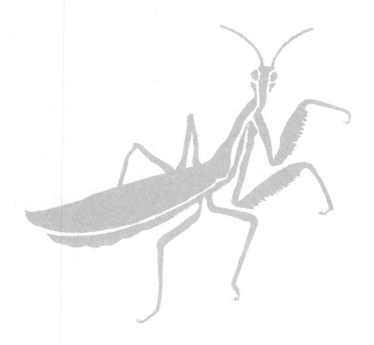

Diane Genero took an Amtrak Express to Philadelphia, grabbed a yellow cab at Thirtieth Street station and went directly to City Hall. She was carrying a single piece of Louis Vuitton luggage and a matching shoulder bag.

She dropped the suitcase on the floor in front of the reception desk.

"May I help you, madam?"

Diane looked into the receptionist's brown eyes. In the periphery of her vision she could see two black security guards, glancing over.

"I'd like to see Mayor Bright. I've called three times from New York and haven't been able to get through."

The young, almost pretty receptionist appeared incredulous. "Have you an appointment with the mayor?"

Diane Genero lowered her shoulderbag before she answered. "No."

"I am afraid, madam, that it is impossible to just walk through the door of City Hall and demand to see the Mayor of Philadelphia. Mr. Bright is a very busy—"

"Do you know who I am?" Diane Genero asked. Her voice was soft and there was nothing imperious in the tone of her question.

One of the security guards was walking towards her. The receptionist exchanged glances with the uniformed man before replying. "I'm afraid I don't."

"My name is Diane Genero. I am the mother of one of the girls—" She hesitated, rephrasing her sentence—"one of the victims in the recent series of murders."

The brown eyes seemed to refocus on the expensively dressed woman.

"May I take a look in this bag, ma'am?" The guard's voice caught her from behind.

"It's all right, Victor," the receptionist said, raising her hand and motioning the man away.

"You're the lady who did the TV interview?" There was a cautious respect in the question.

Diane Genero held the woman's gaze and nodded.

"I believe the mayor is in the middle of a meeting," the receptionist said, hesitated, then picked up her phone. "But let me see what I can do for you."

Ten minutes later Diane Genero walked into the mayor's office. Both Winston Bright and Dan McMullon stood as she approached the big wrap-round desk.

The handsome black man went to extend his hand, appeared to balk in mid-motion, then snatched Jeanette Key's filofax from his desk and tossed it into his top drawer. He locked the drawer before returning his attention to Diane Genero.

"How do you do, Mrs. Genero, I'm Dan McMullon," the soon-to-be-appointed police commissioner covered.

"Please sit down," Winston Bright added, reestablishing his composure.

Diane Genero sat down and got right to the point of her visit.

Lankenau Hospital overlooks Lancaster Avenue, on the Montgomery County side of City Line. It is a rich hospital, patronized by many of Philadelphia's oldest mainline, surburban families.

A large, quiet building, its modern facilities and well-kept surrounds offer a conducive atmosphere for convalescence.

Occasionally, the Philadelphia Police Department will place a recovering officer in Lankenau, away from the noise and bustle of the city. Less accessible to the media and unwelcome visitors.

"Bill, Bill." The nurse's voice was gentle, lifting him carefully from sleep.

"Someone here to see you, Bill." The voice belonged to Stella Stevens. She was Fogarty's favorite nurse. He trusted her, enough to let her administer the sponge baths that he found so humiliating.

"Another asshole investigator?" Fogarty grumbled, keeping his eyes shut. "Tell him I'm in a coma."

"This one is female."

There aren't any female investigators on this case, Fogarty thought, opening his eyes.

"Diane Genero," Nurse Stevens said, hesitating before adding, "She's very beautiful."

"Diane Genero . . . here?"

"Downstairs in reception."

"Christ." Fogarty sounded alarmed. He struggled to sit up. The cast on his leg covered him from ankle to mid-thigh; it felt like it weighed a ton. His bare foot stuck out from the bottom of his white sheet.

"I thought there was a ban on civilians," he said.

"I understand this one was very persuasive," Nurse Stevens commented.

She was delighted to see the lieutenant up; he had been sleeping too much lately and the only people he had been in any way pleased to see were the two doctors, Moyer and Tanaka.

She watched as he ran a hand through his hair, then down, across the stubble on his chin.

"I can hold her off while you shave," she suggested.

Fogarty looked into Stella Stevens' hazel eyes. He appeared at once vulnerable and embarrassed.

The forty-year-old nurse smiled. "What's the matter, Lieutenant?"

"Diane Genero is the mother of one of the murdered girls," he answered.

Stella Stevens held him firm. She liked the lieutenant. She wanted him to get well. His body and his mind.

"That doesn't mean you shouldn't look good when you see her," she replied. Then she went into the bathroom and rounded up his shaving gear.

* * *

She's the most beautiful woman I've ever seen. It was a thought that made him particularly self-conscious. He resisted his habitual urge to half turn his face away as Diane Genero walked towards him.

"How the hell did you get in here?" he asked.

"Special permission from the mayor," Diane Genero answered, adding softly, "On the condition that I don't speak to any more press people."

She stood awkwardly at the foot of his bed, hardly able to meet his eyes. For a moment she regretted coming. The whole thing was too personal; she had no business being here. Her awkwardness intensified.

"I came to apologize."

Fogarty remained silent, trying to get a handle on the feelings that threatened to swamp him. She looked different from how he'd remembered. Her face seemed more full, her features more defined. How many times had he tried to recall her face? Finally he had settled on a memory that was, at best, a poor facsimile.

"For the interview. For the way it all came across. Like I was being critical."

Apologize? Her daughter got killed in my town and she's come to apologize, Fogarty thought. He half turned from her.

Diane Genero focused on the fresh pink circle of scar tissue beneath the lieutenant's neck, the heavy cast that held his right leg in a partially bent position beneath the sheet and single wool blanket.

"I'm sorry, really sorry," she managed. Then she turned and reached for the handle of the door.

"Please. Sit down," Fogarty said. His voice sounded raspy, almost gruff.

Their eyes met again. The feeling of loneliness, the same feeling that had touched them when they had met for the first time, was there. This time the feeling stayed, like a third presence, hovering above them.

Diane Genero sat in the chair to the side of Fogarty's bed.

She's cut her hair, that's it. Shortened it so it frames her face, Fogarty observed. He wasn't conscious of his own half-smile.

She looked at him and saw the same face that had stared at her from the newspaper. As if the chemistry between them had washed the years away, erasing the scars, clearing the tiredness from his eyes, refilling them with hope.

"You look like a fucking angel . . ." The words slipped from his mouth. He regretted the "fucking" a second after he'd said it.

"You look like a fucking mess," she replied.

He laughed for the first time in weeks. The laughter hurt, inside and out. It stretched his throat and sealed his fears. Pulling him back into the world of the living. A world in which he knew that Bill Fogarty, the policeman, was finished.

Silence followed. Something had vanished from the room. The loneliness was gone.

"How are you?" Fogarty started again.

Diane Genero considered before answering. "As good as I can be right now."

Fogarty nodded.

"How about you? Aside from all this?" she said, running the length of his body with her eyes.

"I'll survive." Fogarty hardly believed his own bravado.

"You found him, didn't you? He's the one who did this to you. You didn't make any mistake." She stated it as fact.

"I found him," Fogarty answered. He prayed she wouldn't ask him what he was going to do about it. He didn't have an answer. Not yet.

She nodded. "I knew you would."

Then, smiling, as if to acknowledge his unspoken wish, Diane Genero changed the subject.

"Ever been out west?"

"A few times. Once to San Francisco and a couple more to LA," Fogarty replied.

"I never thought of California as out west. I meant more like Arizona or New Mexico," Diane Genero continued. She wasn't exactly sure where she was headed but the exchange felt comfortable.

Fogarty shook his head.

"Santa Fe has the best natural light in the world. That's why so many artists live there."

"I always had an eye for American Indian jewelery. Silver and turquoise. Comes from out there, doesn't it?"

"Not so much as it used to. More of a tourist industry now; the good stuff is all in private collections. Funny, you don't look like a turquoise and silver man to me," she said thoughtfully.

Fogarty shrugged, as if to say, "caught me." "It was really my wife. My wife loved—"What was the word? Ethnic. Yeah, that was it"—all that ethnic jewelery," he answered. "There's a town about fifty miles from here called New Hope. Sort of an art colony, at least it used to be twenty years ago. Every weekend it's full of outdoor markets. A lot of silver bracelets and necklaces, that kind of thing . . . Sarah used to spend hours in those markets." *With me sitting in the car, pissed off, waiting for her.* The memory came as an afterthought.

"Sarah. That was your wife's name. Sarah?" Diane Genero asked.

Fogarty nodded. It was the first time he had been able to talk, even think about Sarah without the guilt. The terrible guilt.

"Beautiful name," she said, then changed the subject again.

"One day, you'll have to take a trip out west. Great place to—" Diane Genero hesitated. "Great place to heal. Your body, your mind. Something about the light. Everything seems more clear." For some reason she thought of Vincent Bellows when she said it. She'd seen him less than twenty-four hours ago and already his face was clouded in her mind. She got up from her chair. Her movement was abrupt.

"Thanks for seeing me." She was about to add "Bill." Instead, she said, "Lieutenant."

The loneliness was flooding back into the room. Fogarty wanted her to leave now, if only to save himself the embarrassment of asking her not to.

"Please, let me know what happens. I'd prefer hearing it from you. Not the newspapers."

Fogarty nodded. "Sure. Thank you for coming." Then Diane Genero was gone and the room seemed darker.

XX.

THE NEW PATIENT

Time was of the essence. Thirty-eight days till Christmas, five days till Thanksgiving. If he planned meticulously, he could be ready by the first of the two national holidays. Five days of fasting, internal cleansing and concentrated exercise. The last five days. Five days until permanence.

He sat naked on the edge of his futon. He was tingling, alive with energy. He'd even smiled at the reporters who had doggedly remained on his front lawn. He hadn't spoken to them; there was no need for speech. There would be plenty for them to write about later. Plenty for them to chronicle. What he needed now was concentration. He closed his eyes, breathed in and held the breath. He could feel her in the center of his forehead. Feel the exquisite trembling of her wings. The buzzing was there all the time now, even as he slept. The dream was there all the time, also. Through all his waking hours. The perfect Man-Mantis was inside him, barely hidden beneath the first layers of flesh on his body. How crude that flesh appeared to him now. How crude his efforts to mold and transform it. Like a shiny, festering larva before metamorphosis. Crude, but necessary.

He lifted the phone, dialed information for Philadelphia.

"Tanaka, Doctor Josef Tanaka."

"Have you an address, sir?"

"Rittenhouse Square."

"Just a moment sir, checking."

He knew the address would be correct. It was one of those times when everything fell into order. When everything made sense.

There was a click followed by a computerized voice. "The number you have requested is . . . 215-568-3548. Repeat, the number you have requested is . . . ."

"215-568-3548." He spoke the number. Already committed to memory. Replaced the receiver. Got up and bolted the bedroom door. Returned to the futon and dialed Josef Tanaka's number. It rang five times before someone answered. A woman's voice. High and nasal.

"Doctor Saunders."

"Doctor Saunders?" His voice was barely above a whisper. As if he had misheard the name.

"Doctor Rachel Saunders," the nasal tone confirmed.

Ng flashed back to the pretty woman with long hair, kissing Tanaka, entering the apartment building in Rittenhouse Square. It took him a moment to react. Controlling his excitement, "I'm sorry. I have her number next to Doctor Tanaka's in my book."

"Doctor Tanaka is not at home. You've come through to Doctor Saunders' message service."

Ng thought fast. Realized he was being offered an opportunity. *She* was guiding him. Faster than he could have anticipated. He surrendered to her control.

"I'm actually calling for Doctor Saunders," he said.

"Are you a patient?"

"Yes," Ng answered.

"If you leave me your name and a telephone number, I will page the doctor and I'm sure she'll call you."

"I'm calling for an appointment," Ng replied. He found strength in the truth of his words. No need to fabricate.

"Then you should call Doctor Saunders' secretary."

"This was the only number I could find."

"Doctor Saunders' office number at Jefferson Hospital is 568-6767."

"Thank you very much. Sorry to trouble you."

"No trouble, sir. Goodbye."

Ng put down the phone. Closed his eyes. His forehead was vibrating with a warm electricity. 568-6767. The number served as confirmation. There were so many variables, so many ways that it could have gone. He had anticipated disguising his voice, having to hang up, perhaps not ever being able to find Tanaka's number. Instead, it had gone perfectly, according to her plan.

He pulled his feet up on to the bed, folded his legs at the

knees, assuming a lotus posture, straightened his spine and squared his shoulders. He performed a set of deep, cleansing breaths, concentrating on the area of vibration in the center of his forehead. His exercise had the effect of creating a vacuum inside him, amplifying all of his senses within that vacuum. He was getting closer to fulfilment with every conscious breath. Like the chrysalis before transformation. Aware of every change in the fiber of his being. Savoring his last stage before permanence. Then he picked up the phone and dialed Rachel Saunders' office number.

21 November 1990

It had been a cold, dry day. Dusk came at five o'clock. The setting sun coincided with the last listed appointment in Rachel Sanders' diary. J. C. Masters, a new patient, no referral. After Mr. Masters it was going to be a quick trip round the ward with special emphasis on Iva Snow's upper lids, then a brisk twenty lengths in the University Hospital pool. After that, home to bathe and set her hair. The hair would take three hours. That should be all right. He wasn't home from the dojo till nine thirty, so it would be a late dinner.

Last night, before she'd drifted off to sleep, as she curled her naked body into his, the chauvinist Jap had actually had the nerve to grip the layer of flesh around her abdomen and ask if he could borrow it as a spare tire for his new bike.

That bastard, she thought, smiling, then resolved to add ten minutes in the steam room to her new regime. She'd do her hair the way he liked it. Bo Derek style from the film *10*. Ten was right, ten years out of fashion. But it suited her face. Even she admitted that. And Josef loved it. She checked her watch. 5:08. She punched the button on her intercom.

"Has the mysterious Mr. Masters arrived yet, Marge?"

"Nothing yet, Doctor. Two calls from Mrs. Stoll though."

"Oh God, did she say what she wanted?" Rachel Saunders

asked, hoping that it wasn't a further complaint about her imaginary drooping eyelid.

"I think it was just some advice. She's contemplating liposuction on her thighs. Wanted you to recommend someone. I took care of it. Hope that was all right," Marge said.

"Who'd you give her?"

"Doctor Spielman."

Susan laughed. "Sam'll love Patricia Stoll. He's crazy to get into Mainline society anyway. Sucking the fat from Pat will be a great introduction.

"Besides, he's single and she's looking for husband number five," Saunders added.

Margery Yates cackled on the other end of the line. "What do you want me to do with J. C. Masters?"

"Give him another twenty minutes, then refer him to Sam Spielman. I'm going swimming," Rachel Saunders said before putting down the phone.

She used the twenty minutes to arrange her schedule for Monday, after the four-day holiday. Monday was Rachel Saunders' clinic day. The day she worked in serious medicine: car accidents, birth abnormalities, congenital defects. Monday was her day of medical atonement.

It was 5:40 when Marge buzzed her.

"A no-show, heh, Marge?" she pre-empted.

"Looks that way, Doctor. Didn't like his voice anyway. Sounded like a nerd. If we hadn't had a cancellation I'd have made him wait two months."

Rachel chuckled. Marge often prejudged patients by their telephone voices. "That's good enough for me, I'm coming out," she said, closing her briefcase.

"Are you still going on that motorcycle trip?" the tall raven-haired secretary asked as they left the office and walked towards the elevator.

"If the weather holds. I promised," Rachel replied.

Marge smiled. "When you gonna get the tattoo?"

Rachel laughed again. "As soon as I decide which hip needs a butterfly."

Willard Ng was parked in a loading zone on the opposite side of the street, facing the revolving glass doors of the medical building. He had arrived for his appointment, as agreed, at five o'clock. It was Rachel Saunders who was late. At five fifty-three he watched the two women leave the building. He recognized Dr. Saunders instantly. It was the long blonde hair. The longest hair he'd ever seen. He waited while they said their goodbyes, then started his van and followed the doctor as she walked east along Tenth Street.

He had chosen his finest wig for this exercise. He had acquired it in a theatrical costumer's shop, near the Locust Street theater.

"All natural fiber. Probably worn in the last production of *Hamlet*," he had been assured as he handed the seventy-five dollars to the proprietor. It was shoulder-length, curly and so black it appeared to have traces of deep blue when viewed beneath the phosphorescent light of his make-up cupboard. It went perfectly with the clear-lensed wire-rimmed glasses and brown woollen duffle coat.

The body beneath the clothing was shaved smooth and impeccably clean. Five days of fasting coupled with a fastidious regime of gastric and colonic cleansing had resulted in a constant state of heightened awareness. He had come to full realization that his physical shell was no more than the host body from which his higher self would be born.

Rachel Saunders could see the entrance to the hospital gymnasium complex a block away. She stopped to check her watch. When she looked up again Willard Ng was walking towards her. She had never seen him before and made a point not to press Josef for the details of his encounter. Still there was something "not quite right" about the huge man in the spreading duffle coat.

J.C. Masters, five o'clock. A growing paranoia sent warning signals to her limbs.

She looked around. *Christ, it's a crowded sidewalk. I'm safe.* She moved laterally, giving the big man room to pass. He shifted with her; one side of his coat, the side closest to Rachel Saunders, was opening. Like a great, dark wing.

In that instant Rachel knew who the man was. She pivoted, her mouth half-way formed into a cry for help. Her stomach seized; she couldn't find breath. She was slipping into the darkness, felt the coarse wool rub against her cheek. A hand, vice-like, squeezed inward, constricting her windpipe. She was going to die. She knew it. Right here, on a busy city sidewalk, a familiar sidewalk. She was going to suffocate.

Her legs were moving although there was no sensation of her feet touching the pavement. She heard a voice, thin, reedy. Hardly human, it came from above her, close but distant from her senses. "Pardon me, let me through, my wife is sick. Let me through."

Then she was inside a car. Moving. Breathing. Rough, gasping breaths.

Willard Ng looked over at the long hair; it covered his captive's shoulders like a silken blanket. She was slumped forward in the front seat, recovering. Another few minutes and she would be able to talk. He hadn't broken anything inside her. His flat fist had entered her diaphragm just touching her lower ribs. A very satisfying movement, delivered with his right arm, using the forward momentum off his left foot, relaxing the intercostal muscles between her ribs and forcing all air from her lungs. Then his wing wrapped her, guiding her to his van. People moving out of his way. Cooperating, preferring to believe his sick wife lie than to interfere. He looked again, almost certain that she wasn't damaged. In any case he'd examine her thoroughly before he prepared her.

Thirty seconds later Rachel Saunders raised her head. The first thing she noticed in the subdued light of the van was that her attacker was bald and had removed his glasses. The second was that he was smiling.

She was frightened but not panicking. It was a strange, rarified sensation. She'd had it before, a few times, during the course of a particularly difficult surgical procedure. When things had stopped going according to plan. A feeling of intense concentration, propelled by a controlled fear, yet coupled with an ability to divide her consciousness into the doer and the observer. The observer was able to overview a situation without the coloring of emotion. The observer in Rachel Saunders knew she was in trouble; it also knew that she was alive and uninjured. She stayed low, keeping her head forward. Said nothing. Recording every detail of the road and direction. Poised to jump from the van as soon as it slowed down. To scream. Even to attack the monster who sat beside her.

Willard Ng headed towards Vine, driving at a moderate speed, cutting and weaving to avoid the lights. Finally taking a sharp left and accelerating along the wide, lamplit boulevard which circumnavigated the art museum. Flowing into Fairmount Park Drive, then taking a right on to the expressway. Traveling at a steady fifty-five, driving in the slow lane, edging his way towards Thirty-fourth Street.

He had a strong sense of his captive, admired her silence, knew that she would attempt to escape.

Josef Tanaka left the lab at five thirty. He and Bob Moyer tried an exchange of pre-holiday pleasantries, which were strained by the knowledge that their friend was in a mess and there wasn't a damned thing they could do. An official freeze had been placed on the entire investigation, forensics included. Nobody was to speak a word to anyone about Willard Ng.

"As soon as the air clears we'll reopen the investigation and fry the bastard, but while there're jobs on the line, we let it sit." That was the line that Dan McMullon had taken and that was the line they toed. Everybody on the inside knew that the chief inspector had gone out on a limb for Lieutenant Bill Fogarty.

Speculation was that it was to absolve himself of the guilt of having sold Fogarty out four years ago and stealing his promotion.

"Nothin' evens the score for knifing somebody in the back." That's what the old timers were saying. It didn't really matter. At least, for once, Blubberguts had done the right thing.

The van had turned off the expressway at Thirty-fourth; it was moving slower now. Almost slow enough to jump. But to where? There was nothing but desolate parkland and scraggy pines, all lit by the gloom of a few overhead streetlamps. *God. Please. Show me some people. Any people. Winos, gangs, anybody I can scream to.* But the night was cold, it was late in November, and even the windows on the occasional passing cars were rolled up. She kept her head down, not wanting to give the slightest sign of an intended escape. Her watch read 6:23. *God, it's only been twenty-three minutes.* It felt like an eternity. She thought of Josef. Where would he be now?

Tanaka made it to South Forty-fifth Street by six o'clock. The door to the dojo was open and Reuben Daniels, the club secretary, and at seventy-two the oldest practicing member, was alone on the floor. Daniels was performing a passable rendition of Bassai Dai, one of the intermediate forms. Tanaka waited in the cordoned area to the side of the floor until the black man had finished.

"If you were fifty years younger you'd be dangerous," Tanaka quipped as Daniels turned around.

"Ten years ago an' you couldn't a got a hand on me," Daniels answered. Both men laughed as Tanaka crossed the floor and entered the locker room.

Minutes later he was standing in his gi in front of the Maki-wara, a straw-padded striking post. He planted his feet, cocked his arm and slammed a reverse punch into the straw.

After one hundred punches Tanaka's first knuckle had begun to bleed. He had been thinking of Willard Ng, and of what Ng had done to his friend. He was frightened of Ng. Not just in a physical sense, but in a way that seemed to dig right into his psyche, undermining his mental and emotional defenses. It was as if Ng knew him in a way that he was unable to know himself. As if there was a bond between them. He'd felt it for a long time but never so strongly as that morning in Camden; it had haunted him since.

He increased the tempo of his punches. His knuckles were going numb and the numbness seemed to transmit itself to his thoughts. There was still an hour to go before class. In an hour he could pound some real distance between himself and his fear.

Willard Ng drove straight down Thirty-fourth, beneath the Pennsylvania Railroad trestle, and continued past the front entrance of the zoo. Half a mile later he turned right on to Zoological Avenue. He slowed down then, finally cutting his engine. The van coasted the final few yards, stopping within easy walking distance of H Gate.

Rachel Saunders had been in his possession for thirty-five minutes; she had not uttered a word. He sensed a strong discipline. He admired that.

He turned, leaned across her and lifted the lock on her door, indicating that she should get out of the van. Even in the minimal contact of his body against hers, he sensed her tension. She'd probably run the moment the door opened. That would be unfortunate; he didn't want to injure her in the recapture. He wanted her intact. He squeezed across the front seat, pushing against her.

She froze, her stomach contracting. She didn't want to leave the van. At least while they were driving he had been occupied. His attention directed away from her. There had been the possibility of escape. Even the sound of passing traffic had been a reassurance. Now they were alone. *Oh God, I don't want him to touch me. To violate me.* Josef had refused to tell her the things he had done to the others. Did they all feel like this before? *No. I don't want to die. Please.* She stopped herself on the verge of desperation. Caught the whimper before it left her mouth. Alone. She was alone. Once when she was a girl, twelve years old, she had been at the beach with her mother. Swimming, she was a good swimmer, even then. Out a long way, she couldn't touch bottom. In the whitecaps and small breakers. Trying to get to shore. Struggling. Caught in the ebb tide. Embarrassed at first. Too embarrassed to call for help, to admit her distress. Until, finally, when she was exhausted, she waved. Signaled. She was in too deep. She couldn't get back. . . . And no one saw her. No one saw the small hand above the churn of water. No mother. No lifeguard. For a terrible, doomed moment, she knew she would drown. Knew that this was it, on this sunny July day. Disconnected from the warm sand and song of voices. Alone. Somehow, then, way back then, she had pulled herself together. Found an inner calm. Floated with the tide, let the waves take her to shore.

"Where are we going?" She forced the words. Her voice was soft, almost expressionless.

"Inside," Ng answered.

She moved with the weight of his body against hers, stepping down from the van, on to the street. He was right beside her, gripping her arm. There was no give in his fingers. They were like a steel vice. *He's stronger than Josef.* The thought chilled her.

They walked along the dark road, a high chain-link fence to their right, the raised tracks of the railroad to their left. Quiet, desolate tracks. *Please, let a train pass, faces in the window. Someone to see me. To connect to.*

She focused her eyes on the road ahead. Knew that she had to do something. Fight, run, break the terrible grip on her arm. The grip. Even stronger on her mind.

She kept walking, like a prisoner to the gallows. Then she saw the figure, a dark silhouette, walking towards them, on the same side of the road.

The vice tightened on her tricep, fingertips meeting between muscle and bone. She yelped with pain. The grip eased slightly.

It was a man coming towards them, wide, like a football player, broad-shouldered. He was carrying a canvas bag, like an athletic bag. He was no more than fifty yards away.

Keep coming, please, keep coming, Rachel Saunders willed. *Another few steps and I'll scream.*

An instant later, Willard Ng wrapped his left arm up and around her neck, squeezing inwards so tightly against her carotid artery that she temporarily lost consciousness. Her legs went slack and her feet dragged across the concrete. Seconds later, when she came to, she was walking with a limp. It took her a moment to realize that she had lost a shoe. She focused on the man who stood facing them. *Glass eye. He's got a glass eye.* That was her first thought. Then she heard his voice. As if her senses were returning one at a time.

"Let her go, then its down ta you an' me, mate."

She detected the trace of an accent. English Cockney? Australian? Understood that the man was bargaining for her life. He had placed his canvas bag on the ground and his left hand was already bunched into a fist.

"Y'al ready duffed one of me friends. I'd do ya for that alone."

The grip on her arm was less severe, but her body was still close to Ng's; she was aware of a strange vibration coming from his chest. A hollowed resonance, almost a wheeze, like asthma.

"Run, call the police!" Her own voice cut the stillness between them.

Gordon Forrest smiled at her. It was a brave smile. Made a little crooked by the pain in his teeth, far back in his mouth. Always the same pain that came before a migraine. He was flushed in the face, his blood pressure up, the steel plate feeling like it would burst from the front of his head.

"Please go," Rachel implored.

"Can't leave ya with this animal." Forest's last word was more a gasp, breath forced from his diaphragm by the sharp forward motion of his body.

Willard Ng watched the stocky man shift. Perceived Forrest's left arm swing up in a hooking motion, his fist arching towards him. He took a firm grip on his captive's hair before he reacted.

Forrest felt his punch land solidly against Ng's shoulder. He swung his right low, uppercutting into the big man's groin.

Ng exhaled. It was a loud, grunting breath that coincided with a counterclockwise twist away from his attacker's strike.

Rachel was screaming now, loud and piercing. Then she lost her footing. Ng caught her by the hair an inch from the sidewalk, whipping her head upwards, forcing her to look at the struggle above. He pivoted, dragging her with him, twisting, this time clockwise, catching the shorter man's jaw with his elbow. The blow stunned Forrest. He would have fallen had Willard Ng not followed his striking motion with a wrapping wing, securing Forrest's head in a cradle lock, bending him backwards, his neck strained against the weight of his body.

Rachel Saunders couldn't see Gordon Forrest's face. His entire head had been positioned beneath Willard Ng's arm, twisted backwards, allowing only the front of his body, arched unnaturally, to hang before her. She could hear, though, his muffled and agonized gasps. He was crying with pain.

"Stop this! You're killing him! Do you hear me! Killing him!" She screamed, trying to stand beneath the weight of her captor's hand. It was impossible. Then came a noise like the sound of a breaking branch, sharp and loud, like old wood. Before the silence.

She looked up, into Willard Ng's face. He stood still, Gordon Forrest's limp body hanging in his grip. Ng's features were stretched into a grimace. No, not a grimace. A smile.

He stepped laterally and Gordon Forrest dropped to the sidewalk, his neck broken so cleanly that the vertebrae puncturing his windpipe had forced his swollen and bloodied tongue from his mouth.

Ng pulled Rachel Saunders to her feet. She experienced a numbness in her senses, as if she was there in body only. Her emotions had become detached. She understood the feeling.

Like watching her first autopsy. The initial phase of shock. *No. Mustn't let that happen. Mustn't loose awareness. Stay alert. Stay alive.*

Ng picked the dead man up with a single hand, dragging him to the base of the fence. Kicking his body twice, causing him to lie flat against the join of steel and earth.

Finally he lifted Gordon Forrest's carry-all. Tossed it over the razored barbs at the top of the fence. He ignored the single brown glass eye that watched him from the cracked asphalt of the road.

Rachel offered no resistance as they walked the final ten yards to H Gate. They stood a moment at the iron barrier, then Ng knelt down, dragging her with him as he slid through the twelve-inch gap between the black turmac driveway and the bottom rung of the old divide.

Once inside they entered a maze of small, darkened buildings connected by a landscape of concrete walkways. Only the night creatures were aware of their intrusion, screeching their protests from behind steel bars. A hopelessness descended.

He held her less firmly now, secure in this familiar domain. They walked down a wide avenue for fifty yards, then he guided her to the left, up a paved ramp, to a high locked door with the figure of a lizard etched in stone above its sill. He had the keys in his hand. Unlocked the door.

They entered a wide, cavernous room, plated-glass tanks lining its walls. Most of the tanks were dark, two or three glowed with a subdued light. She was aware of creatures in the lighted tanks, curled and staring from hooded eyes.

He urged her forward, his hand gripping her shoulder, guiding. Only his touch kept her from rigidity. She was drenched with terror, every inch of her frightened. His body was so close she could smell him. A sweet, pungent odor. An odor that seemed to belong to the moist, close atmosphere of the room.

His legs moved in synchronicity with her own, his knee brushing the back of her thigh as she shuffled along into the darkness.

She felt as though she was disappearing down a long, black tunnel. Never to resurface, never to see the light again.

He seemed all-powerful. Nothing could ever stop him, no man, no god. He was going to do things to her. Terrible things, intimate things, things that he'd done to the other women, things that Josef would never talk about. She began to shiver. The shiver took control of her, convulsing her flesh. She heard her own voice. She was sobbing, "No one knows where I am. No one." It was her voice but it was from a different time in her life. Before she grew up, became strong, independent. It was a child's voice. A scared child. It angered her. She closed her mind to the child, straightening, walking without the shuffle. And all the time, seconds that seemed like eternity, he was silent beside her. Indifferent to her torment, intent only on what would be.

He tightened his fingers, halting his captive in front of a white door. Pushed his key into the lock. They moved through a small office, past filing cabinets and a desk, out of a rear door and into a corridor lined with grey metal pipes, interconnecting with boiler tanks creaking and groaning with their incessant labor. An overhead light, red and enclosed in wire mesh, lit their journey to the top of some stairs. Thick wet heat rolled in waves from the emptiness below.

Not going down there. Not going down, she vowed, locking the quadricep muscles of her legs. Then she was in the air, his arm wrapped around her chest, squeezing so tight that her scream clogged her throat. Descending into the heat.

More glass tanks in the room at the bottom of the stairs, a labyrinth of glowing cages. Alive with wary eyes. Some marked "Quarantine," others with placards which designated them as Feed. Feed for the reptiles above.

A diamond-back rattlesnake coiled as they passed, its broken rattle twitching a silent warning.

Down a winding corridor, more pipes, metal walls, condensation dripping from them. Hotter now, she was sweating, her feet shuffling when they touched the ground. The corridor narrowing, finally coming to a dead end.

Too dark for Rachel to see what he was doing. The click of a key, the tumbling of a lock. A sliver of red light as the final door opened.

It seemed that she was staring into an oven. Hot. Hotter than hell. She screamed, twisting away from the door, clawing at his face.

He deflected her hand, bending her wrist back at the joint, forcing her to her knees.

She was shrieking, threatening. "Josef will kill you! He'll fucking kill you!" And at the same time hating Josef Tanaka for leading her to this hell.

Josef will kill you. Josef Tanaka. Her promise repeated in his mind as he lifted her in both arms and threw her on to the inner floor. She landed on her back, her skirt rising.

He kept an eye on her as he closed the door and bolted it from the inside. She was wearing tights. He could see the outline of bikini pants beneath the nylon and a dark pattern where her pubic hair fanned out above her opening. It occurred to him, vaguely, that he had never had a woman. Not in the conventional sense. He had always been repulsed by the thought of procreation. The carnality, the earthiness; he had always been drawn to a higher source.

He moved on top of her before she had recovered from the fall. Ripped savagely at her clothing, shredding it from her body. She fought him at first, holding on to pieces of her skirt, her blouse. Clinging pathetically.

Finally she was naked, staring up at him. Fear had been replaced by defiance in her eyes.

He viewed her curiously. Studied her small breasts with their thick, pink nipples. Her long legs and round, full hips. The black girl had been a better specimen, physically. Younger, muscles more developed, more flexible. Flexible? Ng reconsidered. You could never really tell about that till the positioning. And it was hot in the room, that would make everything easier. In any case, it wouldn't be her physicality that attracted the warrior. It would be her intelligence and her determination.

Her will. It was going to be interesting to see how much of the process she understood.

He bent down, securing her to the floor with his knee, pinioning her by pressing inward against her sternum. She gasped for breath. Then he reached between her legs. She held them shut, crossing her ankles. The muscles of her thighs trembled in spasm.

"No. No. No." She repeated the word through clenched teeth. There was a fiery anger in her eyes.

He pinched the outer lips of her opening. Pinched hard and pulled, lifting the lower part of her body from the floor. Her eyes bulged and her legs went slack. He pushed his hand through, finding her anus.

She was fighting with her arms now, punching and scratching. Tearing his flesh, trying to raise her head high enough to bite.

Willard Ng remembered how much it had hurt when his father had gone inside his rectum. Stretching and ripping. That had been the most terrible thing about his father's punishment. But it had stopped him from misbehaving, stopped him from acting up. He pushed hard into her with his first two fingers, then used his thumb to lever from the other side. She screamed. A loud, full scream.

He stared down at her, holding her as he withdrew his hand. She seemed to understand his eyes.

"I'm not going to fight you. I swear." She said it as she sucked for breath.

He nodded, then stood up. He didn't want to hurt her. Wanted her in perfect condition. He stepped back, inviting her to her feet.

Rachel Saunders stood naked in front of him. She felt much smaller without her clothes, vulnerable, yet not, she sensed, sexually threatened. There was a clinical quality to the way he viewed her. As if she was being examined by a physician used to nakedness. It gave her a spell of reprieve.

Ng liked his captive better now that the wave of fear had passed. It permitted her intelligence to show through the cold blue of her eyes. He wanted her that way. Unclouded by fear. A witness.

His touch was gentle, without the insinuation of a caress. He guided her to a chair, heavy wood and sturdy arms. Bolted to the floor.

She tried to take the room in, entrances and exits, anything that would make a weapon. She saw the single bolted door, the work table, the cage, the killing jars on the shelves. Insects inside the jars. A larger bamboo cage. An insect inside, standing upright: it appeared to be watching.

What is it? A grasshopper? she wondered.

"*Lou-prego-dieu.*" His pronunciation was refined, reverent. "The animal that prays to God."

He read my mind, she thought, nodding silently.

He motioned for her to sit in the high-backed chair.

She obeyed as he reached to the table and picked up a full roll of surgical tape.

"You don't need to tie me." She realized her promise was futile.

He worked meticulously, beginning with her ankles and moving up her legs. It required a full twenty minutes to complete the binding.

Once, when Rachel Saunders had been a little girl, she had played Cowboys and Indians. She had been the squaw and her two boyfriends had roped her to a tree. Then, laughing, they'd run away. It was all OK, just a bit boring, until she'd had to urinate. Then she'd felt the full humiliation of her captivity. Standing there in tears, desperately trying to control her bladder, until it felt as if she would burst. Finally she'd wet herself. She never liked her two boyfriends much after that.

She was holding her bladder now. And she hated Willard Ng.

He taped her mouth, pulling her head back tight against the chair. Then he moved the bamboo cage to the side of the table. Rachel wasn't sure whether it was so she could see the insect better, or the other way round.

Satisfied, Ng unbolted the door and exited. When she heard the lock snap shut on the other side, she urinated.

Tanaka closed the door of the apartment, surprised that the hallway and living room were dark. He stood quietly, listening for the sound of the television from the bedroom. Often when Rachel dried her hair she watched one of the eight o'clock reruns; *thirtysomething,* or *Cheers* were favorites. "Helps deaden my mind," she explained when confronted by his inevitable question of "How can you watch this shit?"

Tonight there was no sound of TV. He switched on the light. The sofa and chairs had not been disturbed since he'd left that morning. He walked through the adjoining rooms. Nothing had been disturbed, because Rachel had not returned from work. A flush of irritation caused him to tighten his lips. An emergency, always an emergency. In a profession in which she professed there were no emergencies. Probably some old bitch moaning about the angle of her eyelash. Why tonight? They were going out to dinner tonight, dressing up.

Tanaka sat down on the low, curving sofa. *Don't be so fucking selfish.* He tried to self-administer some of Doctor Saunders' philosophy. And tomorrow they were going to take the bike and ride to the Poconos. A weekend in the mountains. To clear his head. *His* head, more selfishness? Probably, but he needed it. Need to put some space between himself and what had happened.

First they'd stop and see Bill Fogarty. He was in the Lankenau now, moved courtesy of the Philadelphia PD. At least Dan McMullon and Winston Bright could keep a tight rein on who the detective talked to, who made it on to the visitor list. The Philadelphia police force looked silly enough without its offending officer being investigated by the Camden felony squad. Bill had really blown it. No two ways about that. The case. His career. And Willard Ng was still out there. Josef Tanaka knew he was guilty. And what was Josef Tanaka going to do about that?

A ringing telephone interrupted his train of thought.

"Hi, Josef."

He recognized Marge Yates' voice immediately.

"Where is she, Marge?" he said, planning on short-circuiting the excuse he expected to follow.

"I don't know, but I can tell you where she's not."

"What do you mean?"

"I mean I picked up her swimming suit by mistake when I left the office. It was in a plastic bag from Whole Earth and I threw it in with my shopping. She's gonna be pissed," the secretary explained.

"What time was that?" Tanaka asked.

"Just before six."

"And she was headed to the pool?"

"Yes. And then home to do a Bo Derek before you arrived."

Tanaka didn't laugh and Marge Yates wondered if she'd overstepped the mark. "Is something the matter?" she asked meekly.

"No," Tanaka replied, covering for his anxiety. "I got home a little early and she's not here, that's all. When was her last patient?"

"Five o'clock, but the guy never showed up."

"Who was it, do you remember?" Tanaka asked. He was beginning to get a bad feeling.

"He was new. Gave his name as J. C. Masters."

"Who referred him?"

"No referral. Said Doctor Saunders had been recommended by a former patient."

"For what?"

"Deviated septum. Sounded like it might be operable. That's why I gave him the appointment. It was cancel—"

"Can you remember his voice, Marge?"

"Sort of hollow. Echoey. I remember 'cause I always check the new ones out by the sound of their voices. This one sounded like he was in pain. Either that or a real nerd. Something's wrong, isn't it, Josef?" she repeated.

"Where did you last see Rachel?" Tanaka asked. His tone was almost harsh.

"Outside the Jefferson. On her way to the pool."

Tanaka was fighting to keep the panic from his mind. When he spoke again it was as if he was detached from his own voice. "Let me make a few calls and get back to you." It sounded so matter of fact.

"What do you want me to do?" Marge offered. She was putting two and two together. She knew Josef had been involved in the recent police scandal. She was aware of the monster they had been hunting.

"Just hold on to the swimming suit."

It was the type of dismissive reply that always annoyed Margery Yates.

Tanaka was sensitive to the silence on the other end of the phone.

"To hell with making calls. I'm going to the hospital. Maybe she had an emergency. If she isn't there I'll head to the pool. She could've rented a suit. I'll call you later, Marge."

"Thanks, Josef. Hope you find her."

Tanaka ran the seven blocks to the hospital. It took the head nurse three minutes and four phone calls to confirm that Rachel Saunders had not been on any of the wards since one o'clock that afternoon. Then Tanaka went straight to the gymnasium complex at the University. Margery Yates met him in the entrance hall. Tanaka almost expected to see her.

"She never got here," Marge said.

"You sure?"

"The guy who's working the desk has been on since four o'clock. Rachel never signed in." Her voice was very controlled, businesslike.

"No chance of slipping by? Maybe he was away from the desk for a minute?"

Marge shook her head. "She would have had to sign in. No other way to get a locker key."

"I'm going down to look," Tanaka said. He started in the direction of the sign that read "Women."

Marge Yates touched his shoulder as he passed. "You can't do that, Josef. It'll cause all kinds of hell. If you wait here I'll go."

Marge was gone a few minutes. When she returned she was shaking her head. "Rachel hasn't been here. That's definite." She hesitated. "You think we ought to call the police?"

A swirl of anxiety pulled at Tanaka. Involving the police would validate his worst fears. He looked into Marge Yates' brown eyes. She understood.

"Let's go back to the apartment, see if she's there. If she's not, we'll call her service, check for messages. Then we'll decide what to do."

Willard Ng replaced the phone on its hook for the fifth time. Always the same voice. That same high nasal voice that had given him Rachel Saunders' address and office number. He had nothing to say to that voice; it had served its purpose. He looked around. The zoo was deserted. Closed for Thanksgiving. Maybe a skeleton crew would come in the morning to clean and feed the larger mammals. Not till eight o'clock. Sunrise was at six. After that they could do what they wanted. He would be gone. He thought of his captive. He'd been away for half an hour. He had been careful with the tape. Didn't want to stop her circulation. She had to be healthy when he positioned her.

Rachel Saunders could not break her bonds. She had pulled, stretched, flexed her muscles then relaxed, trying to create space inside her restraints. Forced air through her mouth, blowing out into the tape. Nothing. No sound, no give. Even the sweat of her body seemed to settle only around the edges of the cloth, making it itch but affording no movement. It was impossible to estimate how much time had passed since she'd entered the glowing red room; everything had been measured by the secretions of her adrenal glands, causing her fear to rise and fall in waves, crescendoing to unbearable peaks, then leveling out to plateaus of calm. During the peaks she fought hard against her own imagination. What did Willard Ng intend to do with her? It was then that the bruising around her vagina and rectum seemed most painful, as if the areas had swollen and hemorrhaged.

During the calm times she thought of Josef Tanaka. She imagined him entering their apartment, finding her missing. Josef would know what to do. *Dear God, I hope he knows what to do.*

Rachel Saunders was a Catholic, or rather had been a Catholic. She hadn't attended mass in five years. In the hours to come she would pray often.

Another thing that Rachel did during her calm times was to study the small, winged creature sitting before her. The mantis was really very beautiful, long and pale green, its gauze wings closed beneath its slender trunk. There was a certain intelligence to the insect, something in the way it watched and waited.

On the third ring of his seventh call, Willard Ng connected.

He felt the buzz in the center of his forehead before he heard Josef Tanaka's voice.

"Hello." There was a contained anxiety in the tone.

Ng remained quiet, centering himself.

"Hello," Tanaka repeated. He already had a sick feeling in the pit of his stomach. Marge Yates looked up from the sofa.

"Are you alone?"

Josef recognized the hollow voice. His heart sank. He looked at Marge.

"No."

"It is important that you are alone," Ng said, adding a sharpness to his tone.

"Give me five minutes," Tanaka replied.

The connection went dead.

"That was about Rachel, wasn't it?" Marge asked.

Tanaka nodded.

"Is she all right?" Her question was tentative.

Tanaka couldn't waste time. "Marge, you've got to leave now."

She stood. "It's time to call the police, isn't it?" she said.

Tanaka read her eyes. Knew he had to pacify her. "Marge, I work with the police. Every day of my life. And I love Rachel very much. Believe me, when it's time to call the police, I'll call the police."

"You're not going to tell me what's happening?" Marge said, stalling at the open door.

Tanaka firmed up; he'd had enough. "The truth is, I don't know. And I'm not going to find out with you here. Now please, Marge, go home. I'll ring you when I can." He gripped her shoulder, harder than he'd intended. She winced. "Don't make any calls. You understand me?" Tanaka ordered.

Marge nodded her head, looked submissive, as if she'd just been punished for being a bad girl. Tanaka saw the weakness in her eyes. The fear. *Thank God Rachel's not like you,* he thought. "I'll call soon, I promise," he said, then closed the door.

The phone was ringing by the time he'd crossed the room. His heart pounded as he picked it up.

"Alone?" the hollow voice asked.

"Yes."

"You know why I'm calling?" the voice asked, stronger now.

"I think so," Tanaka answered.

"She's got the longest hair I've ever seen," the voice whispered.

Tanaka forced himself to ask the next question. "Is she alive?"

"Yes."

"What do you want?" Tanaka asked.

"I am waiting for you."

Tanaka remained silent. His heart was slowing down, his breathing becoming regular. The connection was beginning, that sense of fate, the same feeling that he had experienced in Ng's presence.

Ng was feeling it too; he had purposely kept his human ego

intact during the preparation. Even during the disposal of the head zookeeper. Like a shield, serving to restrain the Man-Mantis. To keep him fresh for the final becoming. Now he could feel the shield dissolve before a flood of warm electricity. He savored the intertwining of their minds.

"Where are you?" Tanaka asked, breathing the silence. His voice was calm.

"I want to see you. No one else. You. By yourself."

"I understand," Tanaka answered.

"Are you frightened?" There was a certain innocence in Ng's tone. A strange sincerity.

"Yes," Tanaka replied.

"That is how it should be."

Tanaka walked to the bedroom. Almost exactly four hours. That was how long he had till two o'clock. He would have rather it had been immediate. For his sake and for Rachel's. Less time to think, less time to let the fear gnaw at him. *No police, no weapons. No one else must know till it's over.* Over. What did Ng mean by that? *Betray me and I'll know. There will be a hole in the center of your being. I'll sense it, I'll see it. You will have broken the bond between us.* Then Ng had given him the place that they would meet.

Tanaka sat on the edge of the bed. The back of his mouth had the metallic taste of spent adrenalin and his mind felt stretched and hollow. It was important to be rational now, precise and calculating. No time to indulge in guilt trips or martyrdom. It would be his death wish fulfilled. Atonement, Willard Ng had termed it. And Rachel Saunders' life was hanging in the balance of his judgment.

He reached to the night table. Picked up his leatherbound address book, turned to Bob Moyer's home telephone number. Stared at it, already knowing what Moyer would advise him to do. *Play it down the line. Proper police procedure. They're prepared for this type of emergency. Make the meeting, plenty of back-up. Ng wants to talk to you. He needs to confess. Wear a wire. We'll nail him. Save your girl. Save Bill Fogarty.*

XXI.

DEATH WISH

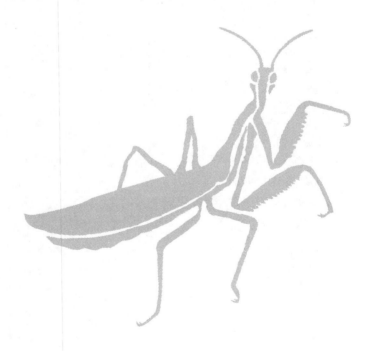

The memory of Gina Genero's body, twisted and raped, kneeling on the wooden trestles of a cold river dock, early-morning sun touching her bare shoulders, drove a wedge through Tanaka's mind. The police had struggled and lost with Willard Ng before. Task forces, psychological profiles, forensics clues, all to little or no avail. In fact Josef Tanaka had been the one to open the case up. And that was on theory bolstered by intuition. *My judgement has been correct.*

He kept telling himself that when the real terror set in. When Rachel Saunders' body replaced Gina Genero's in his imagination. When he wondered if Rachel was still alive.

Then came the deeper, shameful images. Unearthed by old guilt and intense fear. Images of his brother, Hiro, looking up at him from the canvas-covered floor, his neck broken and his eyes forgiving. The same eyes that turned away in humiliation as the stretcher carried his crippled body into their home. And in Josef Tanaka's mind he envisaged his own body upon the stretcher. Beaten and crippled. No good to himself, no good to Rachel Saunders. Atonement? Yes, he understood the desire for atonement. That was what Bill Fogarty had been after. Really, deep down. That was what connected them, Tanaka to Fogarty, both of them to Willard Ng. And Willard Ng understood this . . . Christ, he'd said it. That morning in Camden. That inevitable morning.

Tanaka closed his address book. This would not be a matter of police radios, snipers and back-up teams. Not a time for the contagious spread of nerves and the depersonalized concentration of a tight operation. This was personal; it had always been personal.

Rachel Saunders noticed the change in her captor's demeanor the moment he reentered the room. He seemed to walk differently, his movements sharper, quicker, and his eyes tight and darting.

Ng bolted the door. Then he walked to her, examining her binding, noting that she had stretched it in her efforts to escape. She had estimated the temperature in the room to be in the high seventies. A thin film of perspiration covered her body. She sat still as he tore the tape from her mouth. She made no attempt at speech.

He squatted down, his face even with hers. Stared into her eyes. His pupils were black and dilated; she wondered if he had taken an amphetamine. Something had altered him. He appeared void of emotion. He remained that way a moment, his nostrils opening and closing as he sniffed the air. *The urine. He can smell the urine,* she thought, worried that her offense might enrage him. She held herself back from an apology. *Give him nothing. No stimulus,* she told herself.

He leaned forward, his head dropping to a level beneath her jaw. She fought her urge to scream, pulling back involuntarily as she felt his tongue, rough and dry, rub against the line of her neck. Then across her throat. Working in circles as it traveled up towards the base of her ear. His breath was hot against her skin, growing louder as he licked. His tongue was like a cat's tongue, except thicker and incredibly strong, pushing into her. There was something obscene the way it pushed into her. She felt as though she might retch, closed her eyes, tried to shut him out. It was worse with her eyes closed. The deprivation of sight enhanced the sensation that he was dissolving her flesh. Sucking her blood. Eating her. *Now it's begun. Please God, give me strength.*

As if in answer to her prayer, the licking stopped. Willard Ng drew back his head, viewed her with his face half turned to hers. The tip of his tongue shot outwards, across his lips.

"Salt. You've lost a lot of salt. Your muscles will cramp without salt."

She nodded. Even his voice had changed. It seemed to be coming from a different place. It was higher, thinner, his pronunciation crisp and distinct.

He stood, turned and walked to the shelf, lifted a small container of sodium chloride from amongst his storage bottles.

Poured its contents into a half-full beaker of water. Returned, held the beaker to her lips.

She hesitated. He gripped her chin, squeezing inward, so hard she thought her jaw would splinter. Most of the water spilled, trickling down the front of her neck, on to her chest. The rest got into her mouth. She swallowed.

"Flexible. You must remain flexible," he explained.

"Why?" she asked, watching his head twitch as the word left her lips. As if he was catching the single syllable in flight. Since the revulsion and terror of his tongue against her body had passed, she had settled on a new plateau of calm.

He sensed her calm through the vibration of her voice. It was exactly what was required. He smiled, a shy, innocent smile. Then he went to his shelf and opened a feeding jar. The cockroach was groggy from the heat and hardly kicked as he carried it towards her.

Josef Tanaka emptied his bladder and bowels, shaved his face and bathed his body meticulously. He walked naked from the bathroom through the darkness of the apartment, into the kitchen. He turned on the smallest of the six burners on top of the stove. The glow of heat filled the small room. He placed a full kettle of water on the burner, then walked to the sliding glass doors that led out to their walled balcony. A rush of cold air hit him as he opened the doors. He stepped outside. Leaned against the brick wall, looking out over the bright lights of the city. They seemed far away. As far away as Rachel Saunders.

The night air caused him to shiver. He thought of Willard Ng. Fear welled inside him. Agitated the tiny convulsions of his flesh. He was trembling. Fully afraid. The cold and the fear were conspirators against him. He heard the old-fashioned kettle whistle from the kitchen. Walked inside, to the cupboards above the sink.

The moment his fingers touched the rough, earthenware pot, *chado* began. The traditional tea ceremony, as natural and important to the Samurai as was his skill with the sword. Tanaka began a precise control of his breathing, wiping the tea scoop clean and rinsing the bowl. As if he was performing *kata,* each movement disciplined and precise, the object being to control the flow of thought.

Tonight, because he was alone and preparing for battle, he was both host and guest, or *okyaku.* When the green tea was ready, Tanaka carried his pot and cup to the balcony. He sat down upon the cold brick. Fear tried to reenter him with the chill of the night. Goose bumps ran the length of his arms. He concentrated on the tea, its rich emerald color, its bittersweet bouquet. He sipped slowly, allowing the liquid to warm and replenish him. Fueling his spirit. He allowed his gaze to drift to the stars and the full moon, searching for that central spot of tranquillity inside him. Holding it with closed eyes. Pouring and sipping, in a place beyond fear, outside time.

"Oshimai wo," he whispered, returning his empty cup to the ground. *I am finished.*

Rachel Saunders stared at the six-pointed white star. An instant later the praying mantis struck, seizing the cockroach with its razored grapnels and shredding it. Then the embrace, gauze wings enveloping the twitching creature, pulling it inward to death.

Willard Ng watched from the opposite side of the table, as drawn to the reaction of his captive as to the killing mechanism in the bamboo cage. He had seen her wreak death many hundreds of times, studied and learned from her. Credited her with human intelligence, human evolvement. He had been wrong. For she could never evolve beyond the repetition of killing and eating, fucking, killing and eating. That was her essence. Simple, and perfect within its simplicity.

His captive seemed disturbed by what she had seen; confusion lay like a thin film across her eyes. She had begun to sweat again and the droplets settled in a small pool above the binding on her chest. She exuded discomfort. Soon he would release her from his restraints. In order to position her for the final transition.

He returned his attention to the insect in the cage. He thought of something, a final gesture. A demonstration of his gratitude for what the praying mantis had given him. He stood and walked to his storage jar. The large male was still alive, sulking beneath a dried brown leaf. He lifted it free of the jar, cradling it gently as he moved towards the bamboo cage. The Mantis had not yet finished her first meal when he dropped the male in beside her. She showed no immediate interest and there wasn't enough time to wait. Ng reached through the feeding flap and prised the remains of the cockroach from her. A grapnel attacked his finger, stinging like a bee, a small, insignificant pain. He shook the Mantis loose and closed the feeding flap. It was time to begin his own preparations.

It was midnight when Tanaka rode his motorcycle up the ramp of the underground car park and headed west in the direction of the zoo. Just under two hours until the time that Willard Ng had specified. There was still something that remained undone. One last person that he had to see.

Helen Carter, the receptionist on night duty, did a double-take as the man in black walked into the main foyer of Lankenau Hospital. He was tall and exceptionally handsome, his hair combed straight back and tied in a tight knot behind his head. His clothing was loose, only his trousers belted tight at the waist; he wore a heavy, cotton-knit pullover beneath his black leather jacket. The rubber soles of his training shoes were silent as he strode towards her. His movement was as distinct as his appearance, almost a glide, with long, even steps. He carried a motorcycle helmet in one gloved hand while the other reached into the pocket of his jacket. For a moment Helen Carter thought that he was going to draw a gun. There was that kind of intent in his dark eyes. Maybe this was going to be a drug hold-up. She was relieved when he produced a leather wallet, flipped it open and laid it on her desk.

On closer inspection his brown eyes were as clear and healthy as the ones that stared up at her from his identification. Josef Tanaka, MD, attached to the police forensics division.

"We've had a development in one of our major cases and it is necessary for me to see Lieutenant William Fogarty." His voice left absolutely no room for a negative reply.

Helen Carter felt it wise to check. After all, the lieutenant had been admitted, under guard, with strict orders that all visitors be listed and given a prior OK by the Philadelphia police department. Her hand went for the telephone. Tanaka's covered it, gentle but firm.

"Who are you going to call at twelve thirty at night?" he asked. The gentleness of his touch extended to his voice.

"The police," she replied.

"I am the police, Mrs. Carter."

The tone of his voice, soft but unyielding, made her feel slightly sheepish.

"I'm just trying to follow my instructions," she explained.

A second nurse, standing at the filing cabinet behind Helen Carter, began to pick up on their conversation. Tanaka knew he had to think fast; the last thing he needed was a disturbance. Better just to turn around and leave.

Helen Carter interrupted his hesitation as impatience. She gave in. "I'll take you to the lieutenant's room."

Willard Ng was naked. Standing behind the work table, filling the syringe from a small amber phial. It would be the second syringe he had emptied into his penis.

He completed the injection, laying the used needle on his table, looking down at his engorged organ. The papaverine solution warmed and spread, flooding his capillaries. For a time there was pain; he worried that he had overinjected. It was the biggest he had ever been, pulsing like he would burst. His entire consciousness seemed centered in his groin, then the tingling subsided and his mind found equilibrium.

At first, when he had begun disrobing, she had tried to speak to him. Asked him questions. About the scar across his chest.

The scar, that's what she'd called it. That had upset him. He had expected more in the way of understanding. But *he* understood. Understood that her voice betrayed her. That she was frightened again. That she felt the end coming. That she was stalling for time, trying to establish a rapport with him. Anything which would humanize him in her mind.

He could no longer respond at that level. He had not answered a single one of her questions. About his parents, about his childhood. The same kind of questions that the police psychiatrist had asked him. Dead questions, from a past life. He had continued to undress. Then, when he was naked, he stood and listened. One by one, her words trickled and died. And she was left dumb and silent. Then came the tears. Sad and frustrated. Until, like her words, her tears trickled and died.

She had turned her eyes from him when he began the injections. Staring downwards, at the floor. There was vacancy to her. He sensed a hollowness. As if her spirit had retreated. Not even the coupling insects in the bamboo cage commanded her attention. Just as well, she would be easier to handle.

Rachel Saunders was far away. Hanging on to Josef, on the back of his motorcycle. Breathing in the cold, clean air. High up. Riding in the Pocono mountains, along the winding roads. Dry brown leaves had fallen and there was that wonderful smell of a bonfire. It was Thanksgiving. They were going to be married. They would have children, probably three. Two boys and a girl. And she would taper off her practice, just enough to give her time to spend with her family. She'd waited a long time for the right man. Waited so long that she'd given up. Resigned herself to a life alone. Married to her practice. To a skill she'd been aware of since she was a little girl.

Nine years old, in the back bedroom of her grandfather's cottage on Nantucket Island. With her friend, Betty Bowers, cutting paper dolls from a big cardboard book. Dolls with faces like hearts and big full lips you could color in with red crayon.

Her dolls were always the best, the neatest, no torn edges to her dolls. She was good with her hands, even then.

You could hear the waves roll against the shore from that back bedroom. Sent you right off to sleep at night. Safe, underneath the quilt, with your mom and dad in the middle room and your grandma and grandpa in the one near the bathroom. So Grandpa's flashlight didn't wake anybody in the night, when he stumbled around trying to find the toilet. He must have been about seventy then. The same age her mom and dad would be now. If they were alive. One heart attack. One cancer. Both of them doctors. Both dead within two years of each other. No brothers, no sisters. All alone. Until Josef.

That's why we'll have three kids. So nobody winds up alone. Ever . . .

Willard Ng is close to her now, the tip of his penis touches the bare flesh of her shoulder. There is nothing sexual in its touch; it is more like a dull, blunt instrument. He begins to remove the tape from her body. It makes a sticky, crackling sound. Her skin is fresh and pink beneath the adhesive. So far she has not struggled.

Bill Fogarty was asleep when Helen Carter entered his small, green-papered room. In the dim light she recognized the envelop that had arrived for him yesterday morning. She remembered it because it had been postmarked Santa Fe, New Mexico. She had always wanted to spend a vacation out west and wondered if the policeman had family there. The envelope had been opened and was lying on the bedside table beside a book entitled *Santa Fe, Art and Architecture*. There was a sheet of blue paper in one of the lieutenant's hands. If Nurse Carter was not mistaken there was also the hint of Chanel No.5 in the room. Possibly coming from the expensive notepaper. Bill Fogarty was snoring. *Like a sailor sawing wood,* Helen Carter's father would have said.

"Lieutenant Fogarty." She touched his shoulder. "Bill. Bill."

"Sorry, Sarah," Fogarty mumbled. His snoring changed pitch as he rolled on to his side.

Tanaka walked to the bed, leaning over Fogarty. "Bill. Wake up."

The lieutenant came to with a start. Eyes wide.

"Joey?" His eyes focused. "What's goin' on?"

"Bill, I—" Tanaka didn't want to talk in front of the nurse.

"Thought you were coming tomorrow," the lieutenant added, pushing himself up against the headboard. He knew something was wrong, sensed Tanaka's reluctance. "Sorry. They still got me on medication. It probably is tomorrow." He smiled, placed Diane Genero's letter on the table, then extended his hand. "Jesus, it's good to see you."

Helen Carter stepped forward. "Lieutenant, it's one o'clock in the morning and Doctor Tanaka has insisted he see you. I haven't cleared it with anyone and perhaps—"

"No need to do that. It's all right," Fogarty confirmed. He smiled at her. "Mind leaving us alone?"

Helen Carter left the room.

Fogarty waited. Tanaka's visit was like one of those phone calls in the middle of the night. Bad news.

"Willard Ng has Rachel."

Fogarty's gut tightened.

"He called me at ten o'clock," Tanaka continued.

Fogarty glanced at his watch. 1:03. "Who knows about it?" he asked.

"Nobody outside this room."

What the fuck are you doing, kid! Fogarty wanted to shout it. Instead he stayed quiet.

"Rachel's alive. I know where she is. I know where they both are," Tanaka added.

"What are you going to do?" Fogarty asked, his voice soft.

Tanaka met the policeman's eyes. Full of hardened sympathy.

"Meet him at two o'clock. Do whatever it takes to get her back."

Fogarty felt anger rising. This was no time for anger. He changed tack.

"Listen to me, Joey, listen carefully. . . ." Fogarty hesitated, reached out and touched Tanaka's hand. "The reason I went after Ng was personal. I told myself it was because we needed evidence to close the case. That was bullshit. I did it for myself. To justify the fact that I'm sittin' here with you while my wife and daughter are buried in St. Paul's cemetery. You probably know about that, don't you, Joey?"

Tanaka looked up. His eyes said yes.

Fogarty didn't wait for the answer. "Everybody on the force knows about it."

Tanaka studied the lieutenant's face. There was no trace of self-pity.

"Well I'll tell you somethin' that none of 'em know. Somethin' that I've had to live with." He gripped Tanaka's hand, pulling him closer. "I was drunk when I had that accident. Plastered in the middle of the afternoon, driving my wife and kid home from the shore." His grip on Tanaka's hand tightened. "I wasn't even sure which side of the road I was on. It never came out in court 'cause I had friends in New Jersey. Records got destroyed." Fogarty hesitated. "But I remember. It'll always be the thing that I remember clearest about my life."

In the long silence that followed, Tanaka's thought of Japan, his family, his brother, Rachel Saunders.

"Bill, I've got to do this," he whispered.

"It won't absolve your guilt, Josef. Your brother'll still be a cripple," Fogarty said.

"That's only part of it, Bill," Tanaka answered.

"Let me get a back-up together for you. Guys who won't blow it. Ratigan, John—"

"No." Tanaka's voice was sharp.

Fogarty shut up.

"Willard Ng is tuned in to me. I don't know how or why. He's got a connection with me. Mental. Spiritual. I can't describe it. I've got to play it straight with him. Can't lie. He'll know it."

"You think Rachel is still alive?" Fogarty's voice was harder now. Sceptical.

Tanaka nodded. "She's alive."

"So what do you want me to do?" Fogarty asked.

Tanaka reached into his pocket. Handed Fogarty a smooth, ivory-colored card. Mikio Tanaka's business and private phone numbers along with his home address were positioned below an embossed image of their Samurai family crest.

Fogarty stared at the card.

"If I do not return from my meeting, I would consider it an honor that you notify my family and take care of any arrangements that might be necessary." Tanaka's voice sounded distinctly Japanese.

Fogarty nodded, cleared his throat. "Over there," he pointed towards the closet, "there's a thirty-eight caliber Smith and Wesson. On the shelf, underneath my briefcase—"

Tanaka smiled, began to shake his head.

"Five extra rounds in the pocket of my jacket," he continued, ignoring Tanaka's smile. "You aim for his head. Nowhere else. That's the only chance you got of stoppin' him."

Tanaka was getting up from the chair and Fogarty knew he was losing his last chance at reason.

"Take it, Joey," the lieutenant persisted.

"Thanks, Bill. Thanks for everything," Tanaka said. Then he turned, walking by the closet as he left the room.

Fogarty had his hand on the telephone seconds after the door closed. *Stop him in the lobby. Get a tail on him. Arrest the crazy sonofabitch.* His thoughts raced and collided. He checked his watch. 1:33. Twenty-seven minutes till show-time. Christ, Tanaka wouldn't have left it this late if Ng was in Camden. No. No way. He had to be close. Real close. He took his hand away from the phone.

He was stroking her body, rubbing along the surface of her skin with his rough, bulbed fingers. Massaging her thighs, working upwards in fast, tight circles.

The tape had caused her circulation to stop. She couldn't stand up from the chair. Like she'd been asleep with her arm in an awkward position. Awakened to find a swollen numbness in her limb. Her whole body was that way. Helpless.

Whatever he was going to do would be soon now. She could tell by the speed and precision of his movement. So methodical, as if he had performed the identical ritual many times before. And her naked body was only part of his ritual.

In front of her, in the cage, the coupling had stopped. Something else was going on, a frantic flailing of wings. The larger of the two insects had secured a hold on the smaller. To bite off his head, she knew. She'd studied the praying mantis in high school.

She was aware of everything, yet she was part of nothing. The cessation of feeling in her body had spread mercifully to her mind, disconnecting her from the heat of his breath and the touch of his fingers.

Yet, as he awakened the nerves of her flesh, in sharp, tingling flashes of pain, she experienced a reawakening of her will to resist. She searched the table and shelves with her eyes. Looking for anything that would serve as a weapon. To bludgeon or to cut. Better to cut. His eyes, his throat. She wasn't concerned with the consequences, had stopped thinking of her own life or death. It was more a desire to inflict her self upon him. To defy the impotence of her situation. So she watched and waited. Silent and calm. Resigned to death. Committed to action.

Tanaka bent over Gordon Forrest's body, feeling with his fingers where the third vertebrae of the dead man's neck had snapped inwards, severing his spinal cord. In the moonlight, Tanaka could see there was no skin beneath Forrest's fingernails, no bruising or chafing to his knuckles. Physically, he had been a powerful man, and, as Tanaka remembered, a courageous one. Still, it appeared that he had died without a struggle, handled like a child.

Tanaka stood up. Looked along the desolate street towards

the point at which the high fence was broken by a cluster of outbuildings and a gravel drive. H Gate.

He unfastened the strap of his watch, looked at the dial. 1:51. In nine minutes Willard Ng would be standing behind that gate, waiting for him. He placed the watch in his pocket and walked towards their meeting place.

The numbness was gone. She could have moved easily had she wanted to. Instead she pretended to be stiff and trembling. He guided her to the far corner of the room; he had spread a blanket on the floor, covered it with a white sheet. She knew that whatever he was going to do to her, he was going to do there, on that white sheet. He touched her shoulder, indicating that she should stop.

"Kneel down." His voice was hollow.

She began to kneel, waited for the tension in her quadriceps, then reared backwards, snapping her head up, into his chest.

He exhaled, a sharp hissing breath, reaching for her as she ran. Away from him, midway across the room. Running for the work table, grabbing the discarded syringe. Holding it in front of her, backing towards the door. She had anticipated that he would charge, that it would be a screaming, clawing fight.

Instead he approached slowly, arms rising from his sides, his breath coming like a low growl. There was no more than ten feet between them. *Turn. Open the door. Run!* her mind screamed. But for a moment, a heartbeat, Rachel Saunders slipped into the vacuum of revelation. Linking the man-creature before her, rubbery scar tissue spreading like a six-pointed star across his chest, to the insects in the bamboo cage.

The Man-Mantis sprang forward, covering the ten feet in a single gliding step, catching her as she turned and slid the bolt.

"No!" she screamed, spinning towards him, swiping at his face with the syringe.

Then she was in the air. Flying towards the work table, crashing down, her weight shattering the bamboo cage, the empty syringe hanging from her hand, needle penetrating her palm.

He was bending forward, staring at her, his head twitching, viewing her with predatory eyes. Nothing human in his eyes, nothing she could reason with.

The buzzing. The buzzing has stopped. No connection. The thought registered an instant before he saw his mentor, crushed and broken, lying beside the woman. The head of the male insect was still in her mouth. He paused. Long enough for Rachel Saunders to roll sideways and pull the syringe from her hand.

She stabbed upwards, into his face, missing his right eye by a fraction of an inch, the needle snapping in two on the bridge of his nose. The point remained imbedded. She withdrew the jagged steel, began a second attack. He punched downwards, connecting with her arm as it extended. Fracturing the bone, high up, near her shoulder. The shock of the blow sent waves through her upper body, paralyzing her. He lifted her by her hair, clear off the table, carried her to the sheet and dropped her. She fell on her broken arm, tried to rise and tumbled backwards.

The buzzing had ceased in Willard Ng's head. He was alone now. As he should be, standing on the precipice of the final truth. The Mantis was on the other side. Waiting. Time was short.

He squatted beside her, handling her roughly, forcing her on to her back. She tried to resist, kicking, clawing with her functional hand. He was hardly aware of her efforts, stopping his procedure only once to thrust the heel of his palm into her forehead. That quietened her. Then he concentrated on his work, bending her legs, shaping Rachel Saunders into the last offering.

XXII.

PERMANENCE

Tanaka waited. It was four minutes past two. The moon was full and bright and the night wind whistled through the branches of the trees. He was nervous, and his adrenalized body felt cold and stiff. His left knee ached. He had injured it during an early competition, but hadn't thought of it in years. Tonight it throbbed.

Where is he? Why is he late? Doubts tumbled like dice through his mind.

He pushed against the metal gate. No give. Locked from the inside. There was a space beneath the bottom bar; he could slide under. He squatted down, then held himself back. *Don't deviate, play by his rules. He'll come. He wants me more than he wants Rachel. Rachel is bait. She is alive,* he told himself as he stood up. Another voice told him that something had gone wrong. That he'd fucked up, that he should have called in the police. Taken the gun, or at least told Fogarty where he was going.

The voices stopped when he heard the soft, cat-like footsteps. Hardly audible above the wind. Coming closer.

Tanaka could feel his body preparing, switching on, all systems go. Each of his senses heightened. So much juice flooding him that he trembled. Fight or flight symptom. Every high school biology student had heard of it. The difference between a hero and a coward was only the fine line of control. He breathed in, deep from his lower abdomen, keeping his body revs together. *Don't waste it. Don't waste anything.*

The footsteps stopped. Tanaka searched the shadows with his eyes. Nothing. The only movement was the skeleton tree limbs above him, swaying in their barren dance.

Tanaka wanted to call out, to stop the game. But this was different. This was real. More real than anything before in his life.

He waited and watched. Watched and listened.

At first the sound was indistinguishable from the whine of the branches or the rustling of the brown leaves on the ground. Finally the sound refined, deepened. Tanaka's ears tuned to it.

Then he saw him. Suddenly. As if his eyes had focused, delineating shadow from flesh and blood. Willard Ng was standing facing him, wearing a black silk kimono. As if the huge man had stepped through a wall of invisibility.

Ng waited, measuring time by the beat of his heart, extending the tentacles of his consciousness outwards. Touching and searching, until he was certain that the warrior had not violated their trust, certain that Josef Tanaka was alone.

"Bend down, pull your body beneath the bar," the hollow voice commanded.

At that moment the battle began. Not with fists and teeth, but within their minds, spirits and souls.

Ng motioned Tanaka forward, stepping back to give him safe distance. Tanaka centered on the tight-lidded eyes. Squatted down. Followed instructions.

Vulnerable. I'm completely vulnerable, he realized, maintaining eye contact as he crawled like a soldier under fire. Standing up on the other side. The mantis eyes did not blink as Tanaka walked forward; he halted just beyond arm's reach.

Ng led the way, keeping a half-step ahead, along the deserted stone paths. The calls and cries of the nocturnal animals washed over them. Neither wavered in concentration, nor did they speak. Each footstep carried them further into the darkness from which only one could return.

Willard Ng was profoundly joyful. The warrior was all that he had anticipated, from his cleanly shaven skin to his knotted hair, loose clothes to facilitate movement, light rubber-soled shoes; he was ready for combat, impeccable. The Man-Mantis felt an irrevocable connection. The electricity was alive between them. The buzzing had returned to its place in the center of his forehead. It was soothing, superseding all thought. Giving confirmation to his faith; Willard Ng was complete without the flutter of gauze wings. The praying mantis had been his mentor, his catalyst. Now, her role as teacher had been fulfilled. He was ready to step beyond, to achieve his own permanence. The final transition.

Tanaka felt it too, the electricity. Like a tenuous but unbreakable bond between them. A confirmation of the inevitable.

Ng led him to the front of the reptile building. It was the same route that Tanaka had taken with Fogarty, through the main doors and along the semi-circle of dimly lit exhibition tanks. Then through an "Employees Only" door and into the rear office. Tanaka recognized their location. Behind the closed doors was a boiler room. Down the stairs, a basement. Rooms that he and Fogarty had inspected.

He followed Willard Ng. Everything seemed less familiar in the darkness. The stairs steeper, the ceilings lower. Tiny rodent eyes stared from the feed cages. Tanaka was sweating by the time they turned left, walking down the narrowing corridor, further and further from the subdued light of the tanks. Into another room, hotter now. Darker, enveloped by the smell of fresh-blooded meat. Arriving finally at a narrow iron door. A door that had been overlooked when they had inspected the premises. Revealed behind a wall of parted cages.

Above them, an automatic timer engaged, starting the circulation fan with a grind of metal against metal, sending a jolt through Tanaka's body. A warm stream of air swept the tight passage. The odor of meat and the putrid smell of garbage flowed with the current, as if it was being prised from the damp iron walls.

Ng was directly in front of him. Tanaka could make out his silhouette, black on black. He was removing the padlock from the narrow door. Pushing inwards.

Infrared light flooded the passage. Ng waited, indicating that Tanaka should be the first to enter.

He saw her immediately as he walked through the door. Positioned on the white sheet, in the corner. Legs bent into the full lotus, taped at the ankles, head pushed forward, balanced on her forehead and knees. He could not see her face but there was the strained sound of breathing from the area where her nose crushed inwards against the sheet.

He had seen bodies like this before. Porcelain bodies. Grotesque sculpture. To be cut up and examined. Pieces of his amputation to be used for evidence, or clues. His emotions switched off during those autopsies. It was the only way his humanity could survive. No names attached to the horror. Nothing personal.

He walked towards the body, noticed the redness surrounding the rectum, the bruising along the inner thigh. The lump where the broken bone pushed outwards against the flesh of the upper arm. He didn't want to give this body a name. Didn't want to be responsible for this body. But he was responsible. And this body did have a name.

"Rachel," he whispered, kneeling beside her. His warrior spirit was pierced, caving in around him. Lost beyond anger. He lifted his hand, stroking downwards along her back.

"Don't touch her."

It was the first that William Ng had spoken since they had entered the building. His voice hit Tanaka like a sobering slap. Ng had closed and bolted the door, removed his robe. A thin strip of rubber, like a tourniquet, was fastened around his waist, holding his engorged penis in a flat position against his stomach. He unfastened the restraint, dropped it to the floor.

"I haven't used her yet. Not like the others. Thought you would want to watch."

He walked forward.

Rachel Saunders began to struggle, her shouts muffled by the tape across her mouth.

Tanaka stood between them. His mind was clearing, no time for confusion, no time to question the insanity.

Fogarty was stretched across the back seat, his knee throbbing and his head splitting. If he had been in the hospital he would have dosed up on the pink pills that sat on his night table.

Jim Ratigan and his team would probably be halfway to Camden. Fifteen minutes behind the Jersey cops. They'd find an empty house. Fogarty was almost certain of it. Not so certain that he hadn't made the call. Ten minutes after Tanaka had walked from his room. Ten minutes. It had taken him a full ten minutes to be reborn as a Philadelphia policeman. Before he'd seen Tanaka, before he'd fallen asleep with Diane Genero's letter in his hand, he had decided to move out west. "Bill Fogarty, Insurance Investigator. Bill Fogarty, Private Detective. Buffalo Bill Fogarty, Navaho Jewelery Salesman."

It took a little life and death to glue him back together. To snap him back to reality. He was a cop. On the wrong side of a bad deal, but a cop. He fingered the butt of his .38, wishing he'd had the Colt. *Two loads of Thunderzap. Gotta hit him short and sharp. Temple or throat.* He wasn't interested in an arrest.

Moyer's car was a lot smoother than his Le Mans, and a lot faster. They were at the Thirty-fourth Street exit before he'd begun to remember what it felt like to stand in front of Willard Ng. He had never been helpless in front of any man before. Not helpless like that. And to remember what happened after the beating. What Ng was going to do. What he'd done to the girls, his victims. And would do to Rachel Saunders. Fear began its dance in his stomach, stepping lightly at first. Then it began to kick, good and hard. *Jesus Christ, he's got to die. Got to.*

Willard Ng moved in circles, hands opening and closing, feet gripping then releasing, knees bent, thighs tight, each muscle taking its turn to control the shift of his body. His mouth was closed, nostrils flared; he breathed in, smooth and evenly. Controlled spontaneity. Aware. Totally aware. Eyes and mind focused on Josef Tanaka.

Tanaka shifted another half-step forward, listening to the deep, resonant breathing, concentrating on its synchronicity. In perfect time with his own beating heart. He focused on the cold, dead eyes. Felt their pull, like gravity, drawing him to a place he had never been before. Not in any dojo, not on any street. To a membrane in time, fine and tenuous, between life and death, and through the barrier, to the darkness on the other side.

Tanaka breathed inward, low and slow. Careful not to show the breath. Not to present an opening. Focusing his mind with his exhalation. Deepening his *zanshin*, his state of perfect posture. More a mental posture than a physical one; Tanaka was aware of everything simultaneously: the humidity of the air, the sick, sweet odor of the room, the solitary dripping of a leaking pipe behind him, the beating of his heart, the connection of his soft leather training shoes with the stone floor, the sweat covering the palms of his hands, the man in front of him. Moving.

Stepping laterally, light and graceful on the balls of his feet, his breathing pattern changing, coinciding with the weaving motion of his arms. Long, strangely beautiful arms, as if their muscles had been sculpted from some soft, pliable rubber. Stretching and shaping. In and out. Mesmerizing. Like deadly snakes. Hooking hands, opening and closing with the threat of fanged jaws. Another half-step and Tanaka could see behind the Mantis, to the body on the floor. Rachel Saunders' body. Bound and helpless. Twisted grotesquely.

Kill him. I'm going to kill him, Tanaka vowed.

You will have to, the Mantis mind answered.

Tanaka altered his visual perception, away from Rachel, targeting his opponent's head, throat and upper chest. Searching for an opening. A break in breath. Finding none.

"*Hei!*" Tanaka grunted the word as he began to feint with his fists, shifting his weight forward, moving aggressively towards the hooking hands.

Ng reacted by tightening his stance, drawing his elbows close to his sides, bending slightly at the waist. Inviting Tanaka to attack.

Tanaka waited, refusing to be drawn by the still posture.

He inched closer. Inside striking distance. Listening as the puffing breaths began, low, like an ominous growl. Building. He watched Ng's abdomen rise, fall, then rise . . .

Tanaka began the roundhouse kick midway into Ng's inhalation, lifting the knee and thigh of his kicking leg high, aiming the ball of his right foot at Ng's left temple. Timing his attack to coincide with Ng's peak intake of breath. Pushing with his hips as the roundhouse found its arc, intent on driving his foot straight through Ng's head.

And in that split second, between execution and contact, the Mantis spat the air from his stomach, pivoted and raised his left arm to block.

Tanaka reacted, aborting his kick, dropping his leg, using the same foot to sweep inward against the Achilles tendon of Ng's support leg. Trying to throw him to the floor.

An instant before contact, the Mantis shifted his weight, lifting his lead foot as Josef's swept uselessly below it. Then the Mantis twisted sharply, catching Tanaka with a reverse sweep of his own. Josef punched out as he fell. Connecting with his right fist, good and solid. Landed, rolled and looked up.

The Mantis stared down. Smiling. His nose broken inwards against his face, nostrils no longer visible, skin hanging loose and without structure. Blood gushing.

Still smiling, he reached up, gripped the hanging flesh between his thumb and forefinger. Digging his fingernails inwards, he began to tear. Then, holding his broken nasal bridge with his free hand, he ripped the skin from his face. Dropping it to the floor, leaving two bleeding holes. Stepping backwards as Tanaka regained his feet.

"Good. You are everything I had hoped for. Strong and focused." There was enormous gratitude in the Mantis voice.

And you are completely insane. Tanaka had barely registered the thought when the Mantis leaped towards him, oxygen, mucous and blood spraying from his bared sinuses.

Tanaka punched again, this time with his left hand. Pivoting his hips, clockwise, adding power to his thrust. Aiming at the center of Ng's throat.

His movement was stopped in mid-air by the Mantis's arms, opening like wings, deflecting the blow while stretching the scar tissue across his chest. Forming the star. Arresting Tanaka's eyes, breaking his flow. Ng parried and countered with a single motion. A downward strike to the soft hollow at the base of

Tanaka's windpipe, impacting with callused, bulbed fingertips. Causing Tanaka to choke. An instant before the dragon fist smacked against his forehead, sending Tanaka crashing backwards against the wall.

Stunned, Tanaka moved by sheer instinct, in time to evade Ng's follow-up technique, a claw hand which raked laterally across the surface of his face, narrowly missing his eyes. Sharpened nails tore deep gashes in the skin above Tanaka's cheekbones.

He kicked backwards as he shifted. Felt the heel of his foot dig inwards against Ng's solar plexus. Heard him gasp, sucking air. Tanaka turned, using the momentum of his body to power the knife-edge of his right hand in a slicing strike to Ng's throat.

The Mantis was moving away when the strike landed, smacking against his flesh but doing no real damage. Then they were apart, a body's length between them, circling. Both with the taste of the other's blood.

Tanaka moved quickly, feinting with his fists, dipping his shoulders, all the while stealing time and distance. With three feet to travel, he launched a right front kick, aiming low, at the inside of Ng's thigh, knowing that with any shift in position, his foot would slide up and into Ng's groin.

"*Yei!*" Tanaka shouted, pushing off his back leg, thrusting his hips forward, putting every ounce of his strength and weight behind the kick. Fully committed. He caught Ng in the pelvis, above his single testicle. He could feel his foot bite an instant before Ng flew backwards then dropped to his knees.

Tanaka continued his momentum, lifting his left leg straight up as he raged forward, cutting downwards with the heel of his foot, like an axe, intending to crush Ng's skull.

Ng raised his arms as Tanaka's heel descended, breaking the power of the kick, gripping Tanaka's ankle and calf. Twisting to throw Tanaka to the floor. Then Ng stood, panting for breath.

Tanaka looked up. At a face without a nose and covered in blood; a face that reminded him of some cheap horror mask. A halloween mask. He watched the thin lips move, heard the voice.

"Please continue. You must continue. We are almost there."

Tanaka crawled a couple of paces towards the muscular, hairless legs, began to stand before throwing himself forward, like a football linebacker.

Ng crouched slightly, beginning the power breaths as he lowered his center of balance. Rooting himself, willing his vital energy to flood his veins, connecting him to the floor. Directing the flow downwards, through the stone. He was immovable. Placement of energy, that was the difference between the external and the internal forms. He was about to verbalize his thoughts when Tanaka bit him.

Strong and deep, sinking his teeth into the inside of Ng's thigh. Biting down through skin, muscle and vein, until his teeth met.

The pain reached deep into Willard Ng, through his nerve endings, up his spine and into his brain, piercing his Mantis ego. Breaking his connection with the floor.

Tanaka felt the change. Tucked his head tight to the side of Ng's hip and began to rise. Ng's two hundred and forty pounds rose with him. Then Tanaka ran hard at the wall. The shelf splintered as two rows of bottles and jars shattered on the floor. Killing jars, spilling dead insects, and releasing vapors of cyanide and ether. Tanaka coughed, twisting away from the fumes. Ng clung on, turning Tanaka's body within his grip. Drawing him backwards, wrapping his legs around Tanaka's waist, his forearm locked like a bar across his throat. Arching his own body, pulling Tanaka with him.

Tanaka wrenched down against the forearm, struggling for breath, gasping. His back stretched to breaking point. There was no give. Nothing. Just the hot, even breaths inside his ear. Colors flashed before his eyes, blues and greens, violent reds. Exploding colors. He felt his body cry halt, wanting to give in to the indomitable force against it. He began to relax. Fought against it. *You'll die. Your backbone will break and you'll die.* Death.

Wasn't that why he had come? Alone? This was his death trip. Then he remembered Rachel Saunders. She was going to die too. And she was innocent.

He reached back with both hands, finding Ng's eyes, digging inwards with his thumbs, trying to scoop out the eyeballs.

Fogarty and Moyer were in the reptile house, drawn by the partially opened outer door. Moving back, behind the exhibits, through the office, down the stairs.

They'd found Tanaka's bike, Ng's van. They'd found Gordon Forrest's body.

"Not gonna talk. Kill'm. That's what I'm gonna do, kill'm," Fogarty had vowed. Moyer had nodded his agreement. He had his old army weapon with him. An officer's model .45. He'd kill'm too.

When Tanaka regained consciousness he was seated, his back against the wall. The room had been cleared, the shattered glass swept into a corner. Both his thumbs had been broken.

Willard Ng stood on the opposite side of the room, looking down at Rachel Saunders. She had been struggling, twisting and turning until she lay on her side. He bent and lifted her, repositioning her body.

The Man-Mantis was weeping inside him. Wanting so badly to be free. Perhaps one last empty ejaculation, one last release of the essence of Willard Ng. He turned. Josef Tanaka was crawling towards him.

"If the warrior is not able to perform his task, the warrior will be punished. Forced to watch. And to listen," Ng resolved, reaching down to tear the tape from Rachel's mouth. At first she gasped for breath. Then as he knelt behind her, guiding himself with his hand, forcing her rectum open, Rachel Saunders began to scream.

Tanaka struggled to his feet, grabbing a sliver of bamboo from the broken cage on top of the work table as he ambled forward.

Ng heard him coming, the hobbling footsteps. He didn't

turn, keeping his attention on the offering. She was contracting, forbidding him access.

Ng had just raised his arm, intending to punch her, when the sliver of wood entered the side of his throat, piercing his carotid vein. His blood came in spurts, countertimed to his heart. He was almost inside her when the second strike came. Like a hammer, it drove the splinter deeper in. Then he was being pulled backwards, looking up into the warrior's eyes. Something new about the eyes. They were clear and hard, void of self-doubt. No defeat in the warrior's eyes. Willard Ng knew then that he had been correct in his selection.

He tried to rise once, caught a glimpse of the sole of a training shoe descending towards his head. Blackness. Followed by a feeling of levity. He was climbing. Climbing the staircase. This was reality. He wasn't dreaming.

Josef Tanaka stamped down again. Another thud, dull and strong.

Willard Ng was looking down at his own body. Naked and scarred, blood and gray yoke running from his ears. So very imperfect. Discarded at last, as he had known it had to be. A man was hovering above him, poised to kick again.

He reached the top of the staircase. Looked down for a second time. Two people were walking around his body, trying not to touch it. People he almost recognized. A woman, naked, being supported by a man in black. She appeared to be in a state of shock.

Willard Ng studied the man. He remembered his name. Josef Tanaka. Willard Ng had chosen him for the execution. His own. Chosen him a long time ago. In another plane of existence.

Josef Tanaka was crying. Tears of sorrow, tears of joy, tears of release. Willard Ng had never cried. Not this last time around. Never been allowed to.

Now Josef Tanaka was covering the naked woman with a sheet, holding her.

Then Tanaka walked to the door. Removed the bolt. Opened

it. Let in two more men. One of them was using a crutch, dragging his right leg.

The man with the crutch raised a gun. Aimed it at the body of Willard Ng. The gun smoked five times and Willard Ng's head exploded. The woman in the sheet turned away. The three men stared at the gaping wound. A voice drifted up, through the smoke.

"A cop had to take him down, Joey. I told you that. Remember it when they make the inquiry. Bill Fogarty shot Willard Ng. Nice and neat that way."

Nice and neat that way. The words echoed, repeating from far away. Another time, another dimension.

EPILOGUE

The coroner's report on the body of Willard Ng was filed by Bob Moyer, ME for the city of Philadelphia. Cause of death was given as multiple gunshot wounds to the anterior head region.

Evidence found at the crime scene and a doctor's examination of Rachel Saunders proved, beyond doubt, that Willard Ng had been responsible for the Philadelphia "Mantis Murders."

Lieutenant William Fogarty was presented with a commendation for valor and returned to active duty. Because of injuries sustained during the investigation, he will walk with a slight limp for the rest of his life.

Rachel Saunders continues to practice cosmetic surgery. She has, however, suffered from post-traumatic stress disorder and has required extensive psychotherapy.

Dr. Saunders and Dr. Josef Tanaka, of the police pathology department, intend to marry in the spring. A full family wedding is planned, in Tokyo, Japan.